DARK PROVENANCE SERIES
HEIRESS OF BAEL
DAUGHTER OF DEATH
PARAMOUR OF SIN
PRINCESS OF BAEL
SON OF CHAOS
CAPTIVE OF HELL

 "THE BOND DOESN'T WORK THAT way, Kayla. It's not about absorbing strength from you. It's about our souls."

He released my chin to cup my cheek, his wings spanning out around us to create a cocoon of feathers that left me feeling shielded from the world. Protected. *Cherished*.

My throat worked, my heart hammering in my chest. "What are you doing?" I whispered, uncertain of how I felt about this change.

I... I hated him.

And yet, I felt oddly soothed by his presence. Intoxicated by his essence. Enthralled by the hint of his breath on my lips as his gaze met and held mine once more.

"I'm showing you how it works," he murmured, his pupils twin pools of hypnotic black. "Our bond is in our blood. It's a mating between spirits."

"I know," I said, familiar with how these connections worked.

He shook his head, that subtle action saying I didn't understand. I wanted to argue, to tell him he knew nothing about me or my intelligence, but I was too captivated by his gaze to voice a complaint.

"Archangel bonds differ from those that exist between demons. Ours require life and fidelity, while demonic bonds are founded in protection and loyalty. Being in Hell shielded you from the fractures in our connection. I suspect that's the real reason Bael kept you down there. Although, he told me it was to keep you from killing me."

His lips curled with that last statement, causing my own to curve downward.

"He kept me there to hurt you," I corrected him.

Ezra shook his head again. "No. He knew I would suffer regardless of what plane you resided on. He kept you there to protect you from experiencing the consequences of a neglected bond."

His fingers skimmed the side of my face to run through my hair. I'd taken out my bun, allowing the strands to hang chaotically around my head. He seemed a bit taken with the color, his gaze following his movements as he combed through the knots at the ends.

"Just touching you helps," he whispered. "It's not perfect, and I'm nowhere near healed, but I can breathe a little easier when you're near."

It sounded like a confession, something he hadn't meant to say, but a glimmer of satisfaction warmed his irises to a liquid gold as he returned his focus to my eyes.

"It's not about siphoning your energy, Kayla," he reiterated. "My reason for asking you to eat is to uphold your strength because I need you at full health. Whoever took Kristina's power is going to be a force of nature unlike any I've ever faced. And I need to know my partner—*my mate*—will survive it."

"You say that like you care," I marveled, honestly stunned by his words. "But I know you don't."

He'd lied. He'd tricked me. He'd abandoned me.

Never once had he tried to reach out.

So why would he suddenly care now?

A DARK PROVENANCE NOVEL

Princess
of
Bael

USA TODAY BESTSELLING AUTHOR

LEXI C. FOSS

Princess of Bael

Copyright © 2022 Lexi C. Foss

Editing by: Outthink Editing, LLC

Proofreading by: Katie Schmahl & Jean Bachen

Cover Design: Covers by Juan

Published by: Ninja Newt Publishing, LLC

Print Edition

ISBN: 978-1-68530-091-3

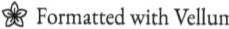 Formatted with Vellum

For Grandma Bonnie, I feel your presence every day, but I really hope you're not reading over my shoulder. This is just as dark as Blood Laws, so please wait until I start writing some clean YA before you peek at my screen <3 Love you always.

And to the readers who have been with Ezra and Kayla since Heiress of Bael first released—I'm sorry this one took so long. I hope you love their story as much as I do.

PRINCESS
of
BAEL

DARK PROVENANCE SERIES
BOOK THREE

**A lifetime of vengeance and decades of pain...
He abandoned her in Hell. She's returned to make
him pay.**

Kay

Once upon a time, I fell for an Archangel's trick.
He bonded me to him for eternity.
Then left me in Hell to survive alone.

I'm no longer the woman I was before.
I'm stronger. Faster. Harder. And lethal.

It's my turn to deliver justice where it's due.

*I'm coming for you, Archangel Ezra.
And your precious Divinity, too.*

Ezra

Once upon a time, I seduced a demon Halfling into helping
me save the balance.
I engaged in a sacred bond.
Then I abandoned her without a word.

I'm no longer the Archangel I was before.

I'm broken. Suffering. Destroyed by my mate.

Now she's coming for me, wielding a blade with the intent to kill.

I won't kneel for you, Princess of Bael.
And I'm prepared to fight.

A Warning from Kay

I'm old.

Like, really, *really* old.

Except I look like I'm maybe twenty-five, thanks to my Archdemon father's blood running through my veins.

And I'm technically only sixty-something human years old. But I spent the last four Earth decades in the underworld. Which equates to roughly fifteen thousand Hell years.

Mind-blowing, right?

One Earth day equals a year in Hell.

Just as one day in Heaven equates to a year on Earth.

I first learned about that mental mindfuck when an Archangel tricked me into a mating bond to help him enter my father's realm in Hell. That Archangel rewarded me afterward by leaving me there to die.

Too bad for him, I survived.

Four Earth decades is a long time to hold a grudge. Given that I spent most of those decades in Hell, it's a considerably old grievance—one I've never forgotten.

And now I have an opportunity to right the scales.

If Hell has taught me anything, it's that sometimes war can be fun.

Grab some knives.

Things are about to get bloody.

KAY'S GLOSSARY

Angel: Powerful beings who consider themselves too good for everyone else.

Archangel: Conniving, cruel, wicked creatures who prey on the innocent and fuck up those innocent lives for sport.

Dark Angel: Eve's pet name for Xai.

Demon: Minions.

Divinity: Three powerful beings who uphold the veil between our worlds. They are children of an Archdemon and Archangel pairing. There are three of them, all female, and my "mate" will do anything to protect them—including leaving me in Hell to rot while he lounges around on his Archangel throne crafted from the blood and tears of those he's betrayed. *Asshole.*

Fallen Angel: Eve. Xai. Angels who actually care about Earth.

Genesis/Dark Provenance: A Nephilim cult. Too bad they don't recruit Halflings.

Halfling: Kick-ass half-demon, half-human beings who have sweet skills and lethal attitudes.

Nephilim: Offspring of angels and mortals.

KAY'S DEMON DICTIONARY

Archdemon: Also known as Princes of Hell. I call mine a sperm donor. Usefulness is still under evaluation.

Blood Demons: Humans call them vampires, but they're much, much worse. And far more deadly to not only mortals but also supernatural beings of all kinds. *Leeches*. Useful in certain situations.

Cyclops: Giant, one-eyed monsters. Not common on Earth. Useless.

Dargarian: Demonic pets that breathe fire and live in a humanoid skin. Not the same as a pyrokinetic, though commonly confused as one. Useful.

Demonic Lord: Leaders who manage separate territories on Earth. Useful.

Ghoul: Demons who enjoy eating dead bodies. Useful.

Guardian: Demonic bodyguards who keep trying to kill me even though I can fry their asses. Not the brightest crayons in the box, but useful little minions.

Incubus: Sexy demons who love to flirt. *Definitely* useful.

Ōrdinātum: Demons who oversee specific regions within a Demonic Lord's territory. Useful.

Orsini Devil: Chatty little demons with gifts of invisibility. Irritating as fuck, but useful.

Pestilence: Humanoid-looking demons that have the ability to create epidemics on Earth. If only they could infect Archangels. Alas, they're useless for my means.

Portal Dweller: Demons who can teleport between planes. Extremely useful.

Royal Guard: Archdemon bodyguard squad. As an Archdemon's daughter, I have my own team. Pretty cool. Useful, but I'm biased.

Scrubber: Demons who can erase mortal memories. Very useful.

Slither: Snakelike creatures that paralyze their victims by covering them in inky crap. Attack from at least ten feet away to avoid projectile spit. Not fucking useful. Kill on sight.

Succubus: Female equivalent of an Incubus. Usefulness is likely, but I've not had the pleasure.

Tracker: Beings who can track demonic auras. Useful unless trying to hide, in which case, *ugh*.

PRINCESS
of
BAEL

Prologue

Ezra

Forty-One Earth Years Ago

Power hummed through the air, the blood vow struck.

Bael couldn't touch Johanna again.

The balance was restored.

And I'd just doomed myself to an eternity of misery.

The cruel glint in Bael's silver-blue eyes told me he knew the agony I'd just accepted as my future. It was why he'd added his own demand—*"Then you will vow never to touch Kayla again."*

I'd agreed with ease, ready to do anything and everything required to protect the precious balance between our worlds.

But inside, my heart had ached and my soul had demanded I decline.

Fortunately, my mind had won. My purpose as the Archangel of Justice was to protect the Divinity. If this was what fate required of me to see my mission through, then so be it.

Kayla wouldn't suffer. If anything, she'd be safer here than on Earth. Her father would introduce her to the powers of her bloodline. He'd ensure she could protect herself.

In that regard, this was a gift.

One her expression suggested wasn't very welcome.

Alas, she'd move on. This wasn't her sacrifice to bear, but mine.

Blood exchanges were meant for angels, after all. Not demons.

What we'd done would be considered forbidden to some. Therefore, my agonized future was a punishment of sorts, one I would accept in exchange for doing what needed to be done.

"Goodbye, Kayla," I said to her.

She didn't reply, her pretty face taking on a vacant expression that almost gave me pause. At least until her caramel-brown irises lit up and focused on me.

Disappointment.

Despair.

Fury.

All the emotions blended into an intoxicating ring of fire that promised retribution.

I held her gaze for a beat, my mouth quirking upward at the sides.

Now there was a fight I welcomed.

One day.

Whenever she earned her Archdemon wings.

Come and get me, little heiress, I dared her with a look. It was a foolish thing to do, something that could potentially destroy the vow I'd just created with Bael. But I'd only agreed not to touch her, not the other way around.

When I turned my attention back to him, I caught the flicker of knowledge in his features because he'd been looking at Johanna with a similar expression.

This isn't over, he seemed to be saying.

But it is for now, I thought. Not that he could hear me. Still, he glanced at me as though he had, his eyebrow arching in challenge. "Until we meet again, Bael," I said, the words a taunt and a promise lined up in a simple phrase.

The twitch of his lips told me he understood.

Demons and angels had been making vows for eternity, our games an endless chess match measured by who could make the best move.

I'd like to say I won this round, but one final glance at Kayla left me uncertain.

She'd been my pawn in this match. And I'd sacrificed her to deliver my form of a checkmate.

Maybe next time she'd be a rook on the board.

Or perhaps, I mused as she straightened her spine, her shoulders squared in defiance. *Perhaps she'll become the most powerful piece of them all. A queen.*

Grabbing Johanna's hand, I unleashed my wings in a flare of power meant to subdue those around me.

Then I left my heart in Hell.

And felt my soul fracture in my wake.

Princess Kayla had broken me irrevocably. When the day came for her to finish the job, I'd be ready.

Not to die.

But to fight.

KAYLA

Forty-One Years Later

WAR. DEATH. VIOLENCE. BLOOD.

Just another day in Hell.

Except this battle appeared to be unfolding on Earth, and the powers that be tended to frown upon that. As a half-human, half-demon hybrid, I understood. Mortals wouldn't react well to our presence in their realm. They'd probably try to enslave us or run dangerous experiments on our blood.

Or worse—turn our existence into a crude political debate. They might even try to promote some of us to positions of power. And not over our own species, but over the human race.

I shuddered at the thought.

Some demons would be excellent politicians.

Not me. I lacked patience and finesse for such matters. Killing people with kindness and placative words didn't appeal to me. I'd rather just kill them.

Like this Tracker demon following me around right now. He was a fucking nuisance that needed to find a new hobby.

I intended to provide him with such an outlet—just as soon as he appeared again—via a knife to the throat. He could choke on that for a while, then focus on regenerating.

I stirred my fruity cocktail with the pretty decorative

umbrella while watching the doorway from my position at the bar.

"Liquid courage?" a deep voice asked from behind me, causing the hairs along my arms to stand on end as the intense energy that came with that voice slithered across my skin.

Shit. I almost knocked over my drink in my hurry to spin around and face the godlike male appearing out of thin air.

Prince Alastor snapped his long, pale fingers, freezing all the mortals in place beneath a wave of impressive telekinetic power.

"You know, when you originally left on this mission, I thought you would go straight to the Divinity," he said conversationally as he took the stool beside me. "But you seem to be wasting quite a bit of time on Earth. Of course, the days might be a bit skewed, what with the time variants and all. Still, I'm surprised to find you..."

He paused to glance around, his dark eyes a hypnotic swirl of energy.

"Where the fuck are we?" he demanded, his perfect lips curling down as he took in the chalkboard and scribbled writing. "Did we fall back in time?"

I snorted and took another sip of my drink before setting it on the bar again. "We're in Fargo, North Dakota," I told him. "I was trying to trap a Tracker, but I'm guessing he ran off at the first scent of you." Which meant I should probably thank him. But his presence here meant we were about to have additional company.

And that complicated things.

"Hmm," he hummed, reaching over the bar to find a bottle of clear liquor. "Well, you're welcome, I suppose. But I really do need you to focus. And I thought Evangeline lived in Nashville?"

"She's all over the map," I muttered. "I also don't need her anymore."

5

"Oh?" He popped the cap off the bottle and tipped the contents into his mouth.

The proof on the label made me gag.

He merely swallowed and arched one of those dark brows at me. "Are you going to keep me in suspense, or elaborate?"

I considered torturing him. It would only be fair after all the decades of torment he'd put me through with his little Pestilence demon pets.

Alas, I didn't want to waste my energy on him.

I pulled out a phone and set it on the bar. "Prince Ashmedai gave me this." It'd been his apology gift after keeping me occupied for several Earth weeks. Our findings had been crucial, the map we'd created one that more than proved the power divide was very real. But it had set me behind on my initial plans to find Ezra.

Then the pesky Tracker had made it worse.

Prince Alastor glanced at the device I'd set on the bar, his expression dubious. "And you're going to what? Call the Archangel of Justice and ask him for a date?" He took in my knee-high boots, black skinny jeans, dark tank top, and leather jacket before settling on my features. "Given that you're mated, I suppose that may work. Although, a naked picture would probably entice him more. Especially as he's had to remain celi—"

"I'm not going to entice him with a date," I snapped, exhausted from popping all over the damn country in an effort to shake that vexing Tracker. I also hadn't slept in, like, a week, thanks to Ashmedai's interference.

At least he'd given me a present before letting me go.

One I very much wanted to use.

I just needed to take care of the damn Tracker first.

And Prince Alastor.

"You're going to ruin my plan," I accused him. "You know Princes of Hell are banned from Earth."

Now it was his turn to snort. "Hate to break this to you, love, but so are Princesses of Hell."

"Ah, but I'm a Halfling," I reminded him. "And I have this," I added, showing him my golden cuff and the silver runes embedded in the metal. It was a gift from Yaz, the head of my Royal Guard.

Prince Alastor flinched in response, his head rearing back. "Warn a demon, would you?"

I shrugged, tugging my sleeve back down. "I'm sure you sensed it already."

He took another sip from the bottle before screwing the cap back onto it and returning the item to the bartender's side of the counter. "I assumed Evangeline gave you a knife."

I scoffed at that. "We're not friends. The only way she'd give me a blade would be the old-fashioned way."

"Good thing you're immune to silver, then." He stood, only to lean an elbow on the wood and stare down at me. "Seriously, what's your plan?"

I finished my cocktail, then focused on him. "Why? Do you want to help?"

"I believe that's your job."

"Then let me do it," I countered.

"I've been waiting seven years, Kayla. Things are not improving."

"I'm aware," I returned, standing and still having to look up to meet Prince Alastor's midnight gaze. He had at least ten inches of height on my five-foot-five frame. My boots didn't help at all.

But that didn't make me powerless here.

He might be hundreds of thousands of Hell years older than me, but I was Archdemon Bael's daughter. I possessed my own bag of tricks.

Fortunately, Prince Alastor had taken a liking to me early

7

on. All his torture had been in the form of tests, just to ensure my strength.

And I had to admit, he'd done a great job fortifying my backbone.

I slipped the phone back into my leather jacket pocket as I said, "I need that Tracker off my tail for this to work. Want to take care of him for me?"

"Are you asking me to create a diversion?"

I smiled. "I am."

He pretended to consider that for a moment. "Well. I'm already here. I may as well enjoy myself a little."

"Just not too much or the Archangels will descend," I warned him, already walking toward the door.

"Oh, they're already on their way," he called after me. "They really frown upon breaking treaties."

The cuff around my wrist burned in warning, telling me he was right. "Then that's my cue." I gave him a little wave with my fingers.

"I want an update in twenty-four Earth hours!" he shouted after me.

Sure, I thought, stroking the cuff around my wrist to engage the portal rune. *I'll get right on that.*

Just like I would update Ashmedai, too.

At some point, I'd taken an assistant job to both Princes of Hell. It wasn't one I'd applied for, or a position I'd actually accepted. Yet Ashmedai and Alastor seemed to be under the impression that I worked for them.

In reality, I was doing this to save my father.

Something I would never have anticipated early on in our relationship.

But the old Archdemon had grown on me throughout our thousands of Hell years together.

And I really didn't want to see his realm—*my birthright*—fall apart as the result of this imbalance.

I also held a soft spot for Earth and the humans here. Which motivated me even more to find a solution to this whole shifting-power issue.

The fact that all of this granted me the opportunity to royally piss off Archangel Ezra certainly added to the appeal.

Because *he* was the one I needed to dethrone to fix this mess.

I would happily drive a blade through his cold, black heart. Then take over his precious Divinity and make the appropriate adjustments.

Too bad I didn't have the knife I needed to properly kill him.

Prince Alastor had one, which was part of our deal. He would give me the tool I needed after I delivered the female he required.

Fine.

I'd need my bond to Ezra to make this work anyway.

He'd used me once. Now it was my turn to use him.

I smiled at the prospect, then engaged the portal energy to find a new location away from Prince Alastor. The cuff had all sorts of helpful magic, allowing me to teleport at will and mask my location.

Which was how I'd picked up a Tracker tail.

He seemed fascinated by my energy signature and would not bugger off.

It was like he saw me as some sort of challenge.

Idiot, I thought, selecting Richmond, Virginia, as my destination. It seemed like the ideal location to set a trap, given my previous human history.

I'd lived in the state of Virginia for twenty-five years before Ezra had turned my world upside down. Seemed like an appropriate place to rekindle this bond with my long-lost mate.

I nearly snorted at the notion of it.

Making him bleed would be incredibly satisfying.

Last time we'd met, he'd been able to snuff out my fire energy. Well, we'd see how well he danced with a blade this time around.

I landed on my old street roughly a block away from my townhome. Unsurprisingly, a new structure stood in its place. Something a bit ritzier than my previous stomping grounds. Actually, it seemed as though the whole neighborhood had leveled up in my absence.

However, the soft mist rolling in off the James River was familiar. As were the hovering clouds fogging the streetlights.

A dangerous ambience.

Yet one I'd always enjoyed while living here.

I meandered around a bit, the sense of being watched a heavy sensation on my mind. That Tracker had obviously made me paranoid.

Or maybe it was the memories coming back to haunt me.

I could almost sense that damn Slither demon here again —the one who had attacked me the night I'd met Ezra. But that was impossible; I'd killed the slithering fucker with a flameball.

Right there, I mused, pausing near the building that stood in my old living space.

An image of the creature oozing black sludge graced my mind, making my nose wrinkle. Being Archdemon Bael's daughter had painted a target on my back all my life, even when I'd lived here in the human world.

Fortunately, thousands of years in Hell had only honed my skills.

If a Slither demon was brave enough to appear now, he'd be dead in seconds.

And he wouldn't be able to subdue me with his paralytic poison, either.

Unlike four decades ago, when the Slither had hit me with some slime right before I'd flamed him.

Which led to Ezra's arrival and him stripping me half-naked to wash the sludge away.

Just before bonding me to him for eternity.

Then tricking me into playing a game in Hell.

A game that is about to end, I thought, pulling Ashmedai's device from my pocket.

To an outsider, it resembled an old-fashioned cell phone. It fit in the palm of my hand and had a shiny, almost mirror-like surface on one side and a matte plastic back on the other.

However, it was something else entirely—an item bespelled to take on an ordinary appearance in case a human saw it. A pretty nifty trick, actually, given how even I couldn't see through the spell. Although, I could sense the power lurking within.

Sort of like me...

I was no longer the half-human, half-demon twenty-five-year-old who'd lived in this town. I'd grown exponentially in my demonic essence during the ensuing centuries. Not just in age, wisdom, and overall skills, but in form, too.

My fancy cuff possessed a lot of abilities, one of which hid my true form from the human world. *No horns here.* Just a head of long, dark hair.

I stared down at Ashmedai's toy and smirked a little, thinking back on how I used to have a mohawk. That trend had died when my horns had arrived. Some Archdemons grew wings. As a Halfling, I'd adopted horns. Totally not fair.

Focus, I told myself, staring at the phone once more. Prince Ashmedai had shown me how to use it.

Flip it open.
Press the Dial button.
Watch the fireworks.

With a shrug, I followed his directions and waited with an arched brow.

Nothing happened.

Glancing around, I searched for any sign of life or a demonic presence that might be—

A burning sensation touched my hand, causing me to drop the phone as it disintegrated into sparks. They swirled around my legs, causing me to jump out of the way just as they shot upward into the sky.

Right over this residential street.

To explode above the houses full of sleeping mortals.

"Shit!"

KAYLA

I spun around, searching for potential human witnesses.

Had I realized it would explode, I would have chosen an empty field, not a damn neighborhood!

Fortunately, everything was quiet. No screaming. No giant boom from the demonic firework. No sound at all.

And from what I could tell, everyone was mostly asleep on this block. Given that it was after midnight on this side of the country, I supposed that made sense.

But that firework remained in the dark sky above, the black hole at the center resembling a tear in the realms.

What the hell, Ashmedai? I thought, irritated. *A warning would have been nice!*

I could almost hear him snickering.

Dick.

I glanced left and right, then up and down, my lips curling down. "Okay, now what?" I demanded into the thin air. With my luck, an army of Archangels would descend and threaten to imprison me for breaching the realms.

Because yeah, that was definitely a fracture in the supernatural veil above my head.

Of course, I would need wings to reach it. Which I didn't possess, even in my demon form, because of my human side.

Pinching my lips to the side, I considered my options.

The cuff let me portal around on Earth and back to Hell. That gave me an escape route, should I need it. My aura would also be masked. At least to an extent.

Although, I questioned that part because of the Tracker's interest.

Or perhaps it was the cuff that had provoked that curiosity.

Regardless, I had a way out if—

The ground began to rumble beneath my feet, causing me to jump behind a nearby bush and crouch down on instinct. A knife fell into my hand, my gaze vigilant on the surrounding area, only to be blinded by a bright light in the sky.

I threw up an arm to protect my eyes from the brilliant, swirling globe of white-gold illumination. It beamed down on the asphalt street like a spotlight from Heaven itself.

Which it was.

Unfortunately.

Three feminine silhouettes formed from the light, floating down from the sky like they were riding a divine elevator. Their dresses and hair fluttered elegantly as they descended, making them look like they were moving in slow motion. As they drew closer and the light stopped blinding me, I could see past the glow to their features, and I recognized the female in the lead—Johanna.

I didn't know her. Yet I was intimately familiar with her at the same time.

My father had kidnapped her forty-one years ago, which was what had inspired Ezra to use me as a one-way ticket to Hell.

He'd traded my life for hers.

Trapping me in the underworld for eternity so that she could be saved.

She landed about ten yards in front of me on a pair of shiny shoes that matched her fitted silver dress. Objectively, I could see the allure—curves, long dirty-blonde hair, brown skin glowing from the crescent moons etched up and down her arms, and a delicate appearance that hid the power beneath.

But none of that made me like her.

Actually, I quite hated her.

Not because of anything she'd done, just what she represented.

She began to chant as two more females gently tapped down to Earth on either side of her, their arms mimicking hers as they began to weave magic into the air with their fingertips and voices.

I had never seen the other two before, but I knew of them.

The raven-haired beauty with the haughty, regal posture was Lucía, while the willowy, doll-like redhead's name was Kristina.

They moved closer together, their chants growing in power, but my attention was drawn away by the appearance of a new silhouette overhead.

A familiar divine being who haunted my dreams.

Ezra, Archangel of Justice, protector of the Divinity, and the one male in all the realms who'd earned my eternal loathing.

He cut an imposing figure as he descended from the light. His velvety black-brown wings stretched behind him to slow his momentum, making him look large and intimidating, especially with his hard body encased in black pants and a matching fitted T-shirt.

His dark boots touched down, and he immediately went into warrior mode with his hands hanging loose at his sides as he strode away from the Divinity to begin surveying the area.

All the black between his ebony feathers and midnight clothes made the white of his hair even more shocking.

The last time I'd seen him, his hair had been a mix of silver and black and hung in long lengths past his shoulders. He'd cut it short, and it was stark white now, thick and messy as though he'd just been roused from sleep. Still looked good, though, much to my chagrin.

However, his protective instincts sucked.

Because he'd clearly missed the obvious threat hiding in the bushes less than ten yards from his precious Divinity—*me*.

As though to confirm my assessment, the imposing Archangel gave me his back as he stalked to the other side of the street. His wings disappeared as well, likely to mask his supernatural presence.

Not that it would help.

Ezra possessed an otherworldly aura that couldn't be disguised.

As did the chanting females before me.

The members of the Divinity were weaving a translucent web of magic into the air, their voices and hand motions causing the enchantment to glow with fiery golden embers.

Can a human see this? I wondered, frowning as I glanced around again for any witnesses. But the street remained silent apart from their voices.

Movement in my periphery caused me to freeze. The stealthy Archangel had stopped right in front of my bush, causing me to retract my earlier statement about him being oblivious to my presence.

Dammit.

"Show yourself," he demanded, his gaze on my hiding spot.

I considered telling him to fuck off, but that wasn't how this game was meant to be played.

Well, here we go, I thought, rising to my feet to meet his gaze. Liquid caramel swirled with dark power in his vibrant irises, his brow furrowing as he took me in.

Not a single sign that he knew me.

16

Or even a note of fear.

It was as though I didn't exist to him. That I wasn't standing here armed and ready to hurt him. That I hadn't spent the last forty-one Earth years *loathing* him.

Which shouldn't surprise me at all, given our history.

But the lack of recognition in his features still stung.

My veins lit with an uncontrollable fire. *Did I mean that little to him? A passing fancy that he left in Hell with his soul-mate bond firmly intact for eternity?*

I wanted to scream at the injustice of it all. How aptly named he was as the Archangel of Justice. If anyone deserved punishment, it was the pompous male in front of me.

And now he had the audacity not to recognize me? His own fucking mate?

A growl clawed at my throat as the knife in my hand burned with my anger. His lips parted, words curling around his tongue as he began to speak. But I wasn't interested in anything he had to say now.

I only wanted blood.

I threw my knife at him, the aim deadly and meant to pierce his chest. Because I wanted him to feel my pain. To understand what it was like to have his heart shredded.

Just like he'd done to me.

Only, the bastard caught my weapon by the blade, his movements still incredibly fast.

I knew better than to try to flame him and instead pulled out another throwing knife.

He dropped the one in his hand to catch the new one, his blood an alluring sight.

"Kayla?" he asked, sounding stunned more than angry. "What the fuck are you doing here?"

"Well, I used to live here," I reminded him. "Until someone tricked me into a mating bond and left me in Hell."

I threw a third knife.

He caught it as well, then tossed it back at me, causing the sharp end to dig into my shoulder. "I see you're still as immature as ever." The disappointment in his voice grated on my nerves.

"Fuck you."

"Yes, that just makes your case," he drawled, folding his arms over his black shirt. He seemed entirely unfazed by the blood on his palm. And why would he be? I'd missed three times, and he'd struck me on his first throw.

"How about you act like an adult for a minute and tell me what you're doing here?" he suggested, his expression hardening even more.

I yanked the blade out of my shoulder, furious at myself for failing to hit my mark. And for letting emotions destroy all my intentions.

Ezra made me irrational.

Which was entirely fair, considering what he'd done to me.

However, to win this match, I needed to be pragmatic and strategic. Just like him.

"The balance is at risk," I informed him flatly.

He arched a perfectly sculpted brow. "Oh?"

"I know you feel it, Ezra." Because I could sense it through my bond with him. I hadn't even needed to overhear my father's concerns or meet with Ashmedai regarding the power shift. I'd already known from my forbidden link to Ezra.

He studied me intently, his expression giving nothing away.

I couldn't hear him. But I sensed the unease swirling around him.

He looked... *tired*. There weren't any stress lines or wrinkles, his expression remaining arrogant and almost bored, but his aura exuded exhaustion. I wasn't sure how I'd caught that —perhaps through our mating connection—but now that I saw it, it became even clearer.

His features resembled that of a thirty-year-old man, although they almost served as a mirage to hide the aging male beneath the façade.

Yet he caught my knife with the reflexes of a powerful Archangel, I reminded myself with a sigh.

I rolled my neck, flinching as my immortal genetics took over and began mending my wound. Using my good arm, I wiped the blade against my black pants. I'd have to sanitize it later.

At least the metal was steel, not silver. While the latter didn't burn me as much as it did a full-blooded demon—hence the silver-etched runes on my cuff—I'd become more and more susceptible to the substance over the years. It seemed to grow in direct contrast with my abilities.

Fortunately, silver had been eradicated on Earth. Humans had never heard of the true element, just a fabricated metal that existed in its place on the periodic table.

Of course, that didn't stop certain immortal beings from illegally creating weapons with it.

Immortals like Eve.

She probably wouldn't have missed, I thought sourly, thinking about my three pitiful throws. *I should have brought a gun.*

"So, what, you came here to warn me?" He phrased it as a question, but his tone suggested it was a mocking one.

"No, I came here to kill you," I admitted without missing a beat. "My warning is for Johanna from Archdemon Bael. He's worried about her."

And I need to borrow one of the Divinity for Alastor, I added to myself. *Then he'll give me a holy blade made of angel bone that will allow me to kill you.*

Up until that moment, none of the Divinity had bothered to spare us a glance, too wrapped up in their weaving and trusting that Ezra would keep them safe. But at my father's name, Johanna paused and glanced over her shoulder, zeroing in on my face. If she recognized me from our one encounter years ago, she didn't give any indication. "Bael?"

"My father," I replied, eliciting yet another arched brow from Ezra. I ignored him, my focus on Johanna. "He's worried about you."

"He's not worried about her," Ezra interjected. "He's worried about himself."

"Sounds familiar," I muttered, unable to stop myself. Then I looked at him again. "You don't know my father like I do. He's worried, so much so that he was considering breaking the vow to see her. I came myself instead."

Not that my father knew that.

He thought I was visiting Prince Alastor to learn more about his governing techniques. But that hadn't gone the way my father had planned, mostly because Prince Alastor had seen through my concern almost immediately.

And that had led to what I'd sensed about the shifting balance, something he'd admitted to feeling as well.

Which had prompted me to travel to Earth to find Eve.

Only to be caught by Ashmedai.

And yeah, it'd been a whirlwind of demonic politics.

Anyway...

"Something's coming. I don't know what, but it doesn't feel natural. It feels—"

A blast cut a swath between the realms, tearing through the quiet street and interrupting my explanation.

I froze, too startled by the sudden violence to react, and then a split second after the first blast, a second explosion lit up the night.

Ezra whirled away from me and drew a sword out of thin air. He held it aloft, his shrewd gaze sweeping the shadows around us.

I knew he was capable of "calling" his weapons from thin

air, because he'd done it once in Hell when we were traveling to Bael's realm. But it hadn't occurred to me that when he'd demanded I show myself a few moments before, he hadn't bothered pulling a weapon on me.

Because he'd never actually considered me to be a threat.

I'll be annoyed by that later, I decided, my gaze dropping to the quaking ground beneath my boots. *What the fuck is that?*

A magical shimmer crackled around us, the sound reminding me of static electricity, only louder and humming dangerously close to my skin.

I blinked hard and shook my head, trying to brush off the weird static hum. But it grew in intensity, until every inch of me vibrated along with the ground.

My insides twisted with the need to vomit.

The horrific reverberations dampened my senses, making it so I couldn't quite see or hear. I thought I heard Ezra shouting, but I couldn't make out his words, and when I tried to focus on him, he was nothing but a blur of colors.

The Divinity's bright light, which still shone on the asphalt a few feet away, was exacerbating my blurry vision. I rubbed my eyes, then glanced away into the darkness for a reprieve.

And found the Tracker demon standing about a hundred yards to my left, entirely too close to the Divinity, staring up at the sky with triumph. His body was encased in a weird sort of armor that seemed to be reflecting the electricity.

It was the same Tracker who'd been following me since Fargo—I recognized his signature.

On any other day, I'd consider him good-looking: olive skin, almond-shaped dark eyes, black hair, tall and athletic... Except for the whole stalker syndrome.

What the hell? I thought, gaping at him.

Ezra started moving toward the Tracker demon, sword

raised, expression grim. But his movements were... off. He appeared to be in slow motion, like he was trying to run underwater rather than on a normal street in Virginia. It was as if everything around us was passing in fractions of time, his speed hampered and belittled by whatever had just occurred.

While Ezra seemed to be trying with all his might to run toward the Tracker, the Tracker appeared to be moving with ease.

I lifted my hand, startled when, instead of moving in slow motion like Ezra, my arm rose as normal.

Whatever was affecting the Archangel hadn't touched me.

I didn't waste any more time. I reached into the holster hanging beneath my jacket and drew a knife. The blade went airborne.

In the same instant, however, the Tracker reached out for the closest Divinity member to him—Kristina. He latched on to her, yanking her against his strange armor. She didn't even have a chance to react. A Portal Dweller appeared right next to them, and then the three of them disappeared.

With my blade embedded in the Tracker's chest.

Ezra, Johanna, and Lucía were still stuck in slow motion, the explosion clearly meant for them and not for me.

Yet the Tracker had obviously followed me here.

He'd tailed me mercilessly all day before finally finding me. But his focus had been on the *sky*, not on me.

In fact, he hadn't tried to grab me at all. It was as though I didn't even exist.

His excitement upon arrival had been about the fracture in the sky.

Then he'd looked at the Divinity and picked the female closest to him. Taking her with him without once looking at me—which was what had allowed me to hit him with the knife.

He wasn't tracking me, I realized. *He... he must have been tracking my device.*

My eyes widened.

That could only mean one thing.

Someone knew my purpose here, and that person had sent the Tracker to follow me... to take a member of the Divinity.

EZRA

FUCK!

I fought the enchantment encasing my limbs, cursing inwardly at my idiocy.

Seeing Kayla had fried my damn brain, causing me to drop my guard and lose sight of my purpose.

A Tracker, I thought, furious. *I let a Tracker capture Kristina.*

Never in my worst nightmares could I have imagined something so simplistic. *A Tracker.* I wanted to laugh and scream at the same time.

All because of Kayla.

Fuck, I hadn't even recognized her at first. She'd... she'd grown up. Like, really grown up. With long, dark waves of hair that framed her delicate curves and nearly reached her ass. Beautiful, caramel-colored eyes. Full, luscious lips that I'd secretly dreamt about for decades. Athletic legs encased in tight black fabric.

Forty-one years.

It'd been *forty-one years*.

And the first thing she'd done was try to stab me.

I wasn't sure if that pissed me off or turned me on.

Her mere presence deteriorated my every thought and instinct, my body craving a touch more than I desired to breathe. I *needed* her, had spent four decades in agony without her, and she'd appeared like some sort of devilish gift dressed in all black and wearing a devious smirk filled with wicked intent.

I groaned inside, my world crumbling at my feet.

Not five minutes in her presence, and the Divinity was already at stake again. Something I'd known would happen if I ever saw her again. Yet I'd forgotten all my concerns, too thrilled to be in her company once more.

It was intoxicating and wrong and reminded me why I'd left her in Hell. Reminded me why I'd sacrificed my own body and heart to protect the balance.

Except I'd just fucked it all up.

Again.

Growling, I pushed all my thoughts aside and focused on the enchantment paralyzing my body. It reminded me of Slither poison. Which was ironic, considering the last one I'd run into had been in this area the night I'd met Kay.

Kay appeared in my periphery, strolling confidently around my paralyzed form. An insidious grin curled up one corner of her lips, and she began to twirl her knife, angling toward me with purpose. She looked like a predator with that new, dangerous look about her.

Great. I knew she hated me for what I'd done to her, and for the last forty-one Earth years, she'd likely carried a homicidal torch for me. Chances were she was a bit more deadly than she'd been during our first encounter.

If she wanted to kill me right now, she could. And I'd be powerless to stop her.

I gritted my teeth, trying to construct a mental wall to fight off whatever enchantment had been cast on me. Forty years ago, it wouldn't have been a problem. My mental acuity against metaphysical attacks had been strong and capable. Then I'd bonded with Kayla and fucked up my skill set.

So much so that now Kristina was in trouble.

But instead of sinking her blade into my chest, Kayla glanced up at the sky, where the tear in the veil between realms still hadn't been fully healed by the Divinity's magic.

She sighed and shook her head, then slipped her knife into a holster beneath her jacket.

I fought harder against the enchantment, keeping one eye on Kayla in case she decided to slice and dice me. She turned her attention to the gold cuff on her wrist as though to casually check the time. Except she tapped one of the glowing runes.

The spell around me disappeared in a blink.

"Still fucking hate Slithers," she muttered, causing me to frown.

A venom bomb? I idly wondered. *Is that what caused time to slow?*

Typically, Slither demons ejaculated venom from their mouths to paralyze their prey, similar to snakes. But demons could technically use that substance to create a weapon to freeze their victims.

"More!" Jo shouted, distracting me as a blast of power left her fingertips.

A curse left Lucía's lips on my opposite side as she shot energy up into the air to pair with Jo's, the two of them immediately falling back into the chant required to mend the sky.

Except they were weakened now by Kristina's disappearance.

A disappearance I'd allowed, thanks to my *mate's* unexpected arrival.

"What happened here?" I demanded, my focus on said *mate*. "Who created the fracture in the veil?" Because that person likely had something to do with Kristina's disappearance, and I intended to go have a stern word with them just as soon as we finished cleaning up this mess.

Kayla's brow furrowed, her hesitant gaze on the sky as she completely ignored my question.

I opened my mouth to repeat myself, only for Jo to sway in my peripheral vision. My wings propelled me to her side, catching her before she could collapse, her brown skin taking on an eerie yellowish tone as the golden crescents on her arms dimmed in brightness.

The equilibrium around us began to shift, making me dizzy as I attempted to stand her upright.

Fuck.

It felt as though I'd just imbibed several dozen alcoholic drinks. My stomach rolled with the intensity, my mind whirling at the disruption to the scales.

The power divide just tilted.

It's tainted.

Officially unbalanced.

Kristina...

My insides churned with the need to go after her, to save her. But I couldn't just leave Johanna and Lucía here without a guard.

Not that I'd done a fabulous job the first time. However, this would only worsen if I left them unprotected.

I'd been struggling with the rift in the balance for years, which was why I'd accompanied them here to fix the veil. Except that Tracker had just come in and taken Kristina with a mere *spell*.

I failed her.

Her presence no longer lingered on this plane, telling me she'd been taken to Heaven or Hell. Most likely the latter, given that a Tracker and a Portal Dweller were her captors.

How the fuck did I let this happen? Although, I knew exactly how. *Kayla.* And not just her presence here today, but also the shattered bond between us.

Four decades of separation had left me weak—a punishment I'd accepted as a result of my crimes against her.

Except now Kristina appeared to be paying the price of my ineptitude.

Fuck. Fuck. Fuck.

Jo released a final flare of power, her breath shuddering out of her from the effort as the sky healed overhead.

Only to be disturbed by a new dark energy.

Archdemon.

And not the half Archdemon beside us. A *new* Archdemon.

I helped Jo stand, my sword materializing once more as Alastor appeared out of thin air, his midnight irises holding a touch of amusement as he took in the surroundings.

Then his gaze went to Kayla as he arched a brow. "So you made that phone call, then?"

Phone call?

She snorted in response, seemingly annoyed.

Which only appeared to amuse Alastor more. An amusement that reached borderline excitement as his gaze shifted to Lucía. "Excellent work, Kayla. I knew I could count on you." He started forward, forcing me to release Jo to intercept him.

However, Alastor disappeared in the next blink, only to reappear at Lucía's side.

Fucking Archdemon, I groused, done with this game.

Lucía's expression told me she felt the same, her multicolored eyes sparkling with murderous intent as Alastor gently drew a finger along her ashen cheek. She might be exhausted from fixing the rift between the realms, but that didn't make her any less powerful.

Just like Kristina.

She'll keep herself alive, I reminded myself. The Divinity possessed the power of the realms. They were the children of specific Archdemon and Archangel matings, thus allowing them to maintain the balance. They didn't die easily.

But they also shouldn't be captured very easily, either.

"You'll do," Alastor murmured, lowering his hand to hold it palm up before her. "Shall we?"

Rolling my eyes, I moved forward with my sword, the tip angling at his neck in the next breath. "I'm in a really bad mood, Alastor. Trust me when I say you don't want to test my patience any more than you already have."

His lips merely curled in response.

Only for a sigh to escape him instead of words as the air around us rippled with heavenly authority.

Azrael and Mietek appeared on either side of Alastor.

Followed by Raziel and Dariel.

And anchored by Zebulon.

The latter wasn't an Archangel but a Demonic Lord. Specifically, the Demonic Lord of North America. He'd likely felt the influx of power in this region, thus drawing him out of his Chicago headquarters to our very location.

He took a glance at the crowd, his dark irises swirling with knowledge, and bowed his head slightly in the respect due to his superiors. Demonic Lords were powerful, sitting at the top of the hierarchy—just under Archdemons. Making Alastor his leader in this situation.

And what a leader Alastor made with his tricks and games.

"Stand down, Ezra," Mietek said, sounding tired.

My blade still touched Alastor's neck, my intent clear and deadly.

Technically, I didn't have to bow to Mietek. He was the Archangel of Chaos, but his powers appeared to be waning of late. Perhaps because his son, Xai, was absorbing them.

Which shouldn't be possible at all.

Archangels didn't lose power; they *gained* power.

Unless, of course, they bonded a Halfling heiress demon and spent four decades away from her.

But Mietek was bonded to the Archangel of Destiny, something that should make him stronger, not weaker.

Is that the imbalance I sense? I wondered, taking in the crowd of Archangels, my lips turning down as I slowly lowered my sword. *No. Not that's not it at all. Something else is very wrong.*

I focused on Azrael and Mietek, deciding to jump straight to the point. "Did you all feel the rift?" I asked, gesturing to the now sealed sky. "Is that what drew you here?"

"Oh, no, they're just following me," Alastor replied, his body far too close to Lucía for my liking. She could handle herself and put up one hell of a fight, but it was my responsibility to protect her. And it didn't feel like she was all that protected at the moment.

"Alastor decided to enjoy himself in Fargo, of all places, then teleported in the middle of our conversation," Mietek explained, his tone indicating how much he did not appreciate Alastor's antics.

The Archdemon merely smiled, saying, "I was bored."

"And what drew you here?" I asked, frowning.

"Me," Kayla replied. "I sent him a text."

I blinked. "A text?"

"Via a phone." She glanced at Alastor. "Felt appropriate."

The Archdemon's devilish grin turned adoring as he studied her. "I've always enjoyed your wit, darling. And I do feel I owe you an apology for underestimating you."

"I'll accept payment as an apology." She held out her hand, but Mietek cleared his throat, drawing Alastor's attention to him before he could respond.

"This is a very serious breach," Mietek informed us, stating the obvious. "The Divinity maintains the balance, which we all know is shifting. Where's Kristina?"

"I don't know," I admitted. "A Tracker and a Portal Dweller took her after bespelling us with some sort of paralyzing agent."

"A venom bomb," Kayla muttered. "Fucking Slithers."

"That wouldn't have impacted you," Alastor said, focusing on the cuff glowing against her wrist. "Right?"

"It didn't impact me, no. I sank a blade into the Tracker while he and the Portal Dweller disappeared."

"Silver?" Alastor asked.

"As I mentioned earlier, I didn't acquire any toys from Evangeline, so no," she replied.

Azrael bristled at the mention of his daughter.

But Mietek spoke before anyone else could. "The balance is at risk. Kristina must be found."

An obvious statement, one I didn't feel the need to echo.

Instead, I glanced at Dariel and Raziel, wondering if they could sense her location. Dariel was the Archangel of Concealment, and his twin brother, Raziel, was the Archangel of Secrets. They functioned as chameleons in this world, their features always shifting to fit the area around them. Right now, they were as dark as the night surrounding them.

"And the rest of the Divinity needs to be protected," Azrael said, drawing my focus back to him.

"Which has been my job for over two thousand Earth years," I pointed out.

It was a task that had been assigned to me when Heaven had first noticed the power shift—something I'd almost said to Kayla when she'd claimed to be here to warn me about the changes. *Yes, I'm very aware of the issue*, I'd nearly told her. *It's been my job for over two thousand years to monitor the situation.*

The variance of power had always been a matter of time, and I'd prolonged the inevitable for as long as I could.

I met Mietek's gaze. "That's why you've been monitoring Earth so closely. You knew it was almost time."

It was also why he'd sent his son, Xai, to Earth around the same time I'd been tasked to manage the Divinity.

We were all players on Mietek's chessboard, meant to help control the fallout as much as we could.

Actually, no, that wasn't quite right.

Mietek was merely the messenger.

His mate, Fate, was the orchestrator behind the scenes. As an oracle, she could see the future, which prompted her to create certain situations to steer our destinies onto the appropriate path.

"Yes, but I didn't anticipate you losing a piece of the Divinity so easily," Mietek returned, his disappointment evident. "*Again.*"

To be fair, the first time I'd "lost" a piece of the Divinity, it was because Bael had tricked Jo into coming to see him.

But this time, it was all on me for failing to observe my surroundings.

"He's been weakened," Azrael pointed out. "And casting blame will not solve the problem."

"No, he'll solve the problem by locating Kristina," Mietek declared, his tone brooking no argument.

As I agreed with that plan, I merely nodded.

"And he'll take Kayla with him," Azrael added.

Now that I didn't agree with.

But Kayla spoke first.

"Yeah, no, that's not happening." She held a hand out to Alastor again. "Blade. Now."

"Hmm," he hummed. "You know, as much as I hate to agree with the divine powers that be, they do have a bit of a point. The balance is wounded enough as is—we can't afford to lose Kristina. Work with Ezra to find her, then we'll talk. In the interim, I offer to guard Lucía."

Blade? I thought, frowning. Then the rest of Alastor's comments filtered through the haze of my mind, causing my frown to flatten into a straight line. "No, that's not happening. You're not equipped to guard Lucía."

"And you are?" he asked, looking me over with a crude glance. "A Tracker just bested you with a venom bomb. Not to mention you falling for Kayla's neat little sky trick." He tsked, but I was too busy translating that last statement.

Kayla's little sky trick.

"*You* did this?" I took a step toward her, and she boldly held her ground.

"Technically, Ashmedai did," she replied. "He gave me the phone and said to use it when I was ready to talk to you. I didn't know it was going to explode into a firework."

"*A firework*?" I repeated, incredulous. "That wasn't a bloody firework, *Princess*. That was a rift in the veil."

"Yes, I know, but it looked like a firework."

"You two can argue semantics later," Mietek interjected before I could respond to Kayla's ridiculous commentary.

A firework.

Un-fucking-believable.

"We need to focus on Johanna and Lucía," Mietek continued. "They need to be guarded while Ezra and Kayla search for Kristina."

"Still not agreeing to that plan," Kayla reminded him, but Mietek wasn't even paying attention to her. His focus had moved to Alastor.

And I really didn't like the way he was looking at the Archdemon.

"Mietek," I started.

He held up a hand. "No. I want to consider this. Alastor has an entire army of Royal Guards, not to mention a hefty front line of defense."

"A compliment?" Alastor pressed his palm to his heart. "Do you hear that, sweetheart? The Archangel likes me."

Lucía curled her lip in response—not in a friendly way, but in a display of disgust.

It didn't seem to register to Alastor, though. His ego would require several lethal blows for it to begin to deflate. And even then, it'd probably only shrink an inch.

"Shall I take them both?" the Archdemon suggested.

"No," I said at the same time as Azrael and Mietek.

"Why not?" Alastor asked. "Ezra had three."

"As the Archangel of Justice," I replied before focusing on Mietek. "How can you even consider trusting him?"

His ebony gaze met mine. "Fate trusts him."

I started at that. "What?"

But he wasn't looking at me anymore, his gaze having moved to Kayla before traveling back to Azrael. "Johanna will be returned to Bael. It'll satisfy the broken vow between him and Ezra."

I folded my arms, irritated. "I haven't broken the vow."

"No, but you will," Mietek replied without looking at me. "And placing Johanna under Bael's protection will ensure he doesn't react."

"I agree," Azrael said with a decisive nod.

"Absolutely—"

Johanna stepped forward, her palm meeting my chest. "He's right," she murmured, her fingers curling into my shirt. "You're going to need your strength to find Kristina, Ez. And for that, you need to be able to touch your mate."

"Oh?" Kayla laughed a little without humor. "No. I've already said no. And no means no. Fuck no, actually. Because I am *not* letting that asshole use me again. Now give me the damn blade, Alastor. A deal is a deal."

"What blade?" I asked, distracted by that comment again. But as I caught the smirk dancing along Alastor's lips, I realized I already knew. "No." I couldn't help the dismay and shock in my voice. "You promised a knife made of angel bone?"

"She really doesn't like you," he replied, shrugging. "I have to admit, I'm on her side with this." He held up a hand before Mietek could respond. "But I also understand the value of finding Kristina. So"—he captured and held Kayla's gaze—"I will give you what you want *after* you find Kristina."

"That sounds familiar," she deadpanned.

His midnight irises practically sparkled. "Doesn't it?" He slipped a cloaked arm around Lucía's stiffening shoulders. "Shall we go, sweetheart?"

She flicked her fingers in a pattern I knew all too well. However, Alastor seemed too amused to understand the danger she'd just created with that skilled move.

"Let's get one thing straight," she murmured, a silver sword appearing in her palm. "I'm not a toy to be manhandled or directed." She pressed the tip of the blade to his throat in the next breath, similar to what I'd done when telling him not to test my patience. "And I am not a doll to be fondled and petted."

Alastor hissed, releasing her immediately.

To which Lucía arched a dark brow. "Do we understand each other, *sweetheart*?"

Alastor's eyes narrowed. "Hmm." A slow smile started at the edges of his mouth. "Yes, you'll absolutely do."

Lucía gaped at him before looking at me and then at Azrael and Mietek. "He's insane. You can't send me with him."

"Done deal," Alastor told her, his palm circling her wrist —the same one holding the sword. "You know where to find us."

They disappeared, the Archdemon far more powerful than I cared to admit.

I growled, the instinct one I couldn't control.

Kayla cursed, her irritation seeming to be over losing her precious blade.

Because she'd intended to kill me.

This whole event had been her way of calling me down and capturing a piece of the Divinity, all in exchange for a rare angel-bone knife.

Which meant she'd just jeopardized the balance for her own selfish vendetta.

My hands curled into fists at my sides, the very notion of it making me want to murder my own fucking mate.

Except Mietek started talking, and his words frustrated me even more.

"You two focus on cleaning up this mess. Meanwhile, Azrael and I will handle Bael and Johanna."

"Actually, I'll take care of that," Lord Zebulon interjected. "Prince Ashmedai requested that I personally handle the delivery to Prince Bael."

"Or I could take her," Kayla offered.

I narrowed my gaze at the little troublemaker. "And, what, hide in Daddy's realm? No. Absolutely not."

"I'm not going to *hide*," she bit back. "Not after how long it took me to escape his realm the first time."

My eyebrows lifted. "You escaped?"

"You sound surprised," she replied. "I'm not the weakling you abandoned in Hell, Ezra."

No, she certainly wasn't. She'd more than grown up. Something I really hated noticing.

Mietek and Azrael ignored the exchange, their conversation shifting back to Johanna.

"She's my charge," I told them. "I can take her."

"We need you to focus on finding Kristina." Azrael's tone remained measured yet authoritative. "You're best suited to find her, Ezra."

Mietek glanced at Azrael. "Not sure about 'best suited.'"

Normally, I would defend myself against the insult. But I rather agreed with him at the moment.

I wasn't at my strongest. Nowhere near it.

When I'd engaged in the bond with Kayla, I'd known there would be ramifications. I just hadn't realized how severe those ramifications would be.

Mietek glanced at me, his ebony gaze assessing. He'd clearly picked up on my lack of a response.

"It'll be good for you," he finally said after a beat. "Use it to recharge."

I knew what he meant. Use *Kayla* to recharge.

Oh, I will, I thought, refocusing on the female in question.

Kristina's kidnapping was a consequence of Kayla's poor attempt at revenge. She'd done all this because she wanted to kill me.

"Were you even really here to talk about the balance?" I asked her. "Or was that your way of making small talk before the Tracker arrived?"

It would make sense for them to work together. She created chaos, gave Alastor a piece of the Divinity, obtained the blade, and killed me. An easy plan. Strategic, too.

"Excuse me?" Her expression and voice suggested I'd offended her. But considering that we were in this present mess because of her selfishness, I wasn't about to apologize.

"I believe that's our cue," Azrael said.

"Yep," Johanna agreed, her fingers leaving my shirt. I hadn't even realized she was still touching me, but given the way Kayla glared at her, she'd certainly noticed.

Hmm, is that a hint of jealousy I detect? I wondered, slightly entertained by the notion. It implied Kayla still didn't fully understand our bond. Because if she did, she'd know I couldn't seek physical comfort from anyone except her.

Hence my four-plus decades of forced celibacy.

That hadn't been nearly as difficult as my weakening

energy or the agony of the dreams I experienced every night. I'd never known how much I could want a woman... until Kayla.

But that was entirely not the point.

The little hellion had come here with the intent to trade a piece of the Divinity for a blade to kill me. Fine. I could almost respect the strategy behind that. But her selfish plan had ended in Kristina's disappearance.

Because she'd created a damn tear in the veil.

Something humans could have seen.

The mundane immaturity of it all floored me.

Was she that blinded by revenge that she couldn't respect the bigger picture? Our fucking existence was at stake, and all she cared about was spilling my blood?

I wanted to throttle her all over again.

Something Mietek and the others clearly picked up on because they grabbed Johanna with a "We'll be in touch" and disappeared as a collective unit. Dariel and Raziel left with them, not saying a single word throughout the exchange. But the judgment in their gazes had spoken volumes.

However, I couldn't focus on their condemnation now.

Not with the feisty demon princess staring me down a mere block away from where we'd first met.

Only this time, she wasn't the meek little Halfling I'd easily manipulated before.

But a woman with a millennia-old need for vengeance.

And a full grasp on her demonic abilities.

All right, little mate, I thought, narrowing my gaze as she crouched into a fighting stance. *Let's dance.*

KAYLA

I'm going to kill Ashmedai, I thought, my focus on Ezra's too-perfect form.

Ashmedai must have known this would happen, that my distraction would end in chaos. The damn Archdemon was always one step ahead of everyone around him, setting up the pieces exactly as he saw fit so they would fall in the order he required.

Including sending me on this chase to find Kristina.

Because I didn't think for a second that this was a coincidence.

He knew the balance was at stake, that certain members from both realms—Hell and Heaven—were growing in power.

"War is coming," he'd told me. *"And if we don't play this exactly right, pandemonium will win."*

I'd played my part, just like he'd intended. Except he'd failed to mention the very negative outcome of this entire mess would result in me having to work with Ezra.

My nemesis.

My *mate*.

I hated him. And I hated more that the others thought they could just dictate to me like some sort of minion.

I'm Princess Kayla of Bael. Not a fucking pawn.

My teeth ground together in protest. This was ridiculous. "I'm not working with you," I said.

"Oh, you absolutely are," Ezra countered. "Even if I have to follow you to Hell and drag you back, you *will* help me fix this."

"Like I did last time?" I asked, arching a brow. "Oh, wait, you can only mate me once. Hmm, so that's out. How will you use me this time?"

"Don't act like this is my fault, little hellion. You're the one who set the trap that allowed Kristina to be taken. And for what? A selfish vendetta." He glared at me. "If your goal here was to punish me, then trust me when I say your job is done. Because I've never been more disappointed than I am right now."

My lips parted. "Excuse me?"

"You heard me. You're a fucking disgrace, and I'm mated to you. It disgusts me."

His words knocked the air right out of my lungs, causing my heart to halt midbeat.

I rose from my fighting crouch and straightened my spine, his statement rolling through my mind on repeat. I'd imagined this moment a million times. Never once had I anticipated his ability to hurt me with a few crude comments.

But I felt each one like an arrow through the damn chest.

I hadn't realized that Ashmedai's *calling card* would explode in the sky. Just as I hadn't anticipated a Tracker showing up and unleashing a venom bomb. Although, I had been immune to it, thanks to my cuff, so I should have acted faster than I had. But I'd been in a bit of shock from his appearance. I'd also completely misunderstood his intentions. By the time I'd figured out what he'd intended to do, it'd been too late.

At least I'd stabbed him.

With a trackable knife, I realized with a start. All my

weapons had runes on them that allowed me to find them again with ease, mostly because I was tired of other demons taking my shit.

But in this case, it might just allow us to find the Tracker who'd taken Kristina.

Which meant we needed to move now before he had a chance to remove it.

We were probably already too late due to all the conversation.

"We need to go," I said, looking at Ezra. "Right fucking now." I was already pulling up the coordinates with the cuff on my wrist.

"What are you talking about?"

"My knife has a locator rune on it." It should give us a near-exact location. I just had to—

"That's convenient," Ezra replied, interrupting my thoughts. "And obviously bullshit. I'm not the gullible one in this relationship, Kayla."

My jaw ticked, the urge to punch him riding my spirit. But we needed to fix this first and argue later.

Despite what he thought about me, I didn't want to make any of this worse.

After everything Ashmedai and I had reviewed, I actually thought giving Alastor a piece of the Divinity would help in the long term. The Archdemons needed a strong partner to ground their powers. They were growing exponentially, something I didn't want to admit to Ezra because my own abilities were also strengthening at impossible rates.

Ashmedai, Alastor, and Bael were all experiencing the same phenomenon. Which meant the other Archdemons likely were as well.

And not all of them were reasonable leaders.

Some valued anarchy and literal world domination.

Hence, we were trying to get ahead of this to stop the eventual war.

But if Kristina had been taken by the wrong Archdemon... then I'd just worsened everything.

Which I firmly blamed on Ashmedai.

And also myself.

Ezra was right. I had acted selfishly. At least a little bit. But I'd thought the phone would just send up a beacon or something, not create a damn hole in the sky.

Regardless, debating the hows and whys was a waste of time.

We could solve this case right now if I located that damn Tracker.

Then Alastor would give me the blade.

And I'd use it on Ezra.

"Are you listening to me?" the asshole Archangel demanded. "We're doing this my way."

I snorted. "We did that last time. It's my turn now."

"I'm not going anywhere with you."

I ignored him in favor of the coordinates populating the space above my cuff. *Got ya*, I thought, grinning to myself. Then I met Ezra's gaze and held out my arm so he could see the location. "Want to tell me how a Tracker ended up in Heaven?"

His brow furrowed, but those pretty gold-brown eyes of his slid to my glowing cuff and the location hovering in the air above it. "How...?"

"Runes," I answered. "And, as I said, I put a tracker mark on my knife. This is where it's at right now." I rotated my wrist, drawing the power back into the metal, and folded my arms. "I think we both know I would never willingly go to Heaven. So. Either you accept my lead and whisk us up there. Or we can stand here and continue to waste time. Up to you."

His square jaw ticked as he studied me. "I don't trust you."

"Likewise, *Ez*," I said, using the nickname Johanna had given him. They were clearly close, and I didn't want to think about *how* close they were. Nor did I want to consider how she felt about him being mated to someone else.

His gaze narrowed. "Don't call me that."

"Why not?"

"Because you're not worthy," he returned.

"You issue these insults like they should mean something to me," I told him, doing my best to pretend like nothing he'd said had bothered me, while knowing full well he'd already struck several chords inside me. "But all you're doing is wasting my time and yours. It's making me wonder if you're purposely drawing this out because you don't want to solve the case."

He grunted. "I'm not drawing anything out. I'm saying I don't fucking trust you."

"Which is fascinating, considering you're the one who betrayed me, *Ezra*, not the other way around." I met and held his gaze. "If you're not willing to follow this lead, then I'll find someone else who is. You have five seconds to decide before I disappear."

Rather than wait for him to insult me again, I started pulling up the rune on my cuff that would allow me to portal.

But his palm curled around my forearm, causing a volt of energy to pass through us. I shivered and he visibly trembled, his irises flaring with liquid gold flames as I met his gaze. "What...?"

He didn't give me a chance to finish my question—which would have been *What is that?*—his teleportation ability wrapping around us and carrying us through time and space.

Sparks sizzled across my skin, an odd sort of power exchange occurring between Ezra and me as we traveled.

Then my stomach began to churn, confirming he'd whisked us up to the heavenly realm—a place I absolutely should never visit. It weakened my demonic senses to a point where I would eventually be almost mortal. Not even my enchanted bracelet would help with that.

I pressed my palm to my abdomen, my knees giving out as we appeared outside on a too-green lawn.

Ezra let me fall, his own hand leaving my forearm as though I'd burned him.

I shuddered, my body protesting everything around me. The cool air. The lack of chaos. The utter perfection of every foreseeable item.

Even the sky was too blue.

I curled into a ball of torment, my sense of purpose disappearing as Ezra left me in the middle of the grassy field.

A breeze caressed my cheeks as his feathers fluttered, his black-brown wings magnificent and sprawling as he used them to propel himself toward a house in the distance.

It was as though he didn't care about me at all.

Leaving me again.

In agony. Suffering. A ball of worthless energy deserted to die.

A flame lit from within me, my heart hardening that much more as fire licked through my veins.

Move, I told myself. *Don't let him do this to you again.*

I gritted my teeth, forcing my body to unfurl.

I'm not that girl anymore. I'm Princess of Bael. A future fucking queen.

Well, not literally.

A future *Archdemon*.

But those semantics didn't matter, because I needed to *move*.

My stomach rolled as I forced myself to shift upward to a

seated position. *One step at a time*, I thought, growling as I attempted to find enough strength to stand.

Seconds turned into minutes, the world spinning around me in an array of brightness that made me more disoriented than the pits of Hell.

I closed my eyes and massaged my temples, my lungs filling as I compelled myself to breathe.

In and out.

There you go.

Archdemons could technically enter Heaven. The more powerful the Archdemon, the more easily they ascended and acclimated.

Clearly, I hadn't reached my full potential yet, because I felt like a withering Slither.

I stole another deep breath through my nose, blew it out of my mouth, and forced myself to my knees. My equilibrium shifted, a sense of weightlessness knocking me off-kilter, but after another handful of breaths, I was able to find my balance and stand.

Now I just needed to walk, something that would have been easier if I didn't feel as though I was floating. The air up here was definitely thinner than the atmosphere on Earth and the murkiness of Hell.

Swallowing, I checked my cuff to confirm that Ezra had brought us to the right place, then I pushed myself forward.

Hours seemed to pass along my very short journey, and when I finally made it to the door, Ezra was already leaving.

His expression told me everything I needed to know. *We're too late*.

My heart skipped a beat, the world shifting around me once more. Perhaps my dizziness had nothing to do with this realm and everything to do with the imbalance of power dissolving around us.

Hellfire, I whispered to myself. *This... can't be good*.

Ezra stepped back as I pushed through the threshold, some part of me needing to see the damage for myself. Because I'd caused this. I'd allowed this to happen. I needed to face the consequences of those actions.

It hadn't been deliberate, and I could lay equal blame at Ashmedai's feet. But that didn't change the fact that this had happened because of my intention to call the Divinity.

I could shoulder that blame. I could handle the aftermath of that decision. Just as I could recognize that I wasn't the one who'd actually carried out the crime.

Except it wasn't Kristina's dead body I found upon entering, but those of the Tracker and the Portal Dweller. I frowned. "My knife didn't do that. It was steel, not silver."

"I know," Ezra replied, leaning against the door with his arms crossed over his chest. "Someone with substantial power killed them. Someone from *my* realm."

Substantial power, I repeated to myself, snorting. Except the latter half of his sentence registered, the truth of the energy signature unmistakable.

There were very few ways to kill a demon.

The easiest of which being to use silver.

And yet... "I don't detect any silver," I admitted, telling Ezra without words that I agreed with his assessment. Minus the *substantial power* jibe.

Although, he might not have meant it the way it'd sounded. However, everything he'd said in the last half hour had been insulting by nature, thus making it hard not to read into such a statement.

"No, whoever killed them did it by force alone." He sounded distracted, like he was evaluating something I couldn't see. Perhaps the energy he'd mentioned had destroyed the two demons.

He spun on his heel to search the house. I followed him through the living area to the kitchen, where he searched the cabinets and refrigerator—all empty. He went to the two bedrooms at the back next, noted the pristinely made beds with a frown, and then went to search the bathroom between them for any evidence of use.

There was none, suggesting this home hadn't been lived in for quite a while. The cleanliness was probably just a heavenly effect.

I left him there and headed toward the office I'd seen near the entry. There was nothing in the desk, just a pen and a piece of blank paper. The cabinets were empty. The bookshelves were clear. And the closet had a solitary jacket.

Ezra stood in the doorway watching me as I finished, his expression unreadable.

He returned to the corpses in the living room, his head tilting as the bodies began to dissolve into ash. Demons usually disintegrated quickly upon death, but time moved differently in this realm. Or maybe the lack of hellish energy slowed the process.

Regardless, that's going to be a bitch to clean, I thought, watching the dust particles dance in the air. Bending, I retrieved my knife from the deteriorating demon and said, "I'll be outside," since there wasn't much I could do inside anyway. I also really didn't want ash in my nose or hair.

Demon corpse wasn't a good look.

Ezra didn't say anything as I left, his attention on the essence he seemed to be tracing all over the house.

Hopefully, he wouldn't take too long, because this realm was giving me a headache. And unfortunately, he was my only ticket back down to Earth.

The irony of that wasn't lost on me. It seemed our relationship would forever be founded on his ability to teleport us at will.

With a grunt, I found a place under a tree to relax.

My legs moved better now, my body seeming to have

acclimated to this world a bit faster than anticipated. Maybe my Archdemon genetics were helping me more than I realized.

Or it's related to the growing power shift, I thought, wincing. *And we've come full circle.*

Because that was why I'd wanted to reach the Divinity.

Lifting my arm, I allowed a flicker of flame to dance across my fingertips. This sort of power shouldn't come so naturally to me here in this plane. Yet I was completely in control of the flaming ability—something I proved by stirring a spiral of fiery energy that swirled up my arm.

It glimmered and purred all around me, responding to my every command and intensifying by the second.

I sighed, momentarily at peace as the substance grounded me in this realm. My eyes fell closed, allowing me to enjoy my surroundings.

A woodsy scent teased my nostrils, lulling me into a state of sublime comfort.

Only to be interrupted by the clearing of a throat.

Ezra.

It took only a second for me to realize the calming scent belonged to him, the undertone of leaves teasing me to full awareness. His golden orbs swirled with power as he stared down at me. He took in the power racing up and down my arms, but rather than snuff it out like the first time we'd met, he merely admired the view.

I almost wanted him to try to steal my fire again, just to see what would happen.

Could he douse my flames with ease like the day we'd first met? Or would I burn him in the process?

Hearing him scream from my fiery embrace would be quite an alluring sound. Alas, his gaze merely returned to mine as he said, "We should go."

"Go where?" I asked, not bothering to call in my power.

Instead, it intensified, roaming up to my neck to flirt with my hair.

"Somewhere safe where we can regroup and decide our next steps," he replied, his focus shifting to my throat.

"And that would be...?" I prompted.

His attention slowly returned to my eyes, his pupils flaring. "My place."

A snort escaped me unbidden. "I'm supposed to feel safe at *your place*?" I nearly laughed. "Right."

He blew out a breath, then palmed the back of his neck while looking skyward, as if searching for patience.

Let me know when you find it, I thought, rolling my eyes and lying down in the grass beside the tree, content to wait here all day. *It really is nice in this place. Soft. Pretty. Peaceful.*

Very different from Hell, where the directions and coordinates changed constantly. I'd spent many years just getting lost down there.

"I trusted you enough to come here. Now it's your turn to trust me enough to go where I suggest." He held out his hand, his gaze taking on a hard glint. "It's that or I leave you here for another angel to find. Unless you've managed to develop a teleportation gift that I'm unaware of? Beyond that trick on your wrist, I mean."

My jaw clenched. But he did have a point. He'd taken us to the coordinates I'd shown him. Now I could let him take me to *his place*.

A realm between the realms.

The precious Divinity.

Wherever the fuck that was.

"Are you going to kill me for knowing too much afterward?" I asked as I pushed myself up off the ground without the assistance of his hand. My flames died in the next instant, but the energy lingered behind, ready for me to call it back at a moment's notice.

"If I kill you, it won't be for knowing too much," he returned, his expression as dark as his tone.

I met his stare with one of my own. "I'm not afraid of you."

He hummed something unintelligible in response, then grabbed my forearm again and wrapped us up in his dark feathers.

I tried to ignore how soft they were against my skin, but it was hard not to notice it when combined with his warm touch.

Butterflies took flight in my abdomen, replacing the earlier queasiness.

Sweet scents tickled my nose.

Ezra's energy surrounded me in a ball of comfort that I'd never known I needed. I nearly leaned into him, craving more, but an eternity of sadness shattered the inclination.

He left me.

Abandoned me.

Betrayed me.

I'd never meant anything to him, just a passing pawn to be used as a one-way ticket to Hell.

There was no comfort in that memory. No happiness. Only soul-destroying agony and a deep-seated need to make him pay.

I'd messed this up by trusting Ashmedai to help me more than himself. Just as I'd trusted Alastor to come through on our deal.

My father had taught me better. As had all my mentors. My supposed friends.

I'd grown up terrified of demons—so many of them had wanted me dead.

Being Bael's daughter had changed all that. At least in his realm. But I wore a target on my back whenever I left, especially when I didn't bring my personal guard.

However, I'd used many of those escape experiences to learn how to properly defend myself. Because I knew there would be a day when I finally found Ezra, and I would need every bit of training I could get in facing powerful beings.

I just hadn't expected his touch to feel so *welcoming*.

My jaw clenched, my eyes closing as I forced myself to ignore it.

This is just part of the bond he tricked me into, I thought. *He's not mine. He will never be mine. And I will never be his.*

I wanted to kill him.

A simple touch wouldn't change that.

Once we finished tracking Kristina down, I'd follow through on my intent. Then no one could accuse me of being selfish in my need for revenge because I would have fixed the problem *before* fulfilling my vengeance.

I opened my eyes to find him scrutinizing my features.

I shut down inside, refusing to let him see any part of me.

I'm not yours. And you will never be mine.

Ezra

Hatred.
Desire.
Fury.
Sadness.

The emotions swirled in Kayla's gaze, each one more devastating than the last. *I did this to her,* I thought, noting the fractures deep in her eyes.

She tried to hide the pain behind a mask of anger, but I could sense each agonized sensation through our bond. Fuck, she'd really grown up.

"I'm not the weakling you abandoned in hell, Ezra," she'd said earlier.

No. She'd blossomed into a warrior female. All hard edges and crude lines founded in anger.

Anger at me.

I swallowed, releasing her with a shove, and stepped back before I did something I regretted. *Like kiss her.*

Just the consideration of it had my insides turning to molten embers, the desire one I'd cultivated and denied for far too long.

Being around her only worsened that longing.

Because she made me feel so damn good. Those mere touches were enough to help me breathe a little easier, lightening my soul and clearing my mind.

It was... intoxicating.

Addictive.

Insane.

Mietek had told me to use her to improve my strength, but now that I'd touched her twice, I wasn't sure I could follow through.

Using her would only deepen my overall craving.

Using her might lead to me keeping her forever.

And using her might break her irrevocably.

I ran my fingers through my hair, blowing out a breath. *Using her isn't an option.*

I wasn't the Archangel I used to be. Once upon a time, I would have done anything to save the balance. But it was too late. The power scales were always intended to tip.

I'd prolonged the inevitable for as long as I could.

Now we needed to work on recovering from it and ensuring the scales tipped in our favor.

Which meant finding Kristina.

I turned away from Kayla to wander away from the foyer I'd teleported us into. Her eyes had fallen to the beige tiles and were now lifting to take in the grand staircase beside us. "It's bright," she muttered.

"Yes. Windows tend to allow light in," I deadpanned, gesturing to the two-story glass windows framing my grand entry door.

"Oh, is that how windows work?" She canted her head to the side. "Fascinating."

Snorting, I continued into the hallway leading to the myriad of kitchens lining the back of my home. Food was my solitary indulgence in life, but as I reached the initial layer of my sanctuary, I realized I wasn't hungry. Rather than explain myself, I merely said, "If you need food, you'll find it here." Because I *felt* Kayla walking behind me, her energy a seductive wave to my senses. It didn't matter that she'd kept ten feet between us. It might as well have been an inch.

Here only five seconds and she's already infiltrating my space, I thought, grumbling to myself. *This was a bad idea.*

But there wasn't anywhere else for us to go. I needed my books and spells, and this area between the realms was relatively safe. At least until the balance fully shifted.

Which wasn't going to happen on my watch.

Kayla and I just needed to solve this puzzle, then we could kill this buzz between us.

By fucking, some dark part of me whispered.

I ignored it, walked by where she stood frozen in the dining area off the first kitchen, and took the hall behind my kitchens toward my study at the end.

Kayla followed, commenting on the size of my estate and asking if I was compensating for something, but I didn't deign to reply to her childish feedback.

Perhaps I'd show her the error of that thought someday.

Perhaps I wouldn't.

More light streamed in through the double doors at the end, the three-story windows beyond framing my library turned study. Or maybe it was a study *and* a library, because the other three walls were all bookshelves up to the ceiling.

"Holy shit," Kayla breathed as she entered the room before me.

"Holy Divinity," I corrected, unfurling my wings and allowing them to touch the ground. I could technically pull them in, but I preferred being in my natural state while in my home. The panes at the top of my windowed wall were glassless, allowing me a direct escape into the sky should I need it.

Kayla ignored my correction, instead wandering to the back windows and the sliding doors in the middle. She opened them without asking permission to step out onto the wrap-around patio outside to take in the view of the pond and trees beyond.

A slice of Heaven, I mused, taking a moment to enjoy the scenery as well.

It never grew old, the rolling hills and blue sky an opulence I adored.

Clouds didn't exist here.

No storms. No need for rain. Just a haven of paradise blessed with perfect temperatures, bright days, and crystal-clear nights.

A stark difference from Hell, something Kayla clearly noticed. As she'd been there the last... I frowned. *How long? Thousands of years?*

My eyebrows lifted.

Shit. No. Ten thousand or fifteen thousand? I glanced at the back of her head. *And she still holds a grudge after all this time?*

Well, I supposed I had ruined her life.

Shaking my head, I unfurled my wings and propelled myself up my shelves to locate the book I desired. Naturally, it was near the top of the room, but the spine fell easily into my hand as I stole it from the shelf.

I flipped the pages open as I descended, my gaze searching the words for the spell that would bring Kristina home.

The last time I'd used this, it had been on Johanna.

And the aftermath of that situation still stood on my veranda outside.

Ignoring Kayla, I settled at my desk with the ancient text in my hand.

"Hmm," I hummed, finding the section I needed and gently laying the book on the polished surface of my desk.

The sweet scent of lilies assaulted my nostrils as Kayla returned, her natural perfume resembling a spike to my senses.

I ignored it, instead inhaling the aroma of the old book

and focusing on my ingredient list. Making a mental list of what I needed, I took off around the room to find each item. I kept them all tucked away in alcoves among the books, not to hide them, just to maintain a certain organization. It made collecting everything simple, with the blank sheet of paper the final item required.

Kayla took over my chair while I flattened the parchment on the desk, her silence an irritation to my senses. Or maybe it was having her at my back that irked me.

However, I refused to comment on it.

And I busied myself with mixing ingredients for the locator spell.

Most of it was blood related, with a pinch of old feathers and some demonic sand from Kristina's father's home realm. The only thing left that I needed was a piece of her hair.

I stepped away from my desk to go to the bookcase in the corner across from the sprawling windows and pulled the book out that would unleash one of the secret doors in the room. It whisked open to reveal the closet beyond it. This compartment contained everything Divinity-related, meaning strands of their hair, old clothes, and anything else that could be used to track them as needed.

Kristina's box was at the back, her strand of hair carefully wrapped within to preserve her energy traits.

I gingerly pulled it out without touching the strand—I didn't want to risk mixing up the power signature—and carried it with the cloth wrapped around it back to the table.

Then I dropped the hair into the liquid and gently stirred it with the wooden spoon I'd plucked off one of the shelves from above.

"What are you doing?" Kayla finally asked as I started sprinkling the concoction over the parchment paper.

"A locator spell," I replied, stating the obvious.

"If you could do that the whole time, why did you follow my lead?" Kayla asked, her tone genuinely curious.

"Because I wanted to see if you were telling the truth," I admitted. "And, on the off chance you were telling the truth, it potentially allowed for a faster resolution."

"Thus allowing me to kill you faster," she replied, nodding. "My thoughts exactly."

I grunted. "You can't kill me."

"Alastor's blade says otherwise."

I paused my task to meet her gaze. "Your aim says otherwise," I corrected, my focus shifting to her leather jacket. "How's your shoulder?"

She shrugged out of the coat in response, letting the material fall to the ground and revealing the tank top beneath. Aside from the dried blood, she appeared fully healed.

"Impressive," I murmured, dropping my gaze to the table in an effort to stop myself from admiring her breasts in that tight top. Because while my comment had been in regard to her ability to heal quickly, I'd meant it more in response to the display of her curves.

Which I really did not need to think about right now.

I refocused on my task, adding the final splash of potion to the paper.

Then I pulled a knife from my pocket to slice my palm—an action that made Kayla grin—and squeezed a trickle of blood onto the center of the page.

The air warmed around us, the only indication that the spell had come to life.

And lines began forming on the page in a light gray ink—lines that defined the locations within the realms.

They appeared and disappeared and reappeared again, the magic shifting through time and space to check every area of all the worlds for Kristina's location.

As the realms were vast, this would take a while.

I blew out a breath. "We should try to sleep while this works," I told her. "We might need our rest for wherever this is going to take us."

Well, *I* needed rest. Something I wouldn't have needed a few decades ago, but that was my consequence to bear.

"Right, then I hope Kristina is still up here and not down there, or an eternity might pass in those seven hours," Kayla muttered.

I blinked at her and frowned. "What do you mean?"

"You know, because of the whole 'one day here is a year on Earth and over three centuries in Hell.'" Her brow furrowed at whatever she saw in my expression. "Right...?"

"You think time moves like Heaven here," I realized aloud, translating what she'd just said. "Time here moves like it does on Earth."

Her eyebrows lifted. "So it's been longer than forty-one days since...?"

It took me another minute to follow what she meant. "Since I left you in Hell? Yeah. It's been over four decades."

Which felt a hell of a lot longer, considering the agony I'd gone through with being fully cut off from my mate. It was through strength and will alone that I'd survived this long. Jo had been about to send me down to Bael to negotiate a truce. But then Kayla had given her the opportunity to take charge with that little stunt in Virginia.

"Huh. I thought it was only, like, a month for you." She looked me up and down. "I guess that explains the aging."

"Aging?" I repeated.

She waved a hand at my head. "Yeah, the white hair and general aura of exhaustion."

My jaw ticked. Johanna commenting on my "aging" had always made me roll my eyes. But hearing Kayla say it bothered me in a way I didn't want to consider.

I look this way because of you.

Because of me.

Because of us.

Rather than say any of that, I merely shrugged and turned back to the growing map. "I'll show you your guest room options, then we'll check the map again in six hours."

I didn't wait for her to agree, just started toward the door and tucked in my wings as I stepped into the hallway once more. The width more than accommodated my feathers, but it still left me feeling a bit boxed in with the ceiling over my head. Twelve feet never felt tall enough, as it would be hard to fly in such a confined space. Fortunately, it only lasted for the length of time it took me to find the kitchens and the back staircase. It was wide open with glassless panes all around it, allowing me to come and go as needed from this space.

Of course, that same area probably left Kayla a bit uneasy since it meant a simple misstep could plummet her to the ground below. I glanced over my shoulder to briefly check on her and found her gazing out into the courtyards—this time with a view of the pool and its waterfalls—with an expression of wonder on her face, not fear.

"Don't let the view distract you," I cautioned. "We have three stories to climb, and I don't want to play 'fetch the falling demon' right now."

She snorted in response but didn't otherwise comment.

I took that as a sign to continue upward along the spiral of stairs. No banister, of course. Not that Kayla seemed to need one.

The third floor, which was technically the second floor in my home, just three stories up, boasted more windowless halls and skylights above that could be opened via a latch.

I led her to the guest quarter wing, then gestured at the three separate doors.

"You can stay in any room, but I recommend this one"—I pointed to the room with windows overlooking the front of the house—"if you want to feel more secure. The other two have open walls meant to accommodate wings. This room, however, has glass doors that lead to a balcony with railings. Towels are in the en-suite bathrooms. There are probably some clothes in the closets, too. Guests come and go."

The Divinity had a lot of admirers, and rather than house angels at their respective residences, I hosted them here where I could watch them.

Steeling myself, I finally allowed myself to face Kayla again.

And felt the air deflate from my lungs.

Stunning.

It was the only word I could use to describe seeing her standing beneath the sun's rays, her hair illuminating in various shades of brown, some of which were tinged with red.

Fuck, it hurt to look at her, to see how beautiful she'd become, and then to catch those agonized layers in her caramel-colored irises.

I cleared my throat and forced my gaze away from her. "Do you need anything else?"

"Alastor's blade?" she asked sweetly.

My eyes slid back to her, my momentary thrall burning to ash at my feet. "Try to sleep, Kayla. And just a reminder, there's food in the kitchens if you need it."

Rather than stand around to wait for whatever retort she imagined, I stepped toward one of the outside exit points and took flight.

Try to sleep, I repeated to myself. *Because I doubt I'll be sleeping at all.* Not with a potential assassin in my home.

As much fun as it would be to engage in a lethal dance with my mate, I had work to do.

And a balance to evaluate.

War is coming, I thought, my feathers bristling in the wind. *What side will we fall on?*

KAYLA

THIS PLACE IS A PALACE, I DECIDED AS I WANDERED down the hall toward the back stairs.

The "guest room" Ezra had given me for the night was more like a full apartment than a room. It had a living area, en-suite kitchen, a half bath near the dining room—which had a table for six in it—another bathroom in the master suite, and a final room set up like an office.

As the daughter of an Archdemon, I was used to opulence. My father's estate was at least four times the size of this one, but he also had an army of staff who lived with him. From what I could tell, Ezra lived here alone.

Which begged the question—where do the members of the Divinity stay?

I wandered down the stairs, my gaze snagging on the exterior once more. Night had fallen while I'd slept, thoroughly confusing my sense of time.

Of course, I'd spent the last ten thousand years or so in Hell. And nothing about the moons' or suns' cycles down there could be considered *typical*. They changed based on mood and the desire to shine.

But Ezra had claimed this place existed in the Earth realm, which implied a day and night schedule similar to what humans experienced.

I made my way downstairs and into the area he'd referred to as the *kitchens*. I hadn't understood the plural before. I did now as I realized he'd meant it literally—there were three kitchens. All in a row. All packed with different types of foods and equipment. All catering to a variety of ethnic cuisines.

"Huh," I marveled, taking in the massive flat grill of the third kitchen. "Hibachi-fried Ezra would be fun to make on this."

A grunt came from behind me, alerting me to *his* presence.

I rolled my eyes and turned around. "Worried I'll find your knives?"

"We've already been over how poorly you manage them. So no." He leaned against the doorway with an apple in his hand. He had on a pair of jeans and a long-sleeved sweater that I guessed tied in the back somewhere to allow his wings room to move.

No socks or shoes.

"Are you dressed modestly for my benefit?" I wondered aloud, aware that clothes were uncomfortable when wings were involved. It was why my father tended to wander around shirtless.

Ezra took a bite of his apple, his striking gold-brown eyes lazily roaming over my outfit. I'd found a pair of jean shorts that fit, paired them with what appeared to be a clean tank top, and reapplied my boots and jacket. This was after enjoying an hour of having every part of me massaged by *three* showerheads.

I'd tossed my still-damp hair up into a bun, ignored the makeup spread in the bathroom cabinet, and slipped the clothes on without underwear.

Because I was not about to put on panties of questionable origin.

"Hmm," he hummed before sinking his teeth into his apple again.

I couldn't tell if that was his reaction to my wardrobe choice or my question. And I didn't care enough to ask for clarification.

Instead, I focused on finding something edible in the fridge. *Sushi.*

I paused, glancing around. I hadn't seen any staff members walking around, but he clearly had them somewhere. Maybe he'd told them to hide from me.

Their loss, my gain, I decided, plucking the tray from the fridge. I found a pair of chopsticks in a drawer, took over a stool at the bar counter near the windowless wall at the back, and went to town while Ezra observed from the doorway.

It wasn't until I popped the last bite into my mouth that he finally said, "That was my lunch."

I chewed slowly, drawing out the moment before swallowing. "Well, it was delicious."

"Of course it was. I made it."

My eyebrows lifted. "You made sushi?"

He rolled his eyes and tossed his apple core into a nearby bin. "You ask that with genuine surprise, as though you know anything about me." He ventured over to the fridge to pull out a green slush from the top shelf and poured himself a glass. "I had left it in there to sit for a moment while I checked on my locator spell."

"Hmm," I hummed, repeating his sound from earlier. "Well. Thanks for lunch, then." *Even though it's, like, midnight outside,* I added in my head.

He poured a second glass of the green goop, brought both cups over to me, set them down, and picked up my empty tray.

I gaped at his soft, feathery wings as he took the dish to the chef-appropriate sink. He rinsed it, soaped it off, washed it again, and placed it on a towel to dry before joining me at the table on the only other stool.

Two straws seemed to magically appear in his hand.

One for each drink.

He tapped his glass against mine, saying, "Cheers," and took a healthy swallow.

"Is it seaweed?" I asked, my nose wrinkling at the thought.

He snorted. "No. It's a green tea smoothie. If you don't want it, I'll drink both." His golden-brown gaze narrowed. "I'll need the calories since someone rudely devoured my lunch."

"You told me to find food if I needed it. I did. It was delicious. End of discussion." I considered that for a moment, frowning. "Actually, no. Not end of discussion. The least you could do is feed me after you betrayed me and left me to suffer in Hell for an eternity."

He ignored me in favor of his drink, but the slight pinch in his brow told me he'd heard me just fine.

Deciding to play his silent game, I taste-tested the green goop and found it surprisingly fruity. "This isn't green tea."

"The base is green tea. I added nutrients." His focus shifted to the night, his gaze drifting up to the moon and the stars. They provided most of our light, something I hadn't really noticed until now.

Everything in this home held a natural appeal to it. Woods. Marbles. White paint. Minimal fluorescent lights. *A lot of glassless windows.*

I mused over it all while I sipped the drink, finding it oddly refreshing. When I was done, I found Ezra's gaze on me again, his expression unreadable.

"What?" I demanded.

"It's strange having you here." His tone implied that he meant *strange* in a negative way.

No surprise there. He'd been an ass when we'd first met, and an ass now.

"You're just as charming as I remember," I drawled, sliding off my stool to carry the cup to the sink. I mimicked his actions with the tray, setting the glass right beside it when done.

He followed suit, cleaning his own cup and the pitcher, while saying, "The locator spell was almost done when I checked. Kristina is in the human realm."

That sounded about right. The shifting of the balance made the energy on Earth chaotic and unpredictable, which would allow someone to hide Kristina rather easily there.

However, rather than comment, I merely nodded. Because I didn't want to hear another mocking "hmm" from Archangel Charming over here.

Ezra finished his kitchen task, then left without another word.

I took that as an invitation to follow and trailed after him to the study and the glorious view it presented of the land-scape outside. If I owned a pair of wings, I would go exploring. Alas, my Archdemon feathers hadn't sprouted yet. It remained unclear if they ever would.

A sigh at the view caught in my throat as I glanced at the desk. My gaze widened, the original parchment having multi-plied into over a dozen maps during my nap.

The eleven realms of Hell glowed red, while the heavenly ones were decorated in soft gray, and Earth unraveled in strokes of black.

Wow.

There were various shades in the different regions as well, causing my lips to curl down. Because they vaguely matched the charts I'd drafted with Ashmedai last week.

I stepped forward to pick up one of the blank pieces of paper and grabbed a pen from Ezra's desk. *I wonder...* I settled on the floor beside one of the fallen parchments and began to draw my own version of a map using the details from my discussion with Ashmedai.

It took several minutes, but the effort proved worth it in the end when I lined up the two maps.

The splotches of color on the parchment matched the power shifts we'd noted.

Narrowing my gaze, I grabbed another piece of blank paper and began drawing the next realm.

Exact match.

Shit.

I took a stack of paper from Ezra's desk, snatched a pack of pens, and settled in among the parchments. I drew everything Ashmedai and I had discussed, including each Archdemon base and their powerful minions. Then I compared the drawings to the maps.

The regions and shades all matched.

But that wasn't what made my stomach churn.

It was the size and colors of the parchment shades that twisted my insides into knots.

Because the parchment shades were just a hair wider than the power outlines Ashmedai and I had drawn last week.

It served as a visual demonstration of how the shift was growing.

Powers were continuing to fluctuate.

The balance is severely at risk.

All things I already knew.

But to see them... *again*... made everything else in this world feel trivial at best.

"*Fuck,*" I whispered to myself. This all proved that Ashmedai's theory about an impending war was absolutely a viable notion.

Whoever took Kristina likely wanted to siphon the power for themselves to use in the upcoming battle. Or perhaps make her an outlet for their abundance of power, which was what my father and Prince Alastor needed pieces of the Divinity to do for them. They were growing too strong and needed the magical conduit to ground them.

Maybe Kristina would be used for a similar purpose.

But the method of her capture suggested otherwise.

This is really bad. A complete understatement, of course. And I'd made it all worse by aiding in Kristina's capture.

"We need to find her right now," I said to myself, standing to scan the maps on Ezra's desk once more. They weren't as easy to read for some reason.

My brow furrowed.

Why are they so dark? The moon had illuminated them perfectly what felt like minutes ago.

I glanced at the windows to find the moon had shifted away to another part of the room, and there wasn't any overhead lighting otherwise. *How long was I...?*

My attention shifted to the floor, noting the myriad of maps littering the ground.

Ezra stood just off to the side, leaning against his desk with his legs casually crossed at the ankles and his hands in the pockets of his jeans. His wings were nowhere in sight.

What...?

Amusement taunted his full lips as he asked, "Are you quite finished?"

I cleared my throat, my mouth having gone dry at finding his intense gaze on me. "I, uh, yes."

Very eloquent, Kay. Great job.

Shaking my head, I pushed away from his desk and took in the mess I'd made of his office. There were drawings and maps everywhere.

"Um..." I glanced at his desk again to find a floating red dot sparking magic in the air. I'd missed it in my daze of trying to read the maps in the dark. "Uh, is that telling us where Kristina is?"

"Yes."

I nodded. "Then we're leaving...?" I prompted.

"Sure," he drawled. "Just as soon as you tell me what the fuck all of this means."

EZRA

I WASN'T BLIND. I COULD PLAINLY SEE WHAT KAYLA had just designed—a war map displaying all the power shifts throughout each realm.

What I really wanted to know was *how* she'd created it.

Because it was... beautiful. Concise. And most importantly, *accurate*.

Every spike of power I'd sensed within the world had been captured in her drawings, as though she'd pulled the information from my soul. As the Archangel of Justice, I could sense imbalances throughout the realms.

Was this a result of our bond? Had she acquired the ability because of my link to her blood? Or was this another talent entirely?

She'd fallen into a trancelike state while drafting these images. Then she'd pieced them all together on the floor as though assembling a puzzle only her mind had understood. Except I'd followed along with every step, aware of where each piece went before she'd placed them.

Did she realize what she'd created?

Or had she fallen under some sort of spell as a result of our link?

"Tell me what this is," I repeated, needing to hear her interpretation of it.

"Maps," she whispered, her expression taking on an

69

unease that reminded me of the old Kayla. The inexperienced, innocent one I'd so easily manipulated.

"Obviously," I replied. "What are they maps of?"

If she said *realms*, I'd snap.

Instead, she bit her lower lip and considered them all, her eyes seeming to clear as she took in her masterpiece.

"The power shifts." She uttered the words softly, but they held a hint of steel beneath them. As though she expected me to deny her claim.

When I remained silent, she glanced up at me and studied my features intently.

I said nothing.

Which only resulted in her saying, "You feel it."

"Of course I do. I'm the Archangel of Justice. Protecting the balance is my job, Kayla."

"Then you understand why Prince Alastor and my father need Lucía and Johanna."

My jaw ticked at the reminder of the two pieces of the Divinity having been taken down into the underworld. That alone caused a disturbance in the energy flow among our worlds, but I understood the purpose. "I imagine it's related to why your father tried to kidnap Johanna four decades ago— to use her as an outlet for his overabundance of power."

"If you knew that, why did you stop him, then? Why trade my life for hers?"

I winced. It wasn't *her* life I'd traded, but my own. Something she'd remarked on just yesterday when she'd asked about my aging. However, she clearly didn't comprehend the impact this mating link had on me or how her residing in Hell while I remained here deteriorated my inner spirit.

Rather than correct her lack of knowledge, I focused on her initial question regarding why I originally stopped Bael. "Because it wasn't time yet and he knew it. He only wanted her as a power play, a way to prove his status to the other Archdemons in the underworld. It had nothing to do with grounding his abilities and everything to do with waving his title around."

"And now?" she prompted, arching a brow.

Her tone told me she was merely testing how much I knew. As she'd essentially just shown me how much she already understood regarding the situation, I supposed I could give her a little insight into my mind in response.

"And now, he's proven he is, in fact, superior." I'd felt it shifting over the last decade, his energy growing substantially heavy in the aura of the underworld. Alastor's power signature had reacted similarly, as had Ashmedai's, Ishkur's, and Morax's. I'd been monitoring them all over the years, aware that they would eventually show promise.

Pushing off my desk, I moved forward to review the maps again. She had pinpointed all eleven Archdemons, noting their auras in a variety of color shades. The darker the red, the stronger their powers. The five Archdemons that I knew were growing were all a ruby shade. She had a few in a standard red and others in a pink.

She'd done the same thing with various Archangels, only using blue.

And then she'd marked several gray and black areas on Earth. "Demons?" I guessed, gesturing to the sprinkle of darker dots in the United States.

"And Nephilim," she replied.

My eyebrows lifted. *That* had been unexpected. "You can sense Nephilim powers?"

She shook her head. "No. Prince Ashmedai acquired the information from Evangeline."

I blinked at her, uncertain of which part of that statement alarmed me more. The fact that Evangeline had willingly given information about Dark Provenance members to an Archdemon, or the implication that she'd been working with said Archdemon.

"Ashmedai?" I prompted. Kayla's connection to the Archdemon concerned me slightly more than the other aspect of her comment.

"Yeah." She pulled the tie out of her hair and ran her fingers through the wavy strands, the texture having crinkled from being scrunched up while wet.

"You've been working with Ashmedai?" I asked incredulously. "Why?"

"It's not like I had a choice," she muttered, her expression hardening as she narrowed her gaze. "I also don't need to explain myself to you."

I arched a brow. "Your recent interior decorating job in my office says otherwise."

She snorted. "Whatever. Do you want to find Kristina or not?" Her focus shifted to the map on the table. She called a flame to her fingertip and used it like a flashlight to highlight the map beneath the red dot. "Vancouver. Great. Shall we go?"

Shutters seemed to fall around her, closing me off from the real Kayla beneath and telling me there was no way in Hell she intended to say another word on the topic.

Because she didn't find me worthy of the knowledge, even though upholding the balance between humanity, Hell, and Heaven was my unequivocal purpose in life.

Rather than push the topic, I allowed her the moment to hide.

She'd already revealed a great deal through all these sketches. They confirmed she knew a lot more about our situation than I could ever have anticipated.

Which meant she could be a valuable partner in this quest.

Or a very dangerous one, I thought, looking her up and down. "All right." I enjoyed a good challenge. Might as well see how this played out.

I picked up the map from the desk, folded it down into a perfect little rectangle, and slipped it into my back pocket. The parchment hummed with magic, telling me it was still working to keep an eye on Kristina's location.

I'd used a similar one to find Johanna all those years ago after Bael had taken her. It was how I'd navigated the underworld. But Kayla had been the reason I'd survived down there, the intense atmosphere not meant for angelic beings.

Our bond had provided me with a literal lifeline, allowing me to thrive in my mate's home environment.

Which was how she'd been able to recover so quickly in Heaven—she'd pulled on my essence to strengthen herself. Not that she seemed to have noticed, but I'd definitely felt it.

Walking past her, I headed toward my bookcase to pull on a book and key in a code on the panel behind it. A door whirred to life, revealing a hidden armory.

Kayla gasped behind me, the only indication that she'd followed me.

Then she brushed by my shoulder to go fondle a pair of my favorite scythes. "Ohhh," she marveled, the sound unmistakably erotic. "This is my kind of kink." She skipped over to a table of daggers before moving on to the wall of ammunition and various mortal guns. "It's really too bad I hate you, Ez," she said, a note of true sadness in her tone. "Otherwise, you would have just become my type."

Type? I repeated to myself, my gaze narrowing at the back of her head. *She has a type?*

That indicated she'd discovered a *type* through trial and error.

Which suggested she'd taken sexual partners. *Plural. Sexual partners* plural.

My jaw ached from clenching it so hard, my desire to wrap my palm around her nape and shove her up against the wall a sudden need that clawed at my insides. I wanted to know who had dared to touch what my soul considered to be *mine*. I wanted to slay them and fuck her in a pool of their blood. I wanted to erase every damn memory in her head and replace them with ones of *me*.

Of course, the only true memories she had of me were unpleasant.

Because I'd used her and then left her in Hell.

A realization that doused cold water over my irrational ire. *She's not really mine*. Our souls were joined, forcing me to remain celibate, but that didn't mean she had to remain faithful to me. Just as it was my spirit that slowly withered and died in her absence, not the other way around.

Had she been a being of Heaven, then our bond would be something else entirely.

But instead, I'd engaged in a forbidden link to bolster myself in my quest, not caring at all for my eventual future.

I didn't regret it.

At least, not in terms of what it did to me.

However, a part of me... a small part... grieved over what I'd done to Kayla. My mate. The female I was supposed to protect.

I hadn't cared about her when we'd engaged in the blood exchange. She'd been a means to an end. A nuisance with a mohawk and a childlike spirit.

By the end... I'd felt somewhat differently.

And seeing the woman before me—the female wielding one of my swords with a grace worthy of an opponent—I felt *very* differently.

She frowned at the handle of my sword, setting it down and picking up another. She tested the weight of two more before she nodded, appeased, and paired it with a holster.

I'd opened this room to find myself a weapon, not give her one of her own. But watching her cinch that holster around her waist had me staying quiet. She looked too good wearing my sword to demand she remove it.

Instead, I focused on finding what I wanted—several knives, some throwing stars, two guns, and a sword of my own.

Kayla helped herself as well, grabbing a pair of daggers that she slipped into her boots and a gun that she loaded with steel bullets instead of silver.

I put silver ones in my mine, something she didn't seem to notice. It had me questioning if silver actually impacted her. She was a Halfling, so, in theory, it should. But silver didn't hurt any of the Divinity members, and they were all part Archdemon.

I would just need to be careful not to accidentally shoot Kayla. Her desire to kill me didn't go both ways.

I very much craved her lively essence.

In more ways than I care to admit.

Clearing my throat, I pulled on a pair of socks and boots from my wardrobe stash in the corner and finished my ensemble with a long black leather jacket that swept the floor near my ankles.

Kayla stood watching me while I finished, her irises flaring with obvious appreciation.

The attraction is mutual, I thought at her. Not that she could hear me. Out loud, I said, "Let's go." I held out my hand, my way of testing her resolve to trust me on another teleportation jump.

She didn't hesitate.

She stepped forward, pressed her palm to mine, and casually asked, "When a member of a mated pair dies, does their partner inherit their previous possessions?"

I grunted, following the path of that question to its clear end. "You're not taking my armory."

Her gaze glittered as she looked up at me. "We'll see."

"No," I promised her. "We won't."

I tugged her into my torso and engaged my ability to traverse the realms before she could spout more nonsense.

And smiled at her sharp intake of air. "Better hold on," I whispered against her ear. "Wouldn't want to risk losing you midflight." Not that I would ever let that happen.

No. If anything, my problem would be letting her go.

Because she felt far too good in my arms.

As though she were meant to be right here with me. *Forever.*

It was the mate-bond fucking with my brain. But at some point, my soul would win this battle of wills. And that would cause the most irrevocable damage of all.

Because when that happened, I'd really make her mine— something she would just have to accept, or something she'd reject, thus fighting me until one of us died.

Maybe she'll inherit my armory after all, I mused.

A concern for another day.

Right now, we had an unknown battle ahead. *It's time to spill some blood.*

KAYLA

EZRA'S ENERGY CARESSED MY SKIN, CASCADING A sense of contentment through my aura.

I tried to ignore it, to fight the sensation of warmth flooding my veins, but my body refused to listen to reason. *Mate. Mine. My Archangel.*

A growl tickled my throat, my frustration mounting.

However, he released me as soon as we arrived, providing me with the space I required to regain control.

Cool air touched my face and hands, a stark contrast to the heat blaring inside me. I grabbed onto the chilly atmosphere, sucking in giant heaps of oxygen, and found my footing on the concrete below.

It only took a few seconds, but it was long enough for Ezra to notice. The glimmer of amusement in his pretty eyes made me want to stab him all over again, something I told him with my gaze.

Which only caused his lips to curl in response. "Save that fight, little heiress," he murmured. "We're going to need it."

I ignored him, instead choosing to focus on our surroundings.

Trees. Snow. More trees.

Apparently, the locator spell sent us north of Vancouver. There weren't any buildings or signs of civilization anywhere.

Just a chilly, wintry mix of icy air and fluffy white landscaping. A very precise location, it seemed.

So that's how Ezra navigated Hell when we first met, I thought, glancing at him. His gaze remained on the snowy evergreens, taking in the scenery and scanning the lands for trouble.

I followed suit, noting how beautiful everything appeared to be. However, the eerie sense of wrongness that lingered in the atmosphere put me on edge.

The winter wonderland reeked of demons. Not literally, just a dark presence in the wind that caused all the hair along my nape to stand on end.

I searched for a source, but my eyes were still acclimating to the dark. The moon peeked through some of the branches, illuminating strips of the ground. It wasn't enough.

Something's here.

I could feel it in the chill skating down my spine.

Ezra stiffened beside me, clearly sensing the same presence.

My cuff tingled with warning in the next instant—a subtle prick to tell me that I was about to need all my strength.

Swallowing, I caressed the rune on the center of my wrist in a star-shaped pattern followed by a slash. Magic hummed over my skin as the cuff granted my power complete freedom. I often used the magic of my bracelet to mask my energy signature and dampen my abilities to controllable levels, but the approaching presence told me I needed to be able to access *every* power at my disposal.

Electricity fizzled across my being, sharpening my instincts and heightening every sense. Which how I heard the subtle shift of snow to my left.

"There," I said, already lifting my gun to take aim.

Boom.

An Orsini Devil appeared out of thin air with a bullet-shaped wound right between his eyes.

Two more popped into view before I could evaluate the scene, the little demons chittering in admonishment. As if that would make me listen.

I sent a round of bullets into their skulls, taking them down before falling into a crouch to prepare for the rest. Because where there was one Orsini Devil, there were several.

And their penchant for invisibility made them difficult to see.

But I could *hear* them.

There were at least two dozen coming at us from all angles. I started firing as each one stroked my senses, and Ezra began slicing with his sword.

"This is a diversion," I told Ezra through my teeth, irritated by the ambush.

Orsini Devils were only good for two things—spying and dying. Their disappearing acts made them useful in some situations.

This was not one of those situations. At least not for us.

But for whoever hired them? Yeah, they were certainly doing their job.

I swapped my gun for a pair of daggers, deciding to save my bullets for whoever really needed them.

And started stabbing at the air.

Demonic screeches echoed off the trees, creating the perfect alarm of sorts while Ezra and I worked to take each Orsini Devil down. They were short and stumpy and invisible, making them difficult to track. But my senses drove me and my blades, slashing through them as I sensed their auras, until the field around us was painted in red snow.

And silence.

I remained crouched for a second longer, surveying the landscape, then I slowly stood to find Ezra staring at me with a glimmer of wonder in his eyes. Rather than comment on his obvious surprise, I focused on the stronger power lurking in the woods—the one the Orsini Devils were attempting to mask.

Now that they were all unconscious and not breathing, I could home in on that intense signature. It flared like a beacon against my demonic senses.

I took off toward it in the next instant with Ezra hot on my heels.

But the aura began to fade as soon as I moved toward it, telling me I was already too late. *He's portaling,* I realized, slowing my pace.

Ezra either didn't care or he didn't notice, because he blew right past me, his steps determined.

I frowned, my steps turning to a stroll. *It's not right. Something's not right.*

I almost uttered the words out loud, but they wouldn't stop Ezra. He continued at full speed ahead.

However, the power was gone. I couldn't sense it at all now.

"Ezra..." I trailed off, noting the desperation in his movements.

My brow furrowed, and my feet picked up speed to follow him. He must have sensed something I couldn't. Or maybe he wasn't sensing anything at all.

No. That wasn't it.

I chased him deeper into the trees, running at his pace now, following whatever lead he'd picked up on, then froze at the sight of him falling to his knees just ten feet away from me.

Fuck.

That was why the power signature had disappeared.

It was... it was *Kristina's* energy I'd felt slipping away, as though siphoned off into another being that had clearly disappeared.

Leaving the precious piece of the Divinity dead... on the forest floor.

My hand covered my mouth, my legs anchored to the ground like blocks of cement. *She's... she's dead. The Divinity is compromised. She's... gone...*

Ezra's head fell back on a bellow that sent a blade right through my heart. It wasn't a sound of solitary sadness, but one of acute fury. A mixture of emotions that swirled all around him, ending in a wave of agony I could feel to my very soul.

The impact fractured a part of me, our link throbbing to life and forcing me to feel every sensation pouring out of his spirit.

Failure.

Admiration.

Despair.

Love.

That last bit gave me pause, allowing me to climb out of this emotional web to the surface, only to be yanked back under a sea of grief.

My knees buckled, sending me to the ground behind him, the sensations drowning me beneath an avalanche of *feeling*.

I sucked in a breath, needing to breathe, yet found myself choking on his fury and sorrow instead. I clawed at the binds around me, only then realizing they were arms.

And it wasn't emotion suffocating me, but his *hands*.

Around my throat.

Because he blamed me for this.

Or am I blaming myself? Is he even strangling me? Is this all a nightmare? Where's my fight? What am I even doing?

I couldn't decide, couldn't see, couldn't fucking *breathe*.

I did this. I'd caused the tear in the veil, the one that had called the Divinity to the human realm, the one that had allowed Kristina to be captured. I hadn't realized it would happen like this because I hadn't known what tool Ashmedai had given me. However, I only had myself to blame for not *asking*. All of this had been done for my own selfish need.

Well, not entirely, but a significant part of it had been tied to my desire for revenge.

I'd wanted to warn Johanna, too. As well as help Alastor. But the largest part had been driven by my need to kill Ezra.

And now Kristina was *dead*.

I deserved this punishment.

I'd caused a fracture in the Divinity.

Sensing Ezra's agony now overshadowed everything with a fresh perspective. Sensing the irreversible shift in the balance did as well.

My needs were futile in the grand scheme of the universe.

Everything is falling apart, I realized, darkness overtaking my vision. *The veil is going to self-destruct. War is coming. Civilization will fall.*

The three realms—Heaven, Earth, and Hell—would converge and collapse onto each other.

Death and destruction would reign.

Pain and suffering.

Blood and soul-crushing devastation.

I could taste it on my tongue, envision it in my dying mind. Part of me knew it wasn't real—not yet—that this was just a nightmarish response to the reality unfolding around me, but it *felt* real.

Just as I could have sworn Ezra's hands had been around my throat moments ago.

However, I couldn't feel him now.

Because he hadn't touched me at all.

It'd been his agony, coupled with the fracture in the balance—along with my own self-blame—strangling me. I blinked to find him still kneeling over Kristina's body.

Then flames danced around us. Invisible to everything but my own eyes.

Flames of despair.

Flames of the future.

Flames of a destiny I'd destroyed through my own selfish means.

The scales have tipped. There's no stopping fate now, I realized, my heart ceasing to beat. *We're already doomed.*

Ezra

Kristina's hair resembled rivers of blood in the snow, her expression vacant, her body lifeless.

Dead.

I kept repeating the word but struggled to comprehend it.

Failed.

Another statement revolving through my mind.

Broken.

A term that described the balance.

Shattered.

An adjective for my spirit. My purpose. My fucking being.

All because I'd been too weak to protect Kristina, too consumed by my mate to fulfill my one task in life. Kayla was very much to blame here. But so was I. Our bond... had destroyed everything.

It had deteriorated my strength, leaving me without my usual skills.

It had provoked anger and hatred in Kayla, driving her need for revenge.

And it had distracted both of us from the inevitable fracturing of the veil.

Fuck.

I ran my fingers through my hair, my jaw aching from clenching it so hard. There was no bringing Kristina back. No fixing what had already been done.

But we're not done with this fight yet, I told myself, swallowing.

The Divinity was always meant to fall, just not like this. My whole purpose in life was to *control* the collapse. Giving in to this setback would prove me worthless.

I refused to accept that fate.

I would find a way to right the scales, to curb this collision course, and... and... uphold... whatever the future may be.

There was no alternative. To give up would mark my entire existence as fruitless. And I could not allow that to happen.

My fingers curled into fists as I forced myself to my feet, my gaze taking in the murder scene, searching for clues, anything that told me *who* had done this. That person needed to die. That being who'd defiled such a sweet, beautiful creature.

I nearly growled, my fury winning over all my other emotions.

Kayla knelt, rooted like a tree, maybe ten feet away, her expression vacant, her eyes unseeing. As though she couldn't accept the scene or admit her guilt in this situation. "You caused this," I accused her, pointing a finger at her and then at Kristina. "That stunt you pulled *caused this*."

Because of me, I thought. But I couldn't voice that part out loud. It spread agony through my veins, directly to my heart, when I realized just how far Kayla would go to destroy me.

But this had all been a result of her own selfish need for revenge. She hadn't considered the repercussions, her fixation on my death blinding her from the consequences of her decisions.

I'd never forgive her for that misstep.

Just as she'd never forgive me for my betrayal.

It didn't make us even; it didn't right the scales. It merely deteriorated our bond that much more, harming both of us in this journey to eternity.

I hated her just as much as I wanted her.

Our bond had been forged in Hell. Cemented in blood. Forbidden by the heavens. And destined to destroy the world.

Because I also hadn't considered the consequences of our mating. I'd been arrogant, deciding I could handle whatever fate threw at me in response to my abandoning Kayla in Hell.

But I'd never anticipated this.

A moment of weakness ending in Kristina's demise.

It was worse than letting Bael keep Johanna—a destiny that had come to be, regardless of my tampering.

I shook my head, sickened and dismayed by it all. Furious at the unraveling of karma and the destruction my choices had caused.

"I know," Kayla whispered, her voice somehow carrying over the chaos in my mind. "I... I didn't mean for this to happen."

I snorted. *Neither did I.* "But that doesn't make it any better, does it?"

"No," she agreed. "It doesn't."

Which was precisely why I needed to find a new path, a way to tempt the scales into our favor before we lost everything. Surveying the ground once more, I searched for hints of where to go. But the entire scene lacked an aura, leaving me without anyone to trace.

Pulling the map from my pocket, I searched for Kristina's essence.

Nothing.

If someone had sucked the power out of her, I should be able to feel a trace of something. Her aura would remain on the map, at least as a distorted texture of an essence that I could follow.

Except there wasn't even a speck left of her.

Unless the being went to another realm, I thought, considering the parchments in my office.

I engaged my ability to traverse time and space, only to freeze as I sensed a powerful being arriving through similar means.

Shit.

I returned to my corporeal state just in time to catch Kayla's broken expression. She quickly masked it behind a look of surprise upon seeing me, then she stood as the aura of the incoming demon touched her senses.

The Demonic Lord of North America materialized before us, his dark appearance and all-black suit blending into the night. His chocolate brown gaze fell to Kristina on the ground before flickering back up to me and shifting to Kayla. His jaw ticked, a glimmer of emotion gracing his usually stoic features.

Fear.

Because he knew as well as we did what this meant.

And as a being growing in power, he also knew we were on the cusp of a war.

More shimmers disturbed the night, announcing the approach of several otherworldly entities.

Azrael.
Mietek.
Dariel.
Scion.
Zerak.
Alastor.
Lucia.
Bael.
Johanna.
Morax.
Valisa.
Ashmedai.
A Nephilim of unknown origin.

They all trickled in, forming a circle of sorts around the crime scene. Only two of them outwardly reacted. *Lucía and Johanna.*

Their ashen features told me they'd already sensed Kristina's passing before arriving, but seeing their fallen member on the ground sent them both to their knees on a wave of sadness I felt all the way to my soul.

I didn't step toward them. I didn't try to comfort them. I wasn't worthy because I'd already failed them all. And that was the worst punishment of it all—I no longer had faith in myself to keep the others safe.

From the gleams in the eyes of my fellow angels, neither did they. Azrael, Mietek, Dariel, Scion, Valisa, and Zerak all wore matching expressions of disappointment.

Valisa's was the most severe. As Kristina's mother, I more than deserved that look. It didn't matter that the two of them had rarely conversed; she'd still created her.

Archdemon Morax, Kristina's father, didn't seem all that bothered. However, he'd merely been the sperm donor in the situation. Kristina might have shared his blood, but she'd held no claims to his heart and vice versa. All he'd really done was give her red hair and contribute to her veil-related abilities.

Valisa, Archangel of Stars, had given Kristina everything else, including her kind blue eyes and willowy frame. She'd also contributed to the veil magic, but in a different way from Morax. He was the darkness, while Valisa represented the light, thus creating the perfect balance in Kristina.

"Well. That's a problem," Alastor muttered.

Lucía glared up at him. "As if you care. You and that Halfling are the reason this even happened. Had she not been trying to capture one of us for you, we wouldn't be here right now."

Alastor's eyebrows drew upward. "I didn't give her that device, sweetheart."

"No. I did," Ashmedai admitted, his ash-blond hair glimmering in the night as his violet eyes went to Kayla and then to me. "I knew it would cause a disturbance. I did not anticipate Archangel Ezra being incapable of handling such a situation."

"You underestimated how weak his bond has made him," Mietek interjected, his irritation palpable. "You and your fucking games, Ashmedai."

"As though you and your brethren are ones to talk," Ashmedai drawled, his irises flicking to the silent Archangel with midnight hair and even darker eyes. "Isn't that right, Scion?"

Rather than reply, Scion merely glanced at the unnamed Nephilim and back at Ashmedai, a murderous glimmer shining in the ebony depths of his gaze. That wasn't all that abnormal, considering he was the Archangel of War. But his expression struck me as protective, or maybe even possessive.

Who is she? I wondered, studying the brunette female. She appeared just as angry, her arms folded tightly as she stood beside Ashmedai in a leather jacket and matching pants. Her high ponytail and hardened jaw suggested a confidence that reminded me a bit of Kayla.

Or what Kayla had looked like prior to arriving at Kristina's murder scene, anyway. Now she just stood off to the side, her gaze on the ground, her shoulders slumped.

I almost moved to stand beside her, not necessarily to offer her comfort but to demonstrate that we were in this hell together. However, the others were already speaking, drawing the conversation back to a blame game of epic proportions where my skills and sanity were questioned and my inability to uphold the balance was flat-out detailed.

Which made my placement in this situation quite evident indeed.

I listened because it wasn't my place to speak.

I'd fucked up.

I owned that.

And from the chagrined line in Kayla's features, I sensed she felt the same. She flinched each time one of them mentioned our forbidden mating and how it had degraded my worth as an Archangel.

"He should have been replaced," Dariel said. "Or the girl should have been destroyed."

Bael bristled, his blue eyes resembling ice. "That's my daughter you're talking about."

"A Halfling," Dariel spat back at him. "Hardly something to be proud of."

"All progeny carry value," Scion murmured softly, his gaze flicking to the Nephilim again as he spoke.

Ashmedai merely smirked in reply.

Azrael appeared ready to kill everyone in the forest.

Valisa's gaze had turned misty.

Morax's expression gave nothing away.

And Zerak just scratched his chin and checked his watch —the technology not of this realm, as it was the Archangel of Time's personal device. The subtle twist of his lips told me the timetable for the war had just shifted and he could see it coming.

"When?" I asked him, interrupting whatever Mietek had just been saying.

Zerak met my gaze, his silvery gray irises the same shade as his skin, hair, and feathers. It wasn't often that he ventured to Earth, his abnormal coloring and striking features marking him as distinctly otherworldly. Even if he tucked in his wings, like Azrael and Mietek were doing now, he would still appear too different to pass for a human.

"Two decades and falling," he replied, blinking. "Eighteen years now. Seventeen. Holding. Eighteen again. Fourteen." He shook his head. "It's... jumping. Rapidly."

"We need to make a decision," Azrael declared, his age and

superiority showing. He wasn't an Archangel like the rest of us, but that didn't diminish his powers in the slightest. "Standing here debating what has happened and casting blame isn't going to fix any of this. We have a chance to alter the path and control the destruction, but the longer we discuss it, the shorter our window becomes."

"Eleven years," Zerak said, his tone one of agreement rather than one of warning.

"What do you recommend?" Dariel asked, the condescension in his tone ruffling my nerves. The Archangel of Concealment always presented himself as this superior being for reasons I didn't understand. He was old, yes, but not nearly as ancient as Azrael. And his claim to fame was his attributes—multicolored eyes and shifting hair—that allowed him to blend in like a chameleon. Just like his brother.

Really fucking magnificent, I thought, narrowing my gaze. *Absolutely worthy of your damn arrogance.*

Of course, Dariel seemed to reserve this side of himself for situations that exclusively involved me. From what I'd heard, he didn't act this way around anyone else. However, because I'd been chosen for the job of guarding the Divinity over him, he enjoyed pointing out my flaws at every turn.

He'd been the one to advocate for my removal after I'd bonded with Kayla.

He'd lost, something he would no doubt bring up again soon and point to this situation as an "I told you so" comment.

"Johanna and Lucía will remain with Bael and Alastor," Azrael stated, glancing at the two females still on their knees.

Dariel opened his mouth, likely to argue, but Azrael silenced him with a raised hand.

"Alastor and Bael have a myriad of guards to protect them and any assets they hold dear." Azrael's tone said this wasn't up for debate. "Hell's terrain is also difficult to traverse and easier to hide in than any other realm. It's the most difficult plane to track power through, too."

He was right. It helped that the realms constantly shifted down there, too. Unlike Heaven, which was one sprawling landscape where all angels lived and traveled freely, similar to how transportation in the human realm worked, only we used our feathers, not airplanes.

"Why Alastor and Bael?" Dariel asked, either not hearing Azrael's implied command not to argue or ignoring it entirely. "Why not send them to their Archdemon fathers?"

"Yes, have they even been notified?" Morax drawled. "Because I certainly wasn't. Not the best alert in the world to be drawn to a place due to the death of a kin."

"Like you ever cared," Valisa spat at him.

"Oh?" He arched a dark red brow. "Was I given a choice in that matter, or was it taken from me?"

"You're not the one who bore her."

"But I did help create her," he bit back.

"The fathers would be too predictable," Mietek interjected, returning the conversation to its course as Zerak hummed at whatever he saw on his watch.

"It could also tip the scales," Ashmedai added. "Orcus and Kore have not shown any signs of growth. Therefore, they do not require the outlet that Bael and Alastor do."

Both Bael and Alastor cast suspicious glances at Ashmedai. "What do you know?" Bael demanded.

"More than either of you," Ashmedai replied succinctly, causing the Nephilim beside him to roll her hazel eyes.

"He has a whole map of power shifts in his office," she informed them. "Feel free to stop by for a look."

"Now, now, Trudy. We've discussed this. No guests allowed, and I certainly won't be tolerating any unsolicited visits from any Archdemons who have grown exponentially in power over the last one hundred years." That last part was spoken with a hint of warning, the underlying context clear. *Enter if you dare.*

Because they weren't the only ones growing in power. I could feel the energy practically pouring off Ashmedai yet sensed nothing from the one he called Trudy. Which was typical for a Nephilim. Their energy signatures varied, with most—if not *all*—being entirely concealed.

I frowned, then pulled out the map again. *Could that be why her aura disappeared?* I wondered, thinking of Kristina and her vanishing essence.

If a Nephilim had somehow absorbed her power, would it be masked to our otherworldly senses?

"What other Archdemons have power fluctuations?" Mietek demanded.

"What other Archangels have power fluctuations?" Ashmedai countered with ease.

"It doesn't matter," Kayla said, sounding irritated. "The power shift has already begun. The veil will fall, causing all the realms to collide."

"Unless we manage the collision," I added.

"I think you've done enough to fuck this all up," Dariel inserted. "Why don't you go back to Heaven and take a holiday, hmm?"

"The Archangel of Justice made a mistake," Azrael agreed. "But he's our best chance at managing the fallout. Actually, *they* are our best chance." He gestured between me and Kayla. "A being of Heaven with a child of Earth and Hell. It's a balance in itself that can be used to alter the scales."

"Nine human years," Zerak hummed, his silver-gray irises flaring with power. "And stalling..."

"Suggesting my statement is accurate," Azrael replied, meeting the gaze of everyone around him. He waited a beat, then arched a white-blond brow at Zerak.

"Still nine years," the Archangel of Time confirmed.

"Brilliant." He met my gaze. "You still have a job to do."

I dipped my chin, accepting the fate. I would hunt down Kristina's killer regardless of his approval, but it was nice to know I'd have his support on the issue. However, there was something I needed. "I want your details on the Nephilim," I told Ashmedai. "All of them."

His eyebrow winged upward before he looked at Kayla. "And here I thought our conversations were private."

"And here I thought you gave me a device that would summon Ezra without putting the universe at risk," she countered without missing a beat. "I guess neither of us was what the other expected."

His responding grin practically sparkled in the night. "On the contrary, sweet princess, you are *exactly* what I anticipated."

"I can't believe you went to him," Bael muttered.

"Not like you were including me in your decisions," Kayla retorted, giving her father a meaningful look. "I was trying to help you."

"And fulfill your penchant for revenge," he replied, his blue eyes as glacial as his tone. "Cute."

She just shook her head. "You still see me as a child, when I'm not."

"You are," he countered.

"She's not," I said, feeling the need to agree with her on this one thing. "But you can handle your family issues later. I want those details on the Nephilim, Ashmedai."

"Why?" Azrael inquired, his tone still holding that authoritative edge to it.

"Because Kristina's aura disappeared," Kayla said before I could speak. "He suspects a Nephilim did this."

Azrael seemed intrigued by that. "And do you suspect the same?"

"I suspect that it's a good place to start," she replied, surprising me at her clear acceptance of my lead.

Maybe there was hope for us after all.

"Ashmedai—"

"I'll do you one better, Ezra," Ashmedai said, cutting off Azrael. "Lord Zebulon will introduce you to one of the Dark Provenance members that helped Evangeline create the list."

I cocked a brow. "Or you could point me in Evangeline's direction, and I could go directly to the source." Seemed more efficient to just ask the Fallen Angel my questions rather than go through an intermediary.

"Ah, you see, I would, but she's currently lost in Hell," Ashmedai murmured, sounding entirely unapologetic about it.

A chorus of "*What*?" followed.

Which merely made Ashmedai grin and say, "I believe we're done here, hmm? Alastor takes Lucía. Bael takes Johanna. Morax fucks off back to his realm and stays there. I keep Trudy. Ezra and Kayla figure out how to find balance in their relationship and hopefully a path forward for us all by tracking down whoever wrongfully inherited Kristina's powers, and we meet again in nine years for a war." He glanced at Zerak for that last part. "Yeah?"

"Nine years," he confirmed.

"Sound," he murmured, wrapping his arm around the Nephilim. "Until then, I recommend steering clear of the Shadow realm." With another of his blinding smiles, he disappeared, leaving Azrael cursing behind him.

He vanished in the next second, his intention to follow the Archdemon clear. Azrael, the Angel of Death, was also Evangeline's father. And it seemed that no amount of aging or superiority could keep a dad from trying to protect his progeny.

Morax grunted. "I don't recall agreeing to a damn thing."

"You're just as charming as I remember," Valisa muttered.

"How is finding Kristina's killer going to help curb the coming war?" Dariel asked incredulously, ignoring them both.

"The fact that you have to ask only proves your lack of qualifications for the job," I said, unable to help the jibe. Because the answer was rather obvious to me—taking back Kristina's power and placing it in a worthier source could right the scales.

In other words, I needed to re-create the missing link to the Divinity.

Which required me to track down her assassin, as he or she had absorbed her essence—it was the only way to permanently slay one as powerful as Kristina.

And the longer we allowed that third party to wander around with power that did not belong to him or her, the more likely the veil would fracture ahead of schedule.

Hence, Zerak's countdown.

I looked at Zebulon. "Where is this member with details on the Nephilim?"

"Nashville," he answered immediately.

"Take us to him." It wasn't a request but a command.

One that Zebulon responded to with a subtle nod of his head.

"That's it?" Dariel demanded. "We just let him run off again and fuck it all up more?"

Mietek leveled a look at him. "Under the right conditions, Ezra will prosper. He just needs to come to terms with those conditions and *use them*." Those last two words were for me, and they served as a reminder of what he'd said just yesterday.

Use her.

He wanted me to absorb Kayla's energy to bolster my own. I gave him a subtle nod, telling him I understood. But that didn't mean I agreed to do it.

Using Kayla as a pawn was what had started this mess.

Doing it again would just worsen everything entirely.

"Right, then. Now that everything's sorted"—Alastor held out a hand for Lucía—"shall we, sweetling?"

He clearly hadn't heeded her warning about the nicknames, something that surprised me because I knew just how deadly Lucía could be with a blade.

"And what? Just leave Kristina here to rot?" she demanded, standing of her own accord. "Absolutely not."

"Agreed," Johanna said, following suit to stand beside her. "Kristina needs a proper burial."

Which could only happen in one place.

I swallowed, my gaze falling to the female on the ground.

Then I nodded.

"We need to bury her," I murmured, echoing their sentiments.

"At home," Johanna reiterated, in case that part hadn't been clear to me.

"I know." I palmed the back of my neck and blew out a breath. "Does it alter the timeline?" I asked, my question for Zerak.

"Steady at nine years," he responded.

I nodded. "All right. Let me know if that changes." I'd probably feel it in the shift of power, but having confirmation would be good. "Tell your contact we'll be coming in two human days," I told Zebulon.

"He'll be ready," the Demonic Lord promised.

Dariel just shook his head. "This is a fucking shitshow." With that beautiful commentary, he disappeared, leaving Mietek to sigh in his wake. His gaze met mine, his statement silent yet loud at the same time. *You know what to do*, his eyes said.

Then he vanished as well.

"Thank you for returning her to the earth, Ezra," Valisa said without meeting my gaze and vanished in the next breath.

I took that as confirmation that she wouldn't be attending the funeral.

"Well. Since I'm clearly not needed for anything..." Morax trailed off and left in a cloud of smoke, the darkness seeming to chase him into the underworld.

Kristina had barely known the Archdemon.

She wouldn't miss him at her burial.

"Nine years," Zerak echoed, then teleported in a manner similar to that of the other angels.

Scion was the last to leave, his expression vacant as he disappeared, leaving me with a horde of Archdemons, an Archdemon's Halfling daughter, a Demonic Lord, and my fractured pieces of the Divinity.

I bent to scoop Kristina into my arms, then I glanced at Johanna. "You know the way. Be sure to take Kayla with you."

Because I didn't have the hands to ensure Kayla's safe passage.

Nor did I trust myself to touch her right now.

Because part of me was still livid with her decision to put the balance at risk for her own need for revenge.

Meanwhile, another part of me wanted to thank her for showing solidarity with me in front of Azrael.

Rather than pick a side, I engaged my gift.

And took Kristina's body home.

Where she would rest for eternity.

KAYLA

Yeah, this isn't awkward at all, I thought, releasing my father's arm the moment my feet touched the green lawn outside Ezra's estate.

His anger resembled a whiplash to my nerves, his overarching disappointment in my actions a palpable emotion between us.

"Look," I started.

"I don't want to hear it, Kay," he said, his arm still around Johanna.

"I was trying to help," I promised, ignoring his comment. "You told Jeremiah—"

"A conversation that was never meant for your ears," he interjected.

"That your power was growing exponentially, and without Johanna, you would erupt," I finished, ignoring him again. "So I did what I thought was best."

"By going to Ashmedai?" Incredulity colored his tone.

"Well, no, I went to Alastor," I informed him. "Then Ashmedai found me in the human realm and forced me to tell him what I knew."

My father's cheeks had taken on a reddish tinge. "*Alastor?*"

"Present," the Archdemon murmured as he appeared with a simmering Lucía in his arms. He didn't release her, his grip remaining firm and reminding me of the grasp my dad had on Johanna.

It didn't appear to be sexual so much as necessary, like they required contact to keep their powers under control.

"You worked with my daughter on this asinine plan?"

"No, I sent her to the human realm to find a piece of the Divinity in exchange for a holy blade," the Archdemon explained as he set his chin on Lucía's slender shoulder.

Okay, well, maybe *his* touch was meant to be sexual.

"A holy blade?" My father's icy gaze returned to me, his short brown hair waving in the late morning breeze—because, yeah, the atmosphere had changed again, making it almost noon here rather than the midnight we'd just experienced in Vancouver.

It'd been night here when we'd left, but perhaps it'd been on the cusp of morning. And who knew how long we'd actually been gone? Time was a fucked-up device between the realms.

"Why did you need a holy blade?" my father asked.

"To kill Ezra," I deadpanned. "Obviously."

My father considered that for a moment. "If that's all you wanted, why not ask me?"

"Because I don't want to owe you any favors." The last time I'd made a deal with him, I'd ended up grounded in Hell for a thousand years with no chance of venturing back to the human realm.

"Yet making a deal with Alastor suited?" he demanded.

"He wanted a piece of the Divinity, which I delivered."

He arched his brow. "And he gave you the knife?"

"Well, no—"

"And you don't see the problem there?" he prompted.

"Oh, I see the problem, but—"

"You tricked my daughter into a one-sided arrangement that you have no intention of fulfilling. That's a direct attack on my kingdom," he stated flatly, his focus having shifted to Alastor.

The dark-haired Archdemon merely grinned. "War between our realms? Sounds delicious."

"Of course you would think that," Lucía snapped. "Death is all you care about."

"Oh, I assure you, sweetling, there are other things I very much care about," he murmured, his lips against her neck.

She growled.

He chuckled.

Then she spun and decked him in the face with an impressive punch, following it up with a knee to his groin—a kick he caught with his thighs before lashing out and grabbing a fistful of her hair. "You want foreplay, baby, and I'll give it to you. But kicking me in the jewels is a hard pass."

She screamed and started attacking him in earnest, her skills quick and nimble as she fought him. *In a dress.* The fabric split at the sides, allowing her fluid motions to carry as she introduced her heel to his cheek. He ducked, but not fast enough, the sharp edge drawing a gash along his face.

Which resulted in another chuckle from the psychopath.

The two of them continued to grapple, causing my father to sigh dramatically. "Be thankful, Johanna."

"For what?" she asked, sounding bored. "That the stalker of my dreams finally made his fantasy a reality?"

My father grinned, his dimples appearing as he gave her an indulgent look. "You enjoyed those dreams just as much as I did, sweetheart."

"Okay, ew," I said, not wanting to listen to any more of *that* conversation. *Where the hell is Ezra?*

I searched the surrounding field for his black-brown feathers and shock of white hair but came up empty.

He probably didn't want to see me anyway.

Because he rightly blamed me for all this.

I swallowed, uneasy with, well, everything. *He* deserved my wrath and retribution, but Kristina hadn't. I could claim all day that I hadn't known what Ashmedai's device would do, and it wouldn't change what had happened.

Kristina was dead because of my actions.

The veil would fall because of my blind need for revenge.

Ezra had used me and left me in Hell. I hated him for it, but I hadn't exactly suffered.

I... I grew into a powerful heiress as a result.

While he'd apparently been weakened.

All those comments in the snowy forest had been eye-opening. The other angels had called him inferior... because of our bond. Because he'd left me in Hell instead of killing me.

It struck me then—the real purpose of my father's blood vow that day and why he'd been so thrilled by the prospect.

"You made that deal with Ezra to punish him. No, to *torture* him as a result of taking away your power outlet," I whispered, interrupting whatever conversation he'd been having with said outlet.

I met my father's devious gaze, my own eyes narrowing.

"You were never thrilled by the prospect of having me home. All those deals that kept me from going to Earth, all the schooling and the training, it was never for my benefit. It was for you, a way to keep me busy in the underworld so I wouldn't find Ezra. Because you wanted to weaken him."

All this time, I'd thought it was a result of my father's obsession with grooming an heiress.

But he'd never come for me on Earth.

He'd never cared when I'd been human.

And I'd forgotten that beneath my intense fury at Ezra using me for his own gain. I'd lost sight of it so completely that I hadn't even been able to see that my own father had used me as a pawn, too.

He'd just played a much longer game.

I almost laughed, my heart and soul already too shattered to break any more.

"Wow" was all I could muster. "Just... *wow*."

"Kayla—"

I held up a hand, taking a play out of Azrael's book. It'd worked for him, so why not me? "I'm good. I don't need your explanation. I understand your penchant for deals, *Dad*. Don't belittle me by trying to make another one."

I started toward the house, already over this little family gathering.

They could all attend the funeral or burial or whatever it would be. I wasn't worthy of it, considering my role in all this. Instead, I'd spend my time in Ezra's office, see what I could figure out from the maps, and try to piece together what I already knew from Ashmedai.

I'd make myself useful, prove myself to be worthier than a pawn in this fucked-up game of fate.

Whoever had taken Kristina's power was a direct threat to the veil. It was one thing to pass on that sort of energy to a worthy candidate, and entirely another to steal it for one's own gain.

I created this mess, so I'll clean it up, I thought as I entered the house via one of the many back doors. This one placed me near the kitchen.

So I grabbed a bottle of water on my way to Ezra's study.

Food would be too much right now, but hydration I could do.

I needed to make this right.

And I would start by reviewing all the maps I'd drawn.

Then I'd create a list of everyone I knew and detail their power shifts.

Someone had taken Kristina and siphoned off her energy. That required significant abilities alone, so it had to be someone of immense power.

And the fact that the signature had disappeared suggested Ezra's suspicion about it being a Nephilim might be right.

I would start there by naming all the powerful Nephilim I knew of.

Beginning with...

Gleason.

EZRA

I set the shovel to the side, the grave site finally ready.

We would have to wait until morning to properly bury Kristina, as she'd preferred the sun, especially in this spot in her favorite garden. I'd left her in her home, lying on her bed, wrapped in her silky linens.

Demons notoriously dissolved into ash upon their deaths, but Kristina had angelic heritage, too. Which left her body corporeal despite her departed soul. Therefore, a proper burial was required. And this was where she'd want to rest for eternity—among the flowers she'd tended to for the last few millennia.

I glanced up at the rising moon, taking in the early evening atmosphere and allowing the air to calm my feathers. Digging had helped clear my mind, providing me with a fresh perspective for the days to come.

Finding the culprit was only one piece of the grand puzzle. We also needed to determine a new host for Kristina's essence because eliminating it would only harm the balance that much more.

Which meant, in addition to tracking Kristina's power, I needed to evaluate all the auras among the angels and demons to locate a potential candidate. Someone willing to provide sturdiness while upholding the greater good. It wasn't an easy feat, hence the reason only three had been chosen through the millennia to bear this burden. It required a specific blend of Hell and Heaven to create such a being.

And from what I knew, there were no recent creations on that front. Archdemons and Archangels inherently harbored resentment toward each other. It'd taken effort just to orchestrate the matings that had created Lucía, Kristina, and Johanna. I strongly doubted any of the parents involved there would be willing to procreate again.

Politics, I thought, sighing as I beat my wings to take me into the air.

Johanna's and Lucía's homes were lit up in the distance, telling me they were both in their respective quarters. I could sense Bael's and Alastor's presence among them, their darkness an itch against my skin that irritated me immensely.

Normally, I would demand they stay in my home.

However, given everything that had happened, it couldn't hurt to add additional security around Johanna and Lucía right now.

It seemed the two Archdemons were of like mind because they had several of their Royal Guards patrolling the estates, their collective presence further irritating my invisible itch.

Several of the guards would likely remain behind to watch over Kayla. I'd allow it because I didn't mind the additional protection where my mate was concerned, but their presence would certainly grate on my nerves.

Interestingly, Kayla didn't have the same impact on me.

Her presence in my home felt... comforting. I could sense her in my office, her aura a beacon that called to my judicial instincts.

Not because I wanted to punish her.

But because I could feel the injustice surrounding her. Something had changed. She felt even more unbalanced than before, her sadness a perceptible pang that pierced my heart.

Was it Kristina's loss? Did she feel as though she'd wronged us all by orchestrating that stunt? I could understand that. She'd acted selfishly. However, her actions were driven by my own, thereby placing the blame collectively between us.

That said, belaboring the past and casting blame would achieve nothing.

We needed to think forward, solve this puzzle, and lay the groundwork for the eventual shift between the realms.

I flew toward my home, circling the back patio to reach the open windows of my den.

Kayla sat inside on the floor, surrounded by papers like earlier, her head bowed as she scribbled something into one of my notebooks—an item she'd clearly found in my desk.

It was on the tip of my tongue to reprimand her for going through my things without permission, but I didn't want to disturb her concentration. So I landed silently on one of my windowsills and sat to observe her.

She didn't seem to notice me, too lost to whatever path she followed in her mind.

We were clearly on the same wavelength in terms of moving forward rather than backward because she appeared to be taking notes on Nephilim.

I frowned, leaving my seat to float down beside her. Plucking a document off the floor, I noticed a list of names with percentages beside them.

When I finished skimming it, I met her exhausted gaze. "It's a list of Nephilim," she explained without me even having to ask. "I'm writing down everything I remember from my meeting with Ashmedai, including the power shifts we noted among the demons and angels. I'm working on that last part now."

She bent her head again, continuing to write.

I started leafing through all that she'd drafted, my jaw hardening with each page. She'd clearly been here all day while

I'd been working on the funeral arrangements. "Have you eaten anything?" I asked.

"Not hungry," she muttered in response, her shoulders seeming to cave a little.

"You need to eat."

She paused to glare up at me. "As I said, I'm not hungry. And besides, this is more important than my body's needs or desires. I was selfish. This is what I deserve."

My eyebrows lifted as she essentially dismissed me by returning to the notebook.

"You..." I trailed off because I'd been about to say, *You weren't selfish*. Which was a lie, and also entirely unrelated to the larger issue at hand. She clearly blamed herself and only herself. "Ashmedai gave you that device."

"Yes, and I used it without considering the ramifications." She pressed the pen just a little harder into the page, her frustration evident. "It was a naïve action on my part, one that will lead to the destruction of life as we know it unless we find out what happened to Kristina's powers and channel them through a more appropriate candidate."

Well, it seemed we were on more than just the same page— she'd taken the plan right from my mind.

Still... "You can't work yourself to death, Kayla. That's not healthy."

"What will it matter if the veil shatters?" she countered, finally looking up at me. "And aren't you supposed to be the Archangel of Justice? Isn't self-punishment one of your values?"

I snorted. "That's not how it works."

"Right. And I suppose if it was, you'd be too weak to handle it anyway. Because of me, apparently. Or our bond. Or whatever."

"A link I initiated knowing full well what the consequences

would be," I said, kneeling beside her to place my palm over the notebook, forcing her to stop writing. "Well, maybe not *all* the consequences," I clarified, thinking of the one we were experiencing now. "But I allowed myself to be weakened. That's on me."

"Just as the events that led to Kristina's kidnapping are on me."

I shook my head. "Those are on both of us. I should have been able to handle a meager Tracker and his Slither-venom bomb."

It still angered me thinking about how easily he'd bested me. I hadn't been prepared at all, when I should have been able to easily thwart his attack. Fuck, I should have been able to *sense* him before he'd even arrived.

Regardless... "Casting blame and punishing ourselves won't fix this, Kayla." I lifted my palm to her cheek, my need to touch her an instinct I couldn't ignore. "We have a long fight ahead, little heiress. We need our strength. So you need to eat."

The last meal we'd shared had been that green tea shake. While we could accomplish a lot with very little sustenance, it would help our brainpower to remain at full strength.

Besides, we'd also exhausted some energy on those damn Orsini Devils.

"Finish your page," I told her, my palm still on her cheek. "I'll go find us some food. Then I expect you to eat."

She blinked at me, her irises holding a note of distrust. "Why?" she whispered. "Will it help you somehow? Make me strong enough for you to borrow energy from?"

I flinched, her question a direct strike to my conscience. She was already anticipating me using her, which I suspected had nothing to do with Mietek's commentary and everything to do with the life she'd lived.

Because of me.

"I can only absorb the strength that you willingly give," I told her.

It wasn't necessarily true.

I could bite her, indulge in her blood, reaffirm our bond, and replenish my low reserves as a result. But I refused to force her.

I wouldn't trick her again, either.

"But I will admit I need to eat more frequently because of my lack of energy," I continued, my palm slipping from her face.

My skin tingled with the residual connection, my soul starved for more. However, I meant it—I wouldn't force her. She'd been used enough in this life. Perhaps with better intentions in mind, but they'd led to... *this*.

And that had me questioning whether any of it had been worth the fragments of pain lingering in her gaze now.

"You rejuvenate me a little just by being here, too," I informed her softly, feeling the need to speak the truth. "It's not enough to provide any true strength, but it makes breathing a little easier."

Clearing my throat, I stood again.

"Finish what you're doing, Kayla. I'll be back with food." Whether she ate it would be another topic entirely, but I'd do my best to tempt her.

I used my wings to gently hoist myself into the air, careful not to exert too much force, as I didn't want the wind to send her pages scattering across the floor. Her eyes followed me up, her brow furrowing as I left through the window.

That look of distrust haunted my thoughts as I flew to the patio nearest the kitchen doors. My hand was on the handle when I felt Bael's approach behind me.

Sighing, I faced him and noted the leathery fabric of his wings. I arched a brow, curious about the physical change. The last time I'd seen him in full demon form, he'd had feathers at his back, not these bat-like wings.

"It's part of the recent shift in Hell," Bael explained, clearly reading the question in my eyes. "I'm surprised Kay didn't tell you."

"She's been a little preoccupied with the notion of killing me." *Just as she's now busy blaming herself for an eon of our rivalry*, I thought darkly but didn't voice it out loud. Bael and I had a history. There was no point in stating the obvious.

"Indeed. Like father, like daughter," he murmured.

Rather than reply to that little comment, I returned to the door and pushed inside, determined to feed said *daughter*.

The invisible itch against my senses grew as Bael followed me into the kitchen, his demonic presence an unwelcome shift in my heavenly atmosphere. However, it was a sensation I would have to become accustomed to, as it would be a permanent existence if the veil fell.

I wandered over to the refrigerator closest to me to pull out a few sandwich items. This was the *Americas* area of my multitude of kitchens, showcasing a variety of foods from the two continents. But a standard turkey sub sounded good right now. It would be easy for Kayla to eat as well.

Bael leaned against the counter beside me as I took a few items out of the pantry to create a meal with our sub. The Archdemon immediately stole the platter of cookies, taking one for himself before setting it down again.

Rather than comment, I added three of the same kind to Kayla's plate—assuming that if Bael enjoyed that brand, then Kayla likely would as well—and snagged a few bags of chips to pair with her sandwich.

Junk food should at least tempt her a little into eating.

That was my hope, anyway.

"My daughter is under the misconception that I used her

to hurt you," Bael informed me, startling me from my task of spreading mustard on a sub roll.

I glanced up at him with an arched brow, a look I often bestowed upon the Archdemon when we were together. "Oh?"

Bael gave me a look. "We both know why she's predisposed to feeling *used*, hmm?"

I grunted, returning to my assembly line of cheese, meat, and bread. "You made that blood vow knowing full well it would weaken me, Bael. Denying it doesn't change your intentions."

The Archdemon fell silent for a moment, then sighed as he moved to take over a stool at the counter across from me. "Fine," he muttered. "Maybe it started that way. But I do care about my daughter."

"Is there a reason you feel I need to know this?" I asked, bored already. "Is this some sort of misguided attempt at having a father-suitor conversation with me? Because I think we're beyond that point, Bael."

"No, Kay can handle herself," he replied. "But there's a reason I hid that holy blade from her all these years, Ezra."

My gaze lifted to his once more, curious. I didn't speak, just told him with my eyes to continue.

"We might share a history, you and I, but that doesn't mean I want you dead," Bael said. "And my daughter is hell-bent on killing you."

I couldn't argue that point. I also couldn't say I blamed her. So I remained silent.

"I kept her in Hell to protect her. I'd also hoped it would help her forgive you in time, to understand that sometimes our choices are for the better good. But I don't think she ever fully grasped your sacrifice in all this." Bael reached over to snag a bag of chips, opening it without asking and stealing a chip.

Rather than comment, I finished putting the sub together and grabbed a knife to cut it down the middle.

"I'm shocked you never came for her," he continued, his voice amused. "I honestly expected you to bend first."

"Why? Because you were cheating by using your dreamwalking abilities to see Johanna despite our agreement?"

He grinned. "I didn't touch her. Not corporeally, anyway."

"Mmm," I hummed, very aware of how he'd circumvented our pact. Technically, he was right in that he'd never truly violated our blood vow. He'd just found other creative ways around it. "Did you think it would entice me to visit?"

"Yes," he answered honestly. "But you proved as honorable as ever."

I scoffed at that. "Not sure Kayla would agree."

"Probably not," Bael murmured. "Which means you're going to have to work very hard to win her over."

"What makes you think I intend to win her over?" I countered. "Maybe I'll kill her instead, like Mietek recommended."

Bael evaluated me for a minute, then slowly shook his head. "No. Your honor won't allow it. And neither will your heart." He pushed off the stool to stand, taking the bag of chips with him. "Tell my daughter to find me tomorrow. We need to talk."

"Sure," I drawled. "I'll pass on the message."

"You will," he agreed, his leathery wings unfurling as he prepared to fly out the door. "Your honor won't allow any other recourse."

With that pronouncement, he flew off into the night, his flight reminding me of a bat more than an Archdemon. Silent, deadly, and swift.

Impressive, I thought, sensing the burst of energy in his wake. *Very impressive.*

He'd definitely grown over the last few decades, marking

now as the right time for him to seek Johanna as an outlet. However, we both knew his desired connection went deeper than a mere need to expel power.

Bael had reached out before his time because he wanted Johanna as a mate. Which was precisely why he'd denied me access to mine as a form of punishment when I'd gone to Hell to take Johanna from him.

It'd all been a twisted, fucked-up version of fate.

One that had played out to an end none of us had enjoyed.

I found a replacement bag of chips—the same brand Bael had taken with him—to go with the subs and assembled it all on a tray.

Then I headed toward my own destiny, wondering if Kayla and I could alter our own ending and perhaps find a new way to coexist without hating each other.

A wishful thought.

One I doubted could be achieved.

But it was a challenge worth fighting for, so I'd give it my all, just like I did with everything else.

And we'd see where we landed.

Either in a pool of each other's blood. Or in a bed littered with feathers.

Maybe both, I mused as I entered the room and found her in the same place as before. *Your choice, little heiress. What'll it be?*

KAYLA

I SENSED EZRA'S APPROACH BEFORE HE ENTERED, HIS energy seeming to precede his arrival. Just like when he'd landed on the window and observed me from above. I hadn't reacted to him, too lost in my notes to allow him to distract me, but I'd felt his eyes on me.

Just as I felt his gaze on me again now.

He didn't speak, just entered, wandered to a pair of high chairs in the corner, and set his tray on the small round table between them.

"Come eat with me, Kayla," he beckoned, his tone holding a silky note to it that caused goose bumps to trail down my exposed arms. I'd discarded my jacket a while ago, leaving myself in jeans and a tank top.

Yet somehow I felt naked, like he could see right through me.

I frowned, not appreciating the sensation.

Vulnerable, I realized. *I feel... vulnerable.* Not necessarily naked in a sexual manner, but unguarded, as though he could penetrate all my natural shields.

It was a result of exhaustion and guilt.

I didn't appreciate it, but I also recognized that this wasn't so much Ezra's fault as it was my own. My decisions had put me here. My actions had driven all of this.

Maybe I deserve to—

"Kayla," Ezra murmured, interrupting my thoughts. "I will tie you to this chair and force-feed you, if I have to."

I blinked. "Excuse me?"

"You heard me."

"Why do you even care if I eat?" I asked him, utterly astounded by the strange surge of protective energy wafting off of him. "I've taken care of myself for thousands of years. Trust me, I can go a few hours without food."

"It's been more than a few hours," he said softly, stalking toward me. "You're going to eat."

"*Why?*" There had to be something he wasn't telling me, some sort of benefit for him, because that was the only way he would possibly push something like this.

From the conversation with the others earlier, I'd gathered that he was severely weakened by our bond. But I didn't know how we fixed that. It felt like electricity hummed through us each time we touched. Was he siphoning energy from me like some sort of Incubus? Just without the sex?

I didn't feel any different.

Perhaps because he hadn't actually started yet. Which could be why he needed me to eat... so I wouldn't notice his antics.

I narrowed my gaze. "I'm not hungry." A true statement. The notion of food made my stomach churn. "So just do whatever you need to do. If I'm hungry afterward, I'll go raid your kitchen."

"Do whatever I need to do?" he repeated.

I waved at him. "You know. To replenish or whatever. Use me. Then leave me alone. I'll figure this out like I always do."

"I'm not going to use you, Kayla."

I rolled my eyes and returned to my list. His lie didn't warrant a reply. I knew my role in his world. I was a pawn to be played.

This game would be so much easier if he just told me the

truth. Of course, then he'd probably grow bored. What fun would it be to give the toy insight into the game before it began?

With a sigh, I reviewed the last name on my list.

Valentino, the Demonic Lord of South America.

Hmm, he'd definitely grown in—

Ezra caught my chin between his thumb and forefinger, forcing my focus to return to him.

I blinked, startled by his unexpected proximity. I hadn't even sensed him move, his wings powering through the space between us without so much as a whisper of sound.

His arrival earlier had been just as silent, only I'd felt his approaching presence like a tidal wave of warmth. But he was already in the room now, his nearness a brand on my aura that made him everywhere at once and impossible to track.

He knelt, his head lowering to bring us eye to eye with one another.

I swallowed, his woodsy scent reminding me of sunshine heating the autumn leaves. It made me think of my old life, my time as a human where I'd experienced wonders like foliage and other seasonal activities.

Hell shifted climates, too. But very differently from the human realm.

"Kayla," he murmured, his grip tightening on my chin. "You need to eat to keep up your strength."

"Because you need to suck it out of me like some kind of leech," I returned. "If you admit it, I'll consider eating." I meant it. The truth would go a long way right now.

But the hardening of his jaw told me he had no interest in making this easy on either of us.

Why were all the men in my life obsessed with using me?

Ezra. Bael. Ashmedai. Even Alastor had proved his intentions when he'd taken Lucía and left me without a blade.

"Just tell me what you need, Ezra," I continued, my tone

more defeated than it had ever been. But after the last two days, could anyone blame me? I'd thought I'd taken charge of my fate and was finally going to achieve a millennia-old revenge.

Alas, no.

Instead, I had put the future of our world at risk, found out the mate I wanted to kill was suffering more than I had realized, and learned that my father had been tricking me into staying in Hell for the sole purpose of torturing a nemesis.

Yep. Great day.

"I need you to eat."

"Why?" I asked, exhausted with all the puzzles. "What difference does it make? Can you not siphon energy off me if I'm starved?"

His golden irises flared with intensity as his gaze dropped to my mouth. "The bond doesn't work that way, Kayla. It's not about absorbing strength from you. It's about our souls."

He released my chin to cup my cheek, his wings spanning out around us to create a cocoon of feathers that left me feeling shielded from the world. Protected. *Cherished.*

My throat worked, my heart hammering in my chest. "What are you doing?" I whispered, uncertain of how I felt about this change.

I... I hated him.

And yet, I felt oddly soothed by his presence. Intoxicated by his essence. Enthralled by the hint of his breath on my lips as his gaze met and held mine once more.

"I'm showing you how it works," he murmured, his pupils twin pools of hypnotic black. "Our bond is in our blood. It's a mating between spirits."

"I know," I said, familiar with how these connections worked.

He shook his head, that subtle action saying I didn't understand. I wanted to argue, to tell him he knew nothing about me or my intelligence, but I was too captivated by his gaze to voice a complaint.

"Archangel bonds differ from those that exist between demons. Ours require life and fidelity, while demonic bonds are founded in protection and loyalty. Being in Hell shielded you from the fractures in our connection. I suspect that's the real reason Bael kept you down there. Although, he told me it was to keep you from killing me."

His lips curled with that last statement, causing my own to curve downward.

"He kept me there to hurt you," I corrected him.

Ezra shook his head again. "No. He knew I would suffer regardless of what plane you resided on. He kept you there to protect you from experiencing the consequences of a neglected bond."

His fingers skimmed the side of my face to run through my hair. I'd taken out my bun, allowing the strands to hang chaotically around my head. He seemed a bit taken with the color, his gaze following his movements as he combed through the knots at the ends.

"Just touching you helps," he whispered. "It's not perfect, and I'm nowhere near healed, but I can breathe a little easier when you're near."

It sounded like a confession, something he hadn't meant to say, but a glimmer of satisfaction warmed his irises to a liquid gold as he returned his focus to my eyes.

"It's not about siphoning your energy, Kayla," he reiterated. "My reason for asking you to eat is to uphold your strength because I need you at full health. Whoever took Kristina's power is going to be a force of nature unlike any I've ever faced. And I need to know my partner—*my mate*—will survive it."

"You say that like you care," I marveled, honestly stunned by his words. "But I know you don't."

He'd lied. He'd tricked me. He'd abandoned me.

Never once had he tried to reach out.

So why would he suddenly care now?

He considered me for a moment, his fingers still combing through my hair. "My instincts don't listen to reason, Kayla. You're my mate. If we're in a situation where you're in danger... I'll struggle to focus on anything other than protecting you."

I snorted at that. "I've been in danger my whole life."

His smile was sad. "Your father would never have let anyone hurt you, little heiress."

My eyebrows rose. "You clearly don't know him like I do."

"I know him very well," he countered. "I know he had guards on you when living in the human realm before we met. Just as I know he would have tested your merit and skills in controlled situations in Hell. You're his only progeny."

"So you're saying you didn't have to worry about me before, but you do now," I translated, unable to hide the incredulity from my tone.

"I've always worried about you," he whispered, the words sounding like another confession. "But this is the first time in a very long while where your protection is my responsibility. Which is why I need you to eat."

His touch returned to my cheek, his thumb drawing along my lower lip.

"I know you can handle yourself, Kayla. I felt your power earlier when you removed whatever shield you keep igniting. But I need you at full strength. I don't want to find ourselves in a situation where I have to choose between you and the balance."

"We've already been in that situation, and you made your choice perfectly clear," I reminded him.

His gaze hardened, his lips flattening. "Being stubborn

doesn't make your point any louder, Kayla. All you're doing is harming yourself through immature actions."

He wasn't wrong. But the notion of food churned my stomach even more. "I don't want to eat," I told him. "Not because I'm rebelling but because... because I'm unsettled by what happened today."

He frowned. "Unsettled how?"

"Are you kidding? You already accused me of being the cause for all this, Ezra. You can't think I'm okay with knowing what I've done, how my *immature actions* have essentially led to the collapse of the veil. I'm a lot of things, but a callous bitch isn't one of them."

I had a heart, too. I could regret decisions just like anyone else.

And I very much regretted my decision to use that device from Ashmedai.

Just as I regretted not trapping that Tracker and killing him.

Ezra studied me, his brow pinching. Then he dropped his hand and sat back on his heels across from me.

The canopy of feathers remained around us, reminding me of a soft nest. I almost reached out to stroke the texture but didn't want to indulge in something I shouldn't. He might be my mate, but that didn't make him mine.

"Your actions are a result of my own," he said after a beat. "Your need for revenge is something I caused. Therefore, this situation is one we created together. Which is why we'll fix it together, too."

My lips parted, his words not ones I expected to hear. The Ezra I remembered was condescending, conniving, and cruel. But this version of him was almost... *compassionate.*

He'd just shared equal blame with me for Kristina's death.

And I wasn't sure how to respond to that.

"In order to fix it, we need to eat. Even if we don't feel up for it," he added quietly. "I made subs because they're easy and provide what we need without being too elaborate. If you prefer something else, I'll see if I have what I need to make it. But we have to eat, Kayla. If not tonight, then in the morning."

I had no idea he could be so reasonable. It sort of turned everything inside out, like he was showing me a side of him not meant for anyone else.

My goose bumps returned, a sense of unease making me shiver. This was too intimate. Too comforting. Too terrifyingly real.

I didn't want to share this moment with him. I didn't want to feel my heart racing at his nearness. I didn't want to experience the warmth in my veins. I didn't want to crave *more*.

I just wanted this to end. To fix our problems and kill him.

Except the latter no longer appealed to me like it once had. I still despised him, but knowing he'd suffered as a result of our bond had weakened my desire for vengeance. Because he'd already been punished. Just in a way I'd never anticipated.

"All right, I'll eat," I finally said, craving a distraction. Food might make me sick, but it would be better than feeling all this warmth toward him.

I also needed a break from his wings. They were too enticing, causing his scent to circle and claim me in a manner I didn't want to acknowledge.

A pang touched my chest as he stood, releasing me from his feathery cage. But I ignored it and inhaled, hoping to replace his cologne with a new fragrance.

Unfortunately, the woodsy aftershave remained, filling my mind with images of foliage and the sun stroking the autumn leaves.

I closed my eyes. In all my thousands of years, I'd never

met a male who'd seduced me on scent alone. Hell, it'd been near impossible to find any who'd even remotely satisfied me.

Yet Ezra's essence left me drunk in his wake, my throat and mouth begging me for another taste.

I swallowed instead, denying the urge, and stood to follow him toward the chairs.

At least eating will make me stop salivating over the Archangel, I thought, taking a seat. *Bon appétit, I guess.*

EZRA

We ate in silence, a soft sort of companionship seeming to fall between us. Afterward, I started reviewing Kayla's notes.

She'd listed hundreds of names, including Nephilim, angels, and demons. Beside them she'd noted their types and known power changes.

I reviewed every detail while she focused on the maps again, circling areas in the human realm where notable Nephilim lived.

"This is impressive," I finally said, unable to hold back the surprise in my tone. "You remembered all these details from talking with Ashmedai?"

She didn't respond for a beat, her attention on a map of North America. Then she blinked up at me.

"A lot of the observations are mine, not Ashmedai's. So they were easy to recall. The Nephilim are new since I don't know much about them and can't sense their auras. Some of the demon details are enhanced as well, but most of these are my notes."

Something about her phrasing clued me in to an important detail. "Can you sense power shifting in demons and angels?"

I didn't know much about how her own abilities had grown during our time apart. When I'd first met her, she'd possessed a childlike control over fire. Now she possessed a beautiful array of skills that I'd only begun to learn about her.

She glanced up at me. "Yes. Can't you?"

"Yes," I admitted. "But that's part of my gifts." I walked around my desk to lean against it, placing me near where she sat on the floor. She seemed to prefer that over chairs. "Can your father sense power shifts?" I knew the answer but wanted to hear her response.

"To an extent," she replied slowly, her expression pensive. "His ability is similar to how Ashmedai can track energy changes. However, they both rely on others to bring them proof."

"While you don't need the proof—you just know," I pressed.

She nodded. "Yeah."

"Like me," I finished, waiting for her to draw the conclusion I'd already arrived at. *You inherited your sense of the balance from our bond.*

It wasn't unheard of for mates to share gifts, but that typically required millennia of intimate bonding. And our link was quite the opposite of that.

"My abilities don't all come from you," she replied, her statement acknowledging what we both knew while also denying that her powers were all related to me.

"No, you're the daughter of an Archdemon. With that comes natural energy that will always be yours. I'm just marveling at how my heritage has influenced your skills. It's quite unique, to say the least."

Rather than harp on that uniqueness, I pushed away from the desk and carefully stretched out my wings. Then I rolled my neck and glanced over my shoulder at the high moon.

"I want to bury Kristina at dawn," I said, changing the subject before Kayla and I could go too deep into the discovery of our shared talents. "Will you join me?"

"In burying Kristina?" Kayla asked, sounding startled.

I found her gaze. "Yes."

"But I...?" She trailed off; however, I followed her train of thought.

"*We* caused it, Kayla," I corrected before she could finish her statement. "And *we* will make amends. Starting with the burial."

Her expression clouded over for a brief second before she dipped her chin. Not a definite acceptance, but it would do.

I sauntered toward her and held out a hand. "Time for bed, little heiress. We need to rest, too."

Either she was exhausted, or she had temporarily forgotten her dislike for me, because she nodded again and slipped her palm into mine. I slowly pulled her up off the floor, guiding her right into my chest.

She startled, her eyes flying up to mine as I palmed her cheek and wrapped my opposite arm around her back. "What are you doing?"

"Saying good night," I whispered, my forehead meeting hers. I didn't kiss her; I just closed my eyes and held her, my need to touch her overriding all my rational thought.

A sense of completion settled through my spirit, my soul rejoicing at having my mate in my arms.

"Hang on," I told her, my grasp around her lower back tightening as I used my wings to lift us from the ground.

She immediately grabbed my shoulders, her shock rippling through us both.

With a quick shuffling of feathers, I took us into the night, choosing a quick flight over the house instead of walking down the hall to the stairs. I flew her up to the balcony off the room she'd stayed in last night and smiled as she shivered in response to our feet touching the ground.

No sounds or words.

No questions.

No callous statements.

Just a silent evening beneath the stars.

She didn't move, her fingers digging into my shoulders as she held on to me as though she feared I might take off again.

We stood like that for several minutes, our souls embracing each other in a manner similar to that of our bodies.

A subtle breeze stroked my feathers and her hair, drawing her sweet scent to my nose. *Lilies*, I thought, inhaling deeply. She reminded me of the garden Kristina had kept near her home.

Most demons carried the stench of Hell with them.

But not Kayla.

I allowed myself another inhale, drawing the moment out as a result of my own weakness for her. I'd missed her without ever really knowing her, and to have her in my arms now resembled a fantasy more than reality.

It could so quickly shift into something dangerous and dark.

Which meant I needed to end it while it was comforting and light.

Kayla's breath feathered over my lips in an unspoken taunt. Rather than give in to the temptation of her mouth, I merely kissed her cheek and whispered, "Sweet dreams, little heiress."

Then I forced myself to release her before I did something I'd regret, and used my wings to carry me from the balcony over to my own rooms.

The sunrise arrived earlier than expected. Despite my best efforts, I'd barely slept, my mind too consumed with thoughts of Kayla to allow me much rest.

Knowing she was down the hall, within touching distance, had my urges kicking into overdrive.

It only proved how weak I'd truly become, because all I could think about was holding a female who despised me.

However, I pushed it all to the back of my mind as I led the burial service outside.

Johanna and Lucía had known my intentions without me having to tell them, both females meeting me at the gardens shortly after dawn.

Kayla had followed me as well, her presence a shadow that soothed my soul. It took serious effort not to reach for her after lowering Kristina into the ground.

No casket.

Just a divine being rejoining the earth.

Johanna and Lucía added flower petals, both of them whispering their goodbyes in soft tones.

It wasn't a mass ceremony with sermons or passages read from ancient texts. Instead, we kept it simple, short, and quiet. Bael and Alastor stood nearby, their heads bowed in respect.

No sarcastic commentary this morning.

No dark humor.

Only peace.

I liked to think it was exactly what Kristina would have wanted.

I gazed down at her red hair, her pale skin, her fragile remains, and picked up the shovel to begin the process of covering her in the rich soil she'd maintained all these years.

The others watched in silence.

Kayla stepped forward as I reached the halfway point, her hand taking the shovel from me without a word as she finished the job. It served as a silent demonstration of partnership, both of us shouldering this responsibility together.

She didn't cry. She didn't even speak. However, I sensed her regret and sadness all the way to my soul. She and Kristina might not have known each other, but Kayla felt her death regardless. We both blamed ourselves. And we both would avenge her, too.

When I glanced at Bael, I found him watching his daughter with a glimmer of respect in his features, his fatherly pride clear in his expression. But she was too caught up in the task to notice.

As the final shovel of dirt met the grave, she kneeled and pressed her palm to the earth. There were no words spoken aloud, just her mental statements that would forever be her own.

Then she stood and faced me with an expectant look.

I nodded, telling her she'd done everything right this morning.

She returned the nod, perhaps agreeing or saying the same thing back.

I wasn't sure, and it didn't really matter. We'd shown up here today as a team, our purposes uniting for the greater good. And together, we would embrace this new path to right the sins of our past.

We turned as one toward my estate, leading everyone back to my home, where we would feast in Kristina's honor. She'd loved to cook, marking this as the best way to celebrate her long life.

Afterward, everyone would go their separate ways.

And then Kayla and I would begin our hunt.

KAYLA

Kristina's funeral and the brunch that followed had been oddly peaceful. I felt as though I'd paid my respects properly and could focus on righting the wrong I'd created. Maybe not entirely, as I couldn't bring her back from the dead, but I could find out who'd done this.

Shortly after brunch, my father had attempted to talk to me about my "misconception" of his games.

"I didn't use you to hurt Ezra. He did that to himself," he'd insisted. "If you consider the greater picture, you'll see that, too."

"Some part of you took glee in his pain, Father," I'd replied, arching a brow that had dared him to argue.

"Of course I did," he'd admitted with a smile. "But I never delight in your pain, Kay."

I'd wanted to believe him, but it was hard to trust anyone in my life when all I'd ever known was betrayal. Instead, I'd just nodded. That'd been enough to satisfy him, allowing him to disappear back to Hell with Johanna.

"When you're done with all this, let me know if you still want that blade, Princess," Alastor had said before grabbing Lucía and following my father's lead in returning to the underworld.

Ezra had grunted in response, then gone to work cleaning up the kitchen while I'd returned to his office.

We'd spent the rest of the day and all of the next reviewing my notes and the maps, deciding on our action plan. We still wanted to meet with Lord Zebulon's Nephilim contact, just to cover our bases. However, we had a decent list of suspects.

No matter what tracking enchantment Ezra did, he couldn't find any traces for Kristina's essence, which confirmed we were dealing with either a Nephilim or a being who could conceal auras.

Or someone working with another skilled in concealment —we weren't discounting that possibility, which, unfortunately, painted a rather long list of suspects and left the very likely possibility that we'd overlooked a candidate.

"We need to consider this from a political standpoint," Ezra said, his arms folded across his chest. He wore another of his sweaters and jeans with no shoes. His wings were artfully tucked into his back as he held the plumes effortlessly off the floor while he studied the board we'd created.

"You mean we need to decide who has a motive to take Kristina's power. Someone who would want the veil to fall."

He nodded. "Exactly."

"That's hard to do when we don't know the majority of the candidates on the board."

"Agreed." His golden irises flickered as he met my gaze. "We need to do some old-fashioned spying."

My lips twisted as I considered how to pull that off. "We'll have to split the list."

He shook his head. "Most of them are in the same general area because of the Dark Provenance."

He pulled out our map and started shading areas of known Nephilim. I already had a similar one somewhere, but his quick drawing was faster than searching.

When he finished, he pinned it to our growing board and stepped back to evaluate it against our list of names.

While the Nephilim were mostly in North America, they

were still scattered all over the United States and Canada. "It'll take us weeks to cover all that together."

"Yes," he agreed, glancing at me. "So, instead, we'll ask Zebulon's contact to arrange an official gathering."

"Like a follow-up to the interviews Evangeline did with the Dark Provenance members for Prince Ashmedai?"

He shook his head again. "No. A gathering scheduled for me to meet them as the Archangel of Justice. You would attend as my mate, but what you'll be doing is reconnaissance with your magic bracelet." He concluded with a wave at my wrist.

That wasn't exactly how my cuff worked, but his idea held merit. "The Dark Provenance would bend over backward to meet with an Archangel."

They were notoriously enamored with the heavenly beings. And anyone who appeared not so excited to meet Ezra would stick out.

Just as someone trying too hard would also be noticed.

I slowly started nodding. "It's a good place to start." And it put all our potential suspects in one room.

Only the guilty party would know our true intention of being there, and that person might give himself or herself away.

Or better yet, he or she may refuse to attend, I thought.

It was a long shot, but we had an extensive list that would take forever to work through. This would cut down our time spent on the initial review and narrow down our suspects.

Except... I frowned. "Will the Nephilim believe I'm your mate?"

Because if they didn't, I would be the one standing out in the crowd.

Which would make observing them very difficult.

"Nephilim don't really like demons, even Halflings," I

continued as Ezra studied me. "They may not even let me in the building."

"They will if I tell them you're with me."

"Maybe. But then they'll all just wonder why I'm there. They can't sense mating bonds, and we don't exactly look like we're mated."

He arched a brow. "How do mated couples look?"

"I don't know. More sensual?" I guessed, thinking back on the few demon mates that I knew. "For starters, they actually like each other." Most of the time, anyway. Some of them bickered, but their fights always carried a palpable sexual undertone. Like they knew as soon as they solved the conflict, they'd end up fucking. Or maybe fucking while continuing to argue.

But maybe angel mates were different.

"Is it typical for angel mates not to touch?" I wondered out loud. "I guess we're not a normal couple anyway, given that we hate each other and I'm half-Archdemon and you're an Archangel. However, that'll just draw more attention, right?"

I blew out a breath and closed my eyes.

Maybe I can ask Zip for a favor? The little Orsini Devil enjoyed surveillance missions. He accepted cookies as bribes, making him cheap.

But I doubted—

Warm knuckles caressed my cheek, halting my thoughts and causing me to inhale sharply. Ezra's woodsy scent surrounded me in an intoxicating cloud of masculinity and grace.

"I don't hate you, Kayla," he whispered, his hand finding my hip as his opposite palm cupped my jaw. Heat swirled around me, his body seeming to set mine on fire as he pulled me into him. "And there are ways to intensify the sensuality of our bond, too."

I swallowed, my eyes opening to find him standing far too close. "Ezra..."

"Kayla," he returned, his silky voice holding a promise I didn't want to accept, a need I didn't want to hear, a curiosity I didn't want to share. But I could almost taste him, his lips mere inches from mine.

We'd kissed once.

When he'd fed me his blood.

The memory haunted my dreams, always evolving into something explicit and ending with me losing myself to the passion of Ezra's touch.

Only to wake and find myself alone.

Those were both my favorite and most hated moments.

I whispered his name again, my need to push him away disappearing behind a fantastical part of my mind that craved my mate. Desired his touch. Yearned for *more*.

It was an overwhelming combination of temptation, longing, and loathing, all wrapped up together in a fog of confused bliss.

His lips brushed mine.

Soft.

Tender.

Exploring.

Like he was waiting for me to bite him or stab him or shove him away. But my fingers sank into his sweater to pull him closer, my nails digging in just a little harder to make sure he felt my claws through the fabric.

I wanted to make him bleed.

I wanted to devour him.

I wanted to hear him beg me to spare him.

Just as much as I wanted to elicit a groan of approval from his throat.

His golden irises swirled with similar emotions, drawing out the intensity between us and darkening the moment.

Did we want to fuck or kill each other?

Did we want to kiss or fight?

Did we want to taste each other or make each other bleed?

Some wicked combination of all of the above.

I wanted to hurt him, but I also needed to embrace him.

"Fuck, Kayla," he whispered, his breath hot against my parted lips. He sounded broken. Beaten down. Demolished by this mounting lust.

I felt every push and pull, every temptation and hesitation, every intense need mingled with darker desires.

His heart beat with mine. His body tensed. His pupils flared.

I sucked in a breath that was all him.

And he pressed his mouth to mine once more, this time harder, his touch filled with purpose and sinful vows neither of us should entertain.

But his tongue silenced all my reservations, destroyed every wall I could have built between us, and demanded that I forgive him. Just for a moment. Just enough to feed our starving souls.

Flames licked at my skin, my power reacting to Ezra's nearness, his touch, his *kiss*.

His energy swathed mine in the next second, cooling the inferno dancing around me and providing a healing element I'd never known existed.

Fire and ice.

Hell and Heaven.

Archdemon and Archangel.

A beautiful balance. A sweet surrender. An intoxicating embrace I would never forget.

He'd overridden the runes of my cuff, providing me with a solace unlike any other.

I clung to him, needing more, my tongue dueling his in a hungry battle of desire and despair. He engaged me in kind, walking me backward into the bookcase and lifting me up until my legs wrapped around his waist.

"I still hate you," I vowed against his mouth, the words leaving me on a moan.

"I know," he whispered, his tone just as ragged as mine.

My fingers clenched the fabric of his sweater, threatening to tear it. His wings flared around us in response, cocooning me in a nest of feathers, my back pillowed by the spines of his myriad of books.

It was beautifully erotic, perfecting our embrace in a manner I couldn't define. It just felt right, as though we were meant to be here, right now, just like this.

His palm slid from my cheek to my throat, squeezing as he deepened our kiss. His tongue resembled a brand, possessing my mouth in a way only a mate could.

I felt his claim to my very soul, our link thriving with renewed vigor, setting my blood on fire once more, just to be cooled by his own force.

The scales tipped, then righted themselves, then tipped again, only to be yanked back to a level state.

It was overwhelming, leaving me light-headed with wonder.

Is this what it feels like to have him siphon off my energy? I wondered, dizzy from the notion of him feeding off my essence.

His grip tightened on my throat, forcing my attention back to him and causing my eyelids to lift. I wasn't even sure when they'd closed, too lost to his touch and kiss to recall much else.

Golden flares echoed in his vibrant irises, reminding me of the day he'd sealed our bond. *Sunshine*, I marveled. *His eyes are like bursting stars.*

"Sensuality isn't our problem," he said darkly, his opposite hand curling beneath me to palm my ass as he pressed his groin into mine. He used his thumb on my jaw to tilt my head back a little more while his grasp tightened enough to cut off my airflow.

Not that it mattered.

I'd stopped breathing when I'd met the intensity of his stare.

He said nothing, just held my gaze, waiting for some sort of reaction.

Did he want me to fight? To claw at his face and demand he release me? Or was he wondering if I'd let him suffocate me?

What game were we playing now?

Did I even want to win?

I tugged on his sweater, pulling him impossibly closer until our torsos were entirely aligned.

Then I leaned in to take his bottom lip between my teeth.

And bit down.

Hard.

He growled in response.

So I licked the wound and allowed him to see the blood on my tongue before taking it into my mouth and swallowing.

It was a feral instinct, one I didn't regret because his essence tasted like ambrosia—sweet, succulent, *divinity*. I moaned silently, the sound cut off by his palm, my eyes falling shut.

And then his mouth captured mine again, kissing me with a ferocity that was borderline animalistic.

My lungs burned as he released my throat, allowing me to inhale. But it was all him and his scent, no true air, just Ezra giving me life.

He bit down on my lip in the next breath, drawing a sharp gasp from my throat at the spark of pain. His tongue soothed it almost immediately, my blood trickling into his mouth.

Hell's wings, it was vampiric.

Except we weren't Blood demons.

We were a mated pair, rekindling a bond from ages ago that had weakened with time. It still remained, the vow one made for eternity. But it'd dulled. And our little kiss had just reignited the blistering heat between us. Only to be cooled by Ezra's energy once more.

"Are you feeding from my essence?" I asked, my voice a pant as my thighs clenched with unmistakable need.

"No. Our bond is finding a new equilibrium," he replied, his golden irises flaring with power. "You're overflowing with warmth, and I'm providing the outlet you need to stabilize."

"By absorbing my energy," I translated.

He shook his head. "It's not about energy, Kayla. It's about reestablishing our link. You being in Hell and unattainable for decades has left me without a much-needed counterbalance for everything that gives meaning to life. I don't need your energy, little heiress. I need *us*."

I swallowed. "I'm not sure I want to give that to you." A lie. My body absolutely wanted to give him everything. He'd lit a fire within me that only he could appease. But if it meant strengthening our bond to the point where I might be unable to let him go, then I wasn't sure I could do that.

I'd come here to kill him.

I still wanted him dead.

I still wanted him to pay.

But I also... I also just wanted him.

"I know," he said softly, his forehead falling to mine as his hand slid up into my hair to comb through the strands. His mouth brushed mine, both our lips swollen from our bites and harsh kiss. However, he made this embrace feel so tender, like it was warmed by a thousand promises that neither of us voiced yet felt all the way to our souls.

I shivered.

This bond between us was dangerous.

Meanwhile, it could also be one of the best sensations of my life.

I licked his bottom lip, craving more of his blood. Alas, the wound had already closed.

Part of me wanted to do it all over again, but Ezra pulled away before I could, his gaze knowing. Probably because he felt a similar urge. "The Nephilim won't be a problem," he said, the hand on my ass returning to my hip. "Let me handle them. You just observe and see if you can read any of their auras."

I wouldn't be able to, but I nodded anyway.

Mostly because I didn't trust myself to speak.

"We'll leave in the morning," he added, helping me to stand once more. "I'll make sure Zebulon's contact is ready."

With that, he released me. Then he took several steps away from me, his wings ruffling at his back.

And in the next breath, he disappeared through the windows.

Into the late afternoon sky.

EZRA

KISSING KAYLA... HAD BEEN A MISTAKE.

Because now I just wanted more.

Her curves beneath my palms. Her naked flesh sweating against my own. Her lips caressing my throbbing shaft. Her nails against my back. Her slick heat pulsating around me as I drove inside her.

I wanted to taste her arousal, to find out if it was as sweet as it smelled.

I wanted to fucking drown in her.

It was all I could think about, making sleep last night an impossibility and leaving me even more unfulfilled this morning.

Thank fuck I had a distraction waiting for us, or I'd pick up right where we'd left off against that bookcase, remove all the clothes, take her into the sky, and teach her how angels preferred to mate.

I'd been so close to losing control yesterday, a sensation I'd never experienced in my very long life. I thrived at being in charge, but Kayla... she made me feel wildly inept, like I couldn't tell up from down.

I ran a hand over my face, preparing myself for seeing her again. It would take serious restraint not to grab her and kiss her as though I had every right to do so.

Which I should.

She was my fucking mate.

But I'd ruined all chances of us having a normal courtship when I'd abandoned her in Hell.

A twinge of guilt—also a new sensation—clawed at my insides, encouraging me to apologize. However, I knew it would never be enough.

I also wouldn't entirely mean it.

The balance had to come first. Always.

Except a very selfish part of me... wanted Kayla to come first. Just this once. Just for us.

I swallowed, palming the back of my neck, and glanced up at the ceiling of my kitchen.

Which was, of course, how Kayla found me.

She cleared her throat, a note of amusement touching her lips as I met her gaze.

It immediately made me suspicious.

"What did you do?" I asked.

She shrugged. "Nothing."

I narrowed my eyes, then glanced around the too-clean kitchen. She'd clearly eaten in here, and recently, too.

Which meant she'd found the leftovers from my midnight snack.

I opened the fridge, confirming it, and just shook my head. "I had plans for that salad."

"And those plans were positively delicious, too," she drawled.

I fought the urge to smile and lost as I caught her proud expression. "Well. At least you like something about me."

Her dark eyes glittered, her lips curling. "Don't get cocky, Archangel."

"I wouldn't dream of it." I pulled out a bunch of fruit, some juice, and a powder from the pantry, then went to work making a meal smoothie.

Kayla crept forward and hopped up onto the counter

beside where I was working, her long, jean-covered legs crossing at her boot-clad ankles.

I doubled my portions without asking her, preparing her the same liquid lunch for our trip to Nashville. I'd reached out to Zebulon early this morning, and he'd provided me with the contact I needed, saying he would be awaiting our arrival.

I'd recognized the name as one at the top of Kayla's list of Nephilim. *Gleason.* He'd grown exponentially in power, marking him as a suspect. But I'd learned from Zebulon that he'd also been the one to help compile the list, which downgraded my suspicion to mere curiosity.

"We're meeting Gleason in Nashville in an hour," I said before hitting the button to blend all the items together.

Kayla merely watched the ingredients spin around in the glass, her expression giving nothing away. However, the dark circles beneath her gaze suggested she'd slept about as well as I had.

I placed my palm on her thigh, curious to see how she'd react.

She startled, glancing down at it and then up at me with an arched brow, still silent.

Deciding to test these new boundaries, I leaned forward to press my lips to hers while holding her gaze. She didn't kiss me back, but she didn't move away either.

I smiled, humming in approval before returning to the blender. The addictive musk of her arousal slithered around me like a noose, immediately making me regret the decision to test those boundaries.

Because now I wanted to fuck her again.

I swallowed hard, wincing at the tightening of my jeans.

Yeah, definitely not the brightest notion I've ever had, I told myself.

The protein shake didn't prove to be much of a distraction, my body strung tight with a need only Kayla could satiate.

A need I'd repressed for forty-one very long years.

It was a drop in the bucket of time for one as old as I, but it resembled an eternity to my aching cock.

Clearing my throat, I poured our drinks into two separate glasses, found a pair of straws, and handed her one of the shakes without looking at her.

"Thank you," she whispered, the words ones I hadn't expected to ever hear from her.

I glanced up to find her eyes on the drink, not on me, her cheeks a reddish hue that spread down her neck and disappeared beneath her leather jacket.

"You're welcome," I replied, the term sounding odd in the air between us.

Cordiality didn't suit our dynamic.

But rather than fight it, I focused on my liquid lunch and cleaned up my mess.

We both finished around the same time, with Kayla surprising me by taking my cup and washing it out along with hers. When she finished, she faced me and said, "Nashville?"

I nodded.

We were both dressed similarly in boots and jeans, though my shoes cut off at the ankles and hers went up to her knees. And I wore a sweater instead of her tank top and leather jacket combo.

Weapons weren't required for this visit, but I had my sword on me—the one I kept enchanted and invisible at all times. And I sensed that Kayla had at least two blades tucked into her knee-high boots with another at her hip.

Which meant we were ready.

I held out my hand. "Let's go."

She didn't hesitate, her skin branding mine as she accepted my offer.

I engaged my ability to portal and navigated to the coordinates Zebulon had provided for the human realm.

It didn't take long, the location closer to where the Divinity resided over the Atlantic Ocean. My home existed on an island of sorts that hovered in the clouds, invisible to the mortals yet tucked inside their realm on a section of floating land. Only those with certain supernatural abilities could find it, and locating it also required very specific directions, thereby keeping out many unwanted demons and angels.

Invitations were mandated for a reason. To arrive without one would trigger all sorts of unpleasant countermeasures.

We touched down in the middle of a backyard, the house before us unexpected. I frowned at it, then glanced around, hoping no humans had seen us teleport into what appeared to be a semi-wealthy suburban neighborhood.

The rising sun suggested it was only six or seven in the morning, making it less likely that mortals were up and about or spying on neighbors' lawns. But still, the location left me frowning. "I must not have heard Zebulon right."

"Oh, you did," Kayla replied, her hand leaving mine. "This is Gwen's old house."

"Gwen?" I repeated.

"Guinevere. Succubus with a bit of a control problem. Best friends with Evangeline. And, given her recent mating with Zebulon, I'm going to assume she's also now Gleason's former roommate. Gleason being the Nephilim that Zebulon wanted us to meet, right?" she guessed.

I blinked at her. "How do you even know all that?"

"I spent a few days stalking them while trying to get an audience with Evangeline. I'd planned to ask her to help me get in touch with Johanna. But then Ashmedai found me. And, well, the rest... you know."

Yes. I definitely knew what had happened then. "I see." I considered the house. "Well. Should we knock?"

"He has an arsenal of silver in there, so I'll let you do the honors," she suggested.

"Silver?" I questioned, arching a brow. The substance had been eradicated on Earth as a safety measure to allow demons to prosper.

"Gleason's a former chemistry professor," Kayla explained, proving she'd learned quite a bit about him while *stalking* Guinevere and the others. "He's also Evangeline's personal weaponsmith."

"I'm sorry; have we met?" a deep voice spoke from the side of the house as a Nephilim with a head of thick auburn hair appeared. Given his commentary and proximity to the home, I assumed he was the Nephilim Zebulon had sent us to meet.

Gleason.

He had a gun in one hand—aimed directly at Kayla's head —and a blade in the other. "Because that's a hell of a lot of private information you just spouted off about me, demon shebitch."

My eyebrows rose.

Kayla just sighed. "Halfling. And if we're picking nicknames, then I prefer 'hellbitch' over 'shebitch.'"

"Excuse me, I'll amend. *Hellbitch*," the Nephilim deadpanned.

"Thank you," she replied with a sweet smile.

Then she threw a knife at the Nephilim's gun, the metal locking with the barrel to render the weapon useless.

Great, I thought, my jaw clenching as Gleason dropped the pistol with a curse. He had a second one in his hand a moment later, the trigger firing as Kayla leapt behind a tangle of bushes.

Gleason unleashed several rounds, the sound deafening.

"*Enough*," I snapped, my sword appearing in my hand and angling toward the reckless Nephilim's neck as I spread my wings wide to make it clear just whom he'd pissed off.

Gleason spun around, ready to fight off my sword, only to freeze as he took in the sight of my feathers.

He fell to his knees in the next moment, his gun lost to the ground beside him.

Because only an Archangel could force their wings out in the human realm, something I clearly should have done upon arrival. But it was typical procedure to take on a humanoid appearance when walking among the unsuspecting mortals.

Kayla's sigh tumbled through the air as she muttered, "You ruined my fun." She rolled out from behind the bushes and picked some leaves from her hair.

I ignored her in favor of the suicidal Nephilim before me. "Did Zebulon fail to mention our arrival?"

The Nephilim proved his penchant for death by shifting back to his feet without my permission. The arrogant bastard had the nerve to meet my gaze, too. "Lord Zebulon told me to expect company, but he didn't tell me what kind to expect."

"And do you typically greet your visitors with insults and weapons?" I demanded.

"Demonic ones that I've never met before?" He glanced at Kayla before looking back at me. "Yes."

"I'm not a demon," I told him through my teeth.

"No, but the hellbitch clearly is," he retorted.

"*Kayla*," I corrected, ready to slice off this jackass's head. "My *mate's* name is Kayla."

KAYLA

EZRA'S WORDS REVERBERATED THROUGH MY MIND on repeat.

"My mate's name is Kayla."

He'd uttered the statement with such vehemence, not because of the meaning behind the phrase but because of the reason he'd felt compelled to voice it.

He's defending me, I realized, noting his protective posture and the positioning of our stances. He'd placed himself between me and the Nephilim. And then he'd told the Nephilim my name after he'd called me a hellbitch again.

"Say it so I know you heard me," Ezra continued. "Perhaps consider including an apology as well."

"That—"

Ezra held up a hand, silencing me, while his opposite hand remained on the glowing sword that he had angled toward the Nephilim.

I glared at Ezra's back, one of my blades falling into my hand on impulse.

But then Gleason said, "Kayla, as in Princess Kayla, I presume?" He shifted to see around Ezra, his striking green eyes meeting mine despite the sharp edge pointed directly at his neck. "You stopped by a few weeks ago."

"I did."

"Hmm." He gave me an appraising look. "Eve would have stabbed you on sight."

"Good thing I met Gwen first, then," I replied, meaning it. Evangeline was notorious for throwing silver first and asking questions later. But I'd been prepared to appeal to her humanity by expressing my human side.

Gleason's expression didn't change, but his shoulders marginally relaxed. "I won't apologize because you owe me a new gun."

"You have silver bullets in it," I pointed out. "I didn't feel like dying today." Silver actually didn't impact me that much at all yet—and might not ever truly impact me the way it would a typical demon—but that was a secret I kept close to the chest. I suspected it would save my life one day.

"Fair," Gleason agreed, his focus returning to Ezra. "I was in the middle of making coffee when I felt your arrival. We can talk more after I have a cup."

With that, he turned and walked toward the house.

Completely at ease with the simmering Archangel in his wake.

It was as though Ezra didn't threaten him at all.

Which, of course, made the Archangel of Justice bristle.

I grinned as I stepped up to his side to point at the Nephilim's back. "I like him."

Then I trailed after him, not caring at all that he hadn't voiced an invite. He'd tried to shoot me. That worked as far as invitations went.

Ezra caught my arm as I started after Gleason, pulling me backward for a visual inspection. His eyes roamed over every inch, causing me to raise a brow. "Like what you see, Archangel?"

"Yes," he answered bluntly. "But how did he miss you?"

I smiled and lifted my wrist. "Shield rune."

He eyed the gold cuff against my skin. "That's impressive."

"*I'm* impressive," I returned, my lips curling at my attempt at a joke.

His gold irises met mine, a startling intensity radiating in his depths as his sword vanished into thin air. "Yes, Kayla. You are."

I blinked, startled by the stark honesty in his statement.

He punctuated his comment with a kiss to my cheek. Then he pressed his palm to my back and said, "Come help me teach this Nephilim some manners."

Ezra's notion of "teaching manners" left a lot to be desired. All he did was stand in the corner of Gleason's kitchen with his arms crossed and brood. I much preferred my method of stealing a mug from the cupboard and helping myself to the coffee maker.

The Nephilim merely smirked in response, then leaned back against the counter and drowned himself in caffeine.

His angelic traits shone in his handsome appearance. I bet he turned a lot of heads on the street with all that thick auburn hair and his magnetic green stare. He obviously spent a lot of time at the gym, too. Although, I doubted those visits had anything to do with his killer physique and everything to do with being a demon hunter.

The Dark Provenance fancied themselves to be a supernatural police force.

Most demons laughed it off.

But Gleason certainly proved to be admirable with his aim. Had I not engaged my shield, he would have hit me at least twice through that bush.

Now he stood in his kitchen wearing the same pajama pants and tight white T-shirt he'd ventured outside in earlier—

no shoes—with his damaged pistol on the counter beside him and his good one strapped once more to his hip.

He seemed completely at ease and unfazed by the presence of Ezra in his kitchen. Instead, he took his time finishing his coffee before looking at my Archangel mate and saying, "So. What do you need?"

Yep. I definitely like this guy, I thought. No idle chitchat was absolutely the way to go in every situation. It was too bad I didn't live nearby. We'd probably be fast friends.

"We need you to help us arrange a gathering of the Dark Provenance members," Ezra informed him. "I want to meet them."

Gleason folded his arms, his expression suspicious. "Why?"

"Do I need to provide a reason as the Archangel of Justice?"

I snorted. *Typical.*

Ezra ignored me in favor of the stoic Nephilim. He stared back at the Archangel without a single hint of fear in his features. Actually, he appeared quite unimpressed. He'd bowed earlier and clearly felt that was enough respect for one day.

Yeah, we were totally best friends in another life, I decided, my lips twitching.

He allowed his arms to fall to his sides as he straightened his shoulders, his posture screaming, *I do not care who the fuck you are; I will not bow again.* However, his voice remained calm as he said, "If you want me to help you arrange a meeting, you're going to tell me why."

Ezra's eyebrows lifted in surprise. "That's not your place to demand."

"But it would make the Nephilim more cooperative," I pointed out as I glanced at Ezra. This time, he acknowledged me, his features holding a touch of annoyance. Maybe because

I'd interrupted. Or more likely because I'd sided with Gleason. But it seemed like an appropriate tribute to kick off our future friendship—something that was absolutely going to happen.

Maybe he'd even help me kill Ezra.

Assuming that was what I still wanted.

"And how would it do that?" the Archangel asked, his tone holding a touch of patience, suggesting he actually wanted my explanation.

I shrugged. "Well, the culprit already knows we're involved. Which means that he or she will know why we want to hold this meeting, right? So why not just be truthful about what's happened and use this as a way to prepare the Nephilim for what's coming?"

Because even if we managed to find Kristina's killer, the balance would continue to shift.

Which meant that we needed to prepare as many allies as possible for the eventual fallout.

Ezra considered me for a moment, his eyes still narrowed. Then he returned his attention to Gleason and sighed.

"She's right," he admitted, shocking me into silence as he jumped straight to the events of what had happened the other day. Except he left out my involvement in his explanation, merely stating that he and the Divinity had been fixing a break in the veil when a demon had ambushed them with a venom bomb.

"A venom bomb?" Gleason repeated.

"Yeah," Ezra muttered. "Made from a Slither."

Gleason visibly shuddered.

And Ezra continued his story, telling the Nephilim about Kristina being kidnapped and later killed.

"We think it's a Nephilim who did it," Ezra concluded.

"Why?" Gleason pressed.

"Because we can't sense her power anywhere," Ezra

explained. "Which means we're dealing with either a Nephilim or a being well versed in concealment."

Gleason's obvious lack of surprise caused my brow to furrow. "Most Nephilim would be quick to argue that point," I told him. "You seem resigned."

"Lord Zebulon clearly didn't tell you about his ex," Gleason replied, causing Ezra and me to share a look.

"His ex?" Ezra prompted.

Gleason just shook his head. "It was a long, drawn-out game of cat and mouse that involved a Nephilim helping her disguise her identity. They attacked Gwen, all in an effort to hurt Lord Zebulon. The Nephilim in question is dead now."

"He helped disguise her identity... through concealment?" Ezra asked, clarifying.

"More or less. He was able to alter her appearance and her aura. But not on camera." Gleason turned to start brewing more coffee. "They framed Gwen for several murders, but it's all been sorted."

I shared a look with Ezra. We might need to learn more about all that.

"And with Eve missing in Hell, who the fuck knows anything anymore? She was taken with an ease that shouldn't be possible, and now no one can sense her aura," Gleason continued, the coffee maker sputtering to life as he faced us once more. "All right, yeah. I can organize a meeting. You can tell them about the shifting balance, and I can help you both assess the masses for any strange reactions or behaviors."

"Eve's aura is missing?" Ezra asked, ignoring the rest of Gleason's statement.

"That's what Gwen told me. But Xai is on it. He'll find her." Gleason sounded confident. "And I pity the assholes who have her." His brow furrowed. "Actually, no, I don't. They deserve whatever Xai plans to do to them."

Ezra nodded. "He'll destroy them. She's his mate. He'll

move Heaven and Hell for her and annihilate anyone who wrongly touched her." He glanced at me and then back at the Nephilim, causing me to grunt. I wasn't going to touch that comment with a ten-foot pole. We both knew it was a load of shit anyway.

"I didn't actually shoot her," Gleason told him.

"You tried," Ezra replied.

I rolled my eyes. "It's history and I'm fine. Let's talk about the gathering—you agreed to help organize the meeting?"

Gleason and Ezra ignored me in favor of staring each other down.

I sighed loudly. "Seriously..." This was the battle Ezra chose to pick in my favor?

"How long do you need to arrange the meeting?" Ezra asked after a heavy beat of silence.

"Probably two or three days," Gleason replied. "Everyone is on high alert right now because of Eve and what just went down with Creek, so it won't be hard to gather everyone. They're all amped up and ready to do something."

I frowned. "Like what?" I wondered out loud, genuinely curious. The Nephilim were more powerful than humans, but nowhere near as strong as angels or demons. "What could you do?"

Gleason finally took his focus away from Ezra to meet my gaze. "That's precisely the problem. We don't know what to do, just that we want to help in some way. And our two guides —Eve and Xai—are busy in Hell."

"How did that happen?" Ezra asked, some of his icy facade seeming to break. "I mean, Ashmedai mentioned Evangeline being lost in Hell, and you said her aura has disappeared, but how?"

"All I know is Xai suffered a bullet to the head and someone took Eve. Remy has popped in a few times to give Gwen updates, and she's sent them to me via text, but no one knows where Eve is or who has her." He sounded a little less confident now than he had when he'd said Xai was handling it. Which implied a very fucked-up situation indeed.

"That's actually somewhat similar to how Kristina was taken and killed," I said slowly, thinking out loud. "We couldn't sense who did it."

Ezra's brows pinched together. "Yes. Very similar."

"Do you think it's related?" I asked him.

"Potentially," he admitted, his mouth twisting to the side for a second. "Which means this meeting may not help us at all if the culprit is in Hell."

"Not exactly," I replied. "It'll help us narrow down the list. Anyone who doesn't show up will be noted."

He dipped his chin, conceding my point. "True. While Gleason works on gathering the Nephilim, we should review the demon hierarchy again, see if anything stands out with the power fluctuations."

"Yes," I agreed.

Silence fell for a beat before Gleason said, "The power fluctuations are what this is about. The shifting balance, I mean. It's why some of us are growing in abilities."

Ezra glanced at him. "Yes." No elaboration. Just a confirmation.

"And that'll lead to an eventual rift in the veil," Gleason translated.

"Yes," Ezra repeated.

"Well..." Some of Gleason's bravado slipped into an expression of uncertainty. "I guess the Dark Provenance is about to be needed now more than ever before."

Not sure how you all can help, but okay, I nearly replied.

Gleason's sharp green eyes cut toward me, his eyebrow arching. "You have no idea what we're capable of, Princess."

My lips curled down. I hadn't said that out loud. "Did you just...?"

"Read your mind?" he finished for me, his lips curling a little. "Not exactly. But as I said, we're a lot more powerful than any of you give us credit for. Perhaps we'll demonstrate at the meeting." His attention returned to Ezra as the coffee maker dinged. "Reach out in two days. I'll give you a time and a place to meet." He didn't wait for a reply, just turned to refill his mug.

But Ezra nodded anyway. "We'll be in touch," he said, holding his hand out toward me in a clear invitation to leave.

However, I didn't accept it. Instead, I considered Gleason's revelation. He was noted at the top of my Nephilim list for a reason—his powers had increased exponentially over the last few decades—but mind reading wasn't part of the profile I'd reviewed with Ashmedai.

Which led me to saying, "I want the files." That had been the original reason to reach out to Gleason, after all.

Gleason glanced back at me, amusement lightening his features just a little. "Of course." He set his mug down and left the room without another word.

I glanced at Ezra, curious as to whether or not he'd picked up on the admission, only to find him grinning.

What? I nearly demanded, my eyebrow lifting.

But he just shook his head again, instead finding a mug and pouring himself a shot of coffee. He downed it in one go and set the cup in the sink as Gleason returned with a thumb drive.

Ezra took it from him and murmured, "Thanks." I didn't recall seeing a computer in his study, but he must have one somewhere.

This time when he held out his hand, I accepted it.

And the world spun around us once more.

All the way back to his estate.

EZRA

A Little Over Two Days Later

KAYLA'S LUSCIOUS BROWN HAIR GLEAMED IN THE moonlight streaming through my open windows. I wanted to comb my fingers through the silky strands, create a fist-like hold, and drag her into a kiss.

It was a craving that hit me square in the gut, tightening my insides and lighting my blood on fire.

I'd never desired a woman in this manner before.

Every day only intensified my yearning.

Knowing she slept in my home, just down the hall, drove me mad, making sleep impossible. Which was a problem because I needed to be able to focus.

Yet I couldn't.

Because all I wanted to do was grab my mate and devour her.

She stood in front of my back row of bookshelves, eyeing the boards we'd propped up against them. We'd drafted several lists, the first being all eleven Archdemons, their realm attributes, and the Demonic Lords who reported to them.

Ashmedai had Zebulon and Valentino written beneath his name, as he only had two Demonic Lords under his proverbial wings.

Others, such as Bael, had four.

Morax had six—a strategy he used to keep his demons competitive for power.

Kayla had added little notes regarding their power levels, marking Zebulon as one of the most powerful beings in the human realm.

She'd also written some notes on Kristina, Johanna, and Lucía, tying them back to their Archdemon and Archangel parents.

Kristina—Prince Morax and Archangel Valisa.
Johanna—Prince Orcus and Archangel Gloria.
Lucía—Prince Kore and Archangel Stefania.

Then she'd moved on to a list of Archangels, of which there were twenty-seven. Since we all technically shared the same realm in Heaven, she hadn't added any territory notes. But she had included a handful of notes on their abilities.

Beneath my name, she'd written: *Archangel of Justice. Asshole. Betrayer. Soon to be dead.*

I'd chuckled along, allowing her a moment of fun. Then I'd repaid the favor by adding my own notes beneath Bael.

Kayla. Halfling. Princess of Bael. Beautiful. Cunning. Brat.

She'd narrowed her eyes at that last part, then shrugged and gone back to her list of Archangels and angels.

But two days later, we were no closer to solving this mystery than when we'd begun. It was almost time to meet Gleason again, and we still had no idea who could be behind Evangeline's kidnapping in Hell. However, we felt certain it was related to what had happened to Kristina.

"I think we're dealing with more than one individual," Kayla eventually stated.

I agreed.

The questions remained: What group? And who was part of said group?

Kayla shook her head as though hearing my questions and

being unable to answer them. With a sigh, she faced me, her caramel-colored irises flaring with power. She kept most of it hidden beneath that cuff, making me wonder what she could do.

Would she be able to kill me if she removed it and allowed me to feel the full force of her energy? I mused. It was a dangerous thought, yet it intrigued me.

I liked how powerful my mate had become.

However, I didn't like how much she hated me. Even now, I could feel her anger at what I'd done to her. And I couldn't blame her for being furious with me.

"Part of me wants to apologize," I admitted out loud. "But I wouldn't mean it."

"No, you wouldn't," she agreed, immediately knowing what I meant. "Even knowing what you do now, you'd make the same decision."

"I would, yes." While she might be vengeful and full of hate, she was still powerful, beautiful, and a force of nature. "Who would you be had I not left you with Bael?" I wondered out loud. "Who would I be had I let the balance fail four decades ago? What would have become of the world?"

"How do you know the balance would have failed?" she countered.

"Because it was always destined to fracture. My whole purpose in this life was to prolong the inevitable, which is a sad existence when you consider that I've always been expected to fail."

She arched a dark brow. "So you left me in Hell, knowing full well it was a moot point anyway?"

"Yes." I leaned back against my desk, my wings fluttering to rest upon the wood as I slid my hands into the pockets of my jeans. "I also knew Bael would never harm you and that you would be safer in his realm while you mastered your powers. You were never meant to reside with the humans. He only did that to gift you the memory of your mother."

Some of the anger tugging at her mouth seemed to dissipate with my words. "How do you know that?"

"Because I've known Bael for a very long time," I replied. "I read his motives almost as well as he reads mine. Which is why he made that blood deal—he knew there would come a day when I couldn't resist staying away from you."

"Yet you never came," she pointed out.

I smiled sadly. "No. You came for me first." And I'd severely underestimated how angry she would be. I'd thought all this time apart would have cleared her head, made her see the bigger picture, and understand that this was the best route for us both.

Alas, that wasn't what had occurred at all.

Because she wasn't me. She didn't view the world as I did. And that'd been the fatal error in my calculation—I hadn't considered *her* feelings at all.

"I don't blame you for hating me," I said, continuing my line of honesty.

There was nothing else to lose here between us.

Besides, she more than deserved to hear my truth.

"I didn't consider how my choice would impact you," I confessed. "Not entirely, anyway. I knew what it would do to me. And it was a consequence I felt I deserved. Not just for failing Johanna in the first place, but for what I did to you as my mate. However, I didn't know it would infuriate you to the point where you would willingly trust other Archdemons to help you track me down."

That part wasn't meant as an accusation, even if it sounded like one.

It was meant to be the truth because I had honestly never anticipated her going to such lengths to seek revenge on me.

"I thought you would forget all about me," I continued.

"You're the Princess of Bael. We might be mated by my rules, but most demons don't engage in blood bonds. I know the connection between us weighs more heavily on me than it does on you. Which is partly why I didn't anticipate your residual anger. I expected it to be temporary."

"You tricked me into a mate-bond and left me in Hell," she retorted, her voice a low purr of angry energy that vibrated the air around us. "How could my anger over something like that be *temporary*?"

"That's where I misjudged our situation," I told her. "I never took *your* reactions into account, only my own. I knew I would suffer, and I accepted it for the greater good. Given the one-sided nature of our bond, I never even considered your feelings because I knew it wouldn't hurt you. It felt... insignificant."

"It wasn't insignificant to me."

"I see that now," I replied, stating the obvious. "What I'm saying is, I failed to account for your emotional reaction to what I'd done."

"So you're saying I'm reacting emotionally," she deadpanned.

I cleared my throat, very aware of the dangerous web she was weaving around my words. "No, I'm telling you that I didn't account for either of our emotions or how we would feel about my actions. I took a practical stance that I now see was wrong. But I also don't regret it."

"Because you acted in the best interest of humanity while knowing full well you would eventually fail anyway, thereby making all this pain a *moot point*," she summarized, her tone telling me how she felt about everything I'd just said.

"What would the world be like today had Bael taken Johanna four decades ago?" I asked, reiterating my earlier question. "His power only began to shift over the last decade or so. He needs her now for balance. But what would have happened had he taken her too early? Would she have balanced him prior to his increase in power, thereby shifting that energy to someone else? Someone less... worthy?"

It was all a delicate dance of righting the scales. To tip them too soon caused the other side to experience an unexpected fluctuation that could create a ripple effect.

I walked over to the board to draw it, showing the scales and adding Bael's name to one side, mine to the other, and Johanna at the top. "Had he taken her, she may have stabilized his energy too soon, but that wave of power would have had to go somewhere," I said, drawing a line from Jo to Bael.

I added Kayla to my side of the scales, showing the temporary stability had we chosen that path four decades ago.

"But the shift has always been coming, so what happens?" I continued, drawing a zigzag line of electricity around both couples and the spark-like ripples away from their balance. "You wouldn't be nearly as powerful as you are now"—something I demonstrated with a red marker, showing the sparks of energy leaving her for somewhere else —"and I would be more or less the same. So who would have inherited the power destined for you? What about Bael? And would Kristina and Lucía have been enough to maintain the veil?"

I turned to find Kayla studying my crude drawing with a skeptical expression.

"Maybe it's not the best illustration," I started.

"No, you are definitely not an artist," she informed me, her tone deadly serious.

I smirked. "True, but you can see where the paths begin to shift."

"Sort of." She didn't sound very convinced.

So I attempted a new method of explanation.

"We've felt this divine shift for several millennia, the first of which occurred when the Divinity was born. All three came into existence around the same time, stirring a fresh power dynamic. You're aware of this part?" I guessed.

"To an extent," she hedged.

"Then I'll elaborate," I said. "Heaven and Hell agreed on a balanced approach to uphold the veil."

"That part I know."

"Right, but agreeing on the balance and upholding it are two entirely separate topics. As a result, there are those who have fought to ensure that the veil remains steady and those who have attempted to tear it down. Two sides to every coin. And not everyone agreed to the purpose of the Divinity that day, only those with the highest ranks of power—ranks that are now shifting."

She considered that for a long moment. "Give me an example."

"Mietek and Xai," I said immediately. "Mietek is the Archangel of Chaos, one of the original Archangels who agreed to the Divinity's purpose. But Xai is growing in power now and will very soon surpass his father."

"Is that not normal?"

"No, it's not," I told her. "Archangels don't lose power unless there is an external influence, such as a strained mating bond. But they can always regain their energy. Mietek has weakened as his son has strengthened, and they're not the only ones experiencing this phenomenon. It's like the universe is trying to bring in a new era of leadership."

"Yet some of the Archdemons are growing in power."

"Yes, but so are some of their underlings, like Zebulon. Which means there are those losing power, too. Will Zebulon grow into an Archdemon and claim his own realm?" I asked, the question a hypothetical one. "Will Xai rise to take over leading the Archangels?"

It was all a guessing game at this point, but one aspect was abundantly clear.

"Not everyone rising in power has good intentions. Now is the perfect time to orchestrate a coup d'état," I concluded.

She rubbed the space between her eyes, signifying that I'd given her a headache.

It was a lot of philosophical conjecture.

But the fact remained... "Had I chosen you four decades ago, it would have reshaped the power divide. The whole point of my role is to control the fallout, and that's precisely what I did by prolonging the inevitable. Hurting you was never my intention. I merely wanted to draw out the endgame."

"And I ruined that by summoning you with Prince Ashmedai's device," she muttered.

"Yes," I said, agreeing to an extent. "But perhaps we will find that it was meant to play out that way." Because I couldn't deny the rightness of having her beside me, almost as though we were intended to exist in this moment, right now, just like this.

She started massaging her temple. "This is a lot."

"It is," I agreed, checking my watch. "We still have a few hours before we're scheduled to meet Gleason for an update. Can I tempt you to have a late dinner with me?"

Kayla's brow furrowed, then she glanced up at me with those hypnotically beautiful eyes. "Are you making it?"

I smiled. "Yes."

She pretended to consider, then shrugged. "Then sure. I could eat."

As could I, I thought, admiring her stunning form as she stretched her arms over her head. She'd worn a tank top with no jacket tonight, leaving me with an alluring view of her breasts and flat abdomen.

If she noticed my hungry stare, she didn't show it. She merely gathered up all the markers, set them in a line on my desk, and sauntered toward the door.

"It's going to take an eternity of well-prepared meals to convince me to forgive you," she said, turning to meet my gaze. "You may as well start now." With that, she flipped her hair over her shoulder and disappeared, leaving me grinning in her wake.

That sounded like a challenge.

One I might just accept.

Kayla

Ezra had made pizza.

From. Scratch.

I nearly died when the first taste of tomato, cheese, and garlic touched my tongue. It redefined the meaning of *divine*.

Not that I admitted it to him.

Out loud I just said, "Not bad." But inside, I was melting. Because, dear realms, it was delicious.

I kept repeating everything he'd said in his office, too, his almost-an-apology a heavy topic that weighed down my thoughts. He'd provided a viewpoint I hadn't wanted to consider—*his point of view.*

"I never even considered your feelings because I knew it wouldn't hurt you." Yet he went into that situation knowing full well what it would do to him. And I'd seen the evidence of his suffering over the last few days. He was not the Archangel I'd mated four human decades ago.

He was... irrevocably changed.

Weakened, but stronger at the same time. Like he'd lived through a lot more than I had, and he'd gained some sort of clarity in the process. An intelligence I couldn't even begin to comprehend.

Or maybe that had always been him.

We hadn't spent much time together before he'd abandoned me. I hadn't even realized the purpose of our bond until he and my father had spelled it out for me. And by then, it'd been far too late to do anything about it.

I'd spent millennia hating Ezra, creating this monster in my head meant to be slayed.

But sitting across from him now, watching as he finished the final bite of a delicious meal, all I could see was a man.

My mate.

Beautiful. Otherworldly. Strong. Intelligent.

It could all be a trick of the imagination—a hopeful thought of a young girl who wanted her knight to be real, to save her from the darkness of Hell.

He's playing me again, I told myself. *Don't fall for this. It's an act meant to subdue me until he shows his true intentions.*

That was the voice of the female I'd become. Because of him. Because of what he'd done to me.

And it very quickly drowned out the hopeful girl inside me that longed for him to be real. To actually mean what he said. *To be my mate.*

But I didn't have a mate.

He'd abandoned me to my fate.

And he would do it again just as soon as it suited him.

His gold irises flared with knowledge, making me distinctly uneasy. Sometimes I wondered if he could read my mind. Or perhaps it was my body language he understood.

Because he grinned as though he welcomed whatever challenge I'd lay at his feet.

However, rather than speak, he stood and cleaned up the kitchen. I didn't thank him for the food. He didn't ask me if I wanted dessert. We just fell into a charged silence filled with violent undertones. Like we might engage in a battle at any moment.

It caused the hairs along my arms to rise.

I glanced around, searching for any weapon I might be

able to use against him, and inwardly cursed for leaving myself unarmed in his presence.

Except that violent air quickly morphed to something else as he faced me again. His gaze was ablaze with a furious energy that froze me in my chair, my breath halting in my lungs.

Not violence, I realized, thinking back on the undertones I'd misread. *Savage need.*

I felt it swirling around me, choking me with the power of it.

Our bond was *starved* for physical touch. My veins throbbed with the desire to sate this connection between us, my thighs clenching with the yearning to feel him inside me.

Oh, demons, I whispered to myself. *I need to escape.*

Because if I didn't, we'd give in to this growing energy, this intoxicating *need* to recharge our link. I'd ignored it for the last few days, trying to forget Ezra's kiss. But it haunted my dreams, waking me at early hours and heightening the illicit craving inside me.

I fought it at every turn.

I sensed he did as well.

But something had shifted between us these last few days, slowly edging us toward this intense moment where it just... snapped into place. No sound. No physical connection. However, I felt it *click* inside me. Some final link securing us together once more.

His burning gaze told me he'd experienced it, too.

The fiery energy sizzled and demanded we indulge in the dark impulse throbbing between us, drawing a moan from my throat. *Oh, this is bad...* His magnetic pull reminded me of an Incubus, wrapping around my throat like a noose and imploring me to kneel. Supplicate. *Beg.*

What is happening to me? I marveled, my nipples hardening beneath my tank top. *I feel... I feel... so hot. So... in need.*

"Kayla," he growled, his palms gripping the island to hold him back. "*Knives*."

I didn't understand.

Did he want to fight before we fucked? Because I would enjoy that.

Except the sensual spark in his gaze quickly hardened to murderous rage, drawing me out of the blissful haze and pulling my focus to the pulsating heat against my wrist.

My cuff.

It glowed with warning, detecting a spell I'd only just begun to understand.

Ezra reminded me of an Incubus because someone was using a lust bomb on us.

Similar to the venom explosion, only more deadly because it could distract and encumber us both.

I pulled up my runes, selecting my shield, and exhaled heavily as the potency of the charm dissipated. It wasn't entirely gone, mostly because it'd only heightened a true lust that existed inside me, but it diminished it enough to allow me to think.

Ezra was still fighting the impulse, his defensive pose a beautiful display of strength and restraint that immediately appealed to me on a core level.

But I fought the attraction and focused on our surroundings, attempting to figure out what was happening.

However, Ezra grabbed me in the next second, drawing a scream from my throat as his control fractured.

Except a blast of heat sizzled over our heads, telling me he'd just saved me from being hit by something dangerous.

"Hold on," he gritted out, his teleportation gift flaring to life.

I grabbed him, preparing to fly, when his wings caught fire, stirring a bellow of agony from his chest. *What the fuck is going on?* I demanded, glancing around me, trying to find the source of the attack.

Ezra released me, his sword appearing as he used it to block another wave of flames.

I followed the arc of the inferno to the Dargarians outside. There were three of them.

Fucking fire demons, I hissed.

I had no idea how they'd portaled here or why, but my wrist blared with warning that more were coming. From *all* directions. Above. Below. To the sides. Their auras were everywhere, drowning us in a sea of sulfur and malicious intent.

I needed a weapon. *Stat.*

Ezra's wings flared, the feathers sizzling in fiery torment. *Why hasn't he extinguished the inferno?* I wondered, recalling the time I'd tried to hit him with a fireball—he'd smothered it before it'd even left my hand. Dargarian pyrokinetics were similar to my own; Ezra should have been able to handle it.

Yet the pungent stench of burning plumes added to the sulfuric air assaulting us from outside.

I shifted my focus to the kitchen, looking for something to put out the flames, when an explosion rocked the foundation outside.

Ezra cursed as my knees buckled, my sense of equilibrium flying over my head—*literally.*

I blinked, stunned.

Everything was dark.

Black.

Starkly *wrong.*

What the hell is happening? I felt as though I were swimming in a dark sea of dense and murky water, searching for the surface and finding nothing but more inky liquid.

It suffocated me entirely.

Until the burning on my wrist yanked me back.

I wrapped my hand around my cuff, drew my requisite star and slash, and inhaled as all my power hit me full force in the chest.

Fire whispered across my skin as Ezra's blade slashed through the air, sending another of those fiery waves back at the Dargarian assholes outside. Anguish distorted his features, drawing my focus to the molten ash at his back.

His wings... I swallowed. They were gone.

But they would grow back.

They had to.

And I needed to stand up and fucking fight.

This all resembled a bad dream, a nightmare I'd never known I feared. Time seemed to spin off its axis, the world around us crumbling into an unrealistic painting. But I could feel it in my spirit that this was real.

Ezra's sanctuary had been severely breached.

We were under attack.

Only a powerful being could create a portal here that allowed demons into the atmosphere.

Which suggested that whoever had absorbed Kristina's powers had brought the battle to us.

Bring it, I thought, embracing every ounce of my power.

My hands burned with energy, the pale skin shifting to dark embers as my fire took over. I used the force of it to push me to my feet, creating an inferno of my own to send into the Dargarians outside. They shrieked, their assault on Ezra momentarily ending.

There wasn't time to search for another weapon; all I could rely on was my own strength.

My head ached as horns pierced my scalp, my demonic form coming out in full force as I embraced my Archdemon side.

The abilities I'd demonstrated in the forest near Vancouver had only been a small dose of what I could do. The Orsini

Devils hadn't been worthy of my full power. But whoever had opened that portal to this sacred place had absolutely earned my wrath.

I growled, furious heat pouring over my skin as tendrils of fire sprouted from my fingertips like whips.

That portal needed to be shut down. I just had to find it.

I almost voiced that plan out loud to Ezra, but another arc of fire came from behind us, silencing my ability to speak. My power intercepted the flames, sending them back to the originator.

My entire life had been molded in preparation for this moment, as I'd been fighting demons since I was a child.

Maybe Ezra was right—I'd needed time in Bael's realm to perfect my abilities—because my reactions came naturally now. I dodged and swerved, sending fireballs at the demons and grinning when they screamed.

Yeah, you like that? I taunted, creating another zigzag of energy to take out several more Dargarians. Then a horde of Ghouls. *Odd.* They didn't usually fight for their Archdemons.

Actually, they didn't typically fight at all.

When a Pestilence demon appeared next, my eyebrows rose. Because those fuckers belonged to Alastor. But I couldn't sense his royal brand on this one at all.

He appeared to be... *solitary.*

What the fresh hell is this nonsense? I wondered. Demons were pack animals. They generally stayed within their realms and served their masters—otherwise known as Archdemons or Demonic Lords. But these underworld minions appeared to be operating on their own.

How? Why?

My shield ignited as the Pestilence demon attempted to hit me with a blade—one I had no doubt he'd coated in his own vile disease.

Alastor would be pissed if he saw this.

Which was why I had no problem setting this asshole on fire—Alastor would thank me later for it.

The Pestilence demon screamed, his humanoid form very mortal-like in appearance and sound. But the black sludge coming out of his eyes was starkly demon.

He began to melt beneath my fiery fury, and a Cyclops shoved him out of his way to reach me. Only, he couldn't fit through the door to enter the kitchens.

His single eye also wasn't on me but on Ezra.

I spun around to see my Archangel mate fighting for his life as almost all the demons around us focused on him— *not me.*

The Dargarians had only shifted focus to me for my fire.

The Pestilence demon had also appeared to be aiming for me, but maybe I'd misjudged his intentions.

Because all the demonic beings appeared to be trying to kill Ezra.

While leaving me to just... exist.

Which meant I could leave and let him die. Or stay and try to protect him.

It took me all of a second to decide to fight by his side. He was mine to kill, not theirs. And the balance needed him.

No. It needed *us.*

I could feel it wavering all around us, this attack on the Divinity's domain tipping the scales in every direction. The heavens had to feel it. The Archdemons, too.

This is very bad, I decided, focusing yet again on the demons. *I really need to find the portal.*

There wasn't time to explain my intentions to Ezra—I had to use the window of freedom to shut this shit down. He could handle himself with that sword.

With my hands lined in flames, I crept down the hall toward his study to escape through the back doors.

Only to find myself immediately surrounded by Slithers outside.

"Oh, fuck this," I said, flaming their slimy asses before one could so much as spit.

Two went down with screams that touched my heart in the best way, just for a third to sneak up behind me like some sort of ninja snake. His fingers went for one of my horns, yanking me down, only for the hand to be severed at the wrist by a blade.

The Slither's head fell to the ground in the next instant, that same blade having cut right through his elongated neck.

I startled, half expecting to find that Ezra had followed me. Alas, no.

It was a different face that stared at me now—one I knew very well.

"Yaz?" I whispered, shocked to see the head of my Royal Guard standing only a few feet away.

He winked in response, then spun away to take out an incoming Orsini Devil in the next instant.

I gaped at him, then allowed myself to take in the carnage outside.

Bodies littered the grounds.

And at least a dozen members of my guard stood lording over them with savage expressions.

Holy hellfire, I breathed, my lips parting. That's *why none of the demons are attacking me... My Royal Guard is here.*

Which meant either my father had sent them at the first sensation of trouble, or he'd ordered them to remain here in the shadows until I needed them.

It was something for me to evaluate later.

Because more demons were pouring onto the lands and I'd left Ezra behind to defend himself.

"Where's the portal?" I shouted.

Yaz pointed his sword directly up in response, making me

curse as a trio of demons fell from an inky cloud in the night sky.

How the hell am I supposed to close that? I wondered, gaping at it. "Who made it?" I demanded, searching the grounds once more. If I could locate that person, I might be able to take them down and force them to dismantle the portal.

Yaz's expression told me I wasn't going to like his response. "We don't know."

Great. That meant whoever was in charge here was blending in somewhere. *No. Not blending.*

Concealing.

I narrowed my gaze as the pieces of the puzzle began to fall into place. Not many knew how to find this plane of existence. Hell, I hadn't even known and my mate was the Archangel of Justice.

I also doubted Ezra left these grounds unwarded. He probably had runes everywhere.

Therefore, whoever was behind this attack knew not only the location but also his security parameters. Because there hadn't been any warning other than the lust bomb—something that had been deployed *after* the grounds had been breached.

Kristina's powers had probably been used to break the barriers, too.

Shit.

We need to get the fuck out of here. This isn't a battle we can—

My thought halted as a knife sliced through my chest, sending me to my knees. But it wasn't visible. I couldn't see it. Only feel it. The sensation stole the air from my lungs, causing me to curl into a ball as Yaz shouted over my head.

A flurry of activity scattered around me, whispers of blue

silk taking over my vision. *My guard. They're protecting me,* I realized as I wheezed in agony.

I patted my hands against my chest, searching for the blood and the weapon and finding nothing. *I don't understand.*

"They're leaving," one of my guards said. *Baxton, maybe?*

"We need to notify Bael," another replied. That sounded like the low tones of Serena, the guard's second-in-command.

"We need a Portal Dweller! Where's Jinx?" a third demanded, the voice too deep for me to sort. Everything hurt. My mind refused to process, my body shaking beneath an onslaught of pain unlike any I'd ever experienced.

Yet I still couldn't find the wound.

Because it's not mine, a faint part of me realized. *This isn't my pain...*

I blinked. *What?*

I pressed my palm more sternly to my chest, determined to quiet that voice.

But the evidence existed beneath my skin.

I wasn't feeling my own death. I was feeling the death of another.

Ezra.

My throat closed, my chest screaming in agony at the realization of what that meant. *He's dying.*

No.

Impossible.

He was *mine* to kill.

I forced my eyes open, noted all of my guards around me, and shoved off the ground to my feet. Everything swam before me, my vision refusing to acclimate to my sudden movement, but I had to *move*, to *run*, to reach Ezra!

Yaz yelled something in my wake, telling me to stop.

But I didn't answer to him. I answered to myself. To my soul. To my *mate*.

I crashed through the doors of the study and took off at full speed inside the home, not stopping until I reached the kitchens.

To find Ezra bleeding on the floor.

His wings were gone, disintegrated into ash.

But that wasn't what captured my focus.

His torso did that.

And the holy blade sticking out of his chest.

KAYLA

A SHIVER RACED DOWN MY SPINE, THE IMAGE BEFORE me eerily similar to the one I'd dreamt of for thousands of years. I'd fantasized often about this moment, the one where I watched Ezra die.

Yet the elation I'd anticipated didn't come.

Instead, I felt depleted. Wilted. Dead inside. Alone. Miserable. Conflicted. *Dizzy.*

I tried to breathe, but my lungs rejected me.

I tried to speak and couldn't.

I... I couldn't stop staring, waiting for the moment of victory to hit me.

And nothing.

No happiness. No excitement. No sense of triumph.

I swallowed. *This... this isn't how it's supposed to happen.* I was meant to wield the blade, to stab him, to conquer my betrayer through my own strength. Not let someone else do it for me.

That had to be why I felt so empty inside, like I'd failed a monumental task destined for me alone.

"You can't die like this," I finally managed to say, my voice raspy and pained. My knees buckled, sending me to the floor beside him. *"You are not dying like this."*

This was my fight. No one else's. How dare they take this battle from me. He was my mate to punish, not theirs.

My eyes narrowed on the dagger slowly sucking the life out of my mate.

There had to be a way to fix this. A way to save him. A way to right the scales so we could try this again.

"We..." I trailed off, unsure of where to go. Bael's realm wouldn't be able to help him. Ezra was an Archangel. "He needs Heaven," I whispered to myself. "But how...?"

I glanced around, seeking a solution and finding nothing that could assist me in saving him.

This is so messed up, I thought, frantic. *You were supposed to die by my hand. Now I have to save you... to... to kill you myself?* It sounded more like a question than a statement in my mind, some part of me adamantly against repeating this scene.

Because it was all wrong.

It didn't please me to see him like this. It *hurt*. Maybe because I could feel his life slipping away, our bond fracturing a piece of me I hadn't known existed until today.

Think, think, think! I told myself.

There had to be a way to rescue him.

I studied the dagger in his chest, my heart throbbing painfully against my ribs. I swallowed. *Wrong*. It wasn't supposed to look like that. It wasn't supposed to feel like this, either.

Fuck.

If it were anything other than a holy blade, I could rip it out of his chest and wait for him to heal. But he wouldn't be able to mend himself back together with the magic left behind from that weapon.

Which meant it needed to be removed carefully, similar to how one would treat a mortal wound.

My throat worked as I tried futilely to figure out what to do. How to fix him. Help him. *Save* him. "Damn it, Ezra. You are not dying like this."

We were nowhere near done with this battle. And I didn't

just mean the one between us. The balance needed him. *I* needed him. I couldn't do this alone.

Yet already I could feel the trembling of change vibrating through the realms, knocking me deliriously off-kilter. Without Ezra, the veil would fall. Not in nine years. But *now*.

I could sense it fracturing already, the waves of unease ripping through my soul and threatening to tear me apart.

Or maybe that's the sensation of losing Ezra, I marveled, my eyes widening. "Shit!"

His skin looked too pale, his breaths were too shallow, and the blood... *Hellfire*...

"Towels," I said. "I need... I need towels." Something to apply pressure and to stabilize the blade.

Yaz handed them to me in a blink, his presence reminding me that I wasn't alone.

"Fetch me a Portal Dweller. Or an Archdemon. Or someone who can teleport us." Ezra needed his home realm, to be surrounded by healing energy.

But even that might not be enough. I shivered. *No. I refuse to let this be the end of it.*

I'd spent too many damn years fantasizing about this moment to let things go down like this.

I'm not ready for you to die. I glared at him. "*You're not dying here, Ezra.*" It came out on a growl, my irritation mounting by the second. We didn't have time to wait for a Portal Dweller—not that many were even powerful enough to reach Heaven—or someone with teleportation abilities.

Ezra was dying.

I could feel his soul tugging on mine, his breaths growing shallower by the second.

Tell me what to do, I wanted to say. *Tell me how to save you!*

I looked at my cuff, frantic for an option, but my portal charm only went so far. Archdemon powers manifested over tens of thousands of years, and I was still a baby among my kind.

But Ezra isn't, I thought, studying him. *He's older than time itself.*

Which meant I needed to tap into his power, to somehow find the link between us that would allow me to engage his ability to traverse time and space.

I'd avoided our connection for so long that I wasn't sure I could find it.

Except, I'd sensed it during our kiss the other day. It had resembled a brand against my body, my spirit, my *mind*, one that had left me intoxicated and overwhelmed at the same time.

My heart skipped a beat as I tried to find that sensation again, to recall how it'd made me feel beyond the obvious heat simmering in my veins. I needed to locate the heart of it, the soul-bond mating us for eternity.

The very bond I long to break, I thought, swallowing thickly. *But I only want to break it on my terms. Not anyone else's. Just mine.*

"You're mine to kill," I whispered to him, my eyes falling closed. "I refuse to let this be our end, Ezra. It's not time yet."

You didn't suffer nearly enough, I added inside my mind.

But that wasn't exactly true.

He'd suffered a great deal.

However, with each passing second, I began to understand how much *I* would suffer from his death. My soul already throbbed in agony, feeling as though a hot blade had sliced me apart from the inside out. And the hot embers now lingered behind to suck all the energy from my veins in the knife's cutting wake.

I clenched my jaw, forcing myself to concentrate, to locate the link...

Only to realize that I already had a hold on our connection.

That was the source of my pain. His death. His soul crying out for mine. It begged me to follow his pleas, to dive into the pulsing anguish, to embrace it.

To embrace him.

I pressed my palms to his cheeks, my forehead meeting his on impulse.

Yaz said something about a Portal Dweller, but it was too late for that. I couldn't use one now. Ezra was the key. I needed the remainder of his energy to whisk us to safety, to take us to the only plane that could possibly heal him.

Show me, I whispered. *Show me how to save you.*

Nothing happened.

No words.

No guidance.

The only thing I sensed was his weakening pulse and slowing breaths.

So I pushed harder, forcing myself to go deeper into our bond, to find the core of our beings and engage him on a spiritual plane of existence. It was dangerous, dark, and deceptive. A place I'd never wanted to go. A forbidden connection between our souls that shouldn't exist.

But we'd forged it in blood.

Strengthened it through our kiss the other day. *And my bite*, I marveled, feeling the potency of our link spring to life between us.

It was a beacon of fading energy, blinking in and out, whispering at me to take another step. Begging me to creep closer. Urging me to stroke the magic blistering between us, to take what was rightfully mine.

A connection I shouldn't desire.

A mate I despised.

A future... *I craved.*

My heart thumped wildly in my chest, my breathing harsh as I explored the depths of our connection. My Archdemon ancestry coupled with his ancient Archangel bloodline should allow me to find a way to ascend to Heaven.

But the potency of our link overwhelmed me, taking me even deeper into our bond, distorting the reality around us.

I swallowed, my sense of time and space falling into a dark obsidian.

All I could hear was Ezra's failing heartbeat.

All I could feel was his lack of breath.

All I could think about was our dying bond.

This isn't right.

This isn't how you're supposed to go.

Why does this hurt so much?

I hate you.

I want you.

I despise you.

I desire you.

You broke my heart.

Part of me wishes I could forgive you.

The words rolled through my head in some fucked-up twist of voices—both mine and Ezra's statements—only they were my thoughts, not his.

Or maybe they belonged to him, too.

Air combed through my hair, causing my stomach to tighten with wrongness.

I loathed this sensation of loss, this feeling of ineptitude.

How are you doing this to me? Why are you dragging me under with you?

I'd craved this moment for so long, yet it felt as though my very soul was being ripped from my being.

The whirling energy turned icy as water swallowed me whole, pushing me to the depths of the ocean where oxygen didn't exist. I inhaled, sputtering, coughing, *dying.*

Except it wasn't water that filled my lungs.

But air.

How...? I wondered, my eyes unseeing.

Darkness engulfed me entirely.

However, whispers caught my ears, the voices ones I recognized yet couldn't name.

Someone commented about time.

Another mentioned the need to heal.

"It's too late for that," a third voice said, this one deeper. "I told him to use the bond. He didn't listen."

"It's not too late," a female murmured. "Not yet. He just needs more of her blood."

"Yes," another woman agreed, her voice the closest. I could feel her warmth radiating through my skin, her healing energy suffocating my inner Archdemon.

I wanted to moan, to growl, to *fight*, but I remained motionless and paralyzed beneath a wave of power I couldn't define.

Ezra provided my only link to reality.

Yet he wasn't conscious.

What's happening? Where am I?

But on the heels of that thought, another hit my mind like a bolt of lightning.

Heaven.

That was the cause of my discomfort. And the source of the drowning sensation.

I don't belong here.

My soul wept, urging me to return to the safety of Hell.

But Ezra's spirit clung to mine, begging me to stay.

Somehow, he'd teleported us here. Or maybe I'd miraculously engaged in the ability to ascend.

Perhaps someone had even come for us.

It all felt too foreign and impossible to decipher. I was lost to the whims of my dying mate.

Because even in death, he owned me. His energy swirled with mine, dragging me down with him to a grave of despair.

I could fight it. I could cut him off. I could let him die.

The link was a fragile strand, one that wobbled and sizzled with warning. *Too weak. Too neglected. Too degraded.*

It would be so easy to slice through it and let him fall.

Only, my heart refused to allow it. Instead, I found myself clinging to him as though he were my anchor in life, demanding he survive.

To kill him my way, I told myself.

Truth or a lie? I couldn't say.

It didn't matter.

Something sliced my arm, drawing a hiss from my mouth. "He needs this," the female informed me. "Your connection is barely alive."

I wanted to say something about *why* our bond was nearly dead, but I couldn't move my lips. I couldn't even see her. Part of me wasn't even sure any of this was real.

Electricity jolted through my veins, drawing a gasp from my throat.

"See?" the woman said. "He needs your blood, and you need his."

Ambrosia touched my tongue in the next instant, stirring a groan from my chest. *So good*, I marveled, swallowing and humming inside as warmth spread through all my previously chilled limbs.

The decadent flavor made me feel alive.

It calmed the ache in my gut, making it easier to breathe.

Another dose graced my mouth, the essence an addiction I immediately took down my throat. I barely felt the knife wound on my arm, too lost to the intoxicating flavor coating my tongue.

The sensual game continued for hours, or maybe minutes.

I really couldn't determine time, my mind lost to everything except for the buzzing electricity humming through my veins.

Eventually, the darkness abated, revealing a clear blue sky.

I blinked up at it, amused by the dots swimming in the distance. *Angels*, I realized as one swooped down in a twirl of feathers. *Fascinating.*

My vision started to blur, so I let my eyes close.

And when I opened them again, the blue sky had turned dark with night.

No... I narrowed my gaze. *No, not the sky. A ceiling.*

Only, it was about thirty feet over my head and shadowed by the lack of overhead lighting. Curtains were drawn to my left, blocking the windows. Or maybe they were blocking a wall, because they stretched from the floor all the way up to the high ceiling.

I frowned. *Where am I?*

I twisted in the silky sheets, my bare skin clammy and sticking to the fabric.

Why am I naked? This wasn't a fun reality to wake up to at all.

Except... *Ezra.*

He lay beside me, eyes closed and just as naked as me.

I startled, realizing my bare skin wasn't just touching sheets but also touching *Ezra.*

His body acted as a blanket for my side while a thin fabric covered my top. Well, partly, anyway. The blanket seemed to be twisted around our waists.

Which left my chest exposed.

And his chest as well.

I immediately pressed my palm to his ribs, noting the red mark over his chest. The holy blade had been removed, and his skin appeared to be fully mended. Just that dark spot remained, reminding me of a healing bruise.

I traced it with my fingertips while wondering, *Is this real? Or is this a dream?*

He felt warm to the touch, but not overly so. Merely alive. Energy thrummed through him to me and vice versa, our bond stronger than ever before.

Because of the blood exchange, I realized. *Assuming that really happened.*

His skin appeared otherwise unblemished, his coloring normal.

I eyed the spiral of black ink decorating the length of his left arm. He'd mostly worn long-sleeved shirts in my presence, hiding the beautiful design from my view. It reminded me of warrior markings. I nearly traced the ornate tattoo with my fingertips, but I didn't want to risk waking him.

Not with us both naked in bed, anyway.

I inhaled, his woodsy scent swirling around me in a kiss of sunshine mingling with autumn leaves. *Heavenly*, I admitted. Which was appropriate, considering our current location.

Except he was missing his wings.

How long will it take for them to grow back? I wondered, recalling the inferno that had destroyed his plumes. This picture seemed incomplete without his feathers.

I inhaled again, allowing his natural cologne to calm my nerves. *They'll grow back*, I told myself. *They have to grow back.*

My eyes drifted shut once more as I lost myself to his fragrance and the silky texture of his skin. It was a secret indulgence, one I would likely regret later. But I craved his touch right now, his strength, his *existence*.

I curled into his side, my head pillowed against his shoulder, my palm flattening over his healing mark.

Just five minutes, I told myself. *That's all we can afford.*

I also didn't want to risk him waking up to me pressed up against him.

However, his smooth breaths told me he was very much lost to sleep.

Which allowed me my private moment of peace.

For four minutes and fifty more seconds, I thought with a yawn. *Not a second more.*

Serenity engulfed me, a sense of rightness touching my soul.

This is what our lives could have been, I mused groggily. *This blissful warmth and shared existence.*

Ezra had taken all that away from us.

A fact that only made me hate him more.

You ruined us.

So I'm going to ruin you.

Later.

When we're both awake.

I yawned again, losing count of my seconds. So I started over at five minutes.

Again.

And again.

And again.

Until the counting followed me into my dreams, where Ezra taught me how to truly fly. As his bonded mate. As his *equal*.

A dream that would never come to be.

But a fantasy I would forever cherish.

Long after he's gone...

EZRA

KRISTINA MUST BE GARDENING AGAIN, I THOUGHT, the sweet aroma of lilies infiltrating my senses. *She's always gardening.*

Except, no. That's not right.

My brow furrowed as I tried to process the scents and the knowledge in my mind.

Everything swirled together, stirring a headache behind my eyes that had me nearly cursing out loud.

But the warmth of a soft, feminine body against mine kept me from speaking out loud.

Kayla, I marveled, feeling her presence all the way to my very soul.

My heart ached, this dream one I'd experienced so many times, always to wake up alone.

This would be no different.

But I would indulge her in any way I could.

I kissed the top of her head, then pressed my nose to her hair, inhaling the sweet floral scent. *Alluring as always.*

It was a forbidden dream.

An attraction that would never die.

This was the only part of my lifetime sentence that I enjoyed—the part where I controlled the fantasy. Where I mastered my mate and called her *mine*.

Sometimes she fought me.

Sometimes she even killed me.

And I always woke up hard for her as a result.

The lethal edge to our connection drove me wild. Perhaps because I knew she would one day succeed in her mission to destroy me.

She hated me.

For good reason.

But that just made the passion between us burn that much hotter.

At least in dreams like this one.

She started to stir against me, and I wondered if we would fight naked or just go straight to fucking. I couldn't define my current mood, my mind fuzzy and warm in an almost foreign manner.

I sighed, content in a way I hadn't been in a very long time. Almost as though I'd finally reignited our blood bond.

Definitely a dream, I mused. Because that would never happen.

Kayla stretched, her warm body gliding against mine as our legs intertwined. Her head rolled against my shoulder, a soft moan leaving her as she nuzzled her nose against my chest.

My lips curled. "Well, this is certainly new." My voice came out a bit more gravelly than normal, but I ignored it in favor of the naked female pressed up against my side.

Kayla froze. "Wh-what?" The sleep in her voice was an enduring quality I'd not experienced much in these dreams. I rather liked it.

She tilted her head back, her caramel-brown eyes widening in surprise. I tightened my arm around her shoulders, holding her against me.

"Generally, we fight first," I murmured, reaching up with my free hand to draw my fingers through her tangled locks of hair. They were tinted red today, making her normally dark

189

hair a more auburn shade with the brown strands mingling with the red.

I wasn't sure what part of my mind had created this new look, but it certainly matched her usual fiery attitude.

"Then we fuck," I continued, my gaze falling to her plump lips. "But I'm okay with skipping the fight this round, unless you want it for foreplay purposes."

Her brow crinkled. "We've never fucked."

"Oh, we fuck every time I dream of you," I admitted. "But usually we start with our clothes on. Then we battle, I pin you, and our clothes disappear." I dropped my focus to her bare breasts. "However, we're already naked. So we can skip that part, and I can devour you instead."

Because I was longing to taste her, the intrinsic need burned through my soul and demanded I take her mouth. Take *her*. Claim her as mine. Solidify our bond and heal us both.

So I did.

I kissed her.

Because this was my dream, making this my fantasy to control.

Only, Kayla's hand pressed against my chest, pushing me back, her irises glittering like burnt gold as she stared at me. "Ezra."

"Kayla," I returned. "Fancy a fight, then?" An ironic thing to ask since this was all in my head. Because it meant *I* wanted the fight, not her.

Which was strange.

Because I didn't feel physically up for a battle right now.

I actually felt rather weak.

Another bizarre sensation for a dream. In this world, I should feel every bit alive. In power. *Dominant*. My fingers drifted from Kayla's hair to the back of her neck, my inner need taking over.

"I don't want to fight," I told her sternly. "I want to fuck you." I grabbed the back of her neck, forcing her gaze to remain on mine. "You're already naked and this is my fantasy, so we'll do it my way."

"Your fantasy?" she repeated, her eyebrows lifting as her soft breath feathered across my lips.

"My dream," I whispered against her mouth. "My rules."

"How often do you dream about me?"

"Every time I close my eyes," I admitted softly, a bit confused by her questions. This was something she should already know since I'd created this scene in my mind. But maybe I had something to work through.

Or maybe it was a delaying tactic.

A new form of foreplay.

Similar to how her hair resembled a pretty reddish-brown color right now—a gorgeously new attribute. Silky, too.

I moved my hand once more, drawing my fingers through the soft strands. "So beautiful," I marveled. Of course, she'd always been beautiful. Even with her old mohawk. "I wonder what you really look like right now." It was a thought I voiced aloud because I could. I studied her facial features, noting the experience glowing in her caramel-brown gaze before lowering my attention to her full mouth. "I wish I could see you, and I mean really see you. I miss you."

If only I possessed Bael's gift for dreamwalking, then I could actually tell her that truth.

Although, I never would.

It revealed too much.

"You... you miss me?" she asked, her voice almost hoarse.

"You know I do," I replied, grinning as I nuzzled my nose against hers. "I dream of you because I can't have you."

"Why can't you have me?"

"You hate me," I said, sure of it. "Rightly so. Or maybe you don't remember me at all." I almost disliked that expectation more than the other, but for her sake, I hoped it was true. "This was my torment to bear, not yours. But the most important reason is that I can't jeopardize the balance." I spoke those last few words slowly, my brow furrowing as a sense of dizziness touched my thoughts.

The balance.

It... it didn't feel right. It felt... tipped?

Was this dream about to shift into a nightmare? It wouldn't be the first time.

And why was I speaking so much?

These were all statements I already knew. Which marked this as a waste of time, especially if my fantasy was about to turn toward darkness.

"I want you," I whispered. "No more talking."

I captured Kayla's mouth again, not wanting to miss the opportunity to embrace her before everything went to hell.

Her nearness, her touch, her heat, all sent a shock wave of energy through my system. It wasn't real, and I'd soon wake to the coldness of my bed and the weakness of my depleting soul, but for these few moments in time, I intended to indulge in the precious gift of our bond. To be with my mate the way I should have been all those years ago.

"Fuck, Kayla," I breathed, moving her to her back and rolling on top of her. She jolted beneath me, her nails biting into my shoulders as I pressed my aching cock against her slickening folds.

"Ezra, this isn't—"

"No talking," I repeated, my tongue dipping in to silence her.

She growled in response.

So I growled back.

We almost always fought in some way, and it seemed we were going to do it whilst naked.

Fine by me.

She dug her talons into my skin, scorching me with a quick flame, which I doused with ease beneath a wave of power that instantly cooled her inferno. A balance of power. A beautiful display of fire and ice. *Our bond. Our mating. Our soul-deep connection.*

She bit my tongue, then groaned as my blood entered her mouth. I allowed her to take her fill before saying, "You bite me, sweet princess, then I bite you."

Which was one of my favorite parts of this fantasy—the blood exchange. It was what I needed more than anything else in existence.

But I didn't want to sink my teeth into her tongue.

No.

I wanted flesh.

So I went for her breast, marking her in the way I truly craved deep down.

She screamed in response, her fingers threading through my hair to tug me away. I captured her wrists and pushed them up over her head to pin them against the bed.

"Ezra!"

I grinned, my mouth finding my mark to indulge in more of her blood before sliding down to take her nipple between my teeth.

She practically melted beneath me, the pain mingling with pleasure causing a strangled noise to escape her throat. It was more impassioned than I'd ever heard it, making this almost feel real. I groaned, the power flourishing between us stirring a sense of dizziness inside me. I almost felt weak. *Wounded.* A bit lost.

"More," I said, kissing a path back up her body to her throat. "I need more, Kayla." More blood. More taste. More *her*.

She whispered my name against my lips, her touch igniting with fire beneath my palms once more. This time I released her wrists and allowed the magic to burn me, welcoming her brand of pain, which only seemed to fuel her onward as her tongue stroked my own.

The little heiress was softening, giving in to my craving, allowing me to take control of my dream and drive us toward the ecstasy that awaited us both.

I pressed my lower half to hers once more, loving how her wetness coated my bare skin. It served as a welcome kiss to my shaft, urging me to take what I desired.

But I didn't want to rush this.

I wanted to indulge in so much more than a quick fuck.

However, that deep sense of dread continued to prick at my nerves. Something felt wrong. I didn't like it. I wanted to erase the danger and wrongness from the moment, to just exist with my mate.

"Ez," she whispered as I started kissing a path down her neck. "Ez, we need... This isn't..." She shivered as my teeth skimmed her throbbing pulse, her fingers threading through my hair again. "Not a dream." The words came out in a rush, almost sounding more like a single word—*notadream*.

My brow furrowed, my lips continuing their journey back down to the mark I'd left on her chest.

It was a strange thing for her to say, but as I shifted focus upward to read her face, I saw the conflict in her expression. The glimmer in her gaze was just enough to give me pause.

"Not a dream," she repeated, swallowing. "We're in Heaven."

I glanced around, noting the bright lights of my heavenly home—a home I hadn't visited in over a century or so. "That's how I know I'm dreaming."

She shook her head. "You were stabbed. Holy blade." Her grip in my hair tightened, her arm flexing as she pulled me back up her body. I went to engage my feathers, to use them to anchor me against her breasts, but I couldn't sense my wings.

Another sign of this being a dream.

Yet that deep-seated ache of dread continued to pummel at my instincts.

Kayla pressed her palm to my chest, not to push me away but to rest just above my heart. "Here. You're still healing right here."

I went to my elbows on either side of her head and allowed my eyes to drop to where her palm rested against my skin. *Red. Blemished. Almost like a healing bruise.*

I frowned at it, searching for a memory, anything to explain this strange sensation. *I'm in Heaven without wings, and there's a wound healing on my chest.*

An impossible occurrence.

Thereby making this an even more plausible dream.

However, something about Kayla seemed too real to be a fantasy. Unless I'd truly lost my mind. Not a stretch of a conclusion, considering the state of my soul.

"His memories will be the last to heal," a feminine voice informed us.

Raphaela.

A subtle whistle of air followed, suggesting the Angel of Healing had just arrived from one of the many balconies surrounding my room.

"He still needs more blood, too," she added. "And several days of bonding to help regenerate his wings."

I tensed on top of Kayla as Raphaela's pale white feathers fluttered in my peripheral vision. We were vulnerable and naked, something that left me uneasy. Kayla must have felt similarly because her fingertips dug into my scalp, holding me above her.

Rather than roll off of my mate, I kept myself balanced on my elbows and slowly tilted my head toward Raphaela to meet her intelligent gaze.

She stood with her hands clasped before her, wearing a

dress that matched her pristine plumes. She resembled a goddess more than an angel, but that was typical of her line. Her golden hair almost reminded me of a halo, too.

"Raphaela," I greeted. This was starting to feel real now. But also not. *What the fuck am I doing here?*

She started to smile, only for another gust of wind to interrupt her as someone else entered via one of the balconies.

Apparently, calling ahead to request a meeting was no longer common practice in Heaven.

"Well. At least you're awake," a deep voice muttered, causing me to tense even more above Kayla.

Mietek.

Fortunately, I had a blanket around my waist. But if I moved, Kayla would be exposed from the belly up, and I was not about to allow anyone to see my mate unclothed—particularly as this was my first time seeing her naked. Outside of a dream, anyway.

No wonder this is different. It's real.

"You need to use her to heal, Ezra. No more dancing around this bond. Fuck her. Bite her. Do whatever you need to fix this. We need your wings and your sense of purpose."

"Mietek," Raphaela admonished.

"He nearly fucking died, Rafa," he retorted. "He needs to hear this."

Kayla said nothing beneath me, her fingers still locked in my hair. I gazed down at her, confused as hell by everything going on around me. "How did we end up here?" *Where did you even come from? Why can't I remember anything? What's making me so dizzy?*

I only voiced the first question out loud, but the others all traversed my thoughts, each one meant for my mate.

However, Raphaela chose to answer. "Your mate embraced the bond between you, lent you her energy and power, and you ascended with her in your arms. Or, it's possible Kayla did that. It's unclear, but you arrived, and I was waiting for you here with Fate."

Of course. The Archangel of Destiny would have seen us coming, and she would have known that I needed assistance.

My death would cause a final rift in the balance, putting everything in jeopardy.

Already, I could feel the equilibrium shift as though something big had happened.

"Did you stab me?" I asked, looking down at Kayla. It wasn't an accusation, more of a curious statement.

Kayla's here. Beneath me. Naked. How?

I tried to determine when she'd returned, where she'd come from, but everything felt fuzzy and uncertain. My last memory was of... nothing, really. Being home. Reading a book, maybe?

It all seemed like a blur of time and space, my mind fractured from whatever the fuck had happened.

Kayla scoffed. "I wish."

"Use her, Ezra," Mietek repeated, his impatience coming through. "Bite her. Heal. We'll talk in twenty-four hours."

"Is that why I'm naked?" Kayla asked, finally taking her eyes away from mine. "Did you put me here to be used like a fuck doll?"

"Dariel is pushing to have you removed," Mietek continued, ignoring her. "If we don't see improvement, we won't have a choice. You already lost Kristina. Now you've lost your wings. *Fix. It.*"

"Kristina?" I asked, my mind blanking. "What happened to Kristina?"

"Your *mate* got her killed in her quest to destroy you," Mietek replied flatly, causing my eyebrows to fly upward.

"Mietek," Raphaela snapped, the usually docile angel showing her teeth.

"I'm going," he replied, waving her off as his wings

expanded. "Twenty-four hours, Ezra. No more." His dark feathers beat in the air to propel him off the balcony of my bedroom suite without another word. I watched him for a minute, taking in the stunning sky beyond and feeling a pang in my heart. *I miss this place.*

Then his words began to register.

Kristina's been killed.

Because of Kayla and her quest to destroy me.

My brow furrowed as I tried to seek out the truth because something about that felt wrong. I... I felt responsible deep down. Yet I couldn't define why.

"I removed your clothes, Princess Kayla," Raphaela said, responding to Kayla's earlier comments in a soft yet authoritative tone. "The skin-to-skin contact helped facilitate the bond exchange required to bring both of you back. His soul absorbed a lot of energy from you to stay alive—something you enabled by accepting the bond."

"*Acceptance* seems like a stretch," Kayla returned.

"Call it whatever you like." Raphaela sounded amused. "Regardless of your term preference, Kayla, you saved Ezra's life. And in the process of doing so, you both nearly died."

And this was supposed to be after she attempted to destroy me? I wondered. *Or as a result of it?*

I searched my mind for answers and found no recollection of any of this. It was dizzying and maddening and making me tense above Kayla for entirely different reasons than before.

"I forced the blood exchange to bring your souls back," Raphaela continued. "Then you both slept for two Heaven days. However, you need more. Your bond is nearly irreparable in this state. It's dangerous to you both."

"A bond I didn't want," Kayla mumbled, her voice a little less certain than moments ago.

"A bond that could right the scales," a new voice whispered as a flutter of opal wings carried Fate, Mietek's mate, into the room. "A bond that requires healing to prosper. But what will their hearts choose? No one can force them. Only they can decide their paths forward. We've done all we can do, Rafa. It is up to their souls now to decide the future for us all."

That's not ominous, I thought. However, a tickle of awareness stroked my senses, silencing any reply I would have voiced.

I shivered as a warped sense of reality brushed my mind.

Things are very wrong. The scales are forever off-center. Imbalance is taking me down... down... down... into a spiral of darkness and light, mingling with fragments of space and time.

I swallowed, my eyes closing as I tried to find my equilibrium.

Lost. I'm lost.

Everything's unstable.

"Ezra," Kayla said, her voice anchoring me to a space in time, drawing me back to her.

Only for the world to tilt all over again, causing me to fall...

Something sharp prickled my thoughts. Something important. There and gone in an instant, swept up in a tidal wave of sensation.

Until everything suddenly went calm around me. *Within* me.

Kayla.

Her palm was against my cheek.

Her lips near mine.

I blinked but couldn't see.

Everything was off-kilter, the Divinity shattered, the world—

Kayla's lips claimed mine, breathing life into my spirit. I clung to her, trying to swim through the darkness of my soul to find purpose and meaning once more.

Her nails dug into my scalp and then the back of my neck,

dragging me back to Heaven and the bed I hadn't slept in for far too long.

Although, it hadn't even been a Heaven year since I was last here.

Only a few Heaven months.

But it felt like an eternity.

Time was so fucked up.

The world was crumbling around us.

I no longer understood the balance. I sensed the scales raging out of control and could hardly move from the pain radiating through my chest.

But Kayla, she resembled freedom. A redefined existence. An escape from the insanity unfolding around me.

So I indulged in her touch.

I returned her kiss.

And I allowed her to take me under a new wave of darkness.

To a renewed fantasy.

Of us.

Our bond.

Our dark fates.

KAYLA

EZRA'S EXPRESSION HAD VANISHED, THE GOLDEN flames of his irises burning into dark pools of obsidian. My heart had stopped at the sight, fear choking me as I felt his soul withering via our connection.

Raphaela had immediately attempted to bring him back, but the other female had pulled her away, spouting off some nonsense about this being our destiny to walk now. "The Heiress of Bael will know what to do," she'd said cryptically before both females had left in a flurry of wings.

She was wrong.

I didn't know what to do.

Ezra convulsed, his body turning cold above me.

I missed the fire of his embrace, the sensuality of his touch. He'd thought this was a dream, admitted to fantasizing about me every night, but I'd felt compelled to tell him this was real.

Even though it certainly hadn't felt real.

It'd felt like a dream to me, too.

Because Ezra was being nice to me. And I *enjoyed* the sensation of him against my bare skin.

All hot, hard male.

Kissing me.

Touching me.

Biting me.

No one had ever lit me on fire the way he had, and we'd barely even begun.

Because he's my mate, I realized. *Our souls are forever intertwined.*

Not even an Incubus could evoke the reactions from me that Ezra had.

And now he was dying on top of me.

"Ezra," I said as his eyelashes fanned downward over his sharp cheekbones, concealing his darkening irises. He flinched, some life entering his expression, but it lasted for a mere breath before he started shivering all over again.

My heart skipped a beat, fresh memories of his near death flashing behind my eyes. We'd come so far. He'd been awake. He'd been kissing me. He'd been *warm*.

I sank my nails into the back of his neck, my mind reeling at this sudden change.

So cold.

Almost frozen.

My power ignited, sending a wave of warmth through him that parted his lips on a sigh.

Balance, I marveled.

Or was it the bond?

A bond that could right the scales, the angel had said, her tone and words so very oracle-like in nature. *It's up to their souls now to decide the future for us all.*

I swallowed, disliking the sound of that fate.

"Ezra," I whispered, trying to draw him back to me.

But he didn't react this time, his skin cooling again.

I blasted him with more power, then pressed my lips to his in a demand for him to respond. His arms tightened on either side of me, his body immediately tense.

I did the only thing I could think to do and kissed him again.

His fingers wove through my hair in response.

But his eyes remained closed, his trembling form still chilled on top of mine.

"Fuck it," I muttered to myself, cupping the back of his neck and parting his lips with my tongue.

He resembled ice. So I filled him with fire. I poured every ounce of my inner flame into him and demanded his reciprocation.

A groan rumbled from his chest, the sound quickly deepening into a growl. He came alive with a strength that took my breath away, his mouth stealing control of our kiss as his body mastered mine on the bed.

I didn't fight him.

I welcomed him.

I gave in to this building inferno and allowed the heat to swallow us whole. There were no more chilling touches or icy kisses, just a wave of dark intensity underlined in intrinsic *need*.

"Kayla," he breathed, his lips traveling across my jaw to my neck. He buried his nose in my hair, inhaling deeply. "This feels like a dream."

"It's not."

"I know," he whispered. "But I want to pretend it is. I want to erase everything. Start over. Embrace the bond the way a mate should."

The admission was warm against my ear, his body taut above mine.

His lips whispered along my jaw to my throat, his kisses light and reverent and making my toes curl. "It would be so easy," he continued, his breath hot against my skin. "Lose ourselves just for a moment, forget our past, and indulge in our connection."

"So you can use me again?" I asked, my voice raspier than before. "Refuel your spirit, heal yourself, and abandon me when you're done?"

He stilled against me, then his head slowly came up, his golden irises burnt around the edges and darkened with black specks. "That's not how a mating bond works, Kayla. It's about rejuvenating our spirits and embracing the energy thriving between us. If we indulge in our connection, it strengthens both of us, not just me."

His brow furrowed as his gaze went to my mouth and then returned to my eyes.

"Your presence distracted me from when I thought this was a dream. I've grown so used to feeling weak that I didn't even realize I was recovering from a life-threatening injury. That's how impactful our strained bond is on my soul, Kayla. But that's my punishment to bear, not yours. So if you say no, I will respect your decision. I'll never use you again."

The veracity of his tone settled between us, his expression telling me he meant every word.

If I rejected him, refused to help him heal, he would accept it.

And then what? Would he die? Would he wither away to nothing?

He was wingless, weak, and barely recovering from a holy blade to the chest. This was a dream come true for me.

Yet I wasn't enjoying this at all.

It resembled a nightmare more than a fantasy. Because I could feel his pain through our bond, could see it radiating from his gaze.

He studied me for a moment longer, then rolled off of me. It wasn't a graceful movement. And he jolted when his bare back hit the mattress, his eyes falling closed on a grimace.

"I don't blame you for hating me, Kayla," he added. "I can't change what I did to you. And I would never change it. But that doesn't mean I've enjoyed the outcome. The balance is, or *was*, at peace. However, the cost was... high."

"They keep saying you're weak," I said slowly. "Because of

our bond. But I don't feel weak. Or I didn't. However, now I can sense you..."

He nodded. "That's why your father kept you in Hell. It protected you from feeling the deterioration of my spirit. It also ensured that I didn't reach out to you again. He wanted me to suffer for what I'd done to you. But he also wanted to protect you."

He'd mentioned something like that before, that my father hadn't only wanted to hurt Ezra, but he'd also been trying to keep me safe.

Now that I could sense Ezra's pain, I started to question a lot of what I thought I knew.

Is Ezra right? Was my father trying to save me from feeling Ezra's pain?

My father was a complicated Archdemon, always playing games and trying to teach through unconventional methods.

He had never really hurt me, though.

He'd actually hurt others who had taken the lessons too far.

However, he'd done it in a way that had made me feel bad because it'd been my failure to fight them that had led to their punishments.

Or maybe that had just been residual guilt I'd put on myself for my poor performance.

It didn't matter.

"You won't be able to stay around me for much longer," Ezra added softly, his eyes still closed. "Being near me will impact you via our bond. Hell rejuvenates you and hides you from my deterioration."

I frowned at him. "What would happen to you if I left again and never returned?"

"I'm not sure," he replied after a beat.

But something told me he was sure.

He just didn't want to tell me.

And that had me narrowing my gaze at him. "Tell me the truth, Ezra."

"It's not your burden, Kayla." His voice was soft, almost dreamlike. I suspected he was falling asleep again, or retreating into that healing state.

Or dying, I thought, swallowing. "Will you die?"

He didn't answer for so long that I thought perhaps he'd either chosen to ignore me or was unconscious again. But he cleared his throat. "An angel-bone blade pierced my heart. It takes a lot of energy to heal an injury of that nature, energy I don't have."

Which meant he would die.

"Why aren't you taking what you need, then? We're not done fixing the balance. And that's your job, isn't it? That's your purpose? The reason you took me to Hell in the first place?"

He released a long, shuddering breath. "I'm old and I'm tired, Kayla." He didn't say anything else.

"That's not a response."

He grunted but remained silent, his agony throbbing through our link. It wasn't just physical pain but also a mental torment.

He didn't want to fail.

He wanted to fight.

But the only way to do so was by healing our bond.

And he wasn't going to force me. He wasn't going to guilt me into it either. He was merely going to accept his failure, and probably die, instead.

I wanted to yell at him, to call him weak for choosing the cowardly way out.

Yet he wasn't a coward. He was one of the strongest males I'd ever met. But he'd meant what he'd said—he wouldn't use me again.

He wouldn't use our bond to heal himself.

He wouldn't put the balance first.

His entire life's purpose... he'd just put second... *for me*.

Maybe because he was tired. Maybe because he was trying to appeal to my heart. Maybe because he wanted to invoke an emotional game meant to seduce me into helping him willingly.

Or maybe because he truly didn't want to indulge in our bond just to heal himself.

He wanted me to desire him, to *choose* him.

To help him of my own free will.

Not to be duped into a bond that would give him the protection he needed in Hell.

My strong Archangel had truly fallen.

No wings. A barely beating heart. A soul so tarnished that his hair had turned white and his powers were nowhere near their former glory.

While I felt mostly fine, apart from our link tugging at my soul.

Would I eventually die without him? Or would I thrive?

Did I even want to know?

Ezra released a shuddering breath, his skin clammy. This wasn't a trick. He was on the verge of death.

And he'd leave this world knowing he'd failed the balance.

It was such a poetic end, and yet, I couldn't accept it.

He was mine to kill. Mine to punish. Mine to *save*.

I stopped thinking.

I leaned over and kissed him.

If I found out this was all a ploy to use me to heal himself, I'd annihilate him.

Fool me once, shame on you.

Fool me twice, shame on me.

"Please don't make a fool of me, Ezra," I whispered against his mouth. "Now kiss me."

EZRA

Kayla's words flowed through me, her pain a visceral wound in our bond that pierced my heart.

I'd betrayed her so badly that she assumed I was using her again now. Yet her lips still met mine, her supple form pressing against me in delicious invitation.

Because she wanted me to heal.

I had no doubt in my mind that she would try to kill me again if I fucked this up between us. And if that happened, I'd allow it. I wouldn't fight her.

She deserved so much more.

If I couldn't live up to that potential, then I deserved to die for it.

Her tongue parted my lips, her warmth chasing away the chill in my spirit.

I returned her kiss, my fingers weaving through her hair to hold her to me. This felt like a dream again, so unreal and fantastical that I started to wonder if I'd already died.

Maybe this was my afterlife.

A world of Kayla, of lounging in bed and worshipping her with my tongue.

Mmm, that sounded like a solid plan.

I took charge of our kiss, emboldened by her touch and the energy swimming through her aura. It stroked mine, enticing me to consume my mate.

And consume her, I did.

I memorized every inch of her mouth, mastering her and telling her exactly what I wanted to do to her without uttering a single word.

She moaned, her palm cupping my cheek as her leg moved over my thigh to plaster herself to my side.

It wasn't enough.

I needed more.

More skin. More touch. More Kayla.

I fisted her hair, my strength deepening with each blissful second of her embrace, and guided her back into the bed as I rolled onto her once more.

Her thighs spread for me, allowing my lower half to kiss hers intimately.

"So wet," I whispered, groaning as I rocked against her slick heat. It would be so easy to slip inside, to penetrate her deep and make her scream my name.

But I wanted everything from her.

Not just a quick fuck.

If we were going to do this, we would do it the right way— with me making her climax in every conceivable manner known in the heavens.

I wanted to prove to her my intentions, to show her without words what she meant to me.

I missed you.

I meant it.

I want you.

I meant that, too.

And by the time I finished with her, she'd know exactly how I felt about her.

Her nails dug into my scalp as my mouth left hers, her opposite hand going to try to drag me back up to her lips.

I caught her wrist and pushed her hand into the pillow

beside her head, then kissed a path down her neck to her breasts.

She gasped, her grip in my hair loosening just enough to display approval. I nibbled her nipple in response, then took it deep into my mouth while swirling the tender tip with my tongue.

"Ezra," she groaned, her hips bucking up into mine.

Another pulse of energy vibrated between us, causing her to inhale sharply in response. "You feel it, don't you?" I murmured against her creamy skin. "Our bond strengthening?"

She shivered. "Y-yes."

"It's not about taking," I said, my eyes finding hers, my lips still tasting her taut peak. "It's about *sharing*, Kayla."

She would benefit from this exchange just as much as I would. My power would become hers, and hers would become mine.

Our life forces would join as one.

Marrying us on a plane of existence only reachable via our souls.

"Our bond energizes both of us," I continued, then drew a wet circle around her nipple with my tongue before capturing it once more between my teeth.

Her moan went straight to my groin, tightening my muscles along the way and begging me to fuck her.

It'd been so long.

Too long.

But I wouldn't rush this.

Not with her.

Not ever with her.

I wanted this to go on forever, to indulge in these moments and expand them into eternity.

Goose bumps pebbled across her abdomen as I kissed my way down to the sweet spot between her thighs. She whispered my name again, her fingers still in my hair. I met and held her gaze once more as I pressed a kiss to her hot center, then I traced a wet line with my tongue through her slick heat.

She convulsed in response, a glorious moan of approval parting her swollen lips.

I took that as a sign to proceed and licked her deeper.

"You taste so fucking good, Kayla," I told her, my voice lowering to a growl. Because fuck, I could die blissfully in this state, with her essence coating my tongue and sliding down my throat.

I'd happily drown here.

But I wanted to hear her cry out in pleasure first.

I needed that sound to follow me to the afterlife.

To give me something more to dream about. To know whether my fantasies were even realistic at all.

I was betting they weren't, as the heat I felt blistering through my veins now made my dreams feel insignificant in comparison.

Kayla set my soul on fire. Not just because of our connection but because it was *her*. This feisty female with her heart of gold.

She might not see it that way.

But I did.

I *knew* her.

It didn't matter that my memories of however many days or weeks or months or years were tainted by my near death.

I felt the knowledge in my soul that this female was destined to be mine all along.

Those memories would come back soon, but for now, I focused on the feelings and the knowledge of our shared destiny.

And I speared her with my tongue.

Her thighs tightened around me, her body quivering as she shared the pleasure I offered with my mouth. It wasn't enough, something I did on purpose to keep her from falling over the edge too quickly.

I wanted her to soar. To scream. To come so hard she saw stars.

Which meant drawing out the pleasure one lick at a time.

"*Ezra*." My name left her on a sexy little growl that had my lips curling against her.

"Yes, Kayla?" I asked softly, my lips moving upward to the place I knew she desired.

"Stop teasing me and fuck me," she demanded.

"Hmm," I hummed against the little bundle of nerves begging for my attention. "Are you sure that's what you want, sweet heiress?"

She practically vibrated in response, her legs tensing as a curse left her lips.

I ran my palms up and down her legs, widening her even more before trailing my fingertips up her inner thighs.

Something incoherent left her as I slipped a finger inside her pulsing heat. I added a second to create a scissoring motion that made her quiver with delight.

"You want me to fuck you like this?" I asked, my mouth still hovering over her clit. "Or like this?" I took the bud between my lips and rolled it with my tongue.

She bucked beneath me, her grip in my hair tightening as she told me without words to stay right there.

Normally, I'd disobey just to get a rise out of her.

But I wanted her to come more than I wanted to breathe.

So I remained, my tongue swirling around her sensitive bundle and taking her to the precipice of insanity with a few harsh swipes.

Her sheath clenched around my fingers, pulling me deeper. I curled them to find the spot I knew would send her over the edge and groaned as her orgasm rippled through her.

It was the sweetest fucking sound.

It intensified her flavor, giving me a renewed reason to live.

I wanted her arousal on my tongue every day for the rest of my existence.

And I demonstrated that by licking her deeply while penetrating her with my fingers, drawing her to another climax on the heels of her existing one.

She screamed from the onslaught, her sweet body tensing and convulsing in waves of euphoria. I felt each one like a kiss against my spirit, her ecstasy addicting.

Which was why I made her do it a third time.

Our bodies were starved for each other, our souls deprived of this connection for far too long. It became almost imperative that I wring the pleasure from her and push her to a heightened state of existence.

But the tears leaving her eyes drew me back, her emotions overwhelming her beneath the spiral of oblivion that I'd coaxed her into.

I crawled back up her shaking form, noting the blush in her cheeks—it went all the way down to her breasts. She appeared well fucked. Exhausted. Replete. However, we were nowhere near done yet.

I kissed her, allowing her to taste her arousal on my tongue. She wept in response, still trembling with violent quakes of residual rapture.

Cradling her face, I used my thumbs to wipe away her tears as I gifted her this moment to relax, to come back to me in Heaven, to this bed made of white silks and soft, creamy cottons.

It took a few minutes.

But I didn't mind.

I loved kissing her, feeling her tremble beneath me, hearing her quiet little pants of pleasure.

Then those beautiful caramel-brown eyes looked at me,

her pupils blown wide with arousal and wonder at the plea-sure I'd just unleashed upon her.

"I had no idea you could do that," she whispered. "No idea it could feel like *that*."

Which implied she'd tried this with others—something that hurt me more than I'd ever allow her to know. But I'd never hold it against her. She hadn't chosen our bond or me, and it was only fair that she'd tried to live her life without me after I'd left her in Hell.

Another punishment for me to bear.

I would spend the rest of my life erasing those memories from her mind and replacing them with sensual moments shared between us.

Starting with now.

Today.

In this bed.

"We've only just begun, Kayla." I kissed her again, silencing whatever she would have said in reply, and pressed my hips into hers. She responded by wrapping her legs around me, welcoming the connection with clear anticipation. "I'm going to fuck you now."

"Yes," she hissed, her nails drawing a jagged path down my spine. It was hard enough to make me bleed, forcing me to focus on her instead of my missing wings.

I drove into her waiting heat, not bothering with plati-tudes or pleasantries or drawing out the moment.

I'd wanted to be inside her.

She'd wanted me inside.

So I'd entered her.

And then I froze, the damp haven stealing my ability to process anything other than sensation.

"Over forty years," I whispered, burying my face in her neck. "*Fuck*, Kayla."

Four decades was nothing for one as old as me, yet I'd forgotten how this felt.

"It's been thousands of years for me," she said, a note of dry humor in her voice.

But I shook my head because she clearly didn't understand. "I haven't fucked anyone since before I met you, Kayla." I uttered the words against her ear. "And this is so much better than my hand."

Her hand stilled against my back. "What?"

I pulled back enough to stare down at her, wanting her to understand. "You're the only one I will ever fuck for the rest of eternity. *That's* our bond. You're it for me." And I wasn't at all disappointed by that fact, something I hoped she could read in my gaze. Because this woman stole my breath away.

"You haven't been with... anyone else?"

I shook my head.

"Not even Jo?" she pressed, causing my brow to furrow.

The mere notion of fucking Jo had me losing some of my drive and excitement for the moment. "Why would I fuck Jo?"

"I... I just assumed..." Emotion filtered through her features. "*Ez.*"

"A nickname," I said, not following.

But then a memory nagged at my mind of me telling Kayla not to call me that, my anger driving me to say she wasn't worthy of using the name.

I couldn't remember how or why.

However, I felt the wrongness of it now.

"Only you, Kayla," I said, pressing my forehead to hers. "This bond ties my soul to yours for eternity. Always. There will never be anyone else."

"But I've been with—"

"Don't," I breathed, not wanting to hear those stories, not while I was lodged deep inside her. "Please don't. You can torture me with stories after, but not now."

It was what I deserved, but I craved this moment, this union, her pleasure, and our bond. "Please, Kayla," I repeated, not caring at all that she could hear the torment in my voice.

"Ezra." Her fingers trailed back up to my nape, where she threaded her fingers through my hair.

I met her gaze, waiting for her to break the moment.

But her mouth captured mine again instead, her tongue parting my lips as *she* kissed *me*. As *she* devoured *me*. It was a passionate embrace underlined in blatant emotion.

And need.

Her legs tightened around me, her ankles hooking behind my back as she drove up to meet my hips.

I responded with a thrust that caused her to gasp against my mouth.

And then her kiss turned lethal.

Not cruel. Not harsh. Just consuming and dangerously addictive.

She owned me.

Mastered me.

Topped from the bottom.

And there wasn't a damn thing I could do about it other than enjoy the moment.

I grabbed her hips and pounded into her while she clutched my neck and continued to fuck my mouth.

It was so damn hot, her power rolling over me in a fiery wave of energy that threatened to destroy my very being. But I matched it with a push of cool energy, meeting her in the middle to create an inferno of forbidden fire.

Hell and Heaven.

Fire and ice.

Archdemon and Archangel.

The scales tipped and righted themselves in sequence, up and down and all around. It made me dizzy, left me shaking above her as I embraced the savagery of our bond.

It was so wrong.

But fuck if I cared.

She was mine. My mate. My Kayla. And we were marrying our souls in the oldest of ways.

Electricity crackled between us, heightening the moment and fueling us with jolts of intensity. Kayla moaned, her chest vibrating against mine as I rolled us to give her a chance on top. She didn't disappoint, her body moving with mine in a rhythm only our spirits understood.

She sat back, her legs straddling my hips, her palm on my chest, as she gyrated in a sensual rhythm that overpowered every fantasy I'd ever had of her.

She was perfect.

Beautiful.

Strong.

I lifted my hips into her, but I missed the connection between our mouths.

So I sat up and kissed her. She responded by shifting her legs to wrap them around me, then her fingers ventured up to my hair while I grabbed her neck. My opposite palm went to the bed to give my thrusts just a little more power.

Her head fell back on a sound of approval.

But I slid my palm from her throat to her nape and yanked her mouth back to mine.

She'd been in charge for long enough. Now I wanted to devour her. To feel her come around my cock. To make her scream through another orgasm and fill her with my essence.

It was an animalistic need to claim her.

To mark her.

To make her mine.

And I gave in to it, taking her with a ferocity that left us both winded.

If I had my wings, I'd have forced her into the sky, to show her how angels danced.

But all I had was my broken form, and I refused to let her down.

"Touch yourself," I demanded, unwilling to release her nape or lose my balance on the bed. "Now, Kayla. Do it now."

She shivered, her pupils blown wide as she opened her eyes to look at me.

But rather than fight my command, she released my hair and drew her hand down her gorgeous form to the apex between her thighs and stroked that little bud.

I lowered my gaze to watch, loving the way our bodies joined and the sexiness of her finger stroking herself.

"Beautiful," I breathed, arching into her. "So fucking beautiful."

She pressed her forehead to mine as we both enjoyed the view.

Then her lips found mine again as her body began to convulse. She was close. And thank fuck for that because I was ready to explode from the sight alone.

Her tight heat clenched around me, squeezing the life out of my shaft as her pleasure mounted into a cyclone of sensation. I felt it blistering through our bond, demanding I fall with her into dark oblivion.

I didn't fight it.

I embraced it.

I fell for her. With her. Indulging in the hot ecstasy that followed and the drowning sensation of intensified power.

I suffocated on her. On us. And all I could do was groan.

It was the sweetest death. A brilliant embrace. A dark haven of torturous explosions that rippled through every inch of my being.

I could no longer breathe, could no longer feel, could no longer *exist.*

Everything around me and in me was Kayla.

I accepted that. I accepted her. I accepted our bond.

And I felt her acceptance, too.

Her lips were on mine, her nails in my hair again, our bodies moving in unison as we continued to dance in the center of all this power.

We absorbed it.

Expelled it.

Absorbed it again.

And we continued moving against each other in a soundless dance, stoking our inner flames and tumbling into incredible rounds of rapture over and over again.

This was our heaven.

Our escape.

Our connection finally coming to life.

Nothing else mattered, only this blissful sensation stealing my senses.

The twenty-four-hour deadline Mietek had given me no longer applied.

Kayla was all I desired now, all I craved. And our fucked-up version of balance.

The mingled souls of an Archdemon and an Archangel.

A new Divinity.

Our Divinity.

EZRA

I woke to the feeling of fingers combing through my feathers. The sensation calmed me, allowing me to feign a few extra moments of sleep while processing the last few days of healing.

I remembered everything now.

And I was over a day late on Mietek's deadline.

Fate must have intervened, as her mate hadn't shown up to chastise me yet. But I assumed he would be here soon. We'd been in Heaven for five days now. Maybe four and a half, close to five.

I'd slept for the first two days.

Then spent the last two and a half days fucking Kayla between naps.

I was curled around her with her back to my chest. She was using my arm as a pillow and my wing as a blanket. We'd created a nest of a sort out of my wings, and she seemed very content to remain there.

Hence the fingers stroking through my plumes.

I sighed, feeling more at ease than I could ever remember.

The return of my wings had hurt in a beautiful way because it'd meant I was truly healing.

And Kayla had taken care of me through the agonizing procedure.

She'd noticed my wince as the regeneration progress had

begun and had proceeded to distract me with her mouth. It'd given a whole new meaning to pleasure and pain. I'd come down her throat on a groan that bellowed through the heavens, then I'd returned the favor while my spine had burned with divine intensity.

An intoxicating experience.

One I would cherish for the rest of my existence.

Just like this experience of waking up with her in my arms and wings.

I nuzzled her neck, gently nipping her languid pulse. She shivered in response, then tilted her head back toward me for a kiss. My palm went to her cheek, cradling her face as I indulged her with my tongue.

She groaned, rolling toward me to press her breasts to my chest, her thighs automatically wrapping around my hips.

I wanted to wake up to this every day for the rest of my existence. Her—naked, needy, *wet*.

Her arousal met mine, her slick heat a welcome kiss against my hard shaft.

However, the flutter of wings kept me from entering her. Because they were wings that didn't belong to me.

Instead, I swathed her with my feathers, hiding her body from view, and glared over my shoulder at the male now standing in my bedroom. "I'm starting to remember why I prefer my home between the realms."

"It's been destroyed," Mietek retorted flatly.

Kayla froze beneath me, her fingers tightening in my hair. She must not have sensed the Archangel's arrival. Knowing she'd been lost to my touch was a nice ego stroke. But rather than comment on it, I arched a brow at Mietek. "Have you arrived to tell me I've been replaced by Dariel?"

He grunted. "No. I've arrived to let you know four Earth years have passed, almost five, and Zerak says the balance will fail in just over three Earth years."

Which meant our original timeline after Kristina's death of nine Earth years had been reduced by one. Considering all that had happened, I was relieved to hear we hadn't lost more time.

"Scion joined Azrael to help the Dark Provenance prepare for the inevitable. But it also served as a way to evaluate the Nephilim and search for Kristina's assassin. Unfortunately, they haven't found anything, and Azrael had to return to Heaven today to help bolster Raphaela's waning strength."

That was a lot of information in a few short sentences. But I focused on the last one most. "Because she had to heal me?" I guessed.

Mietek shook his head. "No. Evangeline."

That could only mean... "They found her?"

"Yes. In the Shadow realm."

My lips parted, my eyebrows lifting.

"Hellfire," Kayla breathed. "Eve was in the Shadow realm? And she's *alive*?"

"Barely," Mietek replied, a note of emotion glinting in his dark gaze. "Xai saved her."

Pride, I realized. *Relief.*

They were both evidenced in his stare, which provided a nice break from Mietek's typically stoic or angry disposition.

"I'm glad she's okay," I admitted.

"As am I," he confided, his voice soft. "Azrael left Scion with the Dark Provenance for now. But we're running out of time. We need you."

That had to hurt to admit. It was also accompanied by a glint of fear in his dark eyes, one that I felt reverberate down to my very soul.

"What exactly do you know?" I asked.

He shook his head, his expression conveying his exhaustion. "Not anything beyond the obvious."

That wasn't very useful, but I didn't comment on it, as it wouldn't be helpful.

"Any insight on who opened the portal that allowed all those demons to access the homes between the realms?" I asked him instead.

"Whoever did it masked his or her energy signature, likely by using Kristina's powers," Mietek replied. "Bael provided a full report of what Kayla's Royal Guards saw, but there wasn't anything in there to pinpoint a culprit. However, it's clearly related."

"Yes," I agreed, frowning. "Whoever attacked us knows we're a threat to the endgame." Because they wanted me dead, or at the very least, distracted.

And they'd succeeded.

"We need to talk to Gleason," Kayla said, drawing my gaze back to her. Her thighs had released my hips, but her feet were planted on the mattress, keeping our bodies very much connected. Not that she seemed to be distracted by that. Instead, her eyes glowed with curiosity.

"The Nephilim?"

She nodded. "He was the last one we saw before the attack. Maybe someone followed us from his house."

"If he knew something, he would have told Scion or Azrael already," I said, glancing at Mietek. "Right?"

He lifted a shoulder. "I haven't heard anything about a Nephilim named Gleason, but I've not been working with the Dark Provenance. Azrael and Scion would be better ones to talk to. However, as I said, Azrael is indisposed at the moment. And Scion is currently in the human realm."

"Then we pick up where we left off and go from there," Kayla said simply. "Afterward, maybe I can reach out to Yaz for a personal report."

My brow furrowed as I glanced back down at her. "Who the fuck is Yaz?" And what did she mean by "personal report"?

"The head of my Royal Guard," she explained, a smile appearing on her lips.

An amused smile.

A gorgeous smile.

One that momentarily distracted me from everything else in the world. I wasn't even sure what we'd just been discussing.

Maybe I'm still delirious from nearly dying, I mused, staring down at her and returning her grin. *Maybe nothing else in this world matters except for her.*

"We can also see what energy signatures have shifted," she added.

"Whatever you do, report back afterward," Mietek said, reminding me of his presence. "I'll let you know what I learn about Evangeline as well. Because someone with great power took her to that Shadow realm. And I highly doubt that's a coincidence."

"Was it the same person who managed to scrub her aura?" I wondered aloud as I looked over my shoulder at him again. Evangeline had disappeared because no one had been able to sense her. Only a powerful being could accomplish that.

"Likely, yes. But there are still a lot of unknowns. The only certainty we have right now is that a Nephilim is involved, and he isn't working alone." Mietek's jaw clenched. "Fate's seen something. I don't know what. She's being cryptic."

"The Archangel of Destiny? Cryptic?" I feigned surprise. "Shocking."

Mietek snorted, but then his lips curled with a hint of fondness before he shook his head. His serious mask fell into place within a blink, almost concealing the previous display of emotion. But not quite. "Report back tomorrow."

His brown-black feathers fanned out around him as he used them to leave the room on a gust of wind that ruffled my wings.

"You need to invest in proper doors," Kayla murmured

after a beat, making me chuckle as I returned my attention to her.

"I think you may be right," I admitted, sweeping my lips across hers. "But I don't think we'll be staying here often."

"We?" she repeated, arching a brow.

"Yes. *We*." Because now that I'd well and truly tasted her, I intended to keep her. She could try to run, but I'd chase her into the literal depths of Hell to bring her back. And I let her see that with my gaze.

Her eyes narrowed in response. "I still hate you."

A lie, but I played along. "I know."

"And I'm going to kill you when I get the chance."

Another lie, one that made me grin. "I look forward to the fight." Because we'd end up naked and in bed. Just like my dreams.

"I mean it, Ezra. I'm going to kill you."

"You're going to try," I corrected her, my lips brushing hers again. "And I'm going to enjoy the foreplay immensely."

She growled, but it was a half-hearted sound that ended with her tongue in my mouth.

Her sweet heat was still pressed against my groin, proving that our yearning for one another was very much mutual.

She might want to kill me.

But she wanted to fuck me more.

I fell into our kiss, loving her with my tongue for several long minutes.

Her fingers fisted in my hair, pulling me back just enough to allow her to speak.

"I need a shower before we shift realms," Kayla said, her voice a sultry purr against my lips. "Why don't you join me and try to convince me to let you live?"

"Hmm, a challenge."

"A challenge on a deadline," she corrected. "I can feel the balance shifting."

"Me, too." It was an irritant under my skin that demanded action. But my soul required just a little more, a healing touch to help mend two broken hearts.

I went to my knees above her, my wings stretching out along my back. She observed me from beneath hooded eyes, her cheeks a luscious pink shade.

My feathers flexed, lifting me off the bed in a show of strength—my need to prove my worth to my mate riding me hard.

She smiled, clearly aware of my intent.

I grabbed her before she could comment, carrying her to the bathroom and into the shower.

"Start counting, Princess," I said, setting her on the bench, flipping on the water, and going to my knees in front of her.

Her sinful gaze lit with golden flames. "What am I counting, Archangel? Heaven seconds?"

"No, little heiress. Orgasms." My lips went to her inner thigh, my teeth grazing her skin. "I'm giving you at least three before we descend."

Goose bumps pebbled down her legs. "A good way to convince me to let you live."

I grinned, my mouth questing upward to her slick heat. Her little nub was practically pulsating, begging for my tongue. I gave it a lick, my gaze locking on hers. "Don't forget to wash off, Kayla. I'll be taking us to the human realm once you're properly satisfied."

Her nostrils flared, her cheeks turning a dark shade that bordered on red.

"As you said," I whispered, my words vibrating her delicate skin. "We're on a deadline, right?"

KAYLA

My thighs tingled with intimate reminders of Ezra's touch, his mouth having left an imprint behind that hummed beneath my jeans.

Not even my golden cuff could mask that residual pleasure. Although, putting it on again did dampen some of the power flowing between us—a reaction I was grateful for, as I didn't need another reason to desire more from Ezra.

Because, Hell's realms, the things that Archangel could do with his tongue ought to be a sin. Our descent to the human realm almost felt appropriate after that demonstration.

We'd found a stack of clothes waiting for us outside the shower, suggesting someone had dropped off the articles for us to wear—including my cuff.

But I couldn't even be embarrassed by the screams that angel had probably overheard.

Because Ezra was worth the outward praise.

He grinned at me now, his hands on my hips as our feet touched the ground. "You look a little distracted, Princess. Something on your mind?"

I returned his smile with a sweet one of my own. "As a matter of fact, yes. I'm thinking about your cock and the things I'm going to do to it after we're done."

His grin disappeared behind a smoldering look. "Careful, I could easily take us somewhere else."

"Hmm, tick-tock," I replied, my tongue clicking like a clock with the word.

Ezra grabbed me by the back of the neck and pulled me in for a searing kiss that left me winded. His lips curled against mine. "I think you're starting to like me."

"I'm not," I lied.

His smile grew, the golden flecks of his irises swirling with challenge. "We'll see."

"Will we?" I blinked up at him, doing my best to feign innocence and ignore the burn in my cheeks. Because yeah, that wasn't helping my case. But the man had just used that wicked tongue on me. Hardly seemed fair to throw words at me after that.

"We will." His golden-brown irises lit up with wicked promise, his dimples appearing for a split second before a demonic energy rolled across our skin.

My cuff flared with warning, but the familiar brush of power had me instantly relaxing.

Except for the fact that it had grown.

A lot.

Since our last meeting.

Which only felt like days ago, but would have been years ago in this realm.

I whirled in Ezra's arms to face the arriving Demonic Lord, his aura a drugging essence that made me dizzy. "Demons," I breathed, swaying back into Ezra's chest. His hands went to my hips, holding me against him. "Your energy signature reminds me of Prince Ashmedai."

Because Zebulon's power resembled that of an Archdemon now. An extremely powerful one at that.

The male in question appeared with a slight smirk, yet he still bowed his head to me in reverence of my position before dipping his chin in respect for Ezra.

"I'm not sure if that's a compliment or not," Zebulon

admitted. "But perhaps don't mention that to him the next time you see him, hmm?"

"I'm sure he's already aware," I muttered, my mind starting to clear as my own aura protected me from the potent impact of his arrival.

"Yes," he agreed, sounding solemn. "I imagine he is."

Which meant there might be a challenge coming between them because Prince Ashmedai couldn't afford to have such a powerful Demonic Lord beneath him. The chances of an imbalance were too great.

And demons weren't known to tolerate threats to their thrones.

"I assume you're looking for Daniel," Zebulon continued. "He's currently in Chicago with Guinevere. I can escort you there, if you like?"

His gaze met and held mine, some hidden message lurking in his dark chocolate depths.

I considered him for a long moment, evaluating whether or not to trust him. I didn't know him well, and his influx of power didn't make me keen on accepting his offer. But my cuff didn't pick up on any signs of malice, something it would normally hum about if someone nearby possessed ill intentions toward me.

Of course, he could know that.

His new abilities might even render my little bracelet useless as well.

Which meant I needed to rely on my gut—a gut that had led me to this very home to meet with Evangeline. Except I'd met Zebulon's mates, Zane and Guinevere, instead. They'd given me good vibes, especially the Succubus. And not just because they were both sexy as sin.

I nearly opened my mouth to reply, then shut it when I realized Ezra had remained silent behind me throughout the exchange.

Frowning, I glanced over my shoulder and up at him. His focus shifted from Zebulon to me, and he arched a brow. He seemed to be waiting on me to make a decision, which was... odd.

Maybe because this was a demon-related request?

Regardless, I shrugged and returned my attention to Zebulon. "Sure. Give us the address and we'll meet you there."

He shook his bald head, the sun glinting off his dark skin. "I'll need to show you the way. There are certain security measures in place."

My frown returned. "Security measures?"

"A lot has changed in the last few years," he said, his voice holding an edge to it that sent a chill down my spine. "It seems the business with my daughter was only the beginning."

Kalida, I recalled. She was his daughter and had served as his Ōrdinātum until she'd been killed. Except she wasn't actually dead, something Evangeline had discovered since the demonic princess had framed the former assassin for the murder.

I hadn't witnessed the theatrics, but I'd heard about it all through some notorious gossips down in Hell's realms.

"I can tell you more at my estate," he continued. "But I'll need to teleport us there."

I shared another look with Ezra.

He studied me for a moment before focusing on Zebulon. "Are you aware of what happened to my estate between the realms?" His deep voice reverberated from his chest into my back, his hands still clasping my hips to hold me against him.

"I heard about the attack, yes," Zebulon replied. "However, the details of it have been scarce at best."

"But you know I was injured," Ezra hedged as I shifted my attention back to the Demonic Lord.

"Yes," he confirmed.

"So you can understand why my ability to trust may be

rather wounded at present." Ezra's palms shifted, his arms wrapping around me in a backward hug.

I frowned. *Is he going to teleport us?*

"Add to that the possessiveness I'm feeling in regard to my mate, and, well, you can also understand that any extension of trust I may bestow upon you will be tentative at best," Ezra continued, his tone holding a lethal edge to it that sent a shiver across my skin. Or maybe that was the result of his words. *Possessiveness. Mate.* "I would not recommend violating said trust."

Zebulon held his gaze without so much as flinching. "Considering that Daniel is currently having an early dinner with my mates, whom I'm also very possessive of, the same could be said about the trust required for me to invite you into my home."

Silence ticked by for a beat, the two males clearly measuring each other's words. Or, more accurately, their power dicks.

I rolled my eyes. "How about you both whip them out, I'll declare a victor in the size department, and we can move on with our business?" I suggested, looking at Zebulon before returning my gaze to Ezra. "We're on a deadline."

"Interesting that you didn't mention that while in the shower earlier," he returned, a spark of dark amusement glinting in the golden flecks of his gaze. "And the only one you'll be measuring is mine, little heiress."

His lips whispered across mine before I could reply. It lasted a second before he spun me around, placing my chest to his, and captured me with one solid arm. His opposite one stretched out, his hand palm up toward Zebulon.

However, his eyes were on mine, his lips lowering to mine as he said, "You can teleport us. I'll hold Kayla while you take my hand."

My eyebrows lifted. "Ezra—"

The world shifted before I could finish speaking, Zebulon having already taken the opportunity to whisk us through space.

Heat touched my senses, followed by a cool wave of energy from Ezra. His arm remained locked around me, but it didn't feel like enough. Not with him being my anchor.

I grabbed his shoulders, my nails digging into his muscles just enough to let him know I wasn't pleased with this manner of travel. He chuckled in response, his mouth still hovering near mine. I considered biting his lower lip, but a ripple of power had my cuff humming to life. Ezra flinched, the metal having likely zapped him as well.

Darkness swallowed us whole in the next moment, followed by a vibration of soundless electricity that sizzled across my skin.

Ezra's hold on me never wavered, his tension rivaling my own.

Until it all stopped and a warm light graced our senses.

Followed by the appearance of a massive estate littered with demons.

They all bowed as Zebulon appeared, then tensed upon seeing me and Ezra. "Stand down," Zebulon said, releasing Ezra to wave his hand at his demonic minions. Most of them were Dargarians, something that irked me after my last interaction with their kind. Ezra seemed just as uncomfortable, his body taut with tension.

"You realize I can take care of myself, right?" I asked, trying to wiggle away from his death grip.

"I do," he replied. "But we're stronger together than apart." He threaded his fingers through my ponytail and pressed his lips to mine in another quick kiss.

"I would say the possessive instincts wane with time, but I would be lying," Zebulon said casually. "This way."

Ezra grinned, releasing me, just to grab my hand and tug me along after Zebulon.

I only allowed it because my mind was reeling from his insane behavior.

"I'm the daughter of an Archdemon," I finally said. "I... I don't need... *this*." Whatever the hellfire *this* meant. I couldn't pick a term. The one used in their conversation—*possessiveness*—seemed right, but it was deeper than that. He was acting like this behavior between us was natural. Like he truly owned me.

Yes, we'd bonded over the last few days.

But I still wanted to kill him.

Sort of.

Maybe.

I shook my head. It didn't matter. We had a balance to fix first. Then I'd debate his future.

He threaded his fingers through mine, tugging me close to him. "Whether you *need* it or not, I'm yours and you're mine," he whispered against my ear. "And now that I've tasted you, I'm never letting you go again."

My eyes widened. "That's not—"

He caught my mouth with his once more, his hand magically grabbing my neck and holding me in place right on the damn steps of the mansion. I pressed my palms to his chest to push him away, but his wings appeared in the next moment, wrapping around us in a cocoon of feathers and strength.

"We can debate this later. For right now, we need unity." His fingers went to my chin, pulling my gaze up to his. "We're stronger together, Kayla." A repeat of what he'd already said. "Please don't fight me on this."

I narrowed my gaze. "Can you stop manhandling me?"

"I'm touching you because it strengthens us both," he replied. "So no. I will not stop *manhandling* you." He pinched my chin a little, his eyes darkening with intensity. "Physical healing is not the same as spiritual healing, Kayla. I need you right now. I need *us*." He released my chin to draw his fingers through my reddening strands. "And you need me, too."

A tremble worked its way down my spine, his sentences ones I would have translated wrong a few days ago. But having felt the energy exchange between us, I was beginning to understand what he meant about our bond.

It wasn't about siphoning energy from me.

It was about creating energy between us. Energy that bolstered both of our souls, not just his. I'd never felt this alive in all my life, the power thriving through my veins renewed with a vigor that came directly from Ezra.

Not a charade or a lie. Not a way to trick me into helping him. Just a mutual bond we both benefited from.

"I promised never to use you again," he added in a whisper. "I meant it, Kayla."

I swallowed, unsure of how to respond to that. While I understood the power exchange a little better now, I hadn't reached a conclusion on his intentions yet. Or even my own.

However, there was one certainty between us—we shared a goal. We needed to find the one who'd murdered Kristina and try to minimize the fallout of the balance shift as best as possible.

And to do that, we had to work together.

Which meant I needed to accept this *possessive* behavior from him.

Although, accepting it really wasn't the problem.

The problem, deep down, was that a part of me *liked* this side of him. I liked that he couldn't stop touching me. I enjoyed that he felt the need to state I was his mate in front of Zebulon even though the Demonic Lord already knew that. And I was very much enthralled by the shelter of feathers warming my skin now.

He was claiming me in front of all these demons.

Telling everyone who could see us that I belonged to him.

He'd cut them all off with a wing, giving me his entire focus, just to make sure I'd *heard* him. That I'd understood his intentions.

And now his glittering golden eyes were watching me, waiting for me to not only acknowledge his statements but also agree to them.

"Please, Kayla." His thumb traced my jaw before gliding down my neck. "Work with me, not against me."

I stared at him for another beat. "Only if you promise me more orgasms." It was my way of brightening what was otherwise a rather deep conversation.

The tilt of his lips told me it'd worked. "As many as you desire."

My eyebrows lifted. "Yeah? You sure you want to make that offer?"

"If it gives me cause to keep you for eternity, then yes." The serious quality of his words matched his expression. "You deserve an eternity of pleasure after everything I've done to you. If that's the payment you require, consider it given."

"I was trying to lighten the mood," I admitted in a mumble.

He kissed me softly, his lips a heavenly presence that made me sigh. "Be a good little heiress and I'll take you to the stars later," he whispered.

My jaw clenched in response. "Good little heiress?"

His gaze held a teasing glint as he pulled back. "You wanted to lighten the mood."

I rolled my eyes. "That's not lightening the mood, Ezra. That's making me want to kill you again."

"Does that mean you didn't want to kill me for a few minutes there? Because if the answer is yes, I'd say that's progress."

I huffed and shook my head. "Let's just go." Except we

were already here, so that didn't work. But the feathery cocoon and deep conversation had made me forget where we were for a second.

However, I remembered quickly as he released me from his wings, the plumes disappearing as soon as his feathers were behind his back. Which confirmed we were still on Earth, as most Archangels chose not to keep their wings visible in the human realm.

Of course, it would be fine here since Zebulon appeared to have truly warded his property.

He hadn't been kidding about being unable to teleport in here.

I wasn't even sure we could leave without his help.

His focus fell to me as I looked up toward the grand entrance to his home. He said nothing, his expression impassive. But as he glanced at Ezra, a knowing glimmer entered his dark brown gaze. "As I said, the instincts never wane. If anything, they only grow stronger with time."

With that, he entered the home.

Ezra pressed his palm to my lower back to lead me up the stairs.

I allowed it, moving closer to him as we walked. It was my way of agreeing to this temporary alliance.

Together.

For now.

Until he makes me want to kill him again, anyway.

EZRA

ENERGY SIZZLED OVER MY SKIN AS WE STEPPED through the threshold, telling me Zebulon hadn't been upfront about a few key items.

Such as the fact that an Archdemon was currently inside his house.

"I assume Ashmedai commanded you not to tell us of his presence?" I drawled, sensing the familiar power wrapping around us like a thick cloak.

"I advised him to say as little as possible," the Archdemon confirmed as he stepped out into the hallway in a set of royal-blue robes that complemented his navy plumes.

I arched a brow at his current state, surprised to see him in full demon mode in this realm. "Is there something I should be concerned about?" I asked, pausing midstep and pulling Kayla more firmly into my side. "Because you should know that I'm feeling rather reactive after the events of the last few days."

It was a similar threat to the one I'd given Zebulon prior to leaving. And I wasn't afraid to level the same one at Ashmedai now.

Because I meant it.

One false move, and I'd respond with my sword.

"As you should be," Ashmedai said, responding to my

comment about my reactive nature. "And yes, you should be concerned. But not about me."

With that mysterious comment, he left the hallway once more.

Zebulon followed him without a glance or a single word.

My eyes narrowed, but I moved toward the room with my arm wrapped tightly around Kayla's waist. I kept my opposite arm free in case I needed a blade.

However, as we entered, I quickly realized that a sword wouldn't be required.

The three-story library before us had been transformed into a war strategy room, much like my own office—which was likely destroyed now, thanks to the attack on my home.

A gigantic map filled with colorful dots functioned as a curtain against the back wall of windows—something I only knew existed because of the light filtering in near the floor and ceiling.

The need for Ashmedai's wings suddenly made sense.

Zebulon stood near a long table covered by a second map. His two mates were seated there with Daniel Gleason and a Royal Guard I didn't recognize.

"Yaz," Kayla breathed, stepping away from me to embrace the Royal Guard.

My lips flattened as he wrapped his arms around her and pressed his face into her neck.

It was too close.

Too familiar.

Too *intimate.*

I stepped forward and cleared my throat, my need to rip this male from my mate riding me hard. His blue-brown eyes met mine with a hint of challenge. "I see you managed to survive."

"I did," I replied, my tone indicating just how I felt about his arms still being around Kayla. "But my mood is still questionable."

"It's unwise to tempt the fate of a refreshed bond," Ashmedai said conversationally. "So you may want to release her before Ezra rips you in half. Or don't. I would undoubtedly enjoy that demonstration."

"Of course you would," another woman drawled from a ladder perched against the map.

Trudy, I recognized. *The Nephilim with Ashmedai*.

She wore a pair of tight black pants and a tank top, accentuating every curve of her body—a fact Ashmedai appeared to be appreciating as she started her descent.

Or maybe he was watching in case she fell.

However, I suspected it was the former allure that drew his attention.

Just as my gaze returned to Kayla and the male still holding her in his arms.

Only a few seconds had passed, but it was long enough to piss me off. I continued toward them, ready to follow through on Ashmedai's threat, when Kayla stepped out of the embrace and into my path. Her palm went to my chest, her gaze finding mine. "He's the head of my Royal Guard and part of the reason I could save you the other day."

Yes. I knew his identity, thanks to her comments earlier about the *personal report* she desired to receive from him. "I'm aware," I stated shortly, one of my hands grasping her hip as the other went to the back of her neck. "That doesn't make me any less likely to kill him."

I kissed her before she could protest, my need to stake a visual claim consuming my ability to properly focus.

These possessive instincts were all so foreign yet felt too right for me to ignore.

Her nails dug into my shirt hard enough to reach my skin.

I didn't care.

I deepened our kiss with my tongue in response and grinned when she threatened me back with her teeth.

"Now that's some energy I could feed on," a male murmured.

Zane, I guessed. We'd never formally met, but I knew of him because of his ties to Zebulon. The female I'd seen beside him was Zebulon's other mate, Guinevere. She hummed something that sounded like approval now, but I ignored her commentary.

Kayla captivated my focus with her nails digging into my chest and her teeth threatening my tongue. I tightened my grip on her nape, daring her to bite down harder.

She responded by releasing my shirt and grabbing my throat instead. The sensation of fire crawling across my skin made me chuckle against her mouth. I soothed the burn with my own power, instantly putting out her flames.

Then I pulled back enough to stare down at her. She met my gaze with a glower that only amused me more. "You're making me want to kill you again."

I arched a brow. "That sentence alone indicates you no longer want me dead."

She snorted, then shoved me away.

I allowed it only because I'd made my point to the room. *Mine.*

Ashmedai appeared amused.

Zebulon looked bored.

His two mates positively glowed with interest.

Gleason's focus was on the map.

And the Royal Guard gave me a look that suggested he'd enjoy watching me die. I returned that glance with one of my own, warning him to back the fuck off.

"He reminds me of Xai," the Nephilim muttered to Ashmedai as her heeled boots met the ground.

"Mmm," the Archdemon hummed. "Equally stubborn, but less cryptic. Their power levels rival one another, too."

My brow furrowed at the latter half of that statement. I knew Xai was growing in power; however, I hadn't been aware of him reaching my status of an Archangel. "Is that how he saved Eve from the Shadow realm?" I wondered aloud.

"Among other reasons," Ashmedai answered, proving to be just as cryptic as the male in question.

"Is she awake?" Guinevere asked, her sensual interest having disappeared behind a layer of obvious concern. "Is she okay?"

"She was still unconscious when we descended," I replied, aware of the friendship between her and Eve. "But Raphaela is healing her."

"Yes, that's why Azrael left over a year ago," Gleason interjected, his focus finally shifting away from the map to look at me. "You missed the meeting."

"Did I? I hardly noticed," I deadpanned.

"What he means to say is 'We regret missing the meeting and are wondering if you can bring us up to speed,'" Kayla interjected diplomatically.

I glanced at her. "Since when are you the reasonable one?"

"Since you decided to become the possessive asshole in the relationship."

"Does that mean you were a possessive asshole before?" I asked.

"In your dreams, maybe," she responded with a sweetly sarcastic tone. Then she looked at her Royal Guard. "Archangel Mietek stated that your report claimed you didn't see how the portal opened in between the realms. Is that true?"

"Yes," he confirmed. "The portal took a lot of effort to close, too. Prince Bael and Prince Alastor worked with a few Archangels to close it after you and Ezra ascended."

"If the portal wasn't closed prior to our ascension, then what caused the demons to stop attacking us?" I asked, confused by his statement. I'd assumed the portal closing had resulted in the end of the battle. But I'd been nearly dead by that point, so I hadn't actually been aware of anything.

"They started to leave after stabbing you with the holy blade," Kayla replied without looking at me. "So they were really only there to kill Ezra."

Yaz nodded. "They were after you as well, but it seemed to be more of a strategic measure to keep you from protecting Ezra."

She grunted at that. "Well, it backfired since our bond is what saved him."

I ran my finger down her spine, displaying my gratitude without words. Because she was right. Had it not been for her acceptance of our connection, I would not have survived.

"Yes, which means protecting you is about to become an even harder job." Yaz sounded more amused than irritated, but he punctuated the statement with a glower in my direction. "Thanks for that, Archangel."

"Good thing I can protect myself," Kayla inserted before I could reply. "So you still don't know who attacked us in between the realms?"

"No," Yaz confirmed.

She nodded, looking at Gleason and then Ashmedai. "Has anyone learned anything useful during our absence? Anything that we should know before we start chasing nonexistent auras around?"

"You'll need to review the updated power shifts." The Archdemon gestured to the table. "Then you may want to examine the strategy on the map." He pointed to the giant wall of paper. "We've outlined several points of attack that we believe are imminent."

"Yes, I'm here to report those back to Prince Bael," Yaz added. "And to give him an update on your well-being."

Kayla rolled her eyes. "Tell him I'm fine."

"Are you, though?" His attention flickered to me before returning to her, true concern etched into the olive-toned planes of his face.

My wings spread from my back, the action a result of my need to remind this minion from Hell of my status in this world. His gaze returned to me as I hoisted myself up in the air to go have a better look at the map.

"Show-off," Kayla muttered in my wake.

"If you want to join me, all you have to do is ask," I called back to her.

"And now he reminds me of you," Trudy interjected.

"Ah, but my feathers are softer and brighter," Ashmedai returned in that perpetually amused voice of his.

"That's not at all what I meant, and you know it." The Nephilim's tone lacked complete fear, something that caused me to glance down at her in wonder. She stood facing off with the Archdemon as though he were a minion, not a being of incredible power.

The female was either suicidal or dangerously stupid. Perhaps a mixture of both.

I ignored the pair in favor of the map, reviewing the high-lighted areas through the realms. Ashmedai had said these were potential targets, but he hadn't stated exactly what or who he thought might attack them.

I voiced the question, and he responded by joining me toward the top where someone had drawn a rather accurate depiction of Heaven's lands.

"Do you think it's the being who took Kristina's power?" I asked him, my voice softer since he floated beside me now.

"Not a being, but a movement." His striking violet gaze met mine. "Whoever is doing this has several players on the board. We know of a few because of what happened to Evangeline, but there are more. It's also become quite clear that there are numerous Nephilim in the Earth realm that have not been accounted for over the decades."

I frowned. "Isn't that the purpose of the Genesis, or Dark Provenance, or whatever they call themselves now?"

"Dark Provenance." Some of the amusement left his tone, but he didn't elaborate on why. "And yes, that's their primary purpose. But our research over the last few years indicates that many Nephilim have gone unnoticed." He gestured to the brunette below. "Trudy is a prime example. Evangeline found her as a child in a demon trafficking scheme run by Kalida."

I'd heard something about that. It was what had led to the last disruption in the balance and a tear in the veil. Xai and Evangeline had handled it with several others, Ashmedai included.

Actually, Ashmedai had been involved in a lot of events as of late.

Which had me taking another deep look at him and that unnatural blue glow shimmering against his feathers. "You've grown even more powerful." Something that made Zebulon's recent growth not as big a deal as he'd suggested when speaking with Kayla before transporting us here.

"As have you," he returned, his arms folding. "I'm not the one you need to be examining."

"Then who should I be examining?"

"Telling you that would only lead to more questions."

I cocked a brow. "So you have an inkling of who is involved."

"A very strong suspicion." His expression and voice suggested it was more than a strong suspicion—it was a very real conclusion.

"And you're not willing to share this information?" I pressed.

"I will once I prove it."

"Or you could tell me and we could prove it together," I suggested.

His gaze turned solemn. "I wish it were that simple, Ezra."

"Don't bother," Trudy called up to us. "He won't play his cards yet no matter how hard you try."

Ashmedai glanced down at her in amusement. "Eavesdropping again, little warrior?"

She batted her hazel eyes up at him. "Always, Prince Hellspawn."

He chuckled and shook his head. "Careful, sweetling. You know what happens when you provoke me."

The *little warrior* appeared entirely unbothered by the lingering threat in his statement and merely yawned in response.

"You also know what you need to do to make me play my cards." The sensual notes in Ashmedai's velvety voice made the Nephilim snort.

"And you know what I want before I decide," she returned.

He shrugged, his gaze returning to me and giving nothing else away. "Do you find it odd that Trudy was part of a demon trafficking operation as a mere infant?"

"I was a child, not an infant," she shot up at us.

He brushed her away with a flicker of his fingers, his focus remaining on me. "I found it odd. Especially considering her paternal line."

My gaze narrowed. "Stop speaking in riddles."

"Is that what I'm doing?" His dimples flashed. "Well, I'm merely pointing out that there are a lot of Nephilim who appear to be unaccounted for. Which makes Daniel's list a disappointing representation of his kind."

"Meaning you didn't find anything useful in that list." Thus suggesting that it would be a waste of time for me and

Kayla to review it now or attempt another meeting with the Dark Provenance members.

"On the contrary, I found several fascinating items on that list, as well as proof that this power imbalance is absolutely impacting offspring with an angel or demon parent." His gaze moved to Kayla. She stood at the table with the others, pointing at something on the massive sheet of paper and asking a question I couldn't hear from my position.

Zebulon responded, his expression giving nothing away.

Meanwhile, Yaz watched Kayla with stars in his eyes, his devotion to her clear.

Still, I didn't quite appreciate his close proximity to my mate.

There were protective instincts, and then there were possessive instincts. This Royal Guard seemed to be exuding some of both.

Did Kayla play with him in the past?

Do I want the answer to that?

"She's a good example," Ashmedai said quietly, the *she* in his sentence clearly referring to Kayla. "Her power is tempered by that cuff, but she's growing at an exponential rate. Of course, that could also be an influence from you."

I met his gaze again, waiting for him to say more.

"Nephilim are the perfect pawns in this game. No auras. No birth records that can easily be tracked. And an unknown aptitude for magic." His feathers ruffled at his back as he maintained his position beside me, his voice quiet. "They're easy to take advantage of, considering their mortal halves. Almost all of them have daddy issues."

Trudy snorted below, but he didn't pay any attention to her.

I idly wondered how she could hear him from three stories below—something I probably should have considered initially, seeing as I couldn't hear Kayla at all from here.

"It seems to me that there's a reason the Dark Provenance has failed in tracking them all down," Ashmedai continued, distracting me from my thoughts about Trudy. "Of course, that's just my theory."

"Nothing you say is ever just a theory, Ashmedai," I returned.

"No, just riddles," he replied, his lips twitching.

"You've been playing this game as long as I have," I told him, ignoring his commentary. "Maybe even longer."

His violet irises glimmered in response, his expression saying, *Definitely longer*.

"You have more than a theory on who is behind this," I added.

"I'm merely stating all the musings that have led me to certain conclusions." His easy tone belied the heavy meaning behind the words.

"And is that why you've taken on a Nephilim pet?" I asked, referring to Trudy. "Because of these musings?" Because I strongly suspected that it was all related.

His lips quirked. "Now you're thinking like the Archangel of Justice."

"That's not an answer."

"Or maybe it is." He winked and descended to his pet in question, giving her a loving stroke against her hair as he glanced up at me.

She growled in response, causing him to chuckle.

I didn't quite understand the dynamic there or why she'd ended up with him, but it was obviously all linked to whatever Ashmedai suspected about the Nephilim being involved.

He was right about them being ideal pawns.

The question was, who would use them?

The Nephilim would have to be strong enough to handle Kristina's power as well, something very few beings would ever be capable of doing.

Unless they shared the power somehow.

I frowned, considering the possibilities of how that could be facilitated. Someone with a higher-level ability would have to be at the helm.

Or multiple someones.

Maybe it wasn't just a group of Nephilim, but angels or demons, too.

Which Ashmedai had already implied.

"What proof are you waiting for?" I asked as I joined him on the floor.

He stood right beside Trudy, his wing wrapping around her in a suggestive manner. But his feathers weren't touching her.

Actually, she seemed rather oblivious to his nearness.

Or perhaps she was used to it.

"If I told you that, it would give away the endgame. And I'm not ready for that particular move yet." He spoke with the ease of an uncaring man, but I sensed the concern in his gaze. "That's the purpose of this." He pointed to the master map.

"We've drawn out every possible outcome and theory based on what we know for sure, and we've altered some of them with speculations regarding the future." Trudy studied the contents as she spoke, drawing Ashmedai's gaze to her.

Admiration touched his features for a brief second before he nodded, his expression morphing back into one of perpetual amusement. It was a mask of sorts, one he used to hide his true feelings on current events.

It prompted others to doubt his position, thus giving him the upper hand in certain situations.

By allowing others to assume his preference for fucking around, he could hide his true intentions.

The question became, were those intentions good or bad? Or were they simply gray?

If anyone could be orchestrating this whole disaster, it was

Ashmedai with his penchant for riddles and carefree maneuvering. He would be the perfect one to engage in this game of imbalance.

And by pretending to be on this side, to be working through all these scenarios, would be the best way to fuck everyone over.

The power rolling off of him confirmed he was very much benefiting from the imbalance, as was Zebulon—a Demonic Lord under Ashmedai's command.

Ashmedai was also the one who'd given that device to Kayla, thus setting all of this in motion for Kristina to be taken.

"You see it now," he mused, his lips twisting into a wry grin. "You see how everything points to me."

"Yes." *Just as your comment proves what I've always suspected about you—you can read minds.* Not that he would ever admit it.

Now was no different.

He didn't even blink at my mental comment.

But that didn't fool me.

I knew his power had grown, including his ability to hear thoughts.

"Which is how you know it's not me," he said casually, referring to my confirmation about how all the details pointed to him as a probable culprit. Or maybe he meant it in response to his mind-reading ability as well. With Ashmedai, it was hard to say.

Still, I responded with a "Yes" because he was right. I knew he wasn't the one behind all this. "You would never be that obvious."

"I would never be that obvious," he echoed. "But someone clearly thought of every angle, which is what I'm doing now. Because whoever we are up against possesses a similar penchant for strategy."

"War strategy," Trudy echoed.

"Precisely." He reached out to tug on a piece of her hair. "Lucky for us, Trudy shares that gift."

"Still not convinced," she told him.

"You will be soon." He flashed her an indulgent smile before arching a brow at me. "Now, would you like me to review what we know?"

"That is why we're here," Kayla drawled, joining us and stepping up beside me. My wing wrapped around her in response, something she either didn't notice or didn't mind because she kept her focus on Ashmedai. "Please detail the expected events on the map."

The Archdemon smiled. "Well, since you asked so nicely, I believe I will do just that."

KAYLA

ASHMEDAI HAD SPENT MOST OF THE AFTERNOON AND evening walking us through the basic scenarios on his map.

After a late-night dinner, he'd continued into one of the more elaborate strategies that involved taking out key power players in Hell. But then he'd countered that by saying it wouldn't work because of the moves Bael and Alastor had made in taking pieces of the Divinity to help balance themselves.

Ezra had grunted at that but had waved for Ashmedai to continue.

Which had taken us into a conversation about the removal of certain Archangels.

"None of that is plausible," Ezra had finally said. "Heaven is impenetrable."

"So was your home between the realms," Ashmedai had reminded him.

And that had spiraled into a discussion on the portals and their creations.

By dawn, I could barely keep my eyes open. Despite the riveting conversation, I was still feeling a bit under the weather from the last few days and Ezra's near death.

I leaned against Ezra, wondering if he felt the same level of exhaustion that I did.

Heat radiated from him, as did a certain level of energy

that kept me buoyed at his side, almost as though his essence served as a lifeline.

He wrapped his arm around my shoulders, his wings having disappeared into his back hours ago when we'd taken over this couch. Ashmedai and Trudy sat across from us in a similar leather loveseat, while Zebulon, Zane, Gleason, and Gwen took up residence on a third couch. And Yaz relaxed in a chair beside where I sat with Ezra.

I'd asked if he needed to return to my father for a report. He'd flashed some high-tech device at me and said, "Already done."

Which I supposed meant he was staying here to protect me.

Not exactly a surprise, considering his comment about needing to increase my security as a result of healing Ezra. He'd been severely displeased by the development. I couldn't really blame him because it meant more work on his part.

I would argue that I could protect myself, but I'd never win the debate. Yaz's whole purpose in life centered around guarding royals. To tell him to do otherwise equated to a direct insult to his very existence.

So I kept my mouth shut and allowed him to remain.

We weren't exactly close, but I did consider him a friend. I trusted him. And I rather liked him, too. In a purely platonic way.

Ezra's thumb stroked a circle against my shoulder, his strength seeming to swathe my being. But it wasn't enough to chase away the exhaustion mounting inside me.

I tried and failed to fight a yawn, drawing his attention away from Ashmedai and to me.

"I think we need to take a break," he said without looking at the Archdemon. "Is there somewhere we can rest?"

A denial taunted my tongue, but I couldn't seem to voice it. Mostly because I knew that fighting my exhaustion would lead to poor decision-making, and we couldn't afford that right now.

"I've already had a room made up for you," Zane informed us with a smile. "I think you'll find it suits."

My brow furrowed, uncertain of what he meant by that.

It also seemed like one hell of an assumption to put Ezra and me in a room together.

Although, he'd been the one to say "we" in his request.

And we were mates.

So maybe not an outrageous assumption.

"Are you okay with those arrangements, Princess?" Yaz asked.

Ezra bristled beside me, but I placed my hand on his thigh in a warning not to reply. I really couldn't handle another round of his possessiveness right now. It was strange and foreign and...

And I kind of like it.

But I didn't want to evaluate why I felt that way right now. It was probably just a residual sensation from the last few days.

Regardless, I found myself nodding at Yaz. "I'm okay." I could handle sharing a room with Ezra. If he pissed me off, I'd put him on the floor.

Yet somehow I suspected it would be quite the opposite.

I'd probably end up asking him to wrap me up in his wings.

He placed his palm on top of mine, giving my hand a squeeze while keeping his opposite arm wrapped around my shoulders. "Thank you, Zane."

"Trust me, the pleasure is all mine," the Incubus replied with a sexy little grin.

"Stop teasing our guests," Zebulon told him.

"Oh, I think you'll find my teasing will benefit you greatly, my lord." Zane leaned in to press his perfect lips to the Demonic Lord's jaw. The Incubus's silver-blue eyes flickered with pure silver for a moment before he turned toward Gwen and captured her mouth in a kiss that redefined the meaning of lust.

"I think your mates are hungry, Zebulon," Ashmedai said conversationally as he stood. "Go feed them before they incite an orgy."

"Of course, my prince," Zebulon replied dutifully. "Zane. Guinevere."

His two mates pulled away from each other and gazed at him with twin expressions of expectation. I half expected them to pounce, but instead Zane moved fluidly to his feet and bowed toward Prince Ashmedai. "I would only incite an orgy with approval, my prince."

"It's not given," the Archdemon replied, but his tone lacked reprimand.

"Another time, then." Zane winked at him before turning to Ezra. "I'll show you to your room."

"Don't seduce them," Lord Zebulon said as the Incubus started toward the door.

"The only one I intend to seduce is you, my lord," he replied with a cheeky grin. "And that's only because Guinevere is always ready for my tongue."

With that, he cast a come-hither glance toward me and Ezra and stepped into the hallway.

"Don't worry," Gwen murmured, a smile in her voice. "He's a perpetual flirt, but he won't touch you."

Gleason grunted. "Sounds familiar."

"Hmm?" she hummed, her eyes sparkling with devious energy, but Lord Zebulon chose that moment to pull her into his lap.

"That's enough, little one," Lord Zebulon murmured. He bowed his head toward Prince Ashmedai, then teleported from the room with the Succubus in his arms.

Yep. He's definitely as powerful as an Archdemon now, I marveled, impressed.

Fortunately, Prince Ashmedai had grown in power as well, making Lord Zebulon less of a threat to his territory.

They also seemed to work well together.

But that didn't mean much.

Power struggles were abundant in the underworld and often seduced friends into becoming enemies.

"You should go to your room now, Kayla," Prince Ashmedai said mildly. "I would hate for you to suffer from a headache."

I narrowed my eyes at him. *Stop playing in my mind.*

His lips curled as though to say, *Stop making it easy on me, and I'll leave your thoughts alone.*

He'd never actually admitted to being able to read minds, just as he'd never acknowledged the full expanse of his tele-kinetic abilities, but I knew he could do both.

"Good night, Kayla." He uttered the words with a finality that told me I was excused.

I smiled, the edges feeling cold and brittle on my face. "It's morning, Ashmedai." I purposely left off the title, something that caused his nostrils to flare.

But his violet irises glimmered in amusement. "Indeed."

Ezra gave my hand another squeeze and used his arm against my shoulders to guide me upward.

"Yaz. Stay with me." The command in Prince Ashmedai's tone was clear.

The head of my Royal Guard dipped his chin in acknowl-edgment. "I won't be far, Princess. You know how to alert me."

"She'll be fine," Ashmedai replied coolly. "Won't she, Ezra?"

"More than fine," he vowed, his tone underlined in sensual promise.

I was too tired to utter a retort or even think of something witty to say. So I just sighed. Loudly.

Ashmedai chuckled.

And Ezra guided me out of the room to the Incubus lounging against the hallway wall.

"I enjoy foreplay and a good game of delayed gratification," Zane mused. "But there's a finesse to it that you seem to be misunderstanding." He looked us over. "If you ever need a tutor, I volunteer."

"Somehow I doubt your lord would approve," Ezra drawled.

Zane's handsome features melted into a charming grin. "He would allow me to play the part of an instructor so long as I keep my hands to myself."

Ezra remained unfazed. "I think we'll work on our own version of foreplay."

The Incubus shrugged and started down the hallway, his athletic form moving with the grace of a prowling panther. "When you change your mind, let me know. I'll demonstrate on Guinevere while you practice on Kayla."

My eyebrows rose. "Is that your version of a double date?"

The sunlight streaming through the hallway windows seemed to kiss Zane's mane of dark, silky hair as he glanced back at me over his muscular shoulder. "My version of a double date would blow your mind, Princess."

Ezra grunted.

I smiled. "We'll think about it." We really wouldn't. I just wanted to irritate Ezra.

The way his arm tightened around my shoulders suggested I'd succeeded.

Just as the glare he tossed my way said I would regret that statement.

I merely batted my eyes at him in response.

Zane kept the flirting to a minimum as he led us the rest of the way to our room. But he did pause at the door to say, "There are some toys in the chest by the bed. Enjoy."

A sexy little smirk twisted his lips, and then he left without another word.

I started to watch him sashay down the hall, but Ezra yanked me inside and shut the door before I could enjoy the view.

The Archangel glowered down at me.

I smiled back, doing my best to appear as innocent as possible. "What?"

"You're mine, Kayla. And I don't share."

I rolled my eyes. "This again."

"Yeah, *this* again." His palm went to my throat as he backed me up against the door. "You can try to kill me. Fight me. Hate me, if you must. But you're still mine."

Some of my exhaustion fled in favor of a spike of anger. "Because you tricked me into a blood bond."

"Yes. I did. And I don't regret it." His mouth claimed mine in the next breath, keeping me from replying.

I started to push him away, my hands landing on his shoulders to do so, but one of his thighs wedged between mine and short-circuited my brain.

One second, I wanted to shove him.

The next, I was clinging to him as though he were my primary purpose in life.

He unleashed that powerful tongue of his, each swipe against mine coaxing me into submitting. It didn't take much. Because I wanted him. I wanted *this*. And I didn't see the point in denying him.

His palms went to my hips to lift me up against the door. I wrapped my legs and arms around him in response.

And then he carried me to the bed.

He didn't bother opening the chest. And I didn't bother to ask.

We didn't need any toys.

Just each other.

Just *this*.

Our clothes disappeared beneath our hands and our mouths, leaving us naked and entangled on the bed.

But he didn't immediately enter me.

Instead, he kissed a delirious path down my body after saying, "Our version of foreplay."

He bit my nipple, then soothed it with his tongue before continuing his journey to the apex between my thighs.

I moaned. Screamed. Begged. And nearly cried.

All the while, he taunted me with his tongue, owning me entirely with his mouth.

I pulled at his hair, needing more.

But he kept taking me to the edge without letting me fall.

Delayed gratification.

I was going to kill that Incubus later. Just after I killed Ezra.

When I admitted that out loud, my Archangel laughed. Then he sucked my sensitive bundle of nerves into his mouth and unleashed the most exquisite kind of agony through my being.

I felt hot. Cold. Shivering and sweating. Everything burned and froze at the same time, my power spiraling out of control, only to be calmed by Ezra's presence.

Give and take.

Push and pull.

Fire and ice.

Archdemon and Archangel.

"Ezra," I breathed, arching into his mouth and weeping at the perfection of the moment.

"Are you going to come for me, little heiress?" Ezra's low rumble of words vibrated my core, causing my thighs to clench.

"Are you going to let me?"

"Yes, darling, I am. And do you want to know why?" He nipped at my swollen nub, his golden irises intense as he met my gaze.

I swallowed, half-insane with need and half-furious at this game of sensual torment. "Why?"

"Because you're mine," he whispered, his mouth sealing around me again as he stared me down.

His words, coupled with that commanding look, left me breathless and writhing beneath him.

Then his tongue swirled.

And my life ended in a climax that shot me directly to the heavens and the bowels of hell at the same time.

"Because you're mine."

Yes.

Yes, I am.

And you're mine, too.

The words whispered through my mind, rolling around in a hypnotic sequence that pulled me into a new existence of acceptance.

A world with a future I wanted to consider.

A place where I might actually be happy.

In the arms of an Archangel. My mate. The male I wanted to hate. Yet I found a part of myself starting to love him instead.

I nearly wept in response.

But then Ezra's body joined mine, his cock perfectly fitting inside me as he fucked me into a beautiful state of oblivion. Chasing our pleasure. Reinventing our dreams. Cherishing this peaceful moment in time.

His lips whispered promises against mine. Promises I accepted. Promises I craved.

And I returned the sentiment in kind with my tongue.

It was a perfect embrace.

A forbidden desire.

A blissful balance.

"Mine," he asserted.

"Mine," I echoed, my nails scraping down his back in a blatant claim. *At least for now.*

He nipped my lip as though he'd heard that thought.

And maybe he had.

Our souls were dancing now, our spirits mating on a plane neither of us could access.

All the while, our blood bond thrived.

And another part of me that hated this male chipped away into nonexistence.

He might break my heart. Leave me to suffer. Abandon me once more.

Yet I couldn't bring myself to believe those threats any longer.

Because a dangerous part of me longed to hope.

For a future.

With Ezra by my side.

EZRA

A Little Over A Week Later

KAYLA AND I HAD DEVELOPED A ROUTINE OF RESTING during the day and discussing strategy with the others all night.

It'd become apparent quickly that Gleason had more or less relocated to Zebulon's mansion sometime over the last two years. He acted as a Dark Provenance liaison of sorts, delivering information back and forth by traveling with a Portal Dweller named Remy.

Ashmedai had gathered a lot of details through his various sources, allowing him to devise over a dozen scenarios and several long lists of key players to observe.

Yet he wouldn't reveal his suspicions about who was orchestrating all this from behind the scenes, something that pissed me off to no end.

But he just kept saying he wouldn't reveal those cards until the appropriate play.

Whatever the fuck that meant.

Kayla guessed it was because he needed more proof before voicing his accusation, which meant the culprit was important and potentially even considered to be one of our allies.

Or it could be a group of people.

Regardless, I suspected Kayla's assumption was correct.

Ashmedai could be infuriating, but his actions were typically justified by a rational cause.

Of course, he'd also given Kayla the phone that had blown up the veil. So perhaps not.

We all stood around the table now, one I'd memorized every inch of over the last eight days. Gleason had just returned from another of his discussions with the Dark Provenance, the wariness in his green gaze telling us all that we weren't going to like what he had to say.

"There were demon sightings in twelve major cities last night. Scion deployed several groups in response to try to minimize the exposure to mortals, but we're running low on troops." Gleason paused before adding, "That can't be a coincidence."

"I haven't had any requests for passage in my realm," Zebulon replied.

"I've not received any requests either," Ashmedai confirmed, his brow furrowing. "You say this started last night?"

Gleason nodded as he ran his fingers through his auburn hair. The unruly strands fell to his ears in a display that suggested he needed a haircut. His thickening beard suggested he needed a good shave, too.

We all did.

Except for Ashmedai and his perpetually clean jaw.

Even Zebulon had a dusting of dark hairs. However, his head remained smooth, so perhaps he'd focused on that instead of his chin.

Not that any of it mattered.

"London, Paris, New York City, Tokyo..." Gleason continued listing cities as though he were being quizzed. "Over half of the Dark Provenance has been deployed in response."

"Something's coming," Ashmedai translated.

"Something's coming," Gleason echoed.

"Why would Scion deploy so many Nephilim under his command?" I interjected. "I understand the need to respond and to ensure mortals don't discover any demons, but he knows as much as all of you. He has to see that this is a setup." Scion was the fucking Archangel of War. He was a master strategist. "What's his play?"

"A great question indeed," Ashmedai murmured, his expression holding a touch of darkness unlike any I'd ever seen from him before.

I frowned. "What is it?"

He merely shook his head. "I'm trying to see the potential impacts from all angles."

"And?" I prompted.

"I'm still reviewing." He turned away from us to face the giant map of realms.

Trudy stepped up to his side, causing his wing to automatically wrap around her, much like mine did when Kayla stood next to me.

But from what I'd observed of Ashmedai and Trudy, they weren't intimate. Yet he clearly felt the need to protect her.

How does she fit into all this? I wondered for the thousandth time this week. Ashmedai wouldn't have taken her unless she meant something. Her penchant for strategy was evident in the way she bantered back and forth with him as he puzzled out potential scenarios. But it had to go deeper than that.

"Are you ready to give me what I want?" he asked her now.

"No."

He sighed. "I didn't think so." He faced the rest of us. "We need to alert Bael and Alastor. We should also get word up to Azrael." His gaze went to Gleason. "I assume he's not yet returned?"

"Scion is still in charge."

Ashmedai nodded. "I thought that might be the case."

My frown deepened. *What is it you suspect about Scion?* I nearly asked, my gaze going to Trudy and back to Ashmedai.

I surmised that she was Scion's daughter because of how the Archangel had reacted to Ashmedai having her in his custody. So was Scion part of this game? A chess piece for Ashmedai to move around the board?

Or were they engaged in a different kind of battle?

Power struggles were common among Archangels and Archdemons. We had a basic understanding of how to tolerate each other—with the Divinity being the heart of that understanding—but that didn't mean we always played by the rules.

I palmed the back of my neck, my gaze lifting to the ceiling. *I'm overthinking all of this.* I'd spent the last week with Kayla trying to regain my own inner balance, working to heal our bond through touch and worshipping kisses. It'd helped to an extent, but I still felt off-kilter, like I was missing something.

We'd tried several times to locate Kristina's power again, even using some of my locator spells. But without my supplies, I couldn't do much other than rely on my abilities to search for imbalances throughout the realms.

I found several.

Too many, in fact.

Leaving us with far too much to investigate and too little time to do it.

Ashmedai had noted several of those imbalances on a new sheet that now hung off the bookshelves to my right.

There were several dozen power shifts that Kayla had confirmed she sensed, too.

In addition to everything else this group had noted.

"What are you thinking?" Kayla asked me quietly, her eyes searching.

"Wishing you could read my mind?" I countered, my lips

quirking at the thought. Some mates could speak telepathically. I was honestly rather surprised that we couldn't. Perhaps it was a result of too many years apart. Maybe we'd grow into it someday.

Or maybe that was the sense of wrongness I felt inside.

The sense that told me something was missing.

Her trust? Her love? Her desire for a future?

I wasn't naïve. I knew I didn't have any of those things yet. It would take time and a lot of groveling to convince her to give me a real chance.

The problem was, I couldn't really grovel. Not when I didn't regret our bond or why it'd been necessary at the time.

Kayla studied me for a long moment. "I'm not sure I want to know your mind."

"Then you'll never know what I'm thinking." I reached out to tuck a stray strand of reddish-brown hair behind her ear. The new color hadn't seemed to alarm her at all. It was almost as though she hadn't noticed. Or maybe she was avoiding the cause of it.

Me.

Our bond.

Our shared energy and power.

"I'll go inform Prince Bael of the update," Yaz said, interrupting my moment with Kayla. "Is there anything else you'd like me to tell him, Princess?"

She pulled away from me to face him. "No. Just pass on the warning that something is imminent."

He dipped his chin in acknowledgment. "Prince Ashmedai?"

The Archdemon flicked his fingers in dismissal. "Make sure he passes the word on to Alastor."

"I'll request it," Yaz replied, his statement suggesting he didn't expect Bael to agree.

A Portal Dweller appeared then, his hand held out for Yaz.

The Royal Guard must have used his device to call for him while I'd been focused on Kayla.

The two of them vanished before Ashmedai could comment. The Archdemon narrowed his gaze, clearly aware of the Royal Guard's antics. However, his focus moved to me. "Do you want to inform Azrael?"

"Is there a reason you think Scion won't?" I countered.

The Archdemon blinked, his expression exuding an innocence that didn't become him. "Why wouldn't Scion tell him?"

I narrowed my gaze. "If there's something you want to say about the Archangel of War, then I think you should just voice it."

"And insult one of your oldest friends?" He glanced at Trudy. "That would be unwise of me, yes?"

"Oh, you suddenly care how I feel about Scion?" Her tone held an edge to it that made the Prince of Hell grin in response.

"I very much care about how you feel, little warrior. We've been over that several—"

Power rippled through the air, cutting off Ashmedai's response and causing me to grab Kayla by the waist. I tugged her to my chest, my wings enveloping her in a protective cocoon as my mind fought to catch up with the prickling sensation unfolding around us.

Something powerful had just rocked this realm.

Something deadly.

"That happened faster than anticipated," Ashmedai muttered, his own wings having wrapped around Trudy in a manner similar to mine with Kayla.

Another wave of energy sizzled across my skin, the sensation leaving behind a dark kiss of friction. Someone was tapping into a hell of a lot of power somewhere.

"We need to find the source." I captured Kayla's face

between my palms. "Can you sense them at all? Anything that may help?"

"Why are you asking me?"

"Because you're my mate, and that makes you just as sensitive to the power imbalance as I am." I couldn't quite keep the irritation out of my voice. She needed to accept that we were partners in this now.

Had I been an asshole in the past? Yes.

Would I be an asshole now in forcing her to accept us? Also yes.

"Can you sense anything?" she countered.

My jaw clenched. It was a fair question. But it only added to my frustration. "I'm struggling to focus on it," I admitted. "It feels... chaotic." Which was why I'd grabbed her. Why I *needed* her.

Something about our bond felt vital to the process. Which was ridiculous because I'd never needed anyone else before. I was the Archangel of Justice. I upheld the scales.

Yet I felt entirely unbalanced and off-center. As though I needed an anchor that wasn't quite there.

Kayla pressed her palm to my face, partially mimicking the way I held her now. However, her opposite hand went to cover mine against her cheek. Then she closed her eyes.

I released a long breath, her touch grounding me in a way I didn't understand.

Everything had just felt so urgent and broken and disconnected. I'd reacted without understanding my actions. She'd become my lifeline. My anchor. My source of balance.

Holding her helped me concentrate on the insanity spiraling around us, the wavering energy pushing and pulling at the realms, and the wrongness of the power fluctuations.

I closed my eyes, my soul searching for the source of all that dizzying static electricity. The culprit fucking with the levels of existence. The heart of our problem.

A shattered Divinity.

I searched for the fractured pieces of Kristina's essence.

It was as natural as breathing, locating the various strands and following them to their unexpected ends.

"They've opened a portal in the underworld," I heard Ashmedai saying. "It's leading straight into Heaven."

EZRA

An impossibility, I thought, frowning.

But I ignored that and continued chasing Kristina's power. It felt close. *Too* close.

Which caused my brow to furrow.

"They're here," Kayla breathed, clearly sensing a thread similar to the one I continued to tug on.

It wasn't exactly Kristina's essence, but a tainted version of it. And it wasn't an aura I picked up on, just the magic being weaved into the air.

Because someone was expelling a great deal of power.

Power that only the Divinity could maintain and possess.

Power that was mine to protect.

But Kayla felt it as well because of her ties to my spirit. And it was those ties that buoyed me long enough in the moment to navigate away from the frenzy of energy and into a realm of astute understanding.

"Can you track it?" Kayla asked me, confirming her awareness of the energy I'd locked onto.

"Yes," I told her. But I needed something first. *A clear path.* Except a strange buzzing infiltrated my ability to home in on the growing power.

"Lift the wards, Zebulon," Ashmedai demanded. "Ezra needs to be able to fly."

If Zebulon replied, I didn't hear it. Because another burst

of energy cascaded static across my senses, rendering me temporarily immobile.

Every part of me ached.

My soul screamed at the injustice of it all.

And then suddenly it cleared again.

An ethereal tug at my psyche helped me locate the misuse of power once more, the wrongness of the act calling upon my soul in a blatant demand to right the scales.

I reacted, my wings wrapping around Kayla as I teleported us toward the malicious energy.

Belatedly, I realized I should have left her behind.

However, I needed her to help me focus.

She served as my map, helping me navigate this dark sea of tumultuous waves and violent whirlpools. I wasn't sure when our relationship had become this power-driven partnership, but I didn't have time to decipher the hows or the whys of our connection.

We needed to focus on the *now*.

Which was unfolding around us in a landscape similar to the place where Kristina had died.

Only it was warmer here. No snow and ice. But a myriad of trees.

I hadn't paid attention to the location, just the energy signature calling me to this place.

Kayla's palms lit with flames as she spun in my arms to attack those nearby. She threw a sphere of fire right at them, only for the embers to dissolve into ash against an invisible shield.

Four pairs of eyes all widened as they noticed our unexpected arrival.

It all happened in seconds, Kayla already preparing another attack, her flames flickering with blue undertones as she changed her power.

She didn't need a weapon because *she* was the weapon.

I called my swords, one for each hand, and used my wings to carry me toward the barrier. The powerful runes etched into my long blades flickered with magic as I sliced them through the air. They pulsated and absorbed the shield's enchantment, learning the elements laced through their protective barrier and quickly dissolving the incantation.

"*That* is very useful," Kayla mused, fire licking across her skin.

"I'll make you one," I promised her. My version of displaying gratitude for her kiss of strength and her innate balance that had allowed me to regain my focus.

The four beings inside the barrier stood, their gazes darkening with intent. I didn't recognize any of them.

They started to speak, but I couldn't hear them through the shield. A pale-skinned blond male with broad shoulders knelt to touch the ground.

Energy hummed along the earth, causing the land to rumble in response.

Kayla grabbed me as the ground split open beneath her feet. I engaged my wings to keep us upright, my hands otherwise occupied with my swords.

"Wrap your arms around my neck," I instructed. It was a moot point since she'd already begun climbing me like a tree. Thankfully, she'd put away her fireballs before touching me.

"This is going to make fighting difficult," she muttered as her thighs clamped down around my waist.

"Or enjoyable." I couldn't stop the musing reply from leaving my lips, nor did I even try to keep the grin from forming afterward.

Kayla snorted, grumbling something about males.

But a pulse of energy had her freezing against me.

"They're building another portal," I said, aware that she couldn't see them.

"Where's the first one?"

"I'm not sure, but I can feel it." They'd created a dark hole somewhere beyond this barrier, the magic whirling in a chaotic rhythm that allowed beings to traverse straight to Heaven from Hell. "It's like they crafted a tunnel from Hell to Heaven that uses this realm as the passing point."

There was no other way to explain it.

I could sense the demons flowing through Earth to reach the heavens. A feat that shouldn't be possible. Which was the source of the chaos shredding apart my soul and threatening the balance between our realms.

"That's why they wanted the Dark Provenance members distracted. They didn't want to give them a chance to interfere on Earth." Because these beings were controlling the anchor that kept the portals alive. "They won't be able to close them in Hell or in Heaven."

It was a guess, but a very good one based on what I felt emanating from behind the barrier.

"Similar to the portal that opened over your estate in between the realms," she said.

I nodded. Yaz had told us earlier this week about how that portal didn't seem to have an origin or an anchor.

Portals between the realms always required a party on either side to keep it open.

But there hadn't been anyone keeping the portal open near my estate that day. At least according to Yaz.

Something that had struck me as suspicious.

However, the demonstration of power before us suggested this was the cause.

Another rumble touched the earth as the male inside shot power through the atmosphere. My wings easily held us aloft while my swords continued to dismantle the magic within their barricade. "They used Kristina's essence to craft this," I told Kayla, my veins alighting with a fury I felt all the way to my soul. "That's why it's taking so long to cut through."

"It's the same essence as what she used to repair the veil." Kayla's words were a statement, not a question.

Still, I confirmed it with a "Yes." But the fact that she knew that just further proved how our spirits were mingling to create a new dynamic between us. "Her ability combined light and dark to create veil magic. It's why she embodied the perfect balance."

"Dark," Kayla echoed. "From Prince Morax. Dark... like shadows?"

I considered that for a moment. "Similar, yes. But he has no domain over the actual Shadow realm."

"True," she agreed. "But that doesn't mean his power..." She trailed off, then cursed.

Her arm wrapped tightly around my neck as she lifted her opposite hand into the air to create a fiery shield.

I glanced up as an avalanche of fire fell over us.

My lips parted. "How...?"

"I felt it coming," she muttered, shuddering as she fought to keep the embers from touching us. "*Hurry*, Ezra."

I sliced my blades against the barrier again, urging the swords to dismantle the invisible magic. But it wasn't something I could rush. This magic was enchanting and powerful, just like Kristina's gifts had been.

"How are they hitting us with magic through the barrier?" I wondered out loud. "And who has the fire magic?" It wasn't necessarily directed at her, just a general question as I searched the four beings inside.

They were all Nephilim.

Or that was my guess, anyway. Because I couldn't actually read their auras.

Which meant they could technically be Halflings as well.

They could also be under a concealment charm of sorts that blocked their energy signatures from being noticed or felt by others. Their influx of intense energy was the only reason I'd been able to find them at all.

Kayla cursed as sweat began to accumulate on her brow.

"Bite me," I told her. "Take energy from me."

She didn't ask questions or hesitate, her blunt teeth landing on my neck before I even finished speaking. Electricity sizzled around us as our souls danced, our bond igniting and flaring to life with a passion that had only grown fiercer between us over the last week.

We'd indulged in our connection without remorse, allowing our bodies to communicate to each other about our desires and needs.

It wasn't perfect.

It likely wouldn't be for decades or centuries to come.

But it was a start.

The barrier began to fracture, stirring a whirlwind of static in the air that caused all the hairs along my arms and neck to stand on end. I could see the edges of it now, the jagged line looking like a tear in the sky as it traversed downward to meet my blade.

Kayla didn't stop imbibing my essence, her jaw working as her shield above us kept the fire at bay.

"We can't hold it," one of the beings inside said, his voice a deep growl that reminded me of a hellhound. His long black hair hung in thick waves past his shoulders, his bangs hiding his eyes from view. Maybe he was some sort of shifter.

I still couldn't read their auras, all four of them seeming to be no more than human to my senses. Apart from the insane amount of energy they were conjuring, anyway.

The tips of my swords punctured through the barrier, creating another fissure that allowed me to feel the cool intensity of their power.

It was growing with each second as more and more of my swords penetrated their shield.

"Almost done," the lone female of the group said, her spiky black hair reminding me of sharp rocks. She'd knelt on the ground moments ago to begin crafting the new portal.

I peered through the torn edges of the barrier, searching for evidence of the tunnel or whatever they were using to traverse through this realm.

Nothing struck me as out of the ordinary, making me frown.

Then another blast of energy came at me through the cracks, causing me to dislodge my swords as I fluttered backward.

My gaze narrowed. "They should not be able to possess this sort of power." I caught the next blast with my sword and sent it back to them, but it exploded against the barrier. "*Fuck.*"

I flew to the side to start again as Kayla growled something against my neck. She'd released my vein when I'd moved and was still trying to hold back the flames raining down upon us.

I could beat Kristina on a good day.

Hell, I could beat the entire Divinity. We'd sparred on several occasions just to keep my fighting skills sharp. But that'd been decades ago—*pre-Kayla*.

While our rekindled bond had helped bolster my reserves, I was nowhere near what I needed to be to win this battle.

And something was holding me back from tapping into my bond with Kayla to fully replenish my abilities.

I thought it was related to trust and her lack of desire to make this long-term. But a nagging sense told me the cause ran deeper than that. Because she was fully embracing me now, yet it wasn't enough.

Biting her wouldn't solve it, not when she needed my strength to keep that shield above our heads.

"I still don't understand how they're attacking us through this barrier when we can't reach them," I snarled, my swords vibrating with renewed power as the magic inside them battled the invisible enchantment.

That portal they were creating swirled to life, allowing me a glimpse of obsidian flames.

What the fuck? My eyes widened as I realized that wasn't a portal at all, but a shadow creature. The kneeling female winked up at me as she sprung backward.

The barrier crashed down between us, and the shadow being lunged.

I shot upward on instinct.

Kayla shrieked in response, her shield swirling around us in a blaze of heat to protect us from the flames I'd just taken us through.

My wings hummed with the reminder of what had happened the last time I'd come into contact with fire.

But I pushed through it, launching us into the sky as that shadowy creature rose to follow us.

I shot an arc of power from my swords, sheathing the flames in ice.

"Why the fuck didn't you do that before?" Kayla demanded, her voice hoarse from the exertion of power.

"Because my runes were otherwise engaged," I replied, my focus on that smoky figure rising into the sky.

"A warning would have been appreciated," she grumbled, her arms straining as she hugged me to keep from falling.

"That bitch just unleashed a being from the Shadow realm." I couldn't keep the fury from my tone. That creature alone could destroy an entire continent in this world in a matter of hours.

And it appeared to be considering just that.

Already the trees below it were turning to ash as it absorbed the life from its roots, the Succubus-like being a danger to everything in its path.

Dizziness hit my senses once more, the threat to the

balance weighing down my plumes and nearly plummeting us to the ground.

Kayla dug her nails into my neck. "Kill it, Ezra. Kill it now."

Part of me wanted to retort something like, *No shit*. But a baser part of me took her command and ran with it.

She wasn't trying to state the obvious; she was trying to keep me in the moment.

And it worked.

I crossed my swords together to create a beam of light that I shot right into the center of the growing beast.

It howled, stirring dark clouds all around us in an attempt to dispel the source of illumination. But my wings outmaneuvered it, my experience and age and power overcoming the soul-destroying demon as I blasted a steady stream of luminescence right into the heart of its being.

Wind roared around us, the creature attempting to fight its fate.

Kayla's nails bit hard into my neck, grounding me, empowering me, forcing me to concentrate on the task until the shadow exploded into ash to decorate the ruined landscape beneath it.

I didn't give it a second thought, my mind already returning to the four beings that had managed to conjure the being into existence.

They were right where I'd left them, shieldless now.

The bulky blond one looked straight up at me, his lips moving as he warned the others.

I arrowed us downward toward them, my swords ready to destroy.

"Hang on," I told Kayla, increasing my speed.

The spiky-haired female on the ground shot to her feet, her arm lifting. A hint of gold winked in the sunlight.

A cuff.

Her fingers ran over it, and she disappeared into thin air.

The others all followed suit just as we reached them, their wrists decorated in similar items, all of them engaging the ability to portal at will.

Just like Kayla could with her own cuff.

I landed on the ground they'd just occupied, that hint of power gone. Vanished. Nowhere to be found.

And the darkening sensation of imbalance fled with it.

Kayla's legs released me as she took an unsteady step backward, her eyes wild with a mixture of furious confusion. "What the fuck?"

Yeah. My thoughts exactly.

Kayla

I COULD FEEL THE RESIDUAL ENERGY ALL AROUND US, that familiar sensation of a portal jump touching my senses. But it was more than that.

It was the way they'd left.

Not through a portal, but via a rune.

A rune that I knew *very* well. One they shouldn't be able to access.

"Tell me about your cuff," Ezra demanded as though reading my mind. "Where's it from? What exactly does it do?"

I glanced down at the shimmering metal against my wrist, then turned to meet his glittering gaze. The black embers of his irises were burning hotter than the gold.

I swallowed. "I... It grants me additional abilities like portaling." But the magic required to create it was supposed to be rare and difficult to cultivate.

So how did those four Nephilim—or whatever they are—use a similar ability? Was it a cuff? Or was it them? And if it was a cuff, does that make it less rare than I thought?

"The primary purpose is to throttle my power," I added, still frowning at my cuff. "It's useful when around humans because it hides my demonic traits." I'd been rather mortified when my horns had sprouted into existence for the first time. My father didn't have horns, and my human mother sure as hell didn't.

I would much rather have wings.

Alas, that was a conversation for another day.

"It also lets me harness my gifts and provides me with the ability to hone my skills as needed. And it disguises what I am, but doesn't exactly mask my aura either." Maybe those beings were using a similar item to hide their energy signatures as well. Was that why I couldn't sense their supernatural type or origin?

"Is it throttling your power right now?" he asked.

My frown deepened as I studied my hand. "No, I disengaged it." Yet my fingertips were still normal.

I touched my head.

My horns are missing, too.

Maybe I hadn't fully released my powers? Everything had happened so quickly with Ezra grabbing me and whisking us here. I'd drawn my usual symbol over my wrist on instinct, then called forth my hellfire.

My brow furrowed as I recalled how weak I'd felt.

Ezra's blood had given me the strength I'd needed to fight that incoming inferno over our heads.

But I'd felt more drained than I should have.

Because he's been using me to heal?

Or was it something else?

I ran my fingers over my cuff again, drawing the symbol that unleashed my powers. Then I called the flames to my hands once more.

No black fingertips.

My horns weren't appearing either.

Is it my cuff or me?

"Give it to me." Ezra held out his hand with the command. "Now."

Part of me wanted to argue, but it seemed frivolous at this point. "Maybe it's this place messing with my powers," I told him as I drew a rune to unlock my cuff. "Or the imbalance." I held out the enchanted item for him. "Or our bond." Because I hadn't possessed my horns in Heaven, either.

Nor did they come to me now as he took the cuff from my hands.

Fire licked along my fingertips, my skin remaining pale and unchanged.

I still felt weak, too.

"It's not our bond." His tone held a note of confidence that I didn't quite feel. "Something has been holding us back. I think this is it."

"But I wasn't wearing it in Heaven."

"Right. And I didn't feel that block in Heaven," he countered.

My brow furrowed. "You've felt a block?"

He nodded. "Yes."

"Why didn't you mention it?" I wondered aloud.

His gaze hardened. "I assumed it was emotional and your lack of faith in me—which I accepted, as it's warranted. But now I'm wondering if it's related to this." He held it up for me as though I didn't know what *this* meant.

"It's never been a problem before." Nor did it truly feel like one now. But my lack of demonic traits was rather telling, as was the exhaustion flowing through my veins. "Someone took that cuff off of me when we..." I trailed off, uncertain of how to finish that statement. "While in Heaven," I decided on instead. "Maybe someone altered it?"

He opened his mouth as though he wanted to issue a retort or a denial, but then his lips tightened together into a straight line.

His thumb brushed the metal, tracing over the silver markings.

"We should talk to Raphaela," he said after a long beat of silence. "Find out who removed your cuff."

"Okay," I agreed. That seemed like a good place to start.

His chin dipped in acknowledgment, his gaze once more falling to the cuff. "Who gave you this cuff originally? How was it created?"

"Yaz had it commissioned."

His expression told me he didn't like that. "Why?"

"To keep me safe." I folded my arms. "He's like a protective big brother to me, Ezra. You don't need to feel threatened by him."

Ezra snorted. "I don't feel threatened by him."

"Sure you don't. That's why you've been so kind to him, right?"

"I've not been *unkind* to him, if that's what you're implying."

I arched a brow. "No?"

"He's alive, isn't he?" he retorted.

I rolled my eyes. "Yes, because that's kind."

"Trust me. It is."

"So you're kind to me as well, then? Allowing a Halfling mutt to live in your prestigious presence?"

He grabbed me by the back of the neck and yanked me into him so hard that the air was expelled from my lungs in a whoosh of sound that made me dizzy.

"I'm not kind to you, Kayla," he murmured, his mouth brushing mine as his opposite arm wrapped around my lower back. "I fucking worship you."

My lips parted at the ferocity in his tone.

Which he took full advantage of by engaging me in a kiss that blew my mind almost as much as his claim did.

I was only vaguely aware of us ascending to Heaven, his power wrapping around me in a warm blanket of protection and adoration.

It left me winded and helpless to his assault, my tongue submitting to his as he possessed every inch of my mouth.

I felt owned.

Cherished.

Worshipped.

Just like he'd stated.

And I positively melted into him, my instinct to fight having fled beneath a wave of intense emotion.

I'm falling for him, I thought dizzily. *I'm really, truly falling for him.*

The realization sent a chill down my spine.

Before, I'd been a naïve little Halfling without enough world experience to recognize my role in Ezra's game as a pawn.

Now I knew my place, and yet I was still succumbing to his desires. Playing right into his hand. Giving him my heart on a fucking gold platter.

I wanted to hate him for breaking through my barriers and abusing my heart in this way. I wanted to loathe him for his trickery.

But my soul wouldn't allow it.

My spirit intertwined with his in a matrimonial bliss that overwhelmed all my instincts, demanding I worship him in kind.

If he betrayed me again, it would destroy me irrevocably.

Which was the last place I wanted to be.

I didn't want to trust him or love him or *crave* him.

I wanted to be free. I wanted him dead. I wanted to be the queen on the board, not a mere pawn.

Yet his mouth made me feel like I was so much more. His tongue whispered words of partnership and equality. An unspoken promise lingered between us, a vow never to harm me again.

But could I trust it?

Could I allow myself to believe in him?

The sound of metal hitting stone made me flinch. However, Ezra's fingers were in my hair before I could even think about what that meant. He still had his hand around my nape, but his opposite palm was on the back of my head, holding me to him as he laid claim to my soul.

My nails dug into his shoulders, my mind having no idea when I'd grabbed him and not truly caring about the how or the why, just the *now*.

I returned his embrace with a fierceness of my own, telling him with my mouth that if he dared to fuck with me again, I'd end him.

It was a false promise.

One I knew I wouldn't be able to fulfill.

Because I'd nearly lost him already and I refused to experience that again. Not when it took everything in me to bring him back.

He was mine to keep alive. Mine to kill. Mine to *love*.

His palm released my neck, his fingers trailing down my spine to the base. Then he grabbed my hip and began walking backward.

I recognized the scents of his home. Of Heaven. The temporary balance settled around us, putting us at ease. I barely even sensed the ascension, my demonic powers having learned how to thrive in this plane during our last visit.

Or maybe that was the bond. Perhaps it was my link to Ezra allowing me to thrive.

I didn't overthink it. I just accepted it.

He led me to his bed, pushing me down into the soft mattress and crawling over me with his myriad of feathers.

An Archangel laying claim.

An Archangel taking what he wanted.

An Archangel healing his mate.

All those thoughts ran through my mind at once, each one foreign yet right. Because I felt the residual energy crawling across my skin, coaxing me into my true form.

Except my hands remained pale and my horns didn't sprout.

I shivered, not understanding this shifting dynamic or what it meant.

But Ezra's mouth cooled my concern, distracting me beautifully with his skilled tongue.

I moaned, arching into him, and allowed this twist of fate.

"Ezra," I whispered.

"Kayla," he returned, his teeth skimming my lower lip.

There were no other words for me to say. No protests. No demands. I just wanted him, *this*, his mouth on mine.

Every touch seemed to balance the scales, causing everything around us to thrive with energy and rightness.

I wasn't sure how I sensed that or if it was a result of us or the events we'd just endured.

But the very notion of stopping this overpowering connection made me feel faint.

"More," I demanded.

"Yes," he agreed, his palm skating up my stomach to cup my breast beneath my shirt. "Definitely more."

I whimpered against his mouth, begging him without words to cool the fire burning within me. It was threatening to explode, to engulf us both.

My inner demon wanted out.

My power needed an outlet.

My soul was suddenly screaming with *need*.

He blanketed me in his cooling energy in my next breath, grounding me once more, putting me at peace.

Everything felt right.

Heaven. Hell. Earth. All the realms were relaxed. No foreign portals. No abuse of the scales. No intense energy signatures to trace.

Just me and Ezra.

Floating. Kissing. Embracing.

His feathers were everywhere, his wings holding me beneath him on the bed in a cage of silky brown-black plumes.

I clawed at his shirt, needing his skin.

He lifted to remove it.

Then his sword appeared to slice through my own.

There and gone in a blink.

I didn't even have a moment to gasp at the lethality of his power.

His mouth chased away the chill, tracing a line directly to my breasts.

Because he'd sliced the bra as well.

It was new—one of Zebulon's men having bought both of us clothes to wear over the last week—but I didn't mourn the loss. If anything, I wanted him to repeat the action with my pants.

He didn't.

Instead, he kissed a dangerous path down my body and unbuttoned the jeans with his mouth before tugging down the zipper with his teeth.

It was erotic. Intoxicating. *Arousing*.

The fabric whispered down my legs, disappearing over the edge of the bed with my boots and socks.

My panties were next.

And then Ezra rolled off me to remove his clothes as well.

A violent tremble touched my senses, the balance shifting negatively from the loss of his touch. My heart started to pound. My lungs worked frantically in an attempt to inhale, but I couldn't find my connection to the air.

I felt lost.

Falling.

Tumbling into nothing.

Until Ezra caught me with his hand, his body lying over mine once more. I clung to him, my arms wrapping around his neck as I silently wept with gratitude.

The scales corrected themselves again, the worlds all in alignment, the power fluctuating evenly between the realms.

No portals. No tears in the veil. No wrongness.

Just a sense of beautiful harmony that deepened as his mouth met mine.

His thumbs brushed the tears from my cheeks, his lips grounding me in the moment as his hips met mine.

He didn't enter me.

He teased me.

The head of his cock grazing my clit.

His chest rubbing my stiff nipples.

His strong thighs brushing the insides of my legs as I crossed my ankles against his ass.

It all felt so utterly perfect and even more intense than before.

Because I let him in.

I chose to trust him.

I chose to believe in our future.

I chose to make myself vulnerable.

To be the queen to his king.

"I'll never hurt you again," he whispered before I could even begin to fear the faith I'd just allowed myself to experience. "You're mine, Kayla. For eternity."

That's a long time, I almost replied. But I couldn't seem to find my voice. I was drowning in power and enigmatic energy.

Is this healing? I wondered. *Is this what he felt when on the brink of death?*

Or was this something more?

How much energy had I exerted on that inferno? How had it even been created? It'd felt fresh from the bowels of hell.

Just like that shadow monster.

Ezra's teeth skimmed my lower lip, tugging me back into the moment, demanding my complete compliance.

I sighed, submitting to his silent command and giving myself over to the sensations of his body pressed against mine.

Hell and Heaven.

Fire and ice.

A balance of power.

My skin warmed just as his cooled, leaving me in a state of complete serenity.

"Take me, Ezra," I whispered, my thighs squeezing his hips.

"No." He didn't thrust forward. Instead, he rolled, pulling me over his lap. "You take me, Kayla."

A savage tremble threatened my stability, my world continuing to whirl around me as I fought the sudden dizziness mounting inside.

My palms went to his abdomen to hold me steady.

His hands gripped my hips.

And then he lifted me.

"Now, Kayla."

I didn't know what else to do other than to take him inside me, and immediately everything felt right again. Tears blurred my vision, my mind struggling to understand what was happening between us. We'd fucked several times, but this was so very different. It was impactful in a way I couldn't define. Shooting me up into the heavens and down to the pits of Hell with every swivel of my hips.

Imbalance.

Balance.

Imbalance.

Balance.

Ezra sat up, his arms wrapping around me in bands of protective muscle. His wings followed, cocooning me in this temporary insanity and granting me a moment of utter bliss.

Then he thrust up into me and destabilized my sense of rightness once more.

Another thrust made me feel at peace.

A third thrust had me crying out at the spinning sensation overtaking my being.

On it went—a battle of tranquility and chaos.

He kissed away my tears even as he caused more to pour from my eyes.

His energy swathed mine, healing me one moment and killing me the next.

I felt lost and at home all at the same time. On a path to euphoric fate one second and falling off the edge into despair only a blink later.

It was insanity.

It was perfection.

It was *us*.

A relationship of balance between Heaven and Hell, two souls destined to create a new Divinity. A new balance. A new way of life.

A moment of clarity struck me—*we're righting the wrong of our sins*—and then it left me as Ezra tumbled me headfirst in a black oblivion of ecstasy.

Pleasure and pain rippled through my being, stirring a battle inside me that threatened to kill me.

But I embraced it.

I allowed it to take me under.

Granted the balance access to my body and soul to create the future required for all of us to survive.

My penance for all the wrongs in my life.

For starting us down this journey that had led to Kristina's death.

To the imbalance of demon and angel kind.

I took it all, the burden mine to bear alone.

Except I wasn't alone at all.

I had Ezra there with me, his body wrapped tightly around

mine as he followed me down this dark and dangerous path called fate.

He didn't abandon me this time.

He didn't leave me behind.

He held me through it all, his spirit issuing a silent vow never to desert me again.

Mine, I heard him whispering into my thoughts. *You were always meant to be mine.*

Maybe he'd uttered those words out loud.

Maybe we'd created a new connection.

Maybe this was our new shared existence.

The birth of a new Divinity.

A bond forged in lies and emboldened by a second chance.

Trust. Faith. Promises. Love.

I experienced it all at the same time, not just within my own soul, but also within his.

He wasn't going to leave me again.

Until death do us part, his spirit promised. *My mate for eternity.*

He'd chosen that from the very beginning, his decision to bond with me going so much deeper than just a vendetta against my father.

But it wasn't something he actively understood.

Fate worked in mysterious ways.

This was our intertwined path.

A future we'd been destined for all our lives.

We just hadn't understood it until now.

Until this moment.

Until we finally broke through the walls between us and embraced what could be.

Our relationship is Divine, I marveled, only partially aware that Ezra had rolled me to my back again. He was still inside me, his movements slower now. *Worshipping.*

Worshipping, he echoed, his mind somehow linked to mine.

I didn't fight it or him.

I merely wrapped my arms around his neck and kissed him. *Make me see stars, mate.*

He smiled against my mouth. *Mmm, prepared to be blinded, little heiress.*

His cock angled inside me, brushing that place so deep and powerful that I couldn't help moaning against his mouth.

And then he took me beyond the stars.

To the brightest sun.

In a galaxy of our own existence.

A place where our souls thrived.

A euphoric world of fire and ice. Our balance. Our universe. Our very own *Divinity.*

EZRA

KAYLA SLEPT PEACEFULLY IN MY BED, HER REDDISH-brown hair sprawled across the pillows in a silky wave I longed to stroke.

But I didn't want to disturb her.

She'd exerted a lot of energy today, and she needed this time to heal.

It hurt to leave her, my soul irritated by the notion of parting ways after joining so completely. However, I needed to see Raphaela about this cuff. And I wanted to talk to Mietek as well.

I bent to press a kiss to Kayla's forehead. "Rest," I whispered. "I'll be right back."

She didn't respond or even flinch, too lost in her dreams to surface.

It would be so easy to tap into her mind, to find out if she dreamt of me at all, but I didn't want to intrude.

Instead, I used my wings to silently propel me from the room and off the balcony.

I soared over the vibrant green landscape, heading toward the heart of the city, only to frown at the various creatures lying dead along the way.

Vultures, I recognized. They were birdlike demons and a royal pain in the ass to kill. The bastards shot venom from their beaks and possessed wings as large as my own.

Fortunately, these were all dead.

But I had no idea they could leave the underworld.

The same could be said about the dead Cyclops near the city gates.

And the multitude of slain demons on the streets inside.

"Fuck," I breathed, shocked by the display of mayhem taunting the otherwise peaceful landscape.

There didn't appear to be any fallen angels among them, just annihilated demon minions.

Which meant no one had brought a holy blade with them to this fight.

And there weren't any shadow beings called into existence here, either.

"Ezra," Zerak greeted as he met me in the sky.

I'd been so focused on the sights that I hadn't noticed his ascent. "This is madness."

"Indeed," he agreed. "But we are back to just over one human year before the balance is at risk again."

I frowned at him. "Back to a little more than a human year?" I'd lost track of time and years after the last however many days or weeks. It was impossible to keep up with the constant shifting in the balance.

"Your union with Kayla gave us more time." He uttered the words without emotion, his silver-gray features giving nothing away. "Unfortunately, it's not enough to stop the inevitable. But it just may save us."

"You're starting to sound like Fate," I muttered.

He blinked. "I don't work with prophecies, Ezra." With that flat statement, he took his leave, not even bothering with a formal goodbye.

Sighing, I continued onward to Raphaela's home near the center of the city.

I landed on her balcony, my wings ruffling in an angelic version of a knock.

No one replied.

I poked my head inside to find her rooms vacant.

Given the destruction to the city, it was likely because she'd left to heal someone.

I took to the sky again and flew a few streets over to Mietek's estate. It was larger than Raphaela's, his home reminding me more of Zebulon's mansion.

Most Archangels maintained similar estates to demonstrate their power. Mine just happened to reside between the realms.

Well, it used to, anyway.

Kayla and I would rebuild it together. Assuming she agreed to reside with me rather than return to Hell.

It was a conversation we would be having soon. Because I intended to follow her wherever she chose to go.

For better or for worse.

You're mine, little heiress.

I landed near the patio entry to Mietek's office. He wasn't inside, but a soft hum of fluttering feathers above told me where to go.

A boost of my wings took me to the third-floor balcony and to the library full of angels.

Raziel.

Azrael.

Raphaela.

Fate.

And Mietek.

"Looks like I'm late for a meeting," I said, entering the room. It was similar to the group that had arrived after Kristina's death, only Raphaela and Fate had replaced Scion and Dariel.

Well, that and Zerak was missing.

However, he only attended when he had something wise to say. Considering he'd just given me the latest countdown report, he likely didn't have any pertinent information to share with the group.

But I figured I'd start there.

"Zerak says we have just over a human year." Which meant we were down to one Heaven day. As such, we couldn't afford to waste seconds with formalities or reviewing obvious facts. So I held up the cuff instead. "Who took this off of Kayla?"

Everyone glanced at each other in confusion.

"It fell off of her upon arrival," Raphaela said, her golden hair shining like a halo as she stood next to Mietek. He was seated in a chair, his expression more exhausted than I'd ever seen it. And from the way her palm rested on his shoulder, I suspected she was healing him.

Given the wariness in her gray eyes, it likely wasn't helping much. Not even Azrael's presence appeared to be bolstering her now.

"Who exactly touched the cuff?" I asked, studying them all intently.

But no one exuded signs of guilt. If anything, they all appeared confused by my questions.

"Only me." Mietek's gruff tone only added to the exhaustion emanating from his midnight gaze. "I folded all your clothing as Rafa handed them to me. Then I set the cuff on top. Why?"

"It's been tampered with and impacted my mate's powers when we faced the beings possessing Kristina's energy." I spun the cuff around my finger, causing the magic embedded in it to glow via the silver runes. "Kayla uses this to siphon her strengths. Instead, it throttled her abilities and absorbed her essence when she tried to release her gifts."

I'd been able to feel that impact when she'd handed me the cuff in the human realm.

The moment my fingertips had touched the metal, it was as though a bolt of electricity had pierced my soul.

"Someone with knowledge of the cuff tampered with it. And the only time she took it off was when we were here." In other words, someone in Heaven had fucked with my mate.

Not only was that an indirect attack against me, but it also implied someone in Heaven was working against the balance.

"Additionally," I continued, "the four beings in the human realm who created the portal that granted Hell direct access to Heaven wore similar cuffs that allowed them to portal at will. I strongly suspect those cuffs are hiding their true auras as well."

Mietek's eyebrows rose. "They were on Earth?"

"Yes."

Azrael and Mietek shared a look. Raziel didn't move, but his gaze narrowed—the only tell that what I'd said surprised him. As the Archangel of Secrets, it wasn't typical for him to be on the outside of something so clandestine.

About the only one in the room who didn't appear fazed at all was Fate.

Which made sense since she had probably foreseen the entire event.

"They used Kristina's power to create a barrier similar to veil energy, then they unleashed an inferno on us that nearly drained my mate of power because of her faulty cuff, and then they called a shadow being into the human realm." The summary of events possessed the desired impact—*shock*. "So you can see why I'm here."

Mietek held out his hand. "May I see it?"

I strode over and placed it in his palm.

He jolted at the bolt of electricity it delivered, his dark eyes narrowing. "Thanks for the warning."

"I already explained what it did," I drawled. "But at least now you can feel how powerful my mate has become."

Mietek gave me a dry look. "We all felt your balance, yes."

Raziel smirked at that.

I did not. "You were the one who told me to use her, Mietek."

"And I think we can agree that you did a hell of a lot more than that," he returned, his focus falling to the cuff.

That comment didn't deserve a response.

Because obviously it was a hell of a lot more.

I folded my arms as I waited for his assessment. Rather than provide one, he handed the item to Azrael. He didn't react to the vibration of power, instead choosing to pass it on to Raphaela.

She sighed as she took the metal into her hand, her pupils flaring to overtake her light irises. Her lips flattened as she tossed the cuff away. "Damning energy." She shuddered, her eyes falling closed. "That's the opposite of healing."

Azrael stroked the edge of her wing, his opposite arm going around her waist to pull her back against him. She trembled once more, her eyes falling closed as she allowed their bond to heal her.

That's what I want with Kayla, I thought. *That innate trust that I'll be there when she needs to fall.*

We'd taken a major step forward overnight, our bodies joining in a beautiful balance of power and divine energy. But I wanted more.

I wanted to restore her faith in me.

And I would spend eternity trying to achieve that.

"Who had access to my quarters?" I asked, shelving my thoughts and desires for another day. Right now, I wanted answers about who had tried to harm my mate.

"I don't think anyone here did that," Raphaela whispered, her eyes still closed. "I think coming here triggered a fail-safe."

My brow crinkled. "What?"

"It didn't radiate that negative energy when it fell from her wrist," she continued as though I hadn't spoken. "Mietek would have sensed it, too."

He nodded. "Yes, and I didn't."

"The initial trigger caused it to fall from her wrist. When she fastened it once more, the negative pull began." Raphaela's irises were still thin as she reopened her eyes, her pupils black pools of vacant energy. "Who gave her that cuff?"

My jaw clenched. "The Head of her Royal Guard."

Mietek's dark brow met his hairline. "I think you should have a word with him."

"I will." But I also wasn't discounting the possibility that someone here altered that cuff.

While the portal might have been open on Earth, it had reached both realms, suggesting there could have been someone on either side of it functioning as a proxy to anchor the magic.

In theory, that should have been required.

However, nothing was working as expected.

"You saw Johanna and Bael through the portal?" I asked, uncertain of all the events that had occurred here.

Mietek nodded, then quickly brought me up to speed about the influx of demons from Bael's realm that had spilled into the heavens. Apparently, Xai had handled the majority of the Vultures—a fact that didn't surprise me—and he'd ordered everyone to take sentry shifts in three-hour intervals to keep watch while the ancients recovered.

Pride colored Mietek's tones, and it was an emotion brightening Fate's features as well. Her opal feathers seemed to shimmer in response, but that was probably just the lighting.

"How's Evangeline?" I asked.

"Awake," Raphaela confirmed softly. "She's going to be fine."

"Good."

"Did you handle the shadow creature on Earth?" Mietek asked.

Normally, I would give him a look and the retort that kind

of inquiry deserved. But given what I'd told him about the cuff and the impact on Kayla's powers, it seemed a fair question to voice. "Yes."

He dipped his chin. "And the four with the cuffs?"

"Disappeared without a trace. I was only able to track them because they used Kristina's gifts," I explained. "Which means I'll be able to do it again when they make their next move." Zerak's warning seemed to suggest that would be within the next twenty-four Heaven hours or so.

I ran my palm over my face.

There was only one move for us to make.

"We'll talk to Yaz." If he wasn't the one who'd tainted the cuff, then he would have no problem telling Kayla and me who'd made it so we could question that individual.

Or perhaps we would play it from a different angle, monitor his movements, and see whom he spoke to.

He'd been on his way to warn Bael about the Dark Provenance being otherwise engaged.

Interesting timing, considering the portal had opened mere minutes after he'd left.

It also seemed rather beneficial on his part to be privy to all the discussions between Zebulon and Ashmedai, under the guise of reporting to Bael.

Perhaps I would check the accuracy of that account with Bael first and go from there.

Regardless, it gave us a lead to—

A jolt sliced through my heart, nearly buckling my knees as it stole the air from my lungs.

"Ezra?" Raphaela said, her voice sounding distant in my ears as the world began to spin around me.

Something was wrong.

An imbalance.

But it's not time yet.

Zerak said we have another human year. That should give us twenty-four Heaven hours.

I clutched my chest, the ache growing by the second, scattering goose bumps down my arms. *What's happening?*

I felt panicked. On edge. *Lost.*

And very, *very* angry.

My lips curled down. *How...?*

Every part of me boiled with that fury, my veins lighting up with a fire that wasn't my own.

My eyes widened. *Kayla.*

I didn't bother saying goodbye to the others, my need to reach my mate overriding every instinct I possessed. Something was very wrong. She needed me. And she needed me now.

My wings beat harshly at my back as I soared through the pure blue skies toward my loft outside of the city.

Every part of me remained on high alert, searching for the culprit that dared touch my mate.

How stupid had I been?

I'd suspected someone had fucked with her cuff, and then I'd left her alone in my home. Alone in a tower with no way down unless the being possessed wings.

Of which Kayla did not.

It left her at a disadvantage, making it easy to harm her.

And without her cuff, all she had was her demonic traits— traits that would be weakened in this realm.

I pushed myself harder, my heart beating a chaotic rhythm in my chest. I should have known better. I hadn't thought this through. I'd meant to call upon the ones who could likely provide me with answers, and had left my mate vulnerable in my wake.

The balcony of my home came into view, but I didn't see anyone or anything lurking that might be attacking my mate. Yet I felt her mounting ire and fear and...

And sadness?

I touched my cheek to find myself weeping with her.

That ache I felt inside was emotional pain, the agony of having a heart shredded within my chest.

Has she been stabbed?

I landed on my balcony in a flurry of feathers, my swords in my hands as I stepped into my bedroom in search of the one harming my mate.

Only to find Kayla curled into a ball on the bed, her small frame shaking as though being pummeled by invisible forces.

I flew to her, my swords disappearing as I searched the bed with my hands for whatever plagued her.

Had some Orsini Devils snuck into Heaven?

No. I'd hear their chittering.

"Kayla?" I whispered, my hands going to her shoulder as I tried to pull her away from her knees.

She froze in response.

"What's hurting you?" I asked, my wing draping over her like a blanket as I settled into the bed beside her. "Tell me how to fix it."

I didn't like the helplessness I felt, the way her trembling form had made me feel.

When she didn't immediately respond, I broke the barrier between us to search her mind for the cause of her current state.

And felt my world come crashing down as her agony struck me squarely in the heart.

Me.

I did this.

It was written all over her thoughts, her anger at having put her faith in me just to be abandoned again.

He left. Of course he left. Why wouldn't he leave? Her residual thoughts lurked on the outskirts of her mind, all comments she'd been making to herself on repeat. *He always leaves. I was a fool. Again. I fell for his tricks. Again. Let him use me. Again. And now he's left me. Again. But in Heaven, without my cuff, and no way home.*

She'd been furious.

She'd been distraught.

She'd been shattered by the notion of abandonment.

And why wouldn't she feel that way? She'd woken up alone, the balance fully restored between our bond, and I hadn't been here to comfort her.

Rather than reply with words, I yanked her into my thoughts, showing her why I'd left and where I'd gone.

I recounted the conversation with Mietek and the others.

I showed her what they'd said about the cuff.

About Yaz.

She didn't immediately reply, nor did she move. She was barely even breathing.

Because she was questioning whether any of this was real. She was questioning her inner strength. She was questioning *us.*

I wrapped myself around her, ensuring she felt every inch of me. "I'm not going anywhere without you, Kayla," I promised her. And I forced her to see how much I meant it, showed her the truth of it in my mind and in my soul.

Our connection had deepened to impossible depths, granting her access to my very spirit.

Had she only thought to press on that link to find me, she would have known immediately where I'd gone. However, her instinct had been to think the worst.

I told her with my mind that I didn't blame her for that conclusion.

Just as I vowed to spend the rest of our lives together proving her wrong.

After what felt like hours, but was more realistically only a few minutes, she began to thaw. A shudder overtook her, then a tremble, and eventually she began to relax.

Only then did she roll to face me, her caramel-brown eyes displaying the very real pain my actions had caused her in this life.

My strong, beautiful Kayla had been deeply wounded by my actions.

Regret simmered inside me, followed by the righteousness that told me I couldn't have done this any other way.

Alas, there was a voice whispering in the back of my mind, humming *what-ifs,* that made me flinch.

I couldn't change the past. *What's done is done.* What I could do was change the future. What I could do was ensure my mate knew how I felt every day for the rest of our time.

We'd created a new form of Divinity together, our souls intertwined in a balance that could be felt through all the realms.

She was my other half. My partner.

Your queen, she whispered, making me frown.

Except an intangible chessboard appeared in her mind, one where she considered herself a pawn. Yet she was telling herself and me that she wanted to be my queen.

This isn't about chess, Kayla. I cupped her face. *We're not pieces on the board. We're the ones making the moves. The strategists watching the plays unfold. We're the reason the game can exist.*

I kissed her, telling her with my mouth all the words I wouldn't voice out loud.

But she could hear them in my mind, the pledges I made, the emotions I felt, the sadness inside at realizing how badly I'd wounded my mate.

Her energy might be healed. However, her heart remained bruised.

I added my own healing ointment to the injury as I made love to her with my tongue.

It wasn't sexual so much as intimate. This wasn't about pleasure or fucking. This was about us. About our future. About our bond.

By the time I pulled back, her irises appeared a little less chaotic, her mind slightly quieter, her heart beating once more.

It wasn't perfect.

But it was a start.

Because the thought she kept repeating to herself now was, *He didn't leave me. He's here.*

I pressed my forehead to hers. "I will always be with you, Kayla. Even if you run to Hell, I'll be there. Because I'm never letting you go again."

KAYLA

I STUDIED MYSELF IN THE MIRROR, NOTING THE increase of reddish hair mingling with my darker strands. It seemed even more vibrant now than it had the other day, similar to how the gold in my irises seemed to be flickering like miniature flames.

Yet my hands were pale.

And my horns were nowhere to be seen.

It would concern me if I didn't still sense the power rippling beneath my skin.

I opened my palm to create a fireball, the embers burning and sizzling with energy strong enough to take down a lower-level demon.

Ezra stepped into the bathroom behind me, his features unchanged. "Your hair is still white." It'd been dark with some silver in it when we'd first met. Now it was still mostly white.

Except for his eyebrows.

One of which he arched now, the darker color more prevalent than the white. "Do you not like my hair?"

"I'm just trying to figure out why I look different and you don't," I replied.

"Hmm." He moved behind me, his gaze holding mine in the mirror as he wrapped his arms around my waist.

My gaze went to the swirl of black ink decorating his left

arm. The design seemed to pulse with power. Or maybe that was the muscle beneath the obsidian tattoos.

"My power and looks have evolved for the last few decades," he continued, his eyes following mine to his tattoos. "However, those markings are ones I've had for thousands of years."

"Are they related to your power?"

He lifted a shoulder. "They arrived when I ascended into my role as Archangel of Justice, so I suppose they are. But I barely notice them."

I frowned. "My power changed when I grew horns—something I definitely noticed—and my hands started to char. But now I'm normal again."

His lips found the curve of my neck as he laid a kiss against my pulse, his gaze still holding mine in the mirror. "You were never normal, Kayla. You're the daughter of an Archdemon and the mate of an Archangel. That has created an incredible power within you, little heiress. Give it time to flourish."

"We don't have time."

He sighed, his chin going to my shoulder as he continued to stare into my eyes. "You're right. We don't. I propose we go to your father's realm first. I want to question him about Yaz."

"It's not Yaz, Ezra." I was sure of it. "I know he looks guilty because he gave me the cuff, but he would never try to hurt me like that."

"It's not just the cuff, Kayla. He was between the realms with us when the attack began, and he went back to Bael just before the latest attack—where the demons came from his realm to Heaven."

My jaw clenched. I knew it looked bad. But I also knew Yaz. "He's innocent, Ezra."

The Archangel studied me for a long moment, then gave a slight nod and brushed his lips against my pulse again. "Then we'll use this opportunity to prove his innocence."

"Just like that?"

"Just like that," he echoed, his hands going to my hips and giving them a subtle squeeze. "We're a team, Kayla. I trust your judgment." The truth of that statement flourished between us, his mind wide open to mine.

We'd created a new form of Divinity between us, a breed of energy that pulsated through our veins, cementing a new kind of balance.

Ezra's entire purpose in life was to protect the Divinity.

And now *we* were the Divinity.

"Will our future children be like Kristina and the others?" I wondered aloud, frowning as I considered that question more thoroughly. "Wait..." I pressed a palm to my stomach. "Is *that* the power we created? Did you use me—"

"Do not finish that statement," he interjected, his expression going from docile to thunderous in an instant. "I would *never* do that to you, Kayla." And he forced the truth on me through our open bond, his fury at the impending suggestion a whiplash against my senses.

I shivered and swallowed, my eyes falling closed. He grasped my chin and rotated me in his arms to face him. "I understand your innate need to distrust me. I've earned that. But you have full access to my soul, Kayla. *Use* it to see the truth."

He was right.

This knee-jerk reaction to distrust him was hampering my ability to *see* the truth, to believe it, to put my faith in him and in us.

However, we hadn't used protection.

And he'd had a penchant for using me in the past.

Replacing Kristina would be exactly what he needed to do to right the scales, and the best way to do that would be to mate with an Archdemon. I might be a Halfling, but I still possessed the powers required to be that other half for him.

I was also the only one he could be with because of our bond.

"Ezra..."

"Don't," he snapped, his grip on my jaw tightening as he wrapped his opposite arm around my waist. "I can hear what you're thinking, Kayla. And you're wrong."

His bare chest burned through my towel, his wings curling around us in a protective shield of black-brown feathers.

"You're also old enough to know how difficult it is to produce children, Kayla. There's a reason you are your father's only offspring. That's why I chose you in the beginning—because I knew he would never hurt you. And you would be the leverage I needed to save Johanna."

His grip tightened when I tried to look away, the memory of that event the reason I questioned his integrity even now.

"The power inside you is the energy formed by our bond. I meant what I told you—it's not about feeding off each other's auras or spirits. It's about creating a new state of existence. *Together*." He released my chin to palm the back of my neck. "And yes, our future heirs will be children of the Divinity. But that likely won't be for centuries to come."

I swallowed, the intensity of his stare burning a hole straight through my spirit. "I'm—"

"I don't want an apology," he interjected, clearly hearing the one forming in my thoughts. "I know I've hurt you, Kayla. Questioning me and my intentions is only natural. But I need you to be my partner right now." His hands shifted to cup either side of my face. "I need you to hear my mind and to try to believe in me, or we're not going to survive what's coming."

My throat worked as I tried to form the words he wanted to hear. I knew I was being stubborn and borderline petulant, but I'd spent thousands of years hating him.

He'd haunted my dreams and my nightmares. He'd been my primary motivator to wake up and fight every day. He'd been my sole focus, my end goal, the only one I'd ever truly cared about.

Killing him would have freed me from this bond.

Yet losing him now would kill me right along with him.

Accepting that hurt in a way I couldn't even begin to detail.

However, the pain in his eyes now told me he could feel that agony inside me, that it was a burden darkening our connection and piercing his heart just as much as it pierced mine.

I went to my toes and kissed him, needing to feel the rightness of our bond and not the dark past yanking me backward in time.

I wanted to join him in the now. To embrace our future. To believe in him. To be a partner. To be the counterbalance he needed to fight beside in this impending balance.

He wrapped his arms around me, lifting me into the air to sit on the counter. My legs parted for him, granting him closer access. But this wasn't about fucking. It was about healing. It was about *acceptance*.

His mind and soul were wide open for me, proving his intentions and allowing me to experience his emotions as though they were my own.

Regret.
Sadness.
Hope.
Adoration.
Respect.
Love.

I shivered at the last one, the sensation one I immediately wanted to distrust. But our link refused to allow my instincts to shine.

Because it was right there.

Tangible.

Mine.

His heart beat for me. His focus in the world had become me. *We* were the Divinity—*his* Divinity. And he would do everything in his power to protect us.

Even if that meant leaving me behind to face this battle alone.

He wouldn't take me with him unless we could be a true team. He wouldn't risk my life in that way. He'd sacrifice his own instead.

The old me would have embraced that, would have sent him off to die knowing I'd played him at his own game.

But this was no longer a game.

This was *us.*

A fresh balance of power where age no longer mattered and experience ceased to exist.

We were a new dynamic full of intense energy and the ability to make everything right between us. We weren't replacing Kristina or her abilities. We weren't replacing Johanna or Lucía either.

This wasn't about rebuilding a broken network. This was about defining a novel state of being.

His forehead met mine, his breath a pant against my lips as though he'd just finished running a marathon. Our kiss was so much deeper than a natural embrace—it was *life.*

I met his burning gaze.

Stared deep into those beautiful irises of brown and gold, the edges burnt from his near death.

And I felt a profound need to give him everything. All of me. Every heartbeat. Every ounce of trust. A true second chance.

He'd already stated his intentions to chase me, even into Hell.

I believed him.

Because if he ran up to Heaven to hide from me, I'd pursue him, too. Wings be damned.

"Maybe you'll grow a pair," he whispered, his lips curving up at the sides. "I hope they match your hair."

I snorted. "Or they'll look like my father's bat wings."

"Yes, that was a strange development," he replied, his brow furrowed. "We should go to him."

"We should," I agreed, my palm pressing against his chest. "I just need some clothes."

He hummed in agreement and pulled me off the counter before guiding me back into the bedroom with his hands on my hips.

"I'm perfectly capable of dressing myself," I informed him dryly.

"I know." He didn't stop moving me until we stood beside the bed. "But I have a present for you."

"I don't think we have time for presents right now, Ezra."

His lips quirked at the sides. "Not that kind of present, little heiress."

He spun me to face the mattress before I could reply, causing my lips to part at both the motion and the items waiting for me.

Clothes—jeans, a sweater, socks, and a pair of boots. That didn't necessarily impress me, but I appreciated him finding me something to wear.

However, it was the item beside them that had my hands reaching forward with excitement. "A sword."

"A temporary one," he clarified. "I'm giving you one of mine until I can make you a proper one." He pressed his lips to my temple. "Test the weight of it and see how it feels. If it's too heavy, then I'll conjure some daggers instead."

"How do you conjure them?" I asked as I lifted the weapon to examine the handle and the overall feel of the sword.

"It's part of my natural gifts, which means you may one day be able to conjure your own weapons. It's a protection ability tied to delivering justice." His fingers trailed down my arm, his energy humming across my skin. "But it's not something I can do with immediate results. It takes finesse to create the right tool. And unfortunately, I think this one isn't suited to your frame."

Considering how heavy it felt in my hand, I agreed with a nod.

The instrument disappeared, returning to wherever he hid his swords. He held his palm up beside me, calling forth a dagger that glittered with power.

My eyebrows lifted. "Is that a holy blade?"

"No, but it's close. If you stab me with it, I won't be pleased." With those lingering words against my ear, he held it out for me to take from him.

I gripped it, then sliced it through the air before opening my hand and feeling the balance of it against my skin. It buzzed with magic that called to my soul, the rightness of the tool making me grin.

"That's better," he said, obviously feeling my contentment. "But I owe you a sword."

"You owe me an armory," I corrected. "Like the one in your library."

He chuckled, his chest leaving my back as he went into a closet just off the bedroom.

I took that as a cue to get dressed and did. He returned in a black sweater that matched my own and a pair of sturdy boots that should have echoed loudly against the marble floor yet didn't make a sound as he walked toward me.

His wings were tucked up off the ground as well, giving him an assassin-like appeal that had my insides humming in immediate approval. The way he ran his gaze over me said the feeling was mutual, but his expression held a severity to it that defined the moment.

We had work to do.

Starting with a visit to my father.

Then a conversation with Yaz regarding the cuffs.

He handed me a sheath for my dagger, which I attached to my waist. My flames would be my primary weapon, but the knife served as a good backup in case my powers started to weaken again.

"Ready?" he asked, holding out his palm.

I wrapped my arms around his neck instead, pressing my body to his. "Take me on a journey, Archangel."

One of his hands went to my lower back while the opposite grasped my nape. "Our new bond is a journey, little heiress."

The wind whirled around us before I could reply, his power washing over us as he triggered our descent.

I rested my head against his chest, sighing at the rightness of his touch.

Until it began to change.

What started as a pleasant warmth grew hot, singeing my senses and blackening my vision.

In the next breath, ice frosted my lungs, freezing me from the inside out.

Kayla!

I tried to reply, but my mind shut down, my limbs turning to string as the world whirled around me in chaos.

Down. Down. Down.

Wind rippled through my hair, my stomach twisting from the sensation of falling.

So. Hot.

No, icy. Cold. Frigid snow.

Floating.

Falling.

Down. Down. Down.

My eyes refused to open, my body weighed down by a power I couldn't seem to fight. It wrapped around me, swathing me in a dark cloak of death.

It reminded me of thick mud, drowning me, suffocating my lungs, and yanking me deeper and deeper into the abyss.

Flames erupted across my skin, drawing a silent scream from my throat.

My spirit battled.

My senses flared to life.

However, they only lasted a second before another blanket of black energy enveloped my being. I attempted to squirm, to move, to break free of the tangled web, but my body wouldn't listen.

I felt controlled.

Overpowered.

Drained.

What the hell is happening to me? I searched futilely for the source, the dizziness making it difficult to focus.

Then a tug on my consciousness sent me spinning in a new direction. *Ezra.* I swam toward him, searching for his presence. *Our link.*

I grabbed onto the bond and yanked myself through time and space, my soul weeping at the loss of our connection.

Imbalance, I realized after a beat. *The battle has started.*

We'd lost time.

Somewhere along the way, the inevitable had shifted. And my soul was being ripped apart in the process.

Except, no. I wasn't alone. I felt Ezra's energy searching for mine, his power a blade that lashed at my senses, demanding I pay attention.

I reached for him.

And everything stilled.

The sensation of falling. The pain in my abdomen. The dizziness in my mind.

Gone.

For a blink in time.

Until an explosion erupted and sent me spiraling again. Only this time, I could see. *Earth. Sky. Clouds. Wings.*

Ezra's arms locked around me in the next breath, his rage at whatever had just occurred washing over me in a blaze of furious energy. "*Shadows,*" he hissed.

I blurrily glanced over his shoulder to see the Shadow demons in question. My brow furrowed. "How?"

But he didn't answer. Probably because he couldn't hear me over the roar of the wind.

I felt weak. Depleted. On the verge of death.

Ezra pressed my lips to his neck, and I bit down on instinct, taking the energy I needed to regain my focus and strength. Something had interrupted our descent. *Shadows.*

But that wasn't possible.

Unless Ezra had teleported us directly into a trap.

How? I marveled, dizzy from the sensation of tumbling through the sky. Ezra's arms were bands beneath my back and legs, cradling me against his chest. I could barely lift my hand to touch him.

Black, I thought, frowning at my skin. *My hand is black again.*

I shuddered, trying to pull more power into me, but the Shadow demons had sucked the life out of my veins, leaving me a shell of a being no stronger than a human.

My brow furrowed, some link flaring in my mind between the sensation of now and the one I'd felt when battling the inferno.

A connection that had me glancing back up at the Shadow demons chasing us.

The cuff fed off my energy like a Shadow demon, I thought.

Ezra. I think whoever is doing this is siphoning energy from Shadow demons.

Which would also explain why Evangeline had been left in the Shadow realm.

Ezra's feet touched the ground, where he set me down, his wings flaring as he turned to face the demons coming straight for us. He didn't hesitate, his swords appearing as he created a blinding light that cascaded around us like a circular shield.

I closed my eyes, the brightness making me whimper.

An explosion of power followed, the heat of it a welcome impact against my chilled skin.

I shuddered at the impact, my limbs still weak from their assault. However, a hum of energy began to trickle through my veins. It came from Ezra's blood but morphed inside me into an inferno of power that chased the darkness from my limbs.

Ezra knelt beside me what felt like hours later, but was more likely only minutes, his hands running over me. "The veil is falling, Kayla. We need to move. Right fucking now."

EZRA

A trap.

That was the only explanation for that fuckup of a descent.

And there were very few beings in the realms who could pull off a stunt like that.

Not the assholes with the cuffs, but whomever they worked for. Unfortunately, we didn't have time to question Yaz about the origin. I wasn't even sure he'd be of much use to us now anyway.

Because whoever we were up against possessed an insane amount of power.

Power that rivaled my own.

I didn't want to assume an Archangel was involved, but a new theory grew in my mind that supported that suspicion.

Maybe my original notion that someone had tampered with Kayla's cuff in Heaven was correct. But they hadn't just set it up to harm her—they'd mimicked the power to create more like it for their minions.

What if that had been the true purpose of the attack on my home? A way to force me to ascend with Kayla at my side, thus making her vulnerable.

Raphaela had claimed Kayla's cuff had just fallen off.

What if it hadn't?

What if someone had somehow manipulated it into dropping?

Kayla had been too consumed by me to notice. She'd gone days without her cuff.

Who knew what had really occurred while we'd slept? We hadn't been all that more aware during our intimate session afterward, either.

But we should still have more time now—at least a few human months, by my count. Yet I could feel the veil shattering.

Had we somehow lost time? Was the fluctuation due to Kayla's injury?

Or had the Archangel of Time misspoken?

A ripple of energy thundered across the earth as power shifted into chaos.

My head spun with the wrongness of it all, the scales no longer able to maintain any semblance of balance. Kayla was my anchor, the center of my existence. And she was barely able to stand.

Those fucking shadows had sucked the life out of her.

I still didn't understand how that was even possible. And it was making me hesitant to try to teleport again now. But there was no other option. Kayla didn't have her cuff, and the breach in the veil was nowhere near our current location.

This had clearly been meant as a distraction, a way to deviate us from our course.

So did that mean they didn't want us to go to Hell?

Or were they merely anticipating our descension in general?

"Ezra," Kayla said, grabbing my wrist. "I trust you."

I blinked down at her.

"I trust you to teleport us again," she clarified. "I trust you to protect us. And I trust you to right the scales. Let's go."

"It may be another trap," I warned her.

"I know. And if it is, we'll be ready this time." She shivered as she spoke the words, making me question her readiness to fight.

But we didn't have a choice.

The energy wavering around us was going to rip this plane apart if we didn't stop whoever was behind this attack against the balance.

Swallowing, I nodded. "All right." I wrapped my arms around her as tightly as possible, then engaged my ability to transport us through time and space.

She clung to me just as harshly, her lips against my neck, preparing to bite if needed. Or maybe she just felt safest there.

I resisted the urge to bury my nose in her hair and kept my mind alert for potential interference. But all I sensed was the unease rippling from the breach in the veil.

It reminded me of the night Kayla had used that device on the sky, only tens of thousands of times worse. Her antics had created a small crack, whereas what I sensed now was a complete dismantling of the magical wall that protected the human world.

My wings took us to the same area outside of Vancouver where we'd found Kristina's body.

That both surprised me and didn't surprise me. Vancouver was a large enough city where a fallout of this magnitude could be a benefit.

But it also felt too predictable at the same time.

However, predictability no longer mattered in this situation, not with my powers allowing me to sense sources of imbalance. The culprits would have anticipated my arrival regardless, which made their choice of venue moot in the grand scheme of things.

A similar invisible barrier met our arrival, the power irritating my senses.

"Slice it," Kayla said as she released me. Then she crouched on the ground with a shudder as she continued to try to regain her strength. It was returning, just slowly.

"Bite me again if you need to," I told her as I called my swords to me.

I slammed the metallic edges against the shield and growled when the energy pulsated back into my hands and arms.

"I'll be okay." Her voice lacked the assurance I heard in her mind. She wanted to appear weak, to lull the opposition into a false sense of confidence.

Clever, I mused. *It may just coax them into coming out to play.* Because right now, I couldn't see them. There were too many trees. But I felt them nearby, and I could see the swirling black hole in the sky that they'd created. It was silent to me beyond the barrier, but I imagined it was quite loud on the other side.

And it was growing at an alarming rate, the inky abyss swallowing everything around it.

Similar to Shadow magic, Kayla told me. *Just like my cuff.*

I nodded. *Someone is using the Succubus-like energy of that realm to disable the balance.*

That wasn't one of Kristina's gifts, right? she asked, her head bowing in a demonstration of exhaustion. It was a lie. I could feel the power thrumming through her being, her Archdemon heritage rising to the surface and preparing for the fight of her life.

No, I replied as that familiar energy hummed through my sword. *She had no control over shadows or darkness, just the mixture of light and dark within her.*

Is it possible that it manifested differently when—

"Kayla!" Yaz's familiar voice traveled between the trees as he darted toward her. "Shit." He fell to his knees beside her.

I frowned. "How the fuck did you get here?" Royal

Guards couldn't teleport. And I didn't sense anyone else with him.

In fact, I didn't sense *him* at all.

He ignored me, his focus on Kayla. "Are you all right?"

"I was attacked by a Shadow demon." Her voice still held that same note of exhaustion, just as her posture appeared broken as well. It was a continued charade for the beings protected by this barrier, but also one for Yaz.

Because she'd noticed the same things I had about his sudden arrival.

Ezra. Her mental voice resembled a whisper as though she feared Yaz would hear her. *He's wearing a cuff.*

"Shit," Yaz repeated. "I need to call Serena for backup."

He started to move back, but Kayla caught him by the arm. "Yaz."

He startled, his shaggy brown hair falling into his eyes. "Princess?"

"Where did you get that cuff?" she asked slowly, her mind telling me she was preparing herself for a fight. She was almost back at full strength but had mastered the art of appearing wounded.

The Royal Guard's lips curled down. "It's from the same place as yours." A pause followed. "Wait, what happened to yours? You never take it off... That's why I couldn't track you."

"You use my cuff to track me?"

"Of course," he replied. "Guarding you is my primary responsibility. I always follow you."

"Even to Heaven?" I asked flatly.

"Well, no. I can't ascend. Just like Kayla can't." His blue-brown eyes flicked up to me before settling back on her. "What's this abo—"

An explosion interrupted him midsentence, causing the ground to shake around us as a portal opened right behind us.

Demonic screams followed as a horde of hellish creatures poured out of the hole into the realm.

With Morax at the helm.

My eyebrows rose, my swords sizzling with warning beneath my palms. I'd finally cut through the first layer of the barrier.

But I was about to need my weapons for an entirely new purpose.

"You're behind this?" I asked, both stunned and infuriated. "*You* siphoned off your daughter's power?"

"No," another voice said from above, a glint of silver shining brightly in the sun and momentarily blinding me as I tried to find the familiar voice. "He merely helped."

Zerak.

A fiery shield blocked my vision as Kayla's power ignited around us in a protective bubble.

Power slammed into it not a second later, her energy capturing and holding the assault and keeping us alive beneath her blistering inferno.

"*That* is useful," I said, recalling her previous comments about my swords.

She grunted in response. "I can't hold this for long. Not against an Archangel and an Archdemon."

"Serena's coming with backup," Yaz replied, his fingers drawing various runes over his cuff.

Kayla's fire had protected him as well, the reaction one born of instinct. Because she trusted him. Despite seeing his cuff and finding out he'd been tracking her, she still had faith in his innocence.

And given his behavior now, I was inclined to follow her lead with him.

Because either he was a brilliant actor playing the long game, or he truly cared about her.

I pulled my swords in, my wings tucked tight to my back.

Kayla's mind told me we didn't have long before her shield failed.

Another blast hit us from the top, followed by one from the side.

You take Zerak. I'll handle Prince Morax, Kayla suggested.

I shook my head. "That portal is going to be a problem." Via our mental connection, I suggested a different plan. *Have Yaz portal you out. I'll draw Morax and Zerak up into the sky. Then you portal back in and take out that portal.*

How are you going to take on Zerak and Morax without holy blades?

By playing with my swords, I answered simply. *I don't need to kill them, just incapacitate them long enough to detain them.* Which would require a few more Archangels and Archdemons to show up to this fight.

An influx of power through battle would create the beacon required to draw them out.

Assuming they weren't busy engaging in similar battles in the other realms.

I don't like this, she said, her mental voice tired. *But I don't have a better idea.* Her irises resembled liquid gold as she stared me down. *Do not fucking die, Archangel. You're still mine to kill.*

I wouldn't dream of cheating on you, little heiress. My death is forever yours. A fucked-up declaration of love.

But it was one that resulted in her lips twitching subtly because she understood the vow I'd just made to her.

A similar one whispered back to me from her mind, a promise to trust me to survive.

On the count of three, Archangel, she whispered. *Three. Two...*

"Get me out of here, Yaz," she said on the "one" count, her shield disappearing.

I shot up into the sky, my wings leaving a flurry of furious wind in my wake.

And then I caught Zerak's angelfire with my sword.

His expression gave nothing away, his gray skin shimmering with silver glitter beneath the sun. It would make him easy to track in the sky but difficult to focus on at the same time.

However, I didn't need to be able to see the minute details within his features to fight him.

Except he wasn't alone up here, something that registered nearly too late as I ducked another fiery assault.

A being blended into the sky, his wings and hair and skin a light blue.

I narrowed my gaze. "*Raziel*."

The Archangel of Secrets did a little bow. "My brother sends his regards."

Fuck. "How many of you are in favor of destroying the balance?" I demanded. "Do you realize what will happen to this plane when the veil falls?"

"It was always inevitable," Zerak replied, his tone as stoic as ever. "We merely chose a side."

"And unfortunately, it's one you can't join," Raziel added. "It's a bit contradictory to your role. Not to mention your newly established Divinity. So we don't really have a choice but to destroy you."

I wanted to ask them who had led the assault on me between the realms, but Zerak was clearly done speaking. He threw another ball of angelfire at me with Raziel's final word, and then the two of them started chasing me through the sky.

Morax didn't join us.

Kayla?

I'm fine, she snarled. *Focus on those traitors and kill them. I've got this.*

I nearly smiled, her ferocity provoking me into action.

She didn't need my protection.

She was my mate. My partner. My *queen.*

Together we were the new Divinity.

And we would not fall.

"You chose the wrong side," I told Zerak and Raziel as my swords caught both of their balls of angelfire at the same time.

Then I created one of my own with the aid of my weapons and the power thriving inside me. Only to feel the presence of another Archangel arriving in a flurry of blood-red wings.

Scion.

"Indeed," the Archangel of War said, agreeing with my statement about choosing the wrong side. He twirled his swords, his energy signature rivaling mine. "Check."

Azrael appeared on my other side. "Make that 'checkmate.'"

I smiled and unleashed my angelfire, casting the first move.

And the real dance began.

KAYLA

A Few Minutes Earlier

"Get me out of here, Yaz."

My Royal Guard didn't hesitate, his hand grabbing my wrist as he portaled us away from the fight.

But we didn't go far.

Maybe a mile or two away.

Because he knew me well.

I would never leave a man behind to fight on his own. Even one I'd proclaimed to hate for most of my life.

Nor would I abandon the veil during such a dire time of need.

A spark of light shot through the sky, confirming our close proximity to the fight unfolding above. Vibrations of power followed the flash, the trees around us quaking from the impact.

And another jolt hit the earth, the portal nearby expanding to allow more demons to enter this realm. I hadn't gotten a close look at them but suspected there were Portal Dwellers among them. They would be venturing to other areas of the world soon, stirring chaos and mayhem in their wake.

"We need to hurry," I said, goose bumps pebbling across my skin. "That portal needs to be destroyed."

"Yes," Yaz agreed, his focus on his cuff. "Serena will be here soon. She's having to use a Portal Dweller." He skimmed his thumb along a rune and frowned. "There are three illegal portals open in the underworld right now. One is in Morax's realm—which we already know about, obviously. Another is in Alastor's realm. And the third is in our home realm."

"Johanna and Prince Bael have it under control," Serena said as she materialized before us with Jinx.

The Portal Dweller immediately blinked out of view, likely headed back to gather more of my guard.

"It's a minor breach that Prince Bael states is meant to distract him from the real problem," Serena continued in her usual robotic tone. "He suspects the portal in Alastor's realm is a similar diversion, as Xai and Evangeline were headed there earlier today. In Hell time, I mean."

Yaz nodded, his fingers still moving over the cuff. "Sounds right."

"Where did you get our cuffs?" I asked. He hadn't properly answered my question the first time, and I wanted a response now.

Yaz glanced at my bare wrists before meeting my gaze. "Why?"

"Because mine started sucking energy out of me like a fucking Shadow demon. So I want to know where they came from."

"Divine power," a deep voice announced from my left as a pair of blood-red wings fluttered into view. "But we can discuss it more after I save Ezra's ass."

The Archangel of War snapped his fingers as a horde of Nephilim appeared in his wake, all of them wearing golden cuffs.

Gleason stood in the center, a long sword in his hands. "Go. I can lead," he said to Scion.

Or I thought he was talking to Scion until Azrael materialized beside Gleason and replied, "I know."

"Ready?" Scion asked, his gaze on Azrael as another fiery jolt of energy sliced through the sky.

Azrael glanced up warily. "Not really, no. Zerak?"

"So it seems," Scion sighed. "Raziel, too."

Azrael shook his head. "We can't kill them."

"I know."

Azrael nodded, his gaze finding mine. "Don't kill Morax."

My eyebrows rose. "Excuse me?"

"We need them all alive to understand their intentions."

I pointed toward the fracture I felt ripping through the veil. "I think they've made their intentions pretty fucking clear."

As though to punctuate my point, two more flames shot through the sky. Then one giant blast followed.

"We need to question them," Azrael stressed.

I snorted. *Bullshit.*

Handicaps and rules were not my style.

And I did not answer to the Angel of Death.

Kayla? Ezra asked, likely feeling my unease.

I'm fine, I snarled. *Focus on those traitors and kill them. I've got this.*

Whatever *this* was. But he needed to focus on the assholes in the sky, not on me.

Ezra's pride and amusement rolled over me, and then he was gone again.

Another explosion sounded, causing Scion's feathers to ruffle. "That's our cue, Death." A sword appeared in his hand, reminding me a bit of Ezra, and he took off into the sky.

Azrael gave me a warning look, then glanced at Gleason. "Good luck." I wasn't sure if that was in reference to the pending fight or to me, but the Angel of Death disappeared before I could comment.

Whatever.

I didn't bow to him or to the Nephilim before me. He could lead his people, but I was the superior in terms of hierarchy.

"We need to take out the portal," I said, my focus on Gleason so he understood I wouldn't be taking orders from him or the angels he reported to. "And be careful with those cuffs. Mine turned against me."

"But you've had that for millennia," Yaz said, his brow furrowing. "At least in Hell years. I gave it to you when you first grew your horns."

"I know."

"So why did it turn against you now and not before?" he asked.

"We don't have time to discuss this," Gleason interjected as two more of my Royal Guard members arrived via Jinx. "Where's the portal?"

"About a mile north," Yaz said.

I shelved my questions about the cuff and focused on the problem at hand, discussing strategy with Gleason.

He had a team of eight Nephilim.

I had a team of seven Royal Guards and a Portal Dweller.

"Can you portal through the barrier beyond the portal?" I asked Jinx.

"Not sure." He disappeared, presumably to find out.

We needed to stop the beings on the other side of it, destroy the portal, and take down anyone who stood in our way—*including Prince Morax*—by any means necessary. He was a powerful Archdemon. If that meant I had to kill him, I would.

Jinx returned with a frazzled expression, his dark hair standing on end. "No," he wheezed, telling me with his appearance and his pained voice that he couldn't break through the veil magic.

Ezra, I'm going to need your sword to break the veil-like barrier.

Use the dagger, he replied. *It has the same magic.*

How do I ignite it?

Just touch it to the barrier. It'll ignite on its own. His mental voice sounded ragged, yet strength radiated from his spirit to mine.

I couldn't see what was happening, apart from the vibrant clashes of magic in the air. And I felt his fury at the events occurring in the sky.

We need to move, I thought, a chill sweeping down my spine. The longer we stayed here, the more demons would come through that portal.

"Revised plan," I said, glancing at Jinx's battered form before directing my attention to Gleason once more. "Your team can focus on the creatures coming up from Hell. My team will help but will also provide a protective shield around me so I can take down the barrier."

Gleason nodded. "Agreed."

"But be prepared. Those beings inside the barrier are powerful, and we still don't know exactly what they are."

Another nod from the Nephilim. "Noted. Let's go."

The Dark Provenance members began to disappear with their cuffs, the magical sensation in their wake familiar.

"Can you teleport her?" Yaz asked Jinx.

The Portal Dweller dipped his chin, his face still pale. "Yeah."

"Then I'll take Serena and Baxton." Yaz grabbed them both before anyone could speak, the three of them winking out of existence in the next blink.

Jinx blew out a breath and held his hand out for mine.

"Make sure you just drop me off and come back here to take a break."

He shook his head ruefully, his mop of dark hair falling into his eyes. "Nah, I'll portal the others. Then we fight."

I almost argued with him, but he was already moving through time and space to take me to the middle of the war zone.

Yaz, Serena, and Baxton immediately surrounded me, their hands resembling weapons as they shot hellfire from their fingertips at the approaching demons.

Prince Morax stood several yards away, his giant black wings blocking my view as he faced off with some Nephilim. I searched for Gleason and didn't see him.

Which told me he'd likely taken on the Prince of Hell.

I muttered a curse but focused on my task.

If he could stay alive long enough to distract the Archdemon, then I could successfully do my part.

I pulled the dagger from my sheath and stabbed the invisible veil-like wall.

Energy hummed across my hand, the runes in the metal flaring to life like my cuff usually did, only the magic in this was different. It pulsated and swirled, learning the enchantment of the barricade and unraveling it piece by piece.

Movement on the other side caught my focus as the bitch with the spiky black hair appeared. She'd been the one to call that shadow creature last time, and I suspected by the smirk on her face, she'd called the ones that had attacked me today, too.

I'm killing you first, I decided.

So you've promised, Ezra returned shortly.

Not you. The spiky-haired, bitch-faced cunt on the other side of the barrier.

Makes me wonder what kind of nicknames you've given me in the past, he drawled.

Right now? Funny Guy with a Death Wish sounds good.

Cute.

I know.

Don't die.

Likewise, I replied as thunder erupted from the clouds. *Ezra?*

Scion is playing. He sounded a bit out of breath, his mental voice strained.

I glanced up to see the storm brewing overhead, then a shock of heat drew my attention back to the spiky-haired bitch. She stood only a few feet away now, her cuff lit up on her arm as she drew several runes over it.

The ground beneath me began to tremble, causing Yaz to curse at my back.

There had to be a better way to do this. Another side of this barrier that I could penetrate without the beings inside noticing.

But where?

An explosion knocked my feet right out from under me, sending me to the earth with an "Oomph" and a curse. The dagger was still in my hand, but I'd released the barrier.

And the bitch inside was grinning like a lunatic.

I glanced over to see a Cyclops heading right toward my guards.

My very *busy* guards, who were currently engaged in hand-to-hand combat with a bunch of Dargarians.

Fuck.

I jumped up and charged forward with a flame already pooling in my free hand. I threw it right into his solitary eye, causing him to topple backward before he could reach Yaz.

This isn't working, I decided, looking around at the portal and the sea of demons before me. The Nephilim were doing their best, but they were up against demons they'd probably only studied.

Demons that shouldn't be in this plane.

Like Blood demons and Slithers and fucking Cyclopes.

I sent another fireball into a nearby giant's eye, bringing him down before he could take on a trio of Nephilim.

I need wings, I thought at Ezra. *Then I could attack this damn veil thing from the top.*

A thunderous wind rippled around me half a beat later, nearly knocking me off my feet as shadows descended across the sky.

I spun to face that spiky-haired bitch just in time for her to blow me a kiss. *Definitely fucking dying first.*

Screams erupted across the field from Nephilim and demons alike—no one wanted to deal with the horde of shadowy creatures flowing down from the sky.

Kayla! Ezra shouted.

I'm fine! I returned, sprinting alongside the wall in an effort to put some distance between me and the damn shadows. Yaz and the others were right behind me.

But so were all the others.

Shit! I picked up speed, my mind working a mile a minute. *How is she conjuring shit outside of the barrier?* The only way that could be possible was if she had some back door built into that protective siding.

A back door I needed to find.

Last time, she'd tapped the shield to unravel it and allow the shadow being to escape.

This time, she hadn't.

But her buddy had been able to make the ground collapse beneath us.

And someone had shot fire from the sky.

Unless... I frowned, considering the alternative. *Unless there are actually five of them.*

And the four inside were just a diversion for the real power *outside* of the barrier.

Maybe they were just the guards, while the one who had created the rift was actually operating from the outside.

Guards that functioned as decoys.

Distractions from the real threat.

Prince Morax? I wondered. *The Archangels in the sky?*

Or was there another guilty party here, one we hadn't yet suspected?

The earth quaked beneath my feet, sending me flying forward as a whirlwind of energy flooded the air.

Screams echoed behind me, the shadow creatures swooping down and attacking everything in sight.

This isn't right, I thought, staring at the scene unfolding before me. *Why would someone unleash the Shadow realm beings on top of the portal? The same portal that was opened to release demons supposedly fighting on the side of those trying to take down the veil?*

It was as though we had three attacking parties—those who wanted to uphold the veil, those who wanted to take it down, and someone who just desired a bout of insanity.

My head spun as I tried to piece it all together, the ground rumbling again from another explosion nearby.

The trees were all on fire.

The sky flooded with smoke and shadow beings.

There were demons covered in blood.

Nephilim using their cuffs to portal-jump all around.

Prince Morax taking to the sky as he fought off a shadow creature.

And my guard trying to form a defensive line around me as the earth continued to shake.

Ezra, nothing about this is making any sense, I told him.

Silence.

Ezra?

A blinding light erupted from the sky, sending me to my knees as the power behind the eruption rippled down to us on the ground.

I couldn't breathe.

Couldn't see.

It was so intense. So damn hot. So... so... *consuming*.

Ezra, I breathed, feeling his energy everywhere as a fissure split through the atmosphere, the balance turning upside down and the realms shuddering from the aftershocks of the destruction.

The veil, I thought. *The veil!*

It was a thousand times worse than the firework I'd released in Virginia.

A million times worse than I'd ever anticipated.

Because it pulled at my heart and drowned my soul beneath a sea of despair.

We were running out of time.

I had to get through this fucking barrier.

I had to stop them!

But I didn't fucking know how.

And those damn shadows... I shuddered, feeling their cooling presence.

Enough, I thought. *Enough of this!*

Ezra and I were the new Divinity. A balance of all three realms. Heaven. Hell. *And* Earth. Because I was a Halfling.

The daughter of an Archdemon.

I might not be able to feel my mate right now, but I could sense our power, that hum of energy that married our souls.

A perfect balance, I marveled, latching onto it and tightening my grip on the blade. *More,* I demanded, reaching deep inside to that plane where my soul existed with Ezra's spirit. *Give. Me. More.*

I yanked on the power there, pulling it into me, surrounding myself with it, swathing my entire being in blissful balance.

My lungs inflated in response, my body taking a deep, steadying breath.

Yes.

This was what I needed.

A blissful Divinity.

A perfect union.

A place founded in equality and... and *love*.

My heart warmed. My soul rejoiced. My veins pulsated.

Yes. Yes.

I vaguely felt Ezra's reaction through the bond, his exhausted mind intrigued by this shifting of power. Then I felt him lending me his strength, pushing his power to me through the bond.

And then I felt his hand.

His body.

His *feathers*.

He had joined me on the ground, his presence the anchor I needed to latch onto as I pulled the Divinity into me, dragging it away from that safe plane of existence and forcing it into action now.

We needed it.

It was the only way to repair the tears between the realms, the shredding of the veil, to break through that godforsaken *barrier*.

I screamed, the fury pouring out of me on a wave of heat and flames to singe every threat in my wake.

Shadow beings shrieked at the abundance of light.

Do it again, Ezra said. *Do that again right now.*

My soul responded, the furious energy leaving me on a tidal wave of emotion that I'd kept bottled up for thousands of years.

Anger.

Fear.

Torment.

I'd spent my life as a Halfling being, only revered in my own realm because of my ties to the Archdemon who presided over the people there.

Everywhere else, I was shunned. Taunted. Laughed at.

Because of my human heritage.

But it was that mortal side now that grounded me in this plane, forcing me to protect it, to find that perfect harmony between the realms and *mend* the breach threatening this plane.

Again, Ezra whispered, his voice filled with an awe I felt all the way to my soul as I shrieked once more, exploding with the power of the Divinity and demanding balance between the realms.

Sparks ignited all around me.

Growls.

Shouts.

Bloodcurdling screams.

I tried to see them, to understand, but it was too damn bright. Too much light.

No more shadows.

No more barrier, some part of me recognized, my mind seeking and finding the true threat lurking within.

Multiple beings with power that didn't belong to them.

I growled, my soul demanding justice for their wrongdoings.

They'd stolen a divine power and used it to commit unspeakable acts, all with the sole desire to inspire catastrophe across the realms.

To realign the powers.

To make the human plane a war zone.

To take mortal slaves.

To ruin the glorious symmetry established between the crossing worlds.

They craved destruction and darkness.

I craved peace and light.

But I possessed the darkness within me as well, a darkness gifted to me by my father.

It all blended inside, stirring a violent ball of lethality that I longed to release.

I stood, my feet feeling lighter than air.

I still couldn't see anything around me—the white light too blinding—but I *felt* the auras of everyone. No. It was more than that. I could sense their intentions with a part of me I'd never accessed before.

This wasn't about good versus evil.

This was about creating a new reality.

A new existence within the realms.

A new order to the universe.

I spun toward the Dark Provenance members, toward *Gleason.* "*You.*"

He possessed powers that he shouldn't.

All of them did.

The cuffs, I realized, looking in the direction of their wrists. I still couldn't see them beyond the blinding light, their energy signatures resembling lukewarm shadows amid the brightness in my vision.

But their wrists were *beacons* of power.

Scion created them.

What did that mean? Why were they all reminiscent of divine power?

To protect them?

To establish a new sort of balance with the Dark Provenance at the heart of it?

Did they call the Shadow realm here?

My mind spun with all the potential scenarios. However, a pulse of power nearby drew my focus to the splintering veil.

I stepped toward it, only to feel Ezra's hand on my wrist. "It's too late."

"It's not," I said, moving blindly through the field toward the rift. "I can fix it."

The power hummed inside me in agreement, our new Divinity flooding my veins with unspeakable energy.

I was overflowing with it.

Burning my very soul and threatening to expel me from this plane, to force me back to the place I shouldn't be able to reach.

The place where our spirits danced.

I fisted my hands at my sides, belatedly realizing I still held the dagger. My focus shifted toward it, my mind conceptualizing a plan before I even understood it.

A conduit.

I lifted the knife and aimed it toward the tear—a cataclysm I could feel more than see—and unleashed my light.

Kayla!

Shouts unfurled around me.

Power rippled through the air.

And those beings with Kristina's power began to pulsate.

I could feel them now, their auras beacons that called to the energy within me.

That ability doesn't belong to you, I thought at them. *That ability belongs to the Divinity.*

Kayla! Ezra shouted again. *Don't do this!*

It's okay, I whispered back to him, my soul coaching me through each and every move. *It's going to be okay.*

You're not—

The energy inside me roared, overpowering his voice and sending me to my knees.

I slammed the blade into the ground. It shook with the power of an explosion, the rocks splitting all around me as I erupted into a thousand pieces.

Jagged.

Sharp.

Intense.

Kayla... The agony in Ezra's voice shot through my heart.

But the pain left me in the next breath.

My heart no longer existed.

I no longer existed.

For my skin and bones had been ripped apart by my very soul, coaxing me into an ethereal state of existence.

A right state.

The only one that matters.

Electricity buzzed all around me, creating static in my ears.

Blissful silence followed.

The world at peace.

Just for a brief second.

The power righted.

The evil beings destroyed.

My spirit forever changed.

And my body... no more.

Ezra

"Kayla!" I shouted as I caught her falling form, her eyes closing as she stopped breathing. "*Fuck*."

She'd... she'd *erupted*. Like a damn star. Light and energy pouring out of her and knocking out everyone around us.

Then she'd shot that same light up into the sky, her power more intense than Johanna's, Kristina's, and Lucía's combined. They usually required chants to merge their energy to heal fissures in the veil.

Not Kayla.

She'd wielded my dagger like a damn wand and forced the veil to meld back together.

After she'd taken down the barrier.

I'd felt her pulling on my soul, on our bond, and I'd teleported to her, thinking she was injured.

But it hadn't been an injury at all.

It'd been her spirit requiring *more*.

I'd left Scion and Azrael up in the sky, battling Raziel and Zerak. Now all four of them were lying in the field, unconscious from Kayla's eruption.

I didn't know how she'd done it, how she'd managed to pull the Divinity into her like that and use it to balance the scales.

It wasn't a power I possessed.

Just one I'd managed but could never truly access.

That was the power of the Divinity—an energy source meant to be controlled by three beings, not one.

I was just the guard. The warrior in charge of protecting the heart of our universe.

And that heart was now Kayla.

My mate.

A true Queen of Divinity.

I couldn't hear her mind or feel her heart beating. Yet her soul warmed the air around us.

Kayla? I whispered, longing to hear her voice.

She said nothing.

Nor did she move.

Had it been too much power for her to harness? Had it killed her? Wouldn't I feel her death? She was my other half. The literal core of my existence. My purpose for breathing.

My Divinity.

Where are you? I wondered, my eyes scanning the burnt trees as though I might find another version of her wandering between the charred branches.

But instead, all I found was an Archdemon leaning against a tree, his navy blue wings tucked artfully at his back.

He smiled, the expression almost as blinding as the sun. "Well, that was far more impressive than the initial explosion."

I growled under my breath, not at all in the mood to deal with him. Not with Kayla lying unconscious in my arms, still unbreathing. I wasn't sure if she was coming back. I wasn't sure how to save her. I wasn't sure what the fuck had even just happened.

"You may want to lay her down," he suggested conversationally. "I do believe she's about to change."

"What?"

Her body began to convulse half a second after the word left my mouth, her clothes erupting in flames. I dropped her as the heat singed my skin, the inferno covering her from head to toe. "Fuck!" I jumped to my feet, searching for water or something to smother her with.

I started to flutter my wings, thinking to cover the flames, but Ashmedai leapt forward to catch my plumes and yank me back. "Give her a second, Ezra."

"She doesn't have a damn second!" I shouted back at him, my fist aiming for his face.

He caught my wrist and twisted it, then teleported us into the sky. I called my sword to me, but it paused midair as he blocked it with a telekinetic shield.

"I'm going to fucking kill you," I seethed, flipping out of his grip and attempting to punch him again.

But my body froze.

My arm hanging in the air.

My wings sprung wide.

My legs stuck in a sprinting position.

My mouth partially open, allowing me to release a snarl. Because while he'd used his gift to hold me in place, he was still allowing me to breathe.

"You're going to thank me," he corrected, his tone mild. "She's being reborn, Ezra. If you take a breath, you'll sense it and realize I'm right."

Reborn.

Was that why I could feel her yet couldn't at the same time?

My eyebrows attempted to lift, but Ashmedai's telekinesis held me captive. *She's becoming an Archdemon.*

"Not exactly," he replied, making my eyes want to narrow now. I always suspected he could read minds. But those two words proved it. "There's a lot you suspect about me. Some of it is true. But you really should be paying closer attention to those around you, Ezra. I'm not your enemy."

You're not my ally either.

"I am in more ways than you realize." He sighed, the sound tired as he snapped his fingers.

We landed on the ground in an instant, his telekinetic hold dropping immediately as my sword fell to the ground.

Kayla was nowhere to be seen, a cluster of reddish-black feathers on the ground in her place. I ran to the feathers, pulling them back to reveal my beautiful mate beneath the nest of silky plumes. "Kayla," I whispered, the sight of her taking my breath away. The flames were long gone, leaving behind unblemished pale skin.

She still wasn't breathing.

But I sensed her spirit all over this forest, her life a blessing that would soon return to her corporeal state.

"Change," Ashmedai echoed, smiling. "Beautiful, isn't it?"

I glanced up at him. "How did you know?"

"Because it's always been expected. She's too powerful to remain a Halfling, not with Bael's blood running through her veins. And now her ties to you have pushed her into becoming who she was always destined to be—a being of the Divinity. Or a queen, as you earlier thought." He flashed me a grin with that last statement, confirming his mind-reading power yet again.

Not that he needed to.

This was just him being Ashmedai.

His smile disappeared as he casually strolled over to where the portal hummed with residual life. Another snap of his fingers opened it back up.

His wings flared. "*Run.*"

I frowned. "What?" I stood to walk over to him and realized the words were for the demons waiting to come through on the other side.

They scurried at the sight of us standing on the opposite side. Or perhaps it was just Ashmedai's presence that sent them running. His intimidating size was accented by his dangerous aura, his powers flourishing in a manner I'd never witnessed from him before.

He began tossing unconscious demons through the open threshold without touching them, his show of telekinetic ability only further proving he'd grown substantially in power.

"You've been downplaying your changes," I said slowly. "How have you hidden this?"

He faced me as more bodies flew through the portal behind him, his violet eyes blazing with energy. "Trudy."

"The Nephilim?"

"She's much more than that," he replied. "They all are. They're beings of two realms. Children of angels. And no one has really considered what they would become." He paused, glancing at the unconscious angels. "Well, some have absolutely considered the possibilities."

I assumed he meant Azrael and Scion since they'd been training with the members of the Dark Provenance.

However, he shifted focus and pointed to the unconscious beings only a few yards away from Kayla. The spiky-haired female and blond male were ones I recognized as having imbibed Kristina's power.

"They're the product of Nephilim being forced to breed with demons, something that would have likely happened to Trudy had Xai and Evangeline not found her," Ashmedai said.

I arched a brow, surprised by that information. "Why haven't you mentioned this before?"

He ignored me, his next words a continuation of what he'd been saying. "They're creations that defy the balance, or perhaps create a new one. That remains to be seen now that your mate sucked the power out of them. But my point is, the rules are changing."

"And you failed to mention this before because...?" I tried again.

"It's a recent discovery, one I've only just confirmed now that I'm in their presence."

"Yet you think Trudy would have suffered a similar fate?" I pressed, not believing his bullshit about this being *recent*.

"She was part of a human trafficking ring organized by a power-hungry demon," he drawled. "It's an obvious assessment and link. All of the movements over the last forty or so human years have been leading toward the endgame. Every detail matters."

I could agree with that. However... "You could share more of what you know."

"I've shared quite a bit," he countered as he lifted the four Nephilim-demon hybrids up off the ground with his power. "More than you even realize." He snapped their necks beneath his telekinetic grip.

Then a holy blade appeared out of thin air as he stabbed them all without once actually touching them.

The lethal weapon landed at my feet in the next instant. "The blade Alastor originally promised Kayla. Be sure she gets it."

I gritted my teeth. "Is this all a game to you?" I demanded as I faced him once more.

His nonchalant cleanup was fucking unnatural. He'd just killed those four beings without leaving one alive for questioning, and he was shoving all the others through that damn portal.

Except for the Dark Provenance members. He left them alone.

Along with the Archdemon and Archangels.

And Kayla's Royal Guard.

"Yes," he said softly. "A game I intend to win." He picked up Morax. "I'll handle him. I imagine Scion will want to handle Raziel and Zerak. Perhaps the timekeeper will give you a new countdown clock, hmm?"

I narrowed my gaze. "So that's it? You take Morax and go?"

He blinked at me. "You act as though this is over, Ezra." The portal closed behind him as the last of the demonic bodies went through it. The only demons he left behind were members of Kayla's Royal Guard.

"We know who is behind this now," I pointed out. Raziel had implicated his brother. And Zerak was clearly involved with Morax. "The culprits will be tried, and justice will be served."

By my sword.

Ashmedai grinned. "Justice. Yes. Except this game has never been about stopping the veil from falling. It's about surviving when it does."

"So there are more beings involved," I translated.

He glanced at several Nephilim before eyeing the fallen angels nearby. "A new era of existence is upon us, Archangel. There are some who seek to take advantage of such changes, and others who merely want to survive it."

He lifted a shoulder, his attention shifting to Kayla.

His eyes sparkled.

"Your princess is about to wake up," he murmured. "My congratulations to you both."

With that statement, he winked out of existence, taking Morax with him.

Fucking insufferable Archdemon, I muttered, kneeling beside Kayla to check her pulse.

Those words had better not be for me, she replied softly, her mental tone exhausted. *Or I'll kill you when I can move again.*

Kayla... I lifted one of her wings up to peer down at her curled form. She resembled an angel with her reddish-brown hair fanned around her and her long, pale legs tucked up against her chest. *You're here.*

Not sure what that means, but okay.

You have wings, I whispered, stroking the red-tipped plumes. *They're mostly black but edged with red, and utterly beautiful.*

She didn't reply, her silence underscored by a note of shock. *How?*

The veil ruptured, sending everyone to the ground. Then you... you channeled the Divinity and exploded. I wasn't sure how else to explain it. *You absorbed Kristina's former gifts, too. And you knocked everyone out except for me.*

Probably because of our link—it had shielded me from the impact of her eruption.

I ran my fingers along the edge of her wing.

You took down three Archangels, an angel, and an Archdemon. As well as all the Nephilim and demons present, I added. *Maybe even a few Shadow demons. Although, I think most of those were impacted by the light from the veil ripping apart.*

I hadn't really seen that part, my soul being called back to hers within seconds of the veil fracturing.

Then I'd been consumed by Kayla and her need for my strength.

I'd given her everything.

You took them all down in a blink, I whispered, still stunned by the power she'd exuded. *Kayla, it was like a supernova went off. And then you healed the veil.*

I'd never seen anything more beautiful or more terrifying in my life.

Afterward, you passed out and grew wings. It sounded so anticlimactic compared to everything else. Yet her wings really should feel like a much bigger deal. Except it paled in comparison to the Divinity thriving inside her.

This is a really fucked-up dream, she mumbled.

If only, I mused, my gaze flicking over to Scion as he began to stir. He would undoubtedly demand an explanation, which

I didn't really have other than to say the veil and balance were restored.

For now, anyway.

Because Ashmedai had made it clear that this was only the beginning.

Do you remember anything? I wondered. *Or is it all a blur?*

I remember questioning a fifth power. She sounded distant. *And everyone's conflicting auras.*

What do you mean?

I don't know. I'm... I'm still confused.

"Fucking hell," Scion groaned from several yards away.

"Something like that," I replied, releasing Kayla's silky wing.

"What the fuck happened?"

"Kayla happened." I couldn't fight the urge to smile, nor did I even try. "She was magnificent."

"Of course she was," a deep voice replied as Bael appeared with Johanna. "She's my daughter."

EZRA

Johanna glanced around the forest, her lips curling down. "The Divinity feels strong here."

"It's Kayla," I replied, standing again.

"Did she absorb Kristina's power?"

I shook my head. Then nodded. Then shook my head again. "It's not that simple. She... she *is* the Divinity now." Or that was how it felt, anyway.

Because I could no longer sense any divine power in Johanna. There'd always been a draw there to protect her and the others—my soul's sole purpose in life designed to guard the Divinity—but now all my focus fully revolved around Kayla.

It was something I hadn't fully grasped until this moment —until I saw Johanna.

"Do you feel any different?" I asked Johanna, my gaze running over her lengthy form. She wore a robe similar to Bael's, the ruby-red color popping against her tan skin.

It hadn't been long since I'd last seen her, but it felt like centuries ago. Perhaps because it had been that long for her in Hell.

However, she possessed a healthy glow that suggested she was thriving there.

And I hadn't sensed any problems radiating from her or Lucía.

Of course, my attention had been utterly consumed by Kayla and the fluctuating balance.

Johanna shared a glance with Bael, then cleared her throat. "My powers have been changing since moving to the underworld. The same is happening with Lucía. We've been... *evolving*."

That seemed to be a good word for it, as it felt like all of us were *evolving* in some way.

Is this part of the change Ashmedai noted? The blending of the realms? The sharing of power among the different beings of this universe?

"Yes. Evolving in preparation for the new Divinity to rise," Mietek said as he appeared.

He caught Scion by the elbow, pulling him up off the ground as though he'd flown in just to assist the other Archangel to his feet.

Maybe he had.

He was the Archangel of Destiny's mate, after all.

"We have some cleanup to do here, I see," Mietek added conversationally, his dark gaze falling to where Azrael, Zerak, and Raziel were all still unconscious on the ground.

Scion grunted. "An understatement." He glanced around, his expression hardening. "Where are the other demons and Morax?"

"Ashmedai sent them back before taking Morax." The abrupt summary came out through my teeth, my irritation with the Archdemon still lingering.

Scion's gaze narrowed. "I see. Nice of him to stop by and help."

I nearly snorted. "It's Ashmedai." I didn't need to elaborate on that. The Archdemon did whatever the fuck he wanted and often engaged in games for his own personal amusement. This was likely no different for him.

Although, his demonstration of power had felt purposeful.

As had his comments about Trudy.

He'd made it clear that this was only the beginning. But the balance felt at peace now, Kayla's control over the Divinity resolute.

Was it only temporary? Would there be a threat to her in the near future?

"Ashmedai will handle imprisoning Morax." Bael sounded sure of it as he headed toward Kayla.

I almost stepped in between them, but Zerak's groan divided my attention. Scion's sword appeared in a blink, the tip pressing to the Archangel's neck as I bent to retrieve the bloody holy blade Ashmedai had tossed at my feet.

If Zerak so much as fluttered a feather, I'd stab him.

A sentiment Scion clearly stated as he said, "Do not move."

Mietek joined him, his expression cold. "Well, this is even more disappointing than the Dariel development."

"Dariel development?" I echoed, my brow furrowed. I knew about his involvement because of Raziel, but we hadn't reached that point in the conversation yet.

"Xai just killed him in Alastor's realm," Mietek explained without looking at me. "He also ascended into a new role as the Archangel of Shadows."

He uttered that last line like it was a throwaway statement.

"Xai?" I asked, clarifying.

"Yes."

I cocked a brow. "Archangel of Shadows?" That was a new title.

Mietek hummed in confirmation and squatted to look at Zerak. "I'm very disappointed in this development, old friend."

"It was only a matter of time," the Archangel replied, his

voice giving nothing away. No remorse. No shock. No disappointment. Just a stoic phrase that seemed to matter little to him.

I'd worry about him in a second.

"We were attacked by shadows again in this realm," I said, returning to Mietek's comments on Xai. "Is that all related to Xai?" I wasn't asking if the Archangel had sent the shadows, just wondering if it was related to his fresh ascension.

"No, he was always destined to become the Archangel of Shadows, much like Kayla was always destined to become the Archdemoness of Divinity—your perfect counter." His midnight eyes met mine. "You both just needed a little push in the right direction."

Mietek was shifting topics too quickly for me to keep up. But his comment on Kayla momentarily pulled my attention away from the shadow beings and toward his cryptic comment about pushing my mate and me in the right direction.

"Meaning?" I pressed.

"You know what it means." He held my gaze in direct challenge, his black-brown feathers ruffling behind him as he stood.

It took me a moment to understand the challenge in his expression. "The cuff."

Mietek shrugged. "It was a hindrance."

"You let us think someone else had altered it." Not a question, but a statement. Because I'd specifically asked him about it, and he'd feigned surprise and innocence. Then he'd made a suggestion that had me questioning Yaz's loyalty to Kayla.

Another lift and fall of the shoulder from the ancient being. "You weren't ready to embrace the truth, and we didn't have time to waste with your righteous anger. Your mate is fine. More than fine. She's finally coming into her element. You're welcome."

My jaw clenched, my desire to punch the smug bastard in

the face driving me forward two steps before my mind caught up with the action. "You nearly got us killed." I uttered the words through a tightened jaw. "You put my mate at unnecessary risk."

He scoffed at that. "*You* put her at risk when you left her in Hell. And you nearly got yourselves killed by not mating properly," he retorted, his wings flaring with power.

A warning, I realized, my eyes narrowing. His energy signature might suggest a waning of energy on his part, but he was still entirely capable of giving me a good fight.

Which would be a waste of time since we were on the same side.

However, that didn't stop me from imagining his death on repeat in my mind.

Fucking prick.

What's happening? Kayla asked softly, her presence in my mind instantly soothing some of my mounting ire.

Mietek just admitted to fucking with your cuff. Which means he *was the reason you were weakened,* I growled.

Why?

To force our need to bond. To heal my powers. To create the new Divinity. "Your cryptic mate is rubbing off on you," I accused him.

He grinned. "I certainly hope so."

"You wanted me to use her like a disposable toy," I spat at him. "You all but told me to fuck her and leave her behind."

"Words that I knew would inspire the opposite effect," he replied dismissively. "I had faith in you to follow the right path."

"Unbelievable," I muttered, running my fingers through my hair.

Bael stood by with an unreadable expression. "It was a wise play," he finally said. "A dangerous one. But a wise one."

Mietek shrugged. "As I said, I had faith in Ezra."

It almost sounded like a compliment, but I was too infuriated to accept it as such.

"What does this new Divinity mean?" Scion asked, his sword still pointed at Zerak's neck. His gaze was on the male below as well, but the question was clearly for Mietek—the giver of cryptic information.

"Only time will tell," Zerak murmured.

Scion's gaze narrowed. "You've lost your voice in this discussion."

"Have I?" the Archangel of Time asked. "You forget my place in all this."

"You lost your place when you got caught fighting for the other side," he reiterated.

Zerak grinned, the expression oddly chilling in his silver-gray features. "I wonder how that happened, hmm?"

Scion's hand flinched against the sword, causing the tip to draw a dangerous line on Zerak's skin. "Careful, Archangel of Time. I wouldn't suggest pushing me right now."

My brow crinkled a little, surprised at Scion's slip of anger. He usually maintained a perfectly calm facade, his strategic ability counteracting his violent side.

But he appeared ready to kill Zerak right now.

The justice dweller in me agreed that the punishment fit the crime.

However, I wanted more details first.

"Take him back to Heaven," Mietek instructed. "Imprison him. We'll interrogate him properly before we decide his fate."

Scion didn't immediately move, some sort of silent conversation flowing between him and Zerak.

Then he slowly lowered his sword. "Come with me willingly, or face the consequences."

Zerak blinked. "An interesting proposal, considering I'll be facing consequences regardless of my choice."

"You attempted to take down the veil," I reminded him. "You deserve those consequences."

"Did I attempt to take down the veil? Or did I merely choose a side to fall on?" he asked, those eerie gray eyes finding mine. "It's all about survival, right?"

My brow furrowed, his words dangerously close to Ashmedai's comments. Either he hadn't been as unconscious as I'd thought and listened to our conversation, or there was a connection between the Archangel and the Archdemon.

"The veil will fall," Zerak continued. "And soon."

"How many years?" Mietek asked.

Zerak smiled. "I guess you'll have to interrogate that out of me, won't you?"

Scion growled, his sword disappearing as he grabbed Zerak by the neck. The pair of them disappeared, causing Mietek to sigh.

"He's right, you know. The veil is still going to fall. It's always been inevitable." He lifted his gaze to the sky before settling it on me. "This just resets the countdown clock."

"Which means we can't kill Zerak."

"No, we cannot," Mietek agreed. "But I would like to understand his choice to work with Dariel. Raziel isn't a surprise; he always follows Dariel. But Zerak? Zerak is practical to a fault."

I ran my hand over my face and nodded. "True." Understanding his motives would help us decide how to move forward. "I want to know what he can tell us about the shadows in this realm."

"My guess is Morax cast them," Bael interjected, reminding us of his presence. He was squatting beside Kayla, his fingers gently stroking her wing. Johanna stood behind him with a hand on his shoulder, her gaze on Kayla, too. "The Shadow realm is near his own; it's quite possible he's found a way to control them. Which could explain Xai's recent rise to power over them, too. They need a master to protect them."

Mietek released a sardonic snort. "I highly doubt Xai will have any interest in protecting them."

"No, but I suspect he'll have an interest in countering the control of others and ensuring they remain in their own realm," Bael replied.

The Archangel of Chaos considered that for a moment before dipping his chin. "That may be true. I'll talk to him."

"See that you do," Bael said as he started gathering Kayla into his arms. "Now, if you'll excuse me, my daughter requires healing."

I stepped forward. "Bael—"

"You're to follow."

He disappeared with her and Johanna before I could comment or react.

"*Fuck.*" What was with the Archdemons today and pissing me the fuck off?

"You can go to her in a minute," Mietek said. "But I need your help with this cleanup first since it seems Scion isn't coming back down to assist."

My jaw tightened. "I can't just let him take Kayla again."

"And you won't," Mietek replied. "Help me clean up. She'll be safe with him. Go retrieve her when we're done."

"She's not a pet, Mietek," I gritted out, irritated by his casual dismissal.

"No, she's your mate." He met my gaze. "Now stop wasting time and help me clean this up so you can return to her."

The words held a double meaning.

He wanted to clean this all up so he could go to Fate.

Just as I wanted to chase after Kayla.

"Bonds are a powerful creation," he added, his tone almost fatherly. "We cherish them, and we do whatever it takes to keep them safe. Sometimes that means sacrificing time. Sometimes that means infuriating our other halves through our protective decisions. Regardless, it's worth it. Because their souls are what keep us going. Their hearts are what we live for. And the connections are where true power lies."

"This is the kind of lecture I needed in the beginning, not the comments about using her."

His lips twisted into a wry smile as he slowly shook his head. "We both know that's a lie, Ezra. You're ready to hear the words now because you finally understand. She's your new purpose. Keep her safe. Cherish her. And be prepared to grovel a little. You just abandoned her in Hell again. I can't imagine she'll be too pleased with you when she wakes."

My jaw clenched. "Fucking Bael." *I'm coming for you, Kayla. Don't give up on me.*

She didn't reply, either because she couldn't hear me or because I'd already pissed her off by not immediately following her father.

Regardless, Mietek was right.

We had to clean this up.

Then I would descend to Hell to find my mate.

And when I did, I'd make sure she knew she was mine.

For eternity.

KAYLA

I paced my bedroom, my wings dragging along the floor behind me.

It'd been three months since I'd last seen Ezra.

I'd expected him to arrive with my Royal Guard, but Jinx had brought everyone back to my father's realm except my mate.

Because he'd ascended rather than descended.

I'd attempted to follow him, to track him down and demand an explanation, but my teleportation abilities were still developing. I only seemed able to portal through the various realms in Hell, not up to Earth or higher to Heaven.

Which left me waiting for him to come to me.

A nagging presence in my mind wondered if he'd left me here again. My purpose was done. I'd saved his precious Divinity, right?

But my soul refused to give that dark voice much credence.

He's coming for me, I thought. *I can feel it.*

I just wished I could hear him. However, something was blocking me.

It'd better not be you blocking me, Ezra, I told him. *Or I seriously will kill you.*

Because I refused to be used and abandoned twice.

A knock at my door had my heart leaping out of my chest.

Only to plummet at the sight of Yaz on the other side.

He smirked. "Happy to see you, too, Princess."

"Sorry," I muttered, my skirts swishing as I turned back into my room to go toward the balcony doors at the back. "I'm just irritated and bored."

"We could go piss off Alastor again?" Yaz suggested, referring to our antics from last week where I figured out how to enter the Archdemon's realm without invitation via my new powers. His guard had come running, just for Alastor to wave them all off upon realizing it was only me. "He still technically owes you a blade."

"He does," I agreed. The bastard had claimed not to have it when we'd gone for a visit. *Lying bastard.*

I leaned against the obsidian stone balcony wall, my gaze scouring the familiar buildings of my father's realm. "I assume you're not actually here to distract me," I said, glancing at the Head of my Royal Guard. "Did you need something?"

His blue-brown eyes sparkled. "No. I came to tell you that I found out more about the cuffs."

My mood immediately brightened. "Oh? Did you find out what Scion meant about it being *divine* magic?" Because that didn't make sense to me, especially not with my new ties to the Divinity. And when I'd asked Johanna about it, she'd also had no idea what I'd meant.

"They're created from a mix of demon and angel magic," Yaz said. "That's what he meant by *divine*. The metal comes from the Chrysus region of Hell. And an angel is the one who enchants it."

My eyebrows rose. "The Chrysus region?" That was nearly impossible to reach, even by Archdemons. It was an area of Hell made almost entirely of gold and protected by shimmering Sprite demons. I'd never attempted to visit, as it wasn't a recommended experience.

"Yep."

"Who the hell is brave enough to mine in the Chrysus region?" I asked, stunned.

"Ankou," he replied.

I gaped at him. "The Soul Keeper?"

Ankou was the gatekeeper of souls in the underworld.

The literal Grim Reaper.

And he wasn't known to play well with others.

But in terms of recruiting someone to mine gold within the Chrysus region, he would be the top candidate for the job. Because not only did he live there, but he also considered himself to be *king* of that territory. Not a true title since he wasn't an Archdemon, but no one was insane enough to question him on it.

"Who...? No, scratch that. *How* did someone convince him to help?" I asked, still shocked.

"I haven't quite figured that part out yet. But he's been working with Prince Ashmedai."

My lips parted. "What?"

"Prince Ashmedai supplies the gold to Archangel Scion. I don't know who is actually blessing them in Heaven, but that's how they're created."

"Prince Ashmedai is the one who gave you my cuff," I realized aloud. Yaz had never actually told me how he'd procured it, just that it was from a trusted source. "My father would kill you if he found out."

Yaz shrugged. "I don't report to him. I report to you. And it's my job to protect you. Prince Ashmedai gave me a way to do that, and I accepted."

"At what cost?"

"That I keep you safe."

"No, I mean, what did you pay Ashmedai?"

"That was his payment," Yaz replied. "He gave me the cuffs in exchange for a lifetime vow to always protect you."

"And nothing else?"

"Nothing else," he confirmed.

Prince Ashmedai was always playing games. "Maybe we should go play in his territory today," I suggested. "See if we can get him to explain why all the Dark Provenance minions have cuffs now."

"I think Archangel Scion is behind that."

"Well, then we can ask him why he felt so strongly about my protection." Not that Prince Ashmedai would tell us. But it gave us something to do and would keep me from pacing all night.

"I think he knew what you would become," Yaz said quietly. "I think that's why he contacted me about the cuff."

"Wait..." I did a double take. "*He* contacted you about the cuff?"

Yaz nodded.

"I thought you procured it as a way to celebrate the appearance of my demonic traits."

"Yes, I went to his realm to procure it. But he offered first."

"And he went to you, not to my father?"

Yaz dipped his chin again. "Probably because he knew your father would never accept the gift."

"So Prince Ashmedai put your life at risk instead," I translated, my mind working through the puzzle. "No. He *tested* you to see how far you would go for me." I almost laughed at the brilliance of it. Prince Ashmedai was constantly playing all the angles and typically operated several paces ahead of everyone else.

"It worked," Yaz murmured.

"Yeah," I agreed. "Yeah, it did."

Until Archangel Mietek had tainted my cuff, anyway.

Ezra had been so angry with that revelation, his possessive energy singeing my soul and branding me as his to protect.

I missed that feeling.

I missed *him*.

Three months in Hell was only about six hours on Earth. So while it felt like an eternity for me, it wasn't that long for him.

And since he'd traveled up to Heaven, it was even less time.

Maybe minutes rather than months.

Not for the first time, I found myself despising how time worked between the realms.

"Maybe we should pay Prince Ashmedai a visit to ask for another cuff." I could at least use it to ascend to Earth. Of course, Yaz could help me with that, too. *Still...* "After all the shit Prince Ashmedai's pulled, it's the least he could do. Perhaps he'll even add a feature that'll let me jump up to Heaven."

Yaz ran his fingers through his overgrown hair, his lips twisting. "I already asked and he said no."

My eyes widened. "You asked Prince Ashmedai for another cuff?"

He nodded. "I can't help you ascend all the way up. So I asked if he could."

"And... what did he say exactly?"

"That you need to learn to do it on your own." He shrugged. "He also said you no longer need the protection of the cuff because you have Ezra."

"When was this? When did you see Prince Ashmedai?" And how did my father not know? *Or does he know and not care?*

"While I was researching the cuff."

"And he just let you into his realm to discuss it?" I asked incredulously.

He gave me an indiscernible look. "One of Ashmedai's Royal Guards is an old friend."

"What kind of old friend?"

"The kind that I don't want to talk about," he replied, his

voice holding a longing note to it. Then he cleared his throat to wave it all away. "Anyway, I came up to provide the update. And to tell you that your father wants you to join him for dinner."

My head fell back on a groan. "Of course he does." He'd been demanding family dinners several times a week, saying something about wanting to enjoy our time while we have it.

And his version of *enjoying our time* was all about testing my new powers.

"Fine," I said. It wasn't like I had anything better to do since a visit to Prince Ashmedai's realm with Yaz appeared to be off the table.

"I'll leave you to prepare, then," Yaz murmured, bowing. "But my offer to buzz you up to Earth still stands."

I smiled. "I know." He'd made it shortly after I'd woken up. However, there wasn't much point in jumping up there with Ezra being in Heaven.

A part of me also wanted to see if he'd actually come for me down here like he'd threatened.

And my soul recognized the need to be down here for balance.

I'd expelled an enormous amount of energy to heal the veil, more than I could even conceptualize. This was the best place for me to heal and recharge.

Of course, I felt fine now.

I was very ready to find Ezra.

But I would give him time, prove my faith in him, and wait.

You'd better be coming for me, Archangel, I thought. *Or I'm going to find where Alastor put that blade and drive it through your heart.*

These were the one-sided conversations I'd entertained for the last few months.

He never replied.

Which was fine.

For now.

Yaz left as I dressed for dinner in one of my trademark ruby dresses. My father had procured a whole new wardrobe to accommodate my wings, the colors all reds and blacks and browns—the signature colors of his familial line.

I smoothed my hands over my skirts, then made my way down the residential hall of the palace to the royal staircase. Several guards stood stationary along the way, their vibrant blue robes a stark contrast against the red stone walls.

Royal Guards always wore blue, regardless of their home realm. They were distinguished by the familial crests etched into the breast area of their robes.

I didn't acknowledge them, my focus on the grand hall and the dining rooms beyond.

My father typically chose the smaller of the three.

The pair of Royal Guards against the wall by the door told me tonight was no different.

I entered and took my usual chair with Johanna across from me and my father at the head. "Daughter," he greeted.

"Prince Bael," I returned.

His eyes grinned, amused by my formal address. "How was your day?"

"Boring. Yours?"

"Enlightening," he replied as he picked up his wine to take a sip of the red liquid.

I didn't ask him to elaborate.

There wasn't a point.

If he wanted to tell me what was *enlightening* about his day, he would.

And he didn't.

Instead, he shifted to general dinner conversation, boring me with discussion over the food and general inquiries about my power. "Did you practice reading auras like we discussed?"

he asked, referring to my enhancing ability to decipher intent from the atmosphere surrounding other beings.

"All the auras in the palace are loyal," I told him. "Not much to practice on." But I did wander the grounds to test everyone in my path. They were all the same shades in regard to their intent to protect.

Only a few had boasted a hint of fear.

However, that was standard practice when in the company of an Archdemon—something my wings marked me as being. I hadn't figured out how to hide them yet. I also didn't quite know why mine were silky feathers while my father's resembled bat wings, but he didn't seem surprised by them.

"Perhaps we'll arrange a trip to Earth soon so you can test the Dark Provenance auras," he suggested as he set down his fork. "You mentioned they felt off during your last visit."

"During my last visit, I was busy repairing the veil with my new powers," I replied dryly. "I don't think a lot of what I remember is reliable."

Everything from that day was fuzzy in my head. I remembered certain bits, like questioning powers traveling through the barrier, and marveling at the myriad of auras in the forest —*and the cuffs*—but I couldn't recall specific details or why I'd felt certain ways.

"Have you heard anything from the Archangels about Zerak or Raziel?" I asked. "Or anything about Prince Morax?"

He shook his head. "Ashmedai has just said Morax is otherwise indisposed, which I translate to mean he's currently in too much pain to speak. And justice in Heaven will take longer than a few Hell months."

Right. Because of time.

From what Jinx had mentioned, several of the Nephilim had been brought up to Heaven for healing. Those who had been unharmed had returned to their respective homes.

But now I wondered if any of the Nephilim would have to

testify in a trial—assuming angels even had a court for such things. I actually wasn't sure of their process for this, as it was rather unprecedented. However, if everyone had to report on the events from Earth, then the trial would likely take several Hell decades.

At least I would be invited to participate. In theory, anyway.

Then I would find Ezra and have a word.

The rest of dinner with my father and Johanna passed by in a similar manner of flat conversation, ending with my father running a series of tests regarding my new powers. Johanna helped, her previous connection to the Divinity making her a powerful ally in learning these new talents.

However, her skills had definitely changed, her control over the veil magic no longer existent. Her new powers were similar to my father's in nature. While neither of them had admitted anything out loud, I knew they'd mated each other.

Which I assumed had played into her changing abilities. Just as Ezra had influenced my shift toward Divinity magic.

I just wasn't sure if their mating was the primary cause of her shift or if my ascension had been the reason for it. Perhaps a mixture of both.

I still maintained all my former gifts, though. They were actually stronger now. And I possessed this new sense of the balance, an ability within my soul that kept me attuned to potential shifts in power throughout the realms.

I'd used it a few times to check in on Heaven, noting the calmness and tranquility of the angels above.

That told me Zerak and Raziel were still alive.

Though, I didn't expect Ezra to kill them. He would seek justice in a different way.

Unlike Prince Ashmedai—he would absolutely kill Prince Morax at some point. Just after thousands of years of torment first.

Although, I still didn't fully understand Prince Morax's involvement. It felt unexplained. Yes, he was Kristina's father. So that made him capable of absorbing some of her power, or *helping* to absorb and redistribute it, as Zerak had stated.

I just didn't understand what it all meant or what motive he'd possessed to do it.

Insanity was certainly an option, and the reason my father had surmised. He'd also said that Morax had called the shadows to the realm. Again, another speculation.

But something wasn't adding up.

Everything felt balanced for the moment. However, I sensed trouble coming. A ripple waiting for us on the horizon. An eventual fall of the veil.

We would have to find a new way to survive.

What I'd done to restore the scales was just temporary.

I could feel the truth of that down to my soul. It wouldn't happen tomorrow or even next year. It'd be a while. But it was coming.

Because it was inevitable.

I sighed as I made my way back to my room, my mind running over all the scenarios along the way. It wasn't something I would find the answer to tonight, nor was it something I needed to answer anytime soon.

However, one day I would understand.

I just hoped that day wouldn't be too late.

My heels clicked against the stone floor as I walked, the guards nearby all averting their gazes in reverence. Typical.

But there was a hum of magic in the air that had my senses piquing.

A subtle energy that didn't quite belong.

Except none of them seemed to notice it.

My brow furrowed, my instincts firing. *Is it just me?* I wondered as I reached my room. *Is it just that sense of dread from the inevitable?*

I twisted the handle, letting myself into the sitting area of my quarters.

No. No, that's not dread.

The sensation spiked as I shut the door, the electrifying aura hitting my senses like a freight train. *Powerful. Drugging. Strong.*

Hellfire stirred along my palm as I started toward the intruder, my lips flattening. "I am not in the mood for this," I said, aware that whoever had intruded on my space was powerful enough to be an Archdemon. "So either start talking or—"

The fiery element died across my palm as I turned the corner, the familiar cool power a kiss to my senses that nearly had my knees buckling in relief.

"I'm having flashbacks to the night we first met," Ezra drawled from his lounging position on my bed. "What was it I said? Something about firing first and asking questions later?"

"Ezra," I breathed.

"You know, it's almost too bad that I didn't hire a Slither to attack you first. Then I would have cause to strip you and bathe you, just like our first date."

I nearly laughed. "That was not a date."

"I undressed you. That qualifies as a date."

"You didn't fully undress me," I reminded him, my blood heating with the reminder of that night. How he'd bathed me. How we'd exchanged blood. *Our first kiss.*

The gold in his irises flared, drawing me closer to the bed, to *him*.

"How about I undress you fully this time?" he offered, his voice low as he slowly slid off of the mattress. "Bathe you even more thoroughly, not just with my hands, but with my tongue?"

My thighs clenched. "Maybe I still want to kill you."

He continued toward me, his height and strength a very

welcome presence in my bedroom. I wasn't sure how he'd managed to arrive here undetected. Or maybe he had been detected. It would be just like my father to orchestrate dinner as a diversion to keep me from finding out about Ezra's arrival.

Although, I doubted he would be okay with Ezra surprising me in my quarters.

Regardless, none of it mattered.

Because my mate was here.

In my room.

Standing right in front of me.

Ezra brushed his knuckles across my cheek. "I think you'll always want to kill me, my queen. It's part of the allure."

Not *little heiress* or *princess*, but *my queen*.

That was a nickname I could become accustomed to.

"If you're thorough enough, I'll consider allowing you to live," I promised.

"Hmm, a challenge." His knuckles left my face as he palmed the back of my neck, tugging me into him. "Shall we seal the deal with a kiss?"

"Yes," I whispered. "Yes, we should."

He grinned, his lips whispering over mine. "It's been only hours for me, but I missed you."

"I missed you, too," I breathed. "Now stop stalling and kiss me."

"As you wish, my queen."

EZRA

We weren't going to make it to the shower.

The moment our mouths touched, the walls between our minds crumbled and our emotions took over.

Kayla's faith in me to find her.

Her annoyance with time for functioning differently down here.

Her heartfelt joy at seeing me again.

Her *love*.

I drowned in every emotion, feeling them as though they were my own and returning the favor in kind. Sharing my need to find her. Sharing my irritation at the cleanup taking too long. Sharing my relief when she'd walked through that door. Sharing my love for her.

The words weren't spoken.

But they didn't need to be because our mouths were doing all the speaking for us.

I grabbed her hips, pulling her to me and reveling in the silky texture of her dress.

So beautiful, I whispered. *You're so fucking beautiful, Kayla.*

And here I thought I wasn't your type, she replied, referring to the lies I'd spoken the first night we'd met.

She might not have been my type prior to my entering her

home. However, the moment we'd met, she'd become my type. My *only* type.

I proved that knowledge to her with my tongue as I engaged her in a dance of sensuality and grace. *We were made for each other, Kayla.*

The perfect blend of Heaven, Earth, and Hell.

Prove it, Archangel.

I grinned against her mouth as I mentally called for a dagger. I usually called for my swords, but this required a more personal touch.

She froze, obviously sensing the magic since my fingertips were still against her hip as the handle formed against my palm. *Ezra...*

I stepped just enough away from her to have easy access to her gown.

Then I sliced it down the middle with one powerful slash.

Her lips parted, her cheeks blossoming with a shade similar to the ruby silk falling apart around her.

"There's a zipper on the back," she chastised.

"Is there?" I feigned innocence. "This was easier."

I pushed the fabric from her shoulders, causing it to spill to the floor in a fluid wave of shimmering red silk. The under-garments beneath matched, giving me pause.

She possessed the body of a siren with her natural curves and long, athletic legs. Or maybe a Succubus was a better description. Because seeing her like this had me wanting to kneel at her feet and worship her between her thighs.

Well, I had promised to use my tongue on her.

A command taunted my mouth, one that would have her climbing onto that bed and spreading her legs for me.

But a fiery kiss of heat stilled the words before they could leave.

I arched a brow as a flicker of embers fell over me, burning away the fabric of my sweater and jeans, but not singeing the skin beneath. I could have dispelled the power, just like I'd smothered her earlier ball of hellfire.

However, I rather approved of where this was going. So I embraced her energy and allowed her to weave her flames through the fibers of my clothing.

She ran her gaze over me as the scraps of remaining fabric fluttered to the ground around me, leaving me clad in only boxers and shoes.

I kicked the shoes off along with my socks and eyed her heels. "Leave those on and get up on the bed."

Her glittering irises suggested she wanted to argue the command, but her arousal told me she wouldn't.

She kept her eyes on me while she moved backward toward the mattress, her long legs allowing her to climb up onto the bed with ease. Her wings ruffled, sprawling behind her as she lay down with a come-hither glance.

"Stunning," I praised her, loving the way her reddish-black plumes contrasted against her pale skin. "Fucking exquisite."

My little heiress had blossomed into a queen.

Her heels slid across the quilt as she bent her legs. Then she spread them in welcome and lifted her arms up over her head. *Still waiting for you to prove that we're made for each other, Archangel.*

Did you transition into an Archdemon or a Succubus? I asked as I knelt on the bed. *Because I'm struggling to tell the difference.*

I pressed a kiss to her knee and set the dagger down beside her hip. It dissolved in the next second, returning to my weapons vault—which had not been destroyed during the attack because of the magical enchantments I kept around it. But it didn't exactly exist in physical form at the moment, either, unless I touched the item.

Or Kayla touched it.

Her link to me granted her access to everything I owned.

373

Which I supposed meant she really would inherit my armory if I died.

A pleasing realization, she mused, her mind obviously melding with mine and granting her full access to my every thought.

You're the only one allowed to kill me, my queen, I whispered back to her, my lips skating up her inner thigh. *But I'm going to endeavor to prove why you shouldn't even try.*

Oh? The breathy little sound turned to a moan as I pressed a kiss to the damp lace covering her warm center.

Yeah, oh, I murmured in reply. *As much as I enjoy this lingerie, it's hiding the part of you that I intend to devour.* I gripped the sides and snapped the delicate material before she could reply.

But she didn't protest.

Instead, she groaned, her mind continuing to dare me to prove our connection.

Which I proceeded to do thoroughly with my tongue.

I didn't stop until she was panting and on the verge of exploding. Her growl when I lifted my head made me smile. "Proof enough yet, darling? Or do you need more?"

"*Ezra.*"

"That's not an answer."

Fire lanced my spine, her power threatening to burn me. I defused it with a quick balance of icy energy. Kayla's hips arched up in response, but I pushed her back down with my palm against her stomach, my tongue swirling around her tender clit.

She wanted to fly.

I could feel it in the tension radiating through her limbs, her soul demanding a rapturous sensation that only I could give her.

It'd been my intent to torment her for hours, but I

couldn't. I wanted to feel her fall apart. To detonate. To scream with passion.

Two of my fingers slid deep inside her, curling upward to stroke her intimately as I applied pressure with my mouth against her sensitive nub.

She shattered in the next breath, her body clamping down around me as she released my name in prayer from her beautiful lips.

I didn't stop.

I kept licking her.

Nibbling.

Driving her over the edge again and again until tears glistened against her cheek.

But it wasn't enough for her. I could sense the torment inside her, that need to be joined, the desire to feel me properly inside her.

Soft, needy little sounds left her lips, each one of them going straight to my groin. Pleasuring her was such a fucking turn-on. However, it always brought us to this point of need that devastated my ability to think. Ruined my ability to control my movements. Destroyed all my intents and drove me toward one single-minded focus.

Claim her.

She was already mine, but that didn't matter. My soul needed to reaffirm our bond, to solidify our link and ensure she understood her place by my side.

We were destined for each other.

The Archangel of Justice and the Archdemoness of Divinity.

A brilliant balance of all the realms.

An intense mating that overpowered all the others.

You came for me, she whispered, a vulnerable and wounded part seeming to heal with the words. *You really came here for me.*

Of course I did, I replied. *I swore I would.*

You didn't abandon me.

Never again, Kayla. You're mine.

Yes, she agreed, writhing against the bed as I crawled over her.

My boxers disappeared beneath her flame. I removed her bra with my hands in response, cupping her pert breasts for a delirious moment before I settled between her splayed legs.

Then I let her taste her arousal on my tongue.

She squeezed my hips with her thighs, her damp flesh a welcome kiss against my hard shaft. "Make me fly, Archangel."

I slid inside her slowly, the union one that seemed to mean so much more than any of our previous matings. This was about us. Our future. Our intertwined destinies and the eternity we intended to share with one another.

This was a promise between our souls.

A marriage that defied all the laws of the universe.

An Archangel and an Archdemoness uniting as one.

Change, I marveled, Ashmedai's comment echoing in my mind.

Kayla and I were part of that change. We were an example union between the realms, a new manner of existence, a relationship that challenged all the natural order.

We shouldn't be together.

It was forbidden.

However, our souls didn't believe in simple acts of right or wrong.

We were made for each other, something our bodies proved by how well we fit together. My wings brushed hers as our hips joined, our tongues speaking a foreign language only our spirits could understand. A sensual embrace. A perfect one. A beautiful union of pleasure and pain and *love*.

Her nails bit into my shoulders as her climax hit her, the display of ecstasy stealing my breath and forcing me to follow.

But we weren't done. Not even close. This was our version of a wedding, our bodies the ones speaking vows and sealing secret promises between our souls.

I went to my back as she continued to ride me, her wings splaying out around us in a beautiful curtain of red and black.

Then I took her again.

And eventually, we ended up in the sky, her power battling mine as we danced in a way only beings of our kind could.

Naked.

Covered in sweat.

Surrounded by feathers.

A glorious experience that seemed to go on for days. And maybe it did. Time no longer held any meaning between us. Just the present and what we felt right now.

For our bond represented the balance.

Which was safe for now.

There were threats still lingering in the wind and a strong likelihood of war on the horizon, but Kayla was my world now. Mine to protect. Mine to cherish. Mine to love.

My Divinity.

My heart.

My purpose.

Anyone who dared lay a hand on her would meet the end of my sword.

Because I would kill for her. I would die for her. I would *exist* only for her.

My Archdemoness of Divinity. The perfect representation of balance. My mate.

"Until death do us part," she whispered against my ear, making me grin. The phrasing was very humanlike, but it held a double meaning that melted my heart.

"That sounds like an invitation for more foreplay, my queen."

"You did say we often fought before fucking in your

dreams," she replied breathlessly, her wings beating behind her. She'd clearly been practicing using them over the last few months. "How about you elaborate on those dreams now?"

My smile deepened. "How about I show you when we go home?" I offered instead.

"And where is home, exactly?" she asked, pulling back to stare into my eyes. She had her legs wrapped around my waist and her arms encircling my neck, our wings keeping us steady in the sky well above Bael's realm.

"In between the realms," I told her. "But only if you want to help me rebuild."

"Does that mean you would live here if I asked?"

I nodded.

"Even though it weakens you?"

"By your side, I'm never weak," I replied, meaning it. I'd entered the realm with no issues and had found her almost immediately.

Of course, it had helped that Bael had allowed the breach. One of his Royal Guards had met me at the gates before showing me up to Kayla's quarters—by order of her Archdemon father. I hadn't known what he would do when I'd arrived, and I hadn't really cared.

Fortunately, it seemed he approved of my mating his daughter.

"I liked your home between the realms," she said softly, her lips curling. "All those kitchens."

"You just liked stealing my food."

"You are a decent chef."

"Decent?" I echoed, my eyebrow cocking. "Try spectacular."

"Hmm. I'll need you to prove that." Her irises sparkled. "So I guess we'll need to rebuild those kitchens and bookshelves."

"And the armory," I added, aware of her real desire. "Maybe I'll create one for you."

"Promise you will and I'll agree to living between the realms."

"Consider it a vow," I told her.

"Then take me home, Archangel." She pressed her forehead to mine. "Take me to our future."

My lips swept across hers. "Hold on and don't let go, Kayla. I don't want to risk you going *elsewhere*," I whispered to her, echoing words similar to the ones I'd given her during our very first descent to Hell.

But now we were ascending.

Something I'd told her once would be nearly impossible to do, back when I'd known I would have to leave her in Hell with Bael.

Not this time.

This time, I ascended with her in my arms.

Taking her home.

To the center of my world.

To a place where she would rule—*as queen*.

EPILOGUE

KAYLA

Several Months Later

"Is there a reason I need to wear this?" I asked, gesturing at the blindfold covering my eyes. "Because I'm all into kinky shit, but this makes walking a bit difficult."

"Balance with your feathers," Ezra replied, his fingers skating the upper edges of my wings. "And trust me to guide you." His opposite hand tightened against my hip as he continued pushing me forward.

"So this is a game of trust."

"Yes," he confirmed, maneuvering me down another hallway in our newly built home.

It was similar to his former manor, but with a few modifications.

The mansion still had a three-story library with all open-air windows. Five main kitchens framed by a patio for outdoor eating. An entire wing devoted to our personal quarters—equipped with a sparring area, a pair of sitting rooms, another kitchen filled with essentials, a massive bedroom built for beings with wings, and an equally large bathroom crafted to accommodate showering and bathing together.

And two outdoor homes for guests.

My Royal Guard permanently resided in one of them with Yaz serving as the leader. The other home was there for visitors.

Like Johanna and my father.

They'd already stopped by twice.

Because apparently my dad "missed" me. Whatever that meant. He'd spent both visits issuing various tests to measure my growing power.

Ezra had claimed that Bael just wanted to teach.

I remained undecided on that assessment.

"Stop thinking about your dad and focus on your footing," Ezra chastised softly, his mind always in tune with mine.

I would have hated this easy connection only months ago, but I found myself rather enjoying it now. Because I was just as connected to him.

Which was why I trusted him to lead me now.

He had a surprise for me.

Something he'd been working on.

Something that *excited* him.

However, he was doing an excellent job of not giving it away in his head.

I could easily push down the barriers he'd put up, but I didn't want to spoil his fun. So I allowed him to maneuver me through the hallways.

He pressed a kiss against the back of my head as his hands rotated me again.

By my estimation, we were near the kitchens.

Or maybe his library.

It was definitely outside of our quarters, as we'd begun this journey in our bedroom, and we'd walked too far for this to be in our personal wing.

"Almost there," he promised, his voice low.

I shivered in response, the heat from his touch and the deep tone caressing his words two of his allures my body

381

couldn't seem to ignore. It made sparring with him fun, especially when he growled.

My thighs clenched with the reminder of him growling against my sensitive flesh only an hour ago. He'd made me come so hard I'd seen stars.

This life with him certainly had perks.

His tongue being one of them.

His skills in the kitchen being another.

We'd developed a rather peaceful existence, only occasionally bothered by imbalances that required my attention.

The trials for Zerak and Raziel were still in progress, time in Heaven moving at a snail's pace. Ezra went up every few days for an update. Sometimes I joined him.

We hadn't learned much.

I'd asked about how the powers broke through the shield, mentioning my suspicions of a fifth person being involved. Mietek believed it was probably one of the Archangels, or maybe even Morax.

I remained uncertain.

Which kept me on alert for potential tamperings with the veil.

So far, nothing out of the ordinary had happened. Just a few Nephilim playing with their enhancing powers on Earth. Luckily, the Dark Provenance seemed to have most of them under control.

"All right," Ezra said, grasping my hips and pausing me midstep. "Stand right here." He tugged me back a little and I obeyed.

A series of beeps followed, then a soft snick of sound that reminded me of a refrigerator door being opened. I frowned. "Did you make me dinner?"

"No," he replied. "Well, yes, I did. But this isn't for dinner. We'll have that afterward."

"What did you make?"

"A stew. It's been slow-cooking all day and needs at least another hour."

I wasn't sure when he found time to be a chef, but I adored him for it.

Another soft whisper of metal gliding against metal sounded, stirring a slight chill around me as cool air touched my senses. "Are you sure this isn't food related?" Because it really did feel like he'd opened up a refrigerator door. Or maybe one belonging to a freezer.

"Take off your blindfold, Kayla," he said into my ear, his chest against my back as he wrapped his arms around my waist.

I lifted my hands to the silk around my eyes and pulled it down, then blinked a little to acclimate to the lighting inside the—

My jaw dropped.

Oh.

Oh, shit!

"A new armory," I breathed, my feet already moving.

Ezra released me, giving me a chance to explore the beautiful weapons room.

"I think I just came again," I whispered, trembling from the excitement evoked by this room.

My mate chuckled. "You didn't, but I'll note that for later." He moved to a large dresser in the middle of the room, the top of which was covered in a sheet of black marble. There were seven drawers beneath it, all of them protected by fingerprint technology. "Try the top one," he suggested.

I pressed my thumb to the indicator in the middle—it took over the area where a handle typically would reside.

It hissed open, just like the doors had, to reveal a gorgeous sword inside.

My lips parted. "Is this...?"

"The sword I promised you?" His gaze twinkled. "Yes. It is. And it's bespelled to come to you when you call it."

Ezra had explained to me how his weapons worked and the various enchantments that allowed him to compel them at will.

He'd already re-charmed three daggers for my personal use.

And now he'd finally made me a sword.

I picked it up to test the weight, twirling it around and loving the way it felt in my hands. The runes embedded into the metal gleamed, ready to be used. "I really hope sparring is on our agenda tonight."

"It's always on our agenda," he drawled.

Yes. Because he enjoyed a good fight before fucking me.

Foreplay, he called it.

He wasn't wrong.

"I love it," I told him, grinning. "You'll have to teach me how to call it to me."

He nodded. "I will. But how about you check out the other contents in the drawers first."

I returned the sword and did just that.

The second drawer had more daggers.

The third was full of throwing stars and smaller knives.

The next few had special kinds of bullets and guns.

And the final drawer had an item that had me immediately jumping away from it.

"Is that a... a *holy blade*?" I gaped up at him as I crouched on the floor near the bottom drawer. "You put a holy blade in the armory?"

"It's the one Alastor owed you," he replied, leaning casually against the dresser as though he hadn't just revealed a weapon that could *kill* him. "Ashmedai told me to give it to you. I didn't want to be upstaged, so I decided to wait until the armory was done."

"Alastor gave me the blade?" I blinked. "He actually came through on his deal?"

"He did."

"And you're giving it to me now?"

"I am."

"Why?"

"Because I trust you not to use it on me." His expression turned serious. "But it's yours, Kayla. I won't hide it from you. And I'll spend eternity trying to ensure you never feel the need to stab me with it."

"That's a dangerous risk," I pointed out, only partially joking.

He didn't laugh. Instead, he stared me straight in the eyes as he replied, "It's one I'm willing to take."

I glanced at the lethal item again before looking at him. "I want to spar." I nudged that drawer closed and stood. "With my new sword. Not the holy blade." Because I had no intention of ever using that item. But I would keep it for eternity because of what it represented—*trust*.

Ezra knew I wouldn't use it.

However, he'd given me the tool I'd desired for thousands of years to use against him. The lethal blade I'd dreamt about driving into his heart every night for most of my life.

It was the kind of gift only beings like us could understand.

One that provided a dark sense of closure.

We'd entered a new chapter of our existence together. That blade represented my old life. The sword on the top shelf resembled my new one.

As the Archdemoness of Divinity.

The queen to Ezra's king.

I held his gaze as I opened the top drawer. "Let's play, Archangel."

"No, Archdemoness," he returned, a sword appearing in

his hand as his golden irises glittered with intent. "Let's *dance.*"

His feathers flickered around him.

Then he disappeared.

I smiled, sensing where he'd ventured off to.

Virginia.

Back to the street where it all began.

I picked up my new sword, my heart warming with excitement. *There had better not be a Slither nearby.*

Teleport to me and find out, beautiful queen. Then show me what you can do.

A potentially lethal date with my Archangel in the human realm?

Don't mind if I do.

TRUDY

GOLD.

Everywhere.

On the walls. The ceilings. The floors. Even the adornments were gold, including the handles, picture frames, the pictures inside the picture frames, the *lights*. It was all some variant of golden hues, and it was giving me a headache.

Ashmedai's navy wing brushed my shoulders. *Not everything is gold.*

Get out of my head.

No, he returned, his gaze on the ornate throne in front of us.

I sighed. There was no use in telling him to stop. He never listened to me.

That's not true, little warrior. I listen to you more than I do anyone else, he murmured, his feathers teasing my bare arm. I'd worn a sleeveless shirt in preparation for visiting this realm. It was warm here, the fountains outside liquid gold instead of water.

"Ah, Ashmedai," a voice said, one I'd become familiar with over the last few years.

Ankou.

He wasn't exactly an Archdemon, but he certainly possessed the power of one.

Except one had to be truly alive to qualify.

And Ankou was something very other.

The keeper of souls.

"Have you come to review your payment?" Ankou asked as he floated over to his throne in a curtain of black robes. I couldn't see his feet, but I knew they weren't touching the ground. And not because of the inky feathers at his back.

He resembled a ghost—not exactly ethereal, but not corporeal either.

Still, he settled onto his throne as though he could feel it. And maybe he could.

"Yes. Archdemon Morax is requesting proof of receipt," Ashmedai replied, his tone indicating his annoyance at being questioned. Not by Ankou, but by Morax.

He'd played his part in this game, helping Ashmedai by acting as a spy for the other side. All in exchange for the safety of his daughter.

Which Ashmedai had provided.

Sort of, anyway.

Ashmedai's deals were never straightforward. The one he'd made with Morax was no different.

"Drop some comments regarding your irritation over current world rules. As an example, complain about not being able to ascend to Earth at will. Make it believable and make sure you voice these comments around certain parties—I'll provide a list—then allow the mastermind to pull you in. Succeed, and I'll save your daughter from her fate. But you must follow my rules explicitly. Deviation will not be tolerated. And just to be clear, you will not approve of all my requirements. However, they will be necessary for your daughter to survive."

I'd overheard Ashmedai's deal with Morax several Hell decades ago. He'd set up everything flawlessly, ensuring Morax was positioned correctly to be a spy for the opposition and knowing well in advance what the mastermind on the other side would require—Morax's help in absorbing and redistributing Kristina's powers.

Very few possessed the power to accomplish that feat.

But Morax being her father had set him up for the role.

And he'd played right into the opposite side's hands, something Ashmedai had counted on when creating his little deal.

I'd be impressed if the whole thing didn't make me so damn sick to my stomach.

"Is that why the Archdemon is at my gate?" Ankou asked, his long, dark hair flowing around him like his robes. Such an eerie presence. Yet there was no denying his beauty. He possessed the features of a Fallen Angel, his alabaster skin flawless, his eyelashes thick and abundant, and his mouth full in a kissable kind of way.

A false facade that hid the unadulterated power beneath.

"Yes," Ashmedai replied. "He wants to see her for himself."

"Hmm." Ankou scratched his jaw, the dark stubble along his chin the only imperfection on him.

Of course, it didn't look like an imperfection on him. It appeared almost model-worthy.

Keep thinking about Ankou in this manner, and we will have a problem, little warrior, Ashmedai murmured into my mind.

Jealous? I taunted.

No. Because you're mine. His wing wrapped more securely around me. *Something I will remind you of on this gold floor if you continue fantasizing about Ankou.*

I rolled my eyes. *I'm not fantasizing about him. And I don't belong to you.*

A lie, one that burned me to my soul.

All because of a deal we'd made.

One I hadn't fully considered from every angle.

That was before I'd learned about Ashmedai's ways. I knew better now.

Unfortunately, it was too late for me to make a change. I would forever be his captive.

Captive, he repeated, his amusement swirling through my mind. *Ah, sweet warrior. One day you'll find a better term.*

One day I'll figure out how to kill you, I returned. *Then I'll change my status from* captive *to* free.

His chuckle feathered through my thoughts, yet his expression remained utterly stoic. No sign of a smile in those violet eyes. His lips straightened in a bored line. His gaze entirely focused on Ankou as he awaited his verdict.

The Soul Keeper considered us for a long moment, then he lifted his hand and beckoned one of his servants forward.

Sprites, I thought, shivering with the knowledge of the kind of beings that served him in this realm.

Only it wasn't a wispy being that flowed through the wall but a female with long ash-blonde hair moving from a doorway near the corner of the room.

She kept her head bowed, her white robes embroidered with gold and giving her a princess-like flair. The tiara on her head and gold bands decorating her forearms helped with the regal effect, reminding me a bit of ancient Greece with the whole appearance.

"Golden one," Ankou cooed, his fingers still waving in the air as he continued to summon her. She moved gracefully on bare feet across the golden floor, then knelt at his feet, her cheek pressing into his palm.

My eyebrows lifted. *Is that Kristina?*

Yes, Ashmedai replied. *He returned her spirit to her body. But it appears the transition resulted in a few changes. I'm guessing it has something to do with how she was buried between the realms and whatever mechanism Ankou used to retrieve her remains. Or perhaps he just prefers blondes over redheads.*

I ignored his side commentary about her new "look" and focused on the deal he'd made with Morax—how he'd essentially done his part, but with slight modifications. *I suppose she's technically alive. Just like Morax requested.*

Indeed.

Except she's a prisoner here.

She doesn't seem all that upset about it, Ashmedai pointed out. *And she would have died brutally had I not made this deal.*

She did die brutally.

Ashmedai made an impatient sound. *Her father took the power from her and redistributed it, as commanded by the other side.*

You did warn him he would have to do things he wouldn't want to do, I inserted dryly. *Obviously, this was one of those things.* A guess I'd made based on how strongly he'd demanded Ashmedai let him see his daughter. He obviously had a heart somewhere inside him.

It was the only way to truly save her. At least he was able to kill her peacefully, something I doubt would have happened had the other side been forced to extract her power via different means—which they would have eventually tried, Trudy. You've seen enough now to know I speak the truth.

He did.

But that didn't mean I was blinded by his "kindness." I knew the real him now. I understood his plays. Nothing about this situation was a result of him caring about anything other than the endgame.

Don't pretend you saved her from a worse fate, Ash, I drawled. *We both know this was about paying Ankou. He wanted an angelic pet capable of withstanding his demonic side. You provided that in the form of Kristina.*

I didn't say my saving her from a worse fate was my only

motive, he returned casually. *Just a benefit of the arrangement. Two demons, one sacrifice—that's the saying, yes?*

It took effort not to roll my eyes. *Two birds, one stone.*

How human of you, he murmured back, his amusement palpable once more.

"Sweet gold of mine," Ankou said warmly. "Your father is here requesting an audience. Shall I permit him entry?"

Kristina swallowed, her eyes lifting to Ankou. "Yes, please."

His resulting smile was indulgent. "Do you intend to kill him?"

"I don't know, my king. Maybe."

Ankou's opposite hand produced a golden dagger that he handed to her. "The choice is yours, golden one."

"Thank you, my king."

They're giving me weird Hades and Persephone vibes, I decided, their connection seeming like an odd mix of sweet and evil.

Am I to know who they are? Ashmedai asked.

Greek mythology, I returned. *Hades, God of the Underworld?*

I assure you, Hades does not exist in my underworld, Ashmedai replied flatly.

Hence the word mythology.

He didn't reply, his focus entirely on Ankou as he snapped his fingers. "Allow the Archdemon to enter," he called.

Do you think she'll kill him? I wondered, eyeing the fragile-looking female. She was a former piece of the Divinity, which meant she was a lot stronger than she looked. Even without her veil power, she still had the blood of an Archdemon and an Archangel running through her veins.

Johanna and Lucía were proof of what she could be, as they'd both mated their Archdemon counterparts to form a new sort of balance. They were powerful matings. Of course, Lucía and Alastor still pretended to hate each other. But that was their clever way of hiding the power they now shared.

If Kristina had mated Ankou, then she would be just as powerful as Lucía and Johanna were now. Perhaps even more so, given Ankou's ties to the afterlife.

That was how Ashmedai had made this arrangement—gold for an angelic pet in the form of Kristina's soul.

All Ankou had to do was retrieve her soul, which I imagined wasn't very difficult for him, given his reign over that realm of existence.

"After this, our deal is through," Ankou said conversationally to Ashmedai.

Ashmedai dipped his chin in acknowledgment, his mind telling me he'd already fulfilled his goals with this arrangement. He'd only brought Morax here to finish his debt to the Archdemon.

Ashmedai might make deals that benefited him more than his counterparts, but he always did find ways to fulfill his side. This was no different. Just another move on the board to ensure all loose ends were neatly tied up.

You're hoping she'll kill him, I realized when he didn't reply to my musings. *To ensure he can't tell anyone that it was you who told him to open that portal.*

I didn't tell him to open the portal. I told him to do what was necessary to gain the trust of the opposition and to report back to me on all the players involved.

So you're punishing him for opening the portal, then? I guessed.

I don't care about the portal, little warrior. It served its purpose by pushing Kayla's ascension. It might not be how I would have done it, but it worked. His attention shifted to the hallway we'd originally entered from, his expression giving nothing away as Morax came into the throne room. *I've fulfilled my obligations to all parties involved. That's our only purpose for being here.*

I didn't believe him.

Ashmedai worked in layers, his strategy always placing him several steps ahead of his opponents. The only being I'd met so far that seemed to rival him was the one seated on the throne.

Fortunately, Ankou appeared quite content to remain in the Chrysus region of Hell. It wasn't considered a realm because the area lacked an Archdemon to oversee it. However, Ankou certainly maintained the area as his domain, and no one dared enter it without his express permission.

Ankou held his palm out for Kristina as she pushed up off the ground to stand. It was a sinuous movement that suggested this happened often between them.

Definitely Hades and Persephone vibes.

Ashmedai's wing brushed my arm, the stroke a warning more than a caress. He needed me to be quiet so he could focus on the interactions in the room.

I almost reminded him that this connection between our minds was *his* fault, but I wanted to concentrate as well.

Morax's black feathers framed his massive form as he bowed respectfully toward Ankou. "Thank you, King Ankou, for allowing me entry. And thank you for saving my kin."

King, not *Prince.* That was the formal address that many of the Archdemons bestowed upon Ankou. Not because he was a true king, but because of his immense control over the afterlife.

I supposed he could be seen as king of that realm of existence.

"Your kin?" Kristina asked, her head tilting in a way that resembled childlike innocence. "I seem to recall you saying I was no child of yours before you sucked the power from my dying form." She took a step forward, her white gown whispering around her ankles. "I thought you were there to help me. To *save* me. We shared blood, after all. But no. You disowned me. Defiled me. *Killed* me."

"To save you," he replied, gesturing at the room. "Prince Ashmedai told me what needed to be done, and I did it. To *save* you."

"Why?" she asked. "Why would you bother at all?"

A note of curiosity piqued in Ashmedai's mind. He'd wondered about this as well. And now I did, too.

"Because I created you," Morax replied. "You're mine. My daughter. My blood. My legacy. I asked Ashmedai to take you into his protection, to help you find a new balance. He offered me this deal instead."

Pride, I realized. *He saved her because she's his only legacy. Similar to Kayla for Bael.*

Indeed. Ashmedai didn't seem all that entertained by the information. Perhaps he'd hoped to learn something interesting, and he was disappointed to discover the true reason.

He wanted you to mate her like Bael mated Johanna and Alastor mated Lucía, I deduced after a beat. *That's why he went to you.*

Yes, Ashmedai confirmed. *I declined. And we both know why I declined.*

I swallowed. *Yes.* He'd wanted me. Not one of the members of the Divinity. *Was there no one else he could ask?*

No one with enough power to help, Ashmedai confirmed. *So I made him a different sort of offer.*

"So you killed me," Kristina said, her grip tightening against the blade. "To save me."

"Yes. I knew there were those who would seek to benefit from the shifting in the balance, which made you a target. It was the only way I knew how to protect you."

"By killing me," she reiterated. "And trading my soul to King Ankou."

The king in question didn't react, his dark focus entirely on Kristina.

"It was the only way," Morax repeated. "There was no one else in Hell who could offer you balance and protection. I didn't want you to be lost forever. Bael had already chosen Johanna, and I didn't want to risk Alastor choosing Lucía over you. So I preemptively took you, siphoned off your power, and sent you here for the ultimate protection." He bowed his head to Ankou. "Thank you for guarding her."

"Oh, I'm not guarding her," Ankou replied, his fingers weaving through the air and causing her hair to float around her as though he were touching her. "She guards herself."

Kristina played the blade through her fingers. "I do." Her eyes narrowed. Then she looked back at Ankou. "I'm not going to kill him. His power will continue to wane until he loses everything. That's punishment enough."

Well, now that's an interesting statement, Ashmedai thought. *I wonder what she's foreseen.*

Oh? A move you're not fully aware of yet? I asked, feigning curiosity.

More like one that doesn't entirely interest me. Morax has served his purpose. Our deal is done.

I glanced at Ashmedai. *So that's it? You just leave him behind?*

It's what he would do to me, he replied.

Ankou dipped his chin in a regal nod. "So be it, little gold of mine. We shall allow him safe passage home."

"Yes," she agreed as she stepped toward Ankou again to kneel at his feet. She lifted the blade up for him to take, and it disappeared into his black robes.

"You may all leave," Ankou announced. "Unless you have another deal for me, Ashmedai?"

"Not today, King Ankou," Ashmedai replied, bestowing upon him the formal title and giving him a subtle bow.

Always playing political games, I thought at him.

Always, he echoed, rising. "Until we meet again," he said.

"Hopefully not soon," Ankou replied. "But I fear that may not be the case for your mate."

A chill swept down my spine.

"I sense her soul will be with me very soon," Ankou continued, his dark eyes gleaming as he met my gaze. "Until we meet again," he echoed, his cloaks wrapping around him and Kristina as the throne room began to dissolve around us.

Ashmedai's familiar quarters appeared in the next blink, my heart kick-starting in my chest.

I met his violet gaze.

And for once, he allowed me to see something other than amusement.

He granted me a glimpse of true fear.

"I think it's time for you to choose a side, dear mate," he said after a beat. "Before it's too late."

Ashmedai and Trudy's story will continue in *Captive of Hell...*

To find out what happened to Xai & Eve, check out *Son of Chaos.*

Son of Chaos

A simple mission turns deadly as the Daughter of Death is kidnapped by an old enemy seeking revenge. Now it's up to me to find her and I will kill anyone who steps in my path.

The Son of Chaos isn't playing. I'm armed, I'm pissed, and I want my Evangeline back. It's time for Heaven and Hell to meet the real Archangel inside of me.

Everyone will pay.
Many will die.
Silver will slay.

And a new power will ascend from the Shadows...

Captive of Hell

I made a deal with a Prince of Hell.
And now I'm his mate.

All I asked for was my freedom after being captured and
dragged down to the underworld.
Prince Ashmedai agreed to the terms in exchange for a
blood vow.
A blood vow that I belatedly realized tied our souls together
for eternity.

Oh, I'm free all right.
Free to roam his realm.
To live in Hell for the rest of my very long life.
Or short life, according to the infamous *Grim Reaper*.

Because, yeah, it's never a good sign when the demon in charge
of the afterlife says he'll be seeing you soon.

If only I had someone in my life who could help.
Like my absentee Archangel father or my devious Archdemon mate.
Alas, no. That's not how fate works in my world.

The veil is about to fall.
The realms are on the verge of collective chaos.
And the power inside me is the key to our salvation.

I just might have to die in the process to release it.
Something Prince Ashmedai has known all along.
For he's the one wielding the blade.
Essentially holding my life in his proverbial hands.

How about another deal, Archdemon?
Save me and I'll help you save the world.
Kill me and I'll take you down with me.
What'll it be?

USA Today Bestselling Author Lexi C. Foss loves to play in dark worlds, especially the ones that bite. She lives in North Carolina with her family. When not writing, she's busy crossing items off her travel bucket list, or chasing eclipses around the globe. She's quirky, consumes way too much coffee, and loves to swim.

Where To Find Lexi:
www.LexiCFoss.com

Also by Lexi C. Foss

Blood Alliance Series - Dystopian Paranormal

Chastely Bitten

Royally Bitten

Regally Bitten

Rebel Bitten

Kingly Bitten

Cruelly Bitten

Blood Alliance World Related Novels

Blood Day

Crave Me

Dark Provenance Series - Paranormal Romance

Heiress of Bael (FREE!)

Daughter of Death

Son of Chaos

Paramour of Sin

Princess of Bael

Captive of Hell

Elemental Fae Academy - Reverse Harem

Book One

Book Two

Book Three

Elemental Fae Queen

Winter Fae Queen

Hell Fae - Reverse Harem

Hell Fae Captive

Immortal Curse Series - Paranormal Romance

Book One: Blood Laws

Book Two: Forbidden Bonds

Book Three: Blood Heart

Book Four: Blood Bonds

Book Five: Angel Bonds

Book Six: Blood Seeker

Book Seven: Wicked Bonds

Book Eight: Blood King

Immortal Curse World - Short Stories & Bonus Fun

Elder Bonds

Blood Burden

Assassin Bonds

Midnight Fae Academy - Reverse Harem

Ella's Masquerade

Book One

Book Two

Book Three

Book Four

Noir Reformatory - Ménage Paranormal Romance

The Beginning

First Offense

Second Offense

Underworld Royals Series - Dark Paranormal Romance

Happily Ever Crowned

Happily Ever Bitten

X-Clan Series - Dystopian Paranormal

Andorra Sector

X-Clan: The Experiment

Winter's Arrow

Bariloche Sector

Hunted

V-Clan Series - Dystopian Paranormal

Blood Sector

Vampire Dynasty - Dark Paranormal

Violet Slays

Crossed Fates

Other Books

Scarlet Mark - Standalone Romantic Suspense

Rotanev - Standalone Poseidon Tale

Carnage Island - Standalone Reverse Harem Romance

www.ingramcontent.com/pod-product-compliance
Lightning Source LLC
Chambersburg PA
CBHW051514250626
47156CB00001B/90